DEBBIE MACOMBER

Texas Skies

#1 *NEW YORK TIMES* BESTSELLING AUTHOR
DEBBIE MACOMBER

Welcome to Promise, a small town in the heart of Texas where the neighbors are friendly and you might just find love.

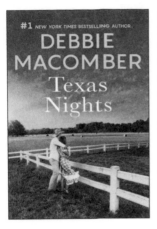

Caroline's Child

No one in town has ever asked who the father of Caroline Daniels's child is. They care about her and little five-year-old Maggie. Especially rancher Grady Weston, who's beginning to realize he cares even more than most...

Dr. Texas

They call her Dr. Texas. Jane Dickinson, a newly graduated physician from California, will be working at the Promise clinic—but just for a couple years. They call *him* Mr. Grouch. And she reminds Cal Patterson too much of the out-of-state ex-fiancée he's trying to forget.

Available May 28 wherever books are sold.

ISBN-13: 978-0-7783-6986-8

9 780778 369868

50899

EAN

DEBBIE MACOMBER

Texas Skies

mira

mira

ISBN-13: 978-0-7783-6986-8

Texas Skies

Copyright © 2019 by Harlequin Books S.A.

The publisher acknowledges the copyright holder of the individual works as follows:

Lonesome Cowboy
Copyright © 1998 by Debbie Macomber

Texas Two-Step
Copyright © 1998 by Debbie Macomber

Recycling programs
for this product may
not exist in your area.

For questions and comments about the quality of this book, please contact us at CustomerService@Harlequin.com.

Harlequin.com

Printed in U.S.A.

Also available from Debbie Macomber and MIRA Books

Midnight Sons

Alaska Skies
(*Brides for Brothers* and
The Marriage Risk)
Alaska Nights
(*Daddy's Little Helper* and
Because of the Baby)
Alaska Home
(*Falling for Him,*
Ending in Marriage and
Midnight Sons and Daughters)

This Matter of Marriage
Montana
Thursdays at Eight
Between Friends
Changing Habits
Married in Seattle
(*First Comes Marriage* and
Wanted: Perfect Partner)
Right Next Door
(*Father's Day* and
The Courtship of Carol Sommars)
Wyoming Brides
(*Denim and Diamonds* and
The Wyoming Kid)
Fairy Tale Weddings
(*Cindy and the Prince* and
Some Kind of Wonderful)
The Man You'll Marry
(*The First Man You Meet* and
The Man You'll Marry)
Orchard Valley Grooms
(*Valerie* and *Stephanie*)
Orchard Valley Brides
(*Norah* and *Lone Star Lovin'*)
The Sooner the Better
An Engagement in Seattle
(*Groom Wanted* and
Bride Wanted)
Out of the Rain
(*Marriage Wanted* and
Laughter in the Rain)
Learning to Love
(*Sugar and Spice* and *Love by Degree*)

You…Again
(*Baby Blessed* and
Yesterday Once More)
The Unexpected Husband
(*Jury of His Peers* and
Any Sunday)
Three Brides, No Groom
Love in Plain Sight
(*Love 'n' Marriage* and
Almost an Angel)
I Left My Heart
(*A Friend or Two* and
No Competition)
Marriage Between Friends
(*White Lace and Promises* and
Friends—And Then Some)
A Man's Heart
(*The Way to a Man's Heart* and
Hasty Wedding)
North to Alaska
(*That Wintry Feeling* and
Borrowed Dreams)
On a Clear Day
(*Starlight* and
Promise Me Forever)
To Love and Protect
(*Shadow Chasing* and
For All My Tomorrows)
Home in Seattle
(*The Playboy and the Widow*
and *Fallen Angel*)
Together Again
(*The Trouble with Caasi* and
Reflections of Yesterday)
The Reluctant Groom
(*All Things Considered* and
Almost Paradise)
A Real Prince
(*The Bachelor Prince* and
Yesterday's Hero)
Private Paradise
(in *That Summer Place*)

Debbie Macomber's
Cedar Cove Cookbook
Debbie Macomber's
Christmas Cookbook

CONTENTS

LONESOME COWBOY

One

Grady had warned her repeatedly. He'd told Savannah that the ghost town was dangerous, that it was a disturbing place. He'd told her over and over not to look for it. And all these years Savannah *had* stayed away. But the more her brother cautioned her, the more convinced she'd become that she had to find it. If for no other reason than the roses. Roses were Savannah's passion—especially old roses, planted before 1867 and now found mostly in cemeteries and abandoned homesteads.

It was because of the roses that she ignored Grady's advice and began to seek out the long-lost town.

After a six-week search, roaming about the rugged Texas hill country, first in the truck, then on horseback and finally on foot with no map and little information, she'd located it. Bitter End. What a strange name, but no stranger than the town itself.

No matter how furious Grady was when he discovered what she'd done, it'd been worth the risk. This certainly wouldn't be the first time she'd defied her older brother. Nor would it be the last. Grady seemed to carry the weight of the world on his shoulders; he rarely smiled anymore. He was as loud and demanding as Savannah was quiet and intense. But her stubbornness was easily a match for his.

Glancing at the truck's speedometer, she pressed her foot to the floor, although it generally wasn't in her nature to rush. However, her chances of escaping Grady's anger were greater if she got back to the house before he returned from his duties around the ranch. Not that she *feared* his anger; she simply preferred to avoid it.

Her brother was so often angry these days, with beef prices dropping and all the other problems associated with running a large cattle ranch. It didn't help that, thanks to Richard, they continued to struggle with debt and financial hardship.

Savannah forced her thoughts away from the unhappy events of six years earlier. It was wrenching enough to have lost both parents in one devastating accident, but Savannah feared that their brother's betrayal, which had followed so soon afterward, would forever taint their lives with bitterness.

"Oh, Richard," she whispered as the truck sped down the winding country road. The pain he'd wrought in her life and Grady's was the kind that even love would never completely heal.

Grady had changed in the years since their parents' tragic deaths—and Richard's betrayal. Finances and other concerns had harassed and tormented him until she barely knew him any longer. Through sheer stubbornness and backbreaking work he'd managed to accomplish the impossible. He'd saved the Yellow Rose Ranch, but at a terrible price. Grady had sacrificed himself and his youth to hold on to the land that had been settled by their great-great-grandfather shortly after the Civil War. Or, as her Southern grandmother called it, the War of the Northern Aggression.

Savannah had wanted to help with their finances; after all, she had a college education. It would be a small thing to return to school and take the necessary courses to obtain her teaching certificate. The Promise school board had repeatedly advertised for substitute teachers, and a full-time position was bound to become available within a few years. Grady, however, wouldn't hear of it. He needed her on the Yellow Rose, and Savannah accepted that. She handled the majority of the paperwork, cooked, cleaned the house and did the gardening. She'd indulged her love for roses, started keeping goats and occasionally hand-raised orphaned or abandoned calves. For six years she'd picked up the slack and made a decent life for herself. But compared to Grady, she didn't feel she was doing nearly enough.

Her desire to contribute to the family income had prompted her to establish a mail-order business for her roses, and while Grady had politely listened to her plans, he hadn't encouraged them. Her small venture was just now starting to show a profit, of which Savannah was extremely proud. In the past few months she'd been spending her evenings working on a catalog.

What Grady needed, in Savannah's opinion, was to marry and start a family. At thirty-five he was well past the age most men settled into family life. He probably would've done so long before now if he hadn't been required to dedicate every waking minute to the ranch. She wondered whether it was too late, whether he'd ever get married. Savannah herself had long since given up any hope of marriage and children. Her maternal urges would have to be satisfied by her animals, she told herself wryly. She'd turned thirty-one her last birthday and hadn't dated in the past four or five years. She rarely thought about having a relationship anymore. Men didn't understand her quiet ways or appreciate her strength or gentleness of spirit. It no longer mattered. She was content with her life. She'd learned to take pleasure in small things—the beauty of flowers, the affection of animals, the comfort of a well-ordered house.

Indian paintbrush, bluebonnets and pink evening primroses, all in bloom, lined the twisting road. Savannah loved spring. The scent of the air brought with it the promise of warm weather and new life. Grady and Wiley, the hired hand who'd been with them so many years he was more family than foreman, had assisted in delivering fourteen calves this week and were looking for that many more in the next couple of days.

Savannah glanced at her watch and hoped Grady had been delayed this afternoon. Otherwise he was going to have a conniption, especially when he realized where she'd gone.

Sighing, she turned the familiar bend in the road and caught sight of an abandoned truck parked close to the ditch. Savannah didn't recognize the vehicle; that in itself was unusual. People who didn't know the area hardly ever wandered this far off the beaten path.

The truck had seen better days. The color had faded badly and a large dent in the side revealed a section where rust had eaten a hole the size of a small plate. With the truck parked as it was, fifteen miles outside of town, far from anywhere, Savannah couldn't help wondering if something was wrong. She might have stopped to investigate if she hadn't been in a hurry.

The decision was taken from her a few miles down the road when she saw a cowboy walking, carrying a saddle. Even from this distance she could see how weary he was; he seemed to be favoring one side, limping discernibly. At the sound of her approach, he straightened, shifted the weight of his saddle and stuck out his thumb.

Never in all her life had Savannah stopped for a hitchhiker, but this man, miles from anywhere and walking in the opposite direction from town, must have been spent.

Savannah pulled over and eased to a stop. She opened the door and climbed out. "Is that your truck parked back there?"

"Yes, ma'am," he answered politely. He was tall and wiry, about her age, she guessed. His Stetson rested low on his brow, shading his face from the afternoon sun. When he touched his fingers to the brim in greeting, she noticed that his eyes were pale blue. "I'd be much obliged for a ride."

Although she'd stopped, Savannah hesitated, unsure what to do. "I wasn't headed toward town."

"As far as you'd take me would be appreciated. Your truck's the first vehicle to come along in more'n two hours." He gave her a tired smile. "I'd hoped to find a ranch and use the phone there, but I haven't seen one yet."

Apparently he didn't realize he was walking away from Promise. "I live ten or so miles down the road." Shielding her eyes from the glare of the sun, she pointed toward the Yellow Rose. Riding with her would only take him farther from where he needed to go. She was about to explain as much, then realized he was tired, hurting and probably hadn't eaten a decent meal in hours, if not days. Grady wouldn't be pleased, but... She shrugged off the prospect of her brother's wrath.

"If you like, you can stay the night in the bunkhouse and I'll drive you to town in the morning."

She could tell that her offer surprised him; his eyes widened briefly. "That's mighty kind of you, ma'am."

The fact that he called her ma'am made her feel dowdy and old-fashioned. She supposed that was exactly what she was, though. No one had to tell her she looked older than her age. She usually wore full-length dresses rather than the more fashionable shirt and jeans; her mother had encouraged this, saying that dresses complimented her tall willowy figure. She'd grown accustomed to working in them, donning an apron for household chores. Her thick, straight, blond hair fell down her back, almost to her waist. Grady had teasingly called her a flower child of the sixties, and in some ways, she did resemble a hippie.

"I'm Savannah Weston."

"Laredo Smith." Again he touched the brim of his hat.

"Pleased to meet you," she said and smiled shyly. "Laredo's an unusual name."

He grinned as if the comment was familiar. "So I've heard." He hitched the saddle higher and added, "My given name's Matthew, but when I was a kid and we moved away from Texas, I wanted to take part of it with me. From that day on I only answered to Laredo. After all these years, I don't know who Matthew is, but Laredo…well, it's a comfortable fit and suits me just fine."

Savannah couldn't have said why, but she had the impression that these details weren't something he shared often. She told herself it was silly to feel honored—but she did, anyway.

She must have smiled because he responded with a grin of his own. It amazed her how a simple smile could transform his drained features. A hint of something warm and kind showed in his sun-weathered face, mesmerizing her for a moment. A little shocked by her own response, Savannah decided she was being fanciful and looked away. Laredo Smith was a stranger and she'd do well to take care.

"If you'd like, you can put your saddle in the truck bed," she offered and walked to the back to lower the tailgate.

The leather creaked as he lifted it from his shoulder and wearily set it down. He hesitated when he saw the roses and reached out a callused hand toward the fragile buds. Gently he fingered a delicate pink petal.

"These are antique roses, aren't they?" He closed his eyes and breathed in the distinctive perfumed scent of the flowers.

His knowledge surprised her. Few people knew about old roses or had heard the term. In her research Savannah had learned that many of the roses found in Texas were of unknown lineage, recovered from hidden corners and byways in an ongoing search-and-rescue mission—like the one she'd been on that very day. Savannah was well aware that some would describe her as a "rose rustler"; it wasn't how she thought of herself. Her overwhelming motivation was her love of the flowers.

"You know about old roses?" she asked.

"My grandmother had a rose garden and she grew roses passed down by her own grandmother. It must be at least twenty years since I saw one. Where'd you ever find these?"

Her pause was long enough for him to notice. "In an old graveyard," she said. "Near, um, an abandoned town." While it was the truth, it wasn't the *entire* truth, but Savannah didn't dare add any details about the ghost town. Only a few people in Promise had even heard of Bitter End. And although Grady had repeatedly warned her against seeking it out, he'd never told her exactly what was so threatening about the long-deserted town.

Only now did Savannah understand her brother's concerns. The dangers weren't found in the crumbling buildings or the abandoned wells; no, they weren't so easily explained. She couldn't help shuddering as she remembered the sensation of…darkness that had come over her when she'd first set foot on the still, silent grounds. Even that didn't adequately describe the emotions she'd experienced. It wasn't a feeling of evil so much as a pressing sadness, a pain and grief so raw that a hundred years hadn't dimmed its intensity.

Knowing little of the town's history, Savannah had felt defenseless and almost afraid. Years earlier, Grady and two of his friends had heard their parents discussing Bitter End, but when Savannah questioned her mother, she'd refused to talk about it. From Grady, Savannah had learned that the town was said to have been settled by Promise's founding fathers. Why they'd moved, what had happened to prompt the relocation, was an unsolved mystery. For all she knew, it was something as mundane as water rights. Although that would hardly account for what she'd felt....

Despite Grady's warnings, Savannah had found Bitter End and dug up the old roses in the graveyard, but she hadn't ventured beyond the fenced area beside the church. She left as quickly as she could. By the time she made it back to the truck, she was pale and trembling.

She'd driven away without looking back. She hadn't investigated any of the other buildings, and she was annoyed now for letting the opportunity pass. She might have found more old roses had she taken the time to search.

"They're beautiful," Laredo said. The light pink bud, perfectly formed, lay like a jewel in the palm of his hand.

"They truly are exquisite, aren't they?" The sheer joy and excitement she'd felt on discovering the roses quickened her voice. "I just couldn't be happier! It's so much more than I hoped to find!"

His gaze held hers and he nodded, seeming to share her enthusiasm.

Warming to her subject, Savannah added, "It's incredible to think they've survived all these years without anyone to care for them."

Laredo gently withdrew his hand from the rosebud.

"Would you be more comfortable if I rode in the back, ma'am?" he asked.

"Savannah," she insisted.

The smile returned again, briefly. "Savannah," he echoed.

"You're welcome to ride in front with me."

He climbed slowly into the cab and she could see that the action pained him considerably.

"I don't suppose you know anyone who's looking for a good wrangler?" he asked.

"I'm sorry, I don't," she said with sincere regret.

He nodded and winced, pressing his hand against his ribs.

"You've been hurt," she said.

"A cracked rib or two," he answered, obviously embarrassed by her concern. "My own damn fault," he muttered.

"A horse?"

"Not exactly." His voice was rueful, a bit ironic. "I got shoved against a fence by a bull. You'd think that after all these years working ranches, I'd know better than to let myself get cornered by a bull."

"My daddy cracked a rib once and he said it left him feeling like he'd been gnawed by a coyote, then dumped over a cliff."

Laredo chuckled. "Your daddy sounds like he's got quite a sense of humor."

"He did," Savannah agreed softly, starting the engine. She knew the tires hitting the ruts in the road would hurt him, so she drove slowly and carefully.

Laredo glanced over his shoulder—to check on his saddle, Savannah suspected. She was surprised when he mentioned the roses a second time. "I never thought to smell roses like those again."

"I'm so glad I found them!" she burst out. "These are the best ones yet." Their scent was sweet and strong and pure, far more aromatic than modern hybrids. These roses from Bitter End were probably White Lady Banks—a rare and precious find.

Savannah talked excitedly about her roses; the cowboy encouraged her, asking interested and knowledgeable questions.

What surprised Savannah was how comfortable she felt with Laredo Smith. They could have talked for hours. Generally when it came to conversation with a man, especially a stranger, Savannah was shy and reticent. The ease with which she talked to Laredo was unprecedented.

It wasn't just roses they talked about, either. Soon Savannah found herself telling him about her gardens at the ranch and the love her mother, Barbara, had for flowers. One topic led swiftly to another. She described Promise and assured him it was a friendly town. He asked about having his truck repaired and she mentioned a couple of reliable garages.

"Oh, my," she said and held her palm to her mouth.

"Is something wrong?"

"I got to chatting away and almost missed the turnoff for the ranch." Such a thing had never happened before. Then, hardly knowing what she was doing, she glanced over at him and said, "The fact is, Laredo, the Yellow Rose could use an extra hand. If you need a job, we'd be happy to offer you one."

Laredo brightened visibly. "I'm good with horses and I'm willing to work hard."

"Grady'll probably have a few questions for you." She added this second part knowing her brother wasn't going to be pleased with her hiring a stranger. In the past he'd always been the one to do the hiring and firing, but if he took offense, he could discuss the matter with her. Every instinct she possessed told her Laredo Smith was worthy of their trust. Besides, they needed extra help, whether Grady was willing to admit it or not.

Laredo grew quiet, and then she felt his eyes on her. "Since you offered me the job, I think it's only fair to tell you I was fired from my last position." He told her he'd been accused of theft, wrongly accused. He neither cast nor accepted blame. "I may be a lot of things, but a thief isn't one of them. If you change your mind, I'll understand."

"I won't," she said, but the instincts that had felt so right moments earlier wavered like dry grass whipped by a harsh summer wind. "I… I appreciate your being honest enough to tell me," Savannah said. Naturally the first thing Grady would want from a stranger, especially one *she'd* taken it upon herself to hire, was references. Well—like everything else about this day—she'd cross that bridge when she came to it.

"You won't be disappointed," Laredo added. "You have my word on that."

A plume of dust followed them as they headed down the pitched dirt driveway leading off the highway. No sooner had Savannah pulled into the yard and turned off the engine than Grady dashed out of the barn and stalked toward her like an avenging angel.

"Just where the bloody hell have you been all afternoon?" her brother demanded, ignoring the shambling black dog that trailed him and nudged the fist clenched at his side.

Savannah inhaled deeply and held her breath while she climbed out of the truck. If she hadn't stopped to pick up Laredo, she might have returned before Grady rode in from the range. Rather than answer his questions, she leaned over and scratched Rocket's ears. The old dog, who'd once belonged to their father, was now well past his prime. He wagged his tail in appreciation.

"You might have left a note." Her brother's ranting continued despite her lack of response.

"I apologize, but—" She wasn't allowed to finish.

"I don't want an apology. I want to know where you were all afternoon." His eyes narrowed on the man beside her. "And I have a feeling I'm not going to like the answer."

It mortified her to have her brother yell at her like this in front of Laredo. "Grady," she said urgently, "perhaps we could discuss this inside."

"You did it, didn't you? Even though I warned you! I *told* you not to look for Bitter End! Doesn't anyone listen to me anymore? I thought you were smarter than this! *Anything* could happen to you up in those hills all by yourself. What's the matter with you, anyway? You should know better than to risk your fool neck over something as ridiculous as a stupid rosebush." His face had turned red with anger.

Disregarding Laredo, her brother advanced toward her. Two steps was as close as he got before her newfound friend moved protectively in front of her, directly in Grady's path.

"Who the hell are you?"

"Grady, this is Laredo Smith," Savannah said evenly, praying she sounded calm and in control. "His truck broke down, and, um, I've offered him a job."

A second of shocked silence followed. "You *what*?"

The anger Grady had shown earlier paled in comparison to the fury that blazed in his eyes now. Savannah didn't acknowledge his outburst. "Dinner's in the Crock-Pot. Chili verde, your favorite."

Grady stared at her, his mouth hanging open, as if he didn't recognize her as his sister.

"I'll have everything ready and on the table in ten minutes. Grady, would you be kind enough to show Laredo to the bunkhouse and ask Wiley to wash up?"

"This is Wiley's poker night," Grady muttered. "But I—"

"So it is," she said and headed up the porch steps and into the kitchen. Her heart pounded like a prairie rabbit's at the approach of a hawk's shadow. "Then there'll just be the three of us."

It didn't take her long to set the table for dinner. When she heard the door swing open, she squared her shoulders and turned to greet her brother and Laredo with a wide smile. "I hope you two had a chance to introduce yourselves."

"We didn't get around to exchanging pleasantries," Grady snarled.

"Laredo, I hope you'll forgive my brother," she said, placing the warm tortillas on a plate. "It's clear he isn't in one of his more cordial moods."

"Your brother?" The words slipped from Laredo's lips in a low whisper of surprise.

"The two of us are equal partners in the Yellow Rose Ranch," she said as a subtle way of reminding Grady that she'd had every right to hire Laredo.

Still grumbling under his breath, Grady pulled out a chair and reached for the blue-checked napkin.

"Can I help you with anything, Savannah?" Laredo asked, looking around for something to do.

"There's a cold pitcher of lemonade in the refrigerator," she said, hoping Grady realized it wouldn't hurt him any to lend her a hand now and then. She tried not to be judgmental of her brother, but lately he'd grown so cranky and irritable. It was more than their perpetual money problems, she suspected, but whatever plagued him, he kept to himself. Savannah wished he'd be more open with her, share his troubles, but that wasn't Grady's way. Like their father he kept everything locked inside, preferring to carry the burden of his problems alone. Once again she wished he'd think about marriage. She had the perfect woman in mind.

Grady Weston was furious with his sister. He didn't know what had come over her. It wasn't like her to openly defy him, nor had he ever known her to pick up a hitchhiker. And never, not once in all these years, had she taken an active role in the management of the ranch. Yet in one single day, his levelheaded younger sister had not only gone against his express orders, she'd gone and hired him additional help. A stranger, no less!

Grady wouldn't have believed it if he hadn't seen it with his own eyes, heard it with his own ears. Savannah wasn't herself. He frowned at Laredo Smith, instinctively distrusting him. One look told Grady the saddle bum was an outsider, a drifter. Not to be trusted. Yet Savannah had invited the man into their home and their lives like a long-lost relative—*and* offered him employment. The problem with Savannah could be reduced to one simple explanation. She couldn't see the bad in people. She was just too damn trusting.

In spite of that, Grady had often admired Savannah for her common sense. But from all appearances, she'd lost every shred of good judgment she'd ever possessed. All within the space of a single day.

"I can't remember when I've tasted better chili," Laredo said, serving himself a second helping when Savannah passed him the bowl.

She lowered her gaze and Grady watched, amazed as color seeped into her cheeks. "I appreciate the compliment, but Nell Bishop's the one who deserves the credit. It's her recipe."

"My compliments to Nell, then, and to you, too."

Savannah's blush deepened. If it wasn't so pathetic, Grady might have rolled his eyes. The town was full of men who were interested in Savannah, but she hadn't given one of them a lick of encouragement. Not a one. *Then she happens on a complete stranger who doesn't look like he's got two dimes to call his own and she practically faints because he compliments her cooking!*

Grady shoved his plate aside, appetite gone. His day had gone poorly. A calf had died after a desperate struggle to save its life, and he wasn't sure the mother was going to make it, either. He'd had the vet out, and they'd done everything they could, but it didn't look promising. If that wasn't bad enough, he'd found a break in the fence line. Luckily he'd been able to repair it before any of the herd had escaped.

The problems never ended. Day in and day out, he faced one crisis after another, each one heaped on top of all the others. He didn't know what it was to laugh anymore, didn't know what it was to spend a night in town drinking with his buddies. Hell, he couldn't even remember the last time he'd kissed a woman.

In six years his life had boiled down to two things—work and worry.

It seemed a million years ago that he'd been young and carefree. Everything had changed for him—and for Savannah—in the course of an afternoon. The life he'd lived before they lost their parents was little more than a vague memory.

After a day like this the last thing he needed was for the one constant, the one sane sensible person in his life, to lose her bearings. Go loco on him. Grady glanced at Savannah and he felt his heart twist with sorrow, frustration, guilt. His sister was as lovely as those roses she cared so much about. She was still young and pretty, although she didn't appear to realize that.

Grady hadn't saved the ranch all on his own, nor was he the only one who'd dedicated his life to building back everything they'd lost. He couldn't have done it without her. Savannah had found a hundred ways to encourage him, lighten his load, and he didn't thank her nearly enough.

Regret settled in the pit of his stomach. He shouldn't have laid into her the way he had when she got home, but damn it all, he'd been worried sick. It wasn't like her to disappear and not tell him where she was going. In the past she'd always been conscientious about that, and with good reason.

Even though the risk of her encountering danger was slim, an accident could always happen. It had to his mother and father. Caught in a flash flood, they'd been swept away in a matter of moments and drowned. Never would he forget the day Sheriff Frank Hennessey had come to deliver the tragic news. So it wasn't that Grady didn't trust Savannah, but her disappearance that afternoon had brought back memories he wished he could forget.

But it was more than the memory of his parents' accident that had distressed him. For three or four months now his sister had been asking him about the ghost town. In the beginning he'd answered her questions and hadn't given her curiosity much thought, but when she persisted, he'd asked her a few questions of his own. That was when she mentioned the old roses. Damn fool woman was willing to risk her neck over something as…as unimportant as flowers. If that didn't beat all, he didn't know what did.

Grady *had* warned her plenty, not that it'd done any good. Hell, he couldn't have found the abandoned frontier town again had he tried. The one and only time he'd ever stepped foot in Bitter End, he'd been about fifteen. Grady and the two Patterson brothers had overheard their parents talking about a ghost town somewhere up in the hills. Without their parents' knowledge the boys had decided to go exploring, to find the place for themselves.

Grady and his friends had set out, thinking it all a grand adventure. As he recalled, they'd spent weeks looking, and when they finally stumbled on the ghost town, it'd spooked them so badly they'd never discussed that day again.

Grady didn't believe in ghosts; he wasn't a superstitious man. But the town was haunted by something he'd been too young to name or understand, something he didn't full comprehend even now. An unfamiliar sensation had descended on him that day, and not only him, but the others, too. He remembered the silence that had come over them, how they'd whispered to each other as if they were afraid someone could hear. He remembered a feeling of deep sadness and an ambiguous kind of threat. It hadn't made sense then and made even less sense now.

What mattered was his sister, and Grady didn't want her wandering around in the country alone in search of some half-dead flowers. Especially if it meant she was wandering around in Bitter End.

"Would you care for another helping?" Savannah asked Laredo, breaking into Grady's thoughts.

Laredo planted his hands on his stomach and shook his head. "As delicious as it is, I don't think I could manage another mouthful. As I said earlier, this is one of the best meals I've had in years. I hope your brother appreciates what a fine cook you are."

Even from across the table Grady could feel Savannah's pleasure at the other man's remark. It *sounded* genuine, but Grady suspected Laredo Smith was a consummate con man, who knew a good thing when he saw it. It was clear to Grady, if no one else, that Laredo Smith was out to take advantage of his sister. Not that he had a raindrop's chance in hell of doing so as long as Grady lived and breathed. The drifter could sweet-talk some other rancher's sister. He'd get nowhere with Savannah; Grady would personally see to that.

"I'll help with the dishes," Laredo offered.

Grady resisted suggesting that Laredo was laying it on a little thick, but he was already out of Savannah's good graces and she wouldn't appreciate his sarcasm.

"I'll do the dishes later," Savannah said. "It's more important that I take care of the roses."

"I could help you with that," he suggested next, and then, as if qualifying his statement, he added, "My grandmother let me help her."

"That…that would be lovely."

Grady couldn't recall the last time he'd seen his sister this flustered.

Like a schoolboy eager to please his teacher, Laredo stood and carried his empty plate to the sink.

Grady couldn't allow this to continue. It was time he set the other man straight. "Before this goes any further, you need to know, Mr. Smith, that there's no work for you here."

"Excuse me," Savannah said, her voice rising, "but *I* was the one who hired Laredo."

"I'll be happy to drive you back into Promise myself," Grady volunteered, ignoring his sister. "Would *now* be convenient?"

The two men glared at each other.

"Grady," Savannah protested, but to no avail. He'd tuned her out, unwilling to listen to her arguments.

When she couldn't attract his attention, Savannah tried reaching Laredo. She said his name, but he, too, ignored her, eyes locked with Grady's. The silent battle of wills didn't last long. Slowly Laredo's shoulders relaxed and he nodded. "Now would be fine."

Grady hadn't expected him to capitulate this easily. If anything, he'd anticipated an argument. Laredo Smith was no fool. The way Savannah had fussed over him at dinner, blushed and made a general idiot of herself, there was no telling how much the drifter could take her for.

"I'll get my saddle."

"No!"

Savannah's cry caught them both off guard. Grady's attention flew to her, as did Laredo's.

Her face was red and her hands had tightened into fists. "If you two had listened to me earlier, I could have cleared this up immediately." She exhaled a long shaky breath. "I was the one who hired Laredo."

"And I said I don't need anyone just now," Grady countered brusquely.

"I didn't say I hired him to help you, Grady. Laredo Smith is working for me."

Two

Laredo sat on the thin mattress and nursed his aching ribs. They hurt a little less now that the aspirin had had time to take effect. Without asking, Savannah had handed him the pills after dinner, as if she knew intuitively how uncomfortable he'd been. She continued to fascinate him, but it was abundantly clear that her big brother wasn't keen on Laredo hanging around her. Not that Laredo blamed him. If Savannah was his sister, he'd keep a close eye on her, too.

Following dinner, they'd transplanted the old roses she'd found that day. Afterward she'd proudly walked him through the flower garden, telling him the names of various plants, describing their characteristics. She grew azaleas, rhododendrons and many others, some of which he'd never seen before. A hedge of sunflowers separated the flowers from a small herb garden. And then there were her roses.

As she led him down the narrow pathways of her rose garden, she stopped to tell him about each one. It was almost, he thought fancifully, as if she were introducing him to her children. Little pieces of her heart, planted and nourished in fertile ground. From the way her roses flourished, she'd obviously lavished them with love and care.

The rows of old roses were what impressed him most—but no less than Savannah's knowledge of their histories. She was able to tell him where each one had come from and when it was first grown. Gesturing in her enthusiasm, she lost her large straw hat; Laredo stooped to pick it up. She smiled as he returned it, but didn't interrupt her history of the Highway 290 Pink Buttons—small roses with double blossoms. Found in this part of Texas, she told him proudly. Her voice was full of reverence as she spoke of the inherent beauty of the old roses, their perfect scent, their ability to survive.

When they'd finished walking around the garden, she wrote out a list of tasks she had in mind for him. Laredo listened carefully, had her show him where he'd find the supplies he'd need and promised to get started first thing in the morning. He was eager to prove she hadn't made a mistake by hiring him, and that her trust in him had been well placed. *Saying* it was one thing, but the proof was in the results.

In the morning, as soon as he finished dealing with his truck, he planned to be in that rose garden working his fool head off. It wasn't wrangling, wasn't what he knew best, but if he treated the roses with the same respect and appreciation he did a good quarter horse, then he'd do fine.

"Cowboy, you got everything you need?" A froggy male voice cut into Laredo's musings, startling him. He swiveled around to find an older man standing just inside the large bunkhouse. Two rows of beds lined the floor—like an army barracks; at the other end was a door leading to the foreman's private room.

"Wiley Rogers," the foreman said.

"Laredo Smith. And yes, thanks, I'm fine for now. I have some stuff in my truck—clothes and such—but I can get those in the morning." He stood and moved toward the man. They exchanged brusque handshakes.

Rogers had to be sixty if he was a day, with legs bowed from too many years in the saddle. "Hear you're workin' for Savannah," he said with a friendly smile.

Laredo nodded.

The foreman chuckled and rubbed his unshaven jaw, eyeing Laredo carefully. Whatever his opinion, he was keeping it to himself. "If that don't beat all," he muttered, still grinning. "Never thought I'd see the day…"

"Beg your pardon?"

"It's nothing," Wiley said. After a moment's reflection he revised his statement. "Actually it *is* something, but you wouldn't understand. Nice meetin' you, Laredo. You need anything else, just give me a holler."

"Thanks, I will." He sat back down on the bed as Wiley retired to his room and closed the door.

Once the lights were out, Laredo lay on his back and stared up at the ceiling, waiting for sleep to claim him. He should've been dead to the world by now. He was exhausted. And for the first time in days the pain in his side had dulled. His belly was full and he had employment, of sorts. He didn't know how long Savannah would find enough tasks to keep him busy, but he didn't imagine this job would last more than a week or two.

As soon as he found out what was wrong with the

truck and had it repaired, he'd hit the road. In hindsight, Earl Chesterton had done him a favor by firing him. Although it sure as hell dented his ego to lose that job, especially under those circumstances. His jaw tightened every time he thought about being accused of theft.

But he was determined to look at this as a blessing in disguise—what his grandmother would have called it. Finding himself unexpectedly jobless was just the incentive he needed to head back to Oklahoma and pursue his dream of breeding and selling quarter horses. After talking about it for years, he was actually going to do it. With the bitterness of being fired from the Triple C Ranch came the sweetness of this chance to live his dream. Even knowing it would mean years of sacrifice, the thought of being his own boss and living on his own land excited Laredo.

Intent on sleeping, he closed his eyes and tried to empty his mind. To his surprise a vivid image of Savannah appeared, clear as anything. He studied her a long while, this warm gentle woman who'd come so fortuitously into his life. She was a comfortable person, and she possessed a kind heart. He liked Savannah Weston, but then it was impossible *not* to like her. In fact—even more than that—he found himself attracted to her. Strongly attracted.

It was years since a woman had captivated him the way Savannah had. She wasn't like other women he'd known. He'd never felt relaxed or easy around the opposite sex, but Savannah brought out his every protective instinct. She was shy but genuine, and he liked that. He liked that a lot. Pretty, too, without being flashy. He sensed that despite her quiet unassuming manner she had courage and strength. She reminded him a bit of the frontier women he'd read about who'd helped tame the territory of Texas. Especially with those long dresses she wore.

Her brother, on the other hand, was another matter. Hardheaded, stubborn, suspicious. Laredo had taken exception to the way Grady spoke to his sister, but it wasn't his place to get involved in their family affairs.

No, sir.

He'd work here while there was work to be had, get his truck back in good running order, then head for Oklahoma as soon as he could arrange it.

That would be the best thing for everyone. For the Westons and for him.

As she'd planned days before, Savannah drove into town the next morning. Her errand list seemed endless. Hardware store, library, the grocery. Finally she was hurrying toward the post office. Her last stop. She realized that the urgency to get back to the ranch had more to do with seeing Laredo again than with any task that waited for her. *Anyone would think you were a schoolgirl!* But she couldn't help the way her heart reacted to the man.

The dinner she planned for that night was Grady's favorite—chicken-fried steak, cream gravy and fresh green beans. A peace offering. He'd barely had a word for her all morning, but then he wasn't communicative at the best of times. Still, there was no mistaking his anger. She'd felt his gaze following her in the kitchen this morning as she'd moved about, preparing breakfast. They'd carefully avoided each other's eyes. Savannah seldom defied her brother, but Grady had left her no option.

Because she'd stood her ground, Laredo was staying. For some reason that made her happier than anything had in years.

Savannah purposely saved the post office until last, hoping Caroline Daniels, the postmistress, would have time to chat. Dovie Boyd, who owned the antique store and the Victorian Tea Room, was just leaving when Savannah pulled into the parking lot. They exchanged cheerful waves.

The interior of the post office was blessedly cool, and Savannah glanced toward the front counter, relieved to see no other patrons. Deciding to pick up her mail first, she found her postbox key and inserted it into the lock. The metal door swung open to reveal Caroline's nose and brown eyes.

"Is it true?" the postmistress demanded.

"True?" Savannah blinked back her surprise at discovering Caroline's face thrust at her through the small opening.

"I thought I was your best friend."

"You are," Savannah said.

"Then one would think you'd have told me about a handsome stranger working at the Yellow Rose."

Savannah felt color explode in her face. Apparently word of her hiring Laredo had already spread through town. In less than twenty-four hours, too! How, she didn't know—didn't even want to know. This was the problem with living in a small town. Nothing was private. Unnerved, she closed the small door and twisted the key, locking it.

"Savannah!" came Caroline's muffled voice.

Reluctantly Savannah unlocked the box and opened the door. "Who told you?" She withdrew the few envelopes from the box and thrust them into her bag.

"Ellie Frasier, and she said he's cute, too."

"Ellie met him?" Savannah asked. Ellie was the daughter of John Frasier, owner of the feed store. She was young and pretty, and she had a lively fun-loving personality. More than once Savannah had hoped Grady would notice her, seeing as he made weekly trips to Frasier's for grain and such. Savannah had hinted a couple of times that he needn't rush home—that maybe he could invite Ellie out for coffee or a cold beer. Her suggestions had met with a glare and a low growl that said he didn't take kindly to her matchmaking efforts.

"So, is he as cute as Ellie says?"

Savannah's blush deepened and she raised her hand to her face. "I... I wouldn't know."

Caroline's chuckle was full of disbelief. "Okay, if you won't answer that, then tell me his name."

No harm there. "Laredo Smith."

"So you were able to talk Grady into hiring another hand. Where'd he happen to meet Laredo?"

This was where the story got difficult. "Grady didn't exactly...hire Laredo."

The brown eyes staring at her from the back of her mailbox darkened perceptibly. "What do you mean?"

Savannah sighed. She might as well explain it once and for all and be done with it. "Laredo isn't working for Grady. I'm the one who hired him."

"You?" Those same eyes narrowed. "Meet me up front."

While Savannah had hoped to discuss the events

of the day before with Caroline, she'd wanted to bring up the subject of Laredo in her own time. She certainly hadn't expected an inquisition, especially this soon. But lately Caroline had been encouraging her to get out more, mingle. Savannah decided to accept her friend's advice the day Caroline took it herself.

"You've got that look again," Caroline teased when Savannah approached the counter.

"What look?"

"The one that says you're...you know, perturbed."

"Well, I am." As far as Savannah was concerned she had every right to feel perturbed, annoyed and downright peeved. The entire town was discussing her life, or soon would be, particularly when it became common knowledge that Laredo Smith worked for her and not Grady. She absolutely deplored gossip and refused to partake in it. She'd never pry into anyone's personal business. Why, she'd been Caroline's best friend for ages, and not once had she asked who'd fathered five-year-old Maggie. If Caroline felt inclined to tell her, then she would, but Savannah would rather die than ask.

"Get over it, Savannah. It isn't every day a handsome stranger wanders into town."

"Laredo didn't exactly wander into Promise." She supposed she'd have to tell Caroline the truth. That'd be preferable to having her hear wild rumors later on.

"I know. His truck broke down. It's the transmission, and with parts and labor it'll be close to fifteen hundred dollars. Plus it's going to take at least ten days for the parts to come in."

Good grief, Caroline knew more about Laredo than she did! "Who told you all that?" Silly question when the answer was obvious. Wiley had mentioned that he was going to help Laredo tow his truck into Powell's Garage that morning. Paul Powell's wife, Louise, did the paperwork and was a known talker. Apparently she'd been at the garage when Wiley and Laredo arrived. To complicate matters, Wiley tended to have a loose tongue himself. Savannah had the sudden urge to sit down with an entire pitcher of iced tea, only she had the feeling that all the iced tea in the world wasn't going to make anything better.

Caroline watched her closely. In a gentler tone of voice she asked, "You hired him yourself?"

"Yes. I've been looking for someone to help me with the garden and—and now that I'm starting to get more orders for my roses, well, it makes sense to hire some help." She could have managed very well on her own, though, and Caroline knew it.

"You like him, don't you, Savannah?"

"Of course I like Laredo. He's kind and thoughtful and…" She couldn't continue. "Grady was just awful! Oh, Caroline, I was mortified." She brought one hand to her mouth, remembering the confrontation between the two men after dinner.

"Grady? What else is new?"

"I offered Laredo a job. I shouldn't have done it without talking to Grady first, but he needed the work and you know how I've been after Grady to hire an extra hand."

"So *you* hired him, and Grady didn't appreciate your…help."

Savannah looked away. "That's putting it mildly. He insisted he didn't need anyone else and offered to drive Laredo into town that very minute. He made it sound as if he wanted him off our property, the sooner the better. I didn't know Grady could be that rude! I was embarrassed, and angry, so I... I stepped in and claimed I'd hired Laredo to work for me."

Caroline's eyes sparked with approval. "I'll bet Grady just hit the roof."

"Put it this way—he wasn't pleased."

Nibbling on her lower lip, Caroline crossed her arms and leaned against the counter. "So, tell me, how'd you meet your new employee?"

The questions weren't getting any easier. "I saw him walking down the road," Savannah admitted wryly, "and I... I stopped and offered him a lift."

Caroline's eyes widened at this, but she didn't comment. Savannah continued. "He asked about work in the area, and before I could stop myself, I said there was a job on the Yellow Rose."

"Which is why Grady took an immediate dislike to him," Caroline muttered.

She knew Grady almost as well as Savannah did. "That's right. He acted like a jerk for no reason other than the fact that *I* was the one to hire him. Oh, Caroline, I don't think I've ever been more furious with my brother."

"So what happened next?"

A sense of pride and satisfaction came to her rescue, and Savannah started to giggle. "If only you could've seen Grady's face when I told him Laredo was working for me. I thought he was going to explode." To give him some credit, Grady had kept his mouth shut. Instead, he'd stormed out of the house like a two-year-old, leaving Savannah and Laredo standing there in awkward silence.

Caroline burst out laughing. "I can see it all now! Oh, Savannah, I'm so proud of you."

"Really?"

"Really. It's about time someone put Grady Weston in his place. Don't get me wrong, I think the world of him, but he's become such a curmudgeon in the past few years. He takes everything so seriously. I can't remember the last time I heard him laugh."

Savannah's heart went out to her brother. What Caroline said was true, but it was only because Grady carried such a heavy load of responsibilities. In only a few years he'd taken the ranch from the edge of bankruptcy and made it viable again. Finances remained tight, but they were no longer in danger of losing the land that had been in their family for generations. Savannah reminded herself of this every time Grady's behavior distressed her. And it had never distressed her more than last night. His opinion of Laredo—and by extension, her—was so scathing. She knew very well that he considered her "a damned fool"—his favorite epithet—for trusting a stranger.

She lowered her eyes, not wanting Caroline to read her face. "Am I a fool, Caroline?"

"You? You're joking, right?"

"No, please, I need to know. I… I'm attracted to Laredo. I've never felt this way about a man. He's not like anyone else. He listens to me, and even though we've barely met, he…he understands me better than my own brother does. We spent an entire hour in my garden last night, and he let me tell him about my roses. His grandmother had old roses and he was genuinely interested in what I'm doing."

Caroline's features softened.

"And he's honest. He told me he'd been fired from his last job and why. He didn't have to do that, but he did and I respect him for it." It sounded foolish now, as if everything her brother had said was true.

"What does your heart tell you?" Caroline asked.

Savannah wavered. When she was with Laredo, there was no doubt how she felt, but in the light of cold reality, she was forced to wonder if she really was as gullible and naive as Grady thought. "I'm not sure anymore."

"Why is it so important that you have all the answers right this moment?"

"I don't know, it's just that—"

Caroline laughed. "Be more patient, Savannah. Life has a way of working things out. And for heaven's sake, quit being so hard on yourself! It isn't a sin to be attracted to a man. Why *shouldn't* you be?"

"But…oh, Caroline, it's been so long since anyone made me feel this way."

"Then I like him already."

"You do?"

"How could I not? He's brought color to your cheeks."

Embarrassed, Savannah raised both her hands to her face.

"He's made your heart smile."

What a nice way of putting it. That was exactly how she felt.

"And I've never seen you look happier."

She *was* happy, Savannah realized. Deliriously so, simply because a kindhearted man had walked in the garden with her and listened as she told him stories about old roses. He'd more than listened; he'd been interested, asking questions, touching her roses with a gentle hand. Savannah had hardly slept the entire night, thinking about their time together.

"I'm too old," she blurted. Of her entire high-school graduating class, she was the only one still unmarried. Two were already on their second marriages, Savannah hadn't even managed to fall in love.

"Nonsense! Too old?" Caroline countered. "That's the most ridiculous thing you've ever said."

"Ellie's right—Laredo *is* handsome. Why would he be interested in someone like me?"

"Because you're beautiful, Savannah, inside and out. He'd be a fool not to recognize that. Now stop worrying and just be yourself."

Savannah felt only slightly reassured. Her biggest fear was that she'd made more of this attraction than there was. She'd barely known Laredo twenty-four hours, and yet it felt as if she'd known him all her life. She was afraid this might be some unrealistic fantasy. It didn't seem possible that he could share her feelings.

"Can you still watch Maggie on Monday night?" Caroline asked hopefully, interrupting Savannah's relentless worries.

"Of course," Savannah told her. She enjoyed having the five-year-old over while Caroline did volunteer work as a math tutor. Grady intimidated the little girl, but Maggie was slowly warming to him, and although Grady wasn't admitting it, he'd come to enjoy Maggie's visits, as well.

"When I drop her off, I can meet your Laredo for myself."

Your Laredo. Savannah blushed and smiled. "He might not be there."

"Then I'm going to plant myself in the living room until he shows up. I'm dying to meet this marvel who's made my very dearest friend finally—*finally*—fall for a man."

"I was thinking of asking him to come to church with me on Sunday," Savannah said. Actually the idea had just occurred to her, and she looked to Caroline for confirmation of its worth.

"Great! I can meet him then. And so can everyone else."

Everyone else. Savannah's heart fell. Tongues were sure to wag if she showed up at Sunday services with a man on her arm. Well, let them, she decided suddenly. She'd speak to him about church this very afternoon.

"I don't want to talk about it," Grady growled at Wiley as they rode back toward the ranch house that afternoon. They'd spent most of the day searching through brush for cows and newborn calves. He was completely drained, mentally and physically. Grady had been up late every night for three weeks, checking on newborn calves in the calving barn. Sleep this time of year was a luxury for any rancher.

Wiley looked offended. "Hey, I didn't say a word."

"That may be, but you're about ready to burst with curiosity, I can tell."

"Seems to me you're wantin' to say your piece, otherwise you wouldn't've mentioned it."

It being Savannah and the hand she'd hired. Even now Grady couldn't believe what she'd done. He had trouble grasping the fact that his own sister could behave like a dithering fool over some saddle bum.

But he'd had an even harder time accepting what

Richard had done. It'd taken weeks for everything to sink in, and even then, Grady couldn't understand how his own brother could betray them. Only when the bills piled up and the federal government had come after the inheritance tax had he been forced to face the truth. Richard was a bastard, pure and simple. As for Smith…

"I don't like him," Grady announced. That was all he intended to say. If Wiley commented, fine. If he didn't, that was fine, too.

"You talkin' about Laredo Smith?"

"Smith," Grady repeated with a snicker. "Mighty convenient surname if you ask me."

"Lots of people called Smith."

"My point exactly," Grady snarled. As a rule Wiley wasn't this obtuse. "I'd bet my snakeskin boots the name's phony."

"He seems like a fine young man to me."

It didn't set well that his friend, his confidant, his foreman would take the other man's side. "What do you mean?"

"He's a real worker. He was up early, wanting to get started in Savannah's garden before I helped tow his truck into town. We had it to Powell's by the time they opened, and Paul took a look at it while we were still there."

"What's wrong with it?" Grady had decided he wanted nothing to do with this hired hand of Savannah's but it was in the best interests of his family to learn what he could.

"Transmission needs to be replaced and the brakes are shot, too. Paul said once he got the parts, he'd have it running in a couple of days."

"Good." Grady suspected the stranger would disappear about the time his truck was repaired.

"He doesn't look like he's got cash enough to pay for it once the work's done."

"What?" Grady groaned.

"You heard me. Why else do you think he was lookin' for a job?"

They headed toward the creek and slipped out of their saddles to allow their horses a long drink of cool water. Grady didn't like the idea of Laredo lingering at the Yellow Rose. He'd seen men like Smith before. Drifters, washed-up rodeo riders, shiftless men with shiftless lives. No roots or families. They spent their money as fast as they earned it without a thought to their next meal, let alone the future. They might work hard, but they also played hard and lived harder. Laredo Smith wasn't the type of man he wanted hanging around his sister, that was for damn sure.

"Find out anything else about him?" Grady asked, kicking a rock with the toe of his boot. His interest was out in the open now, no reason to hide it.

Not waiting for Wiley's reply, Grady climbed back into the saddle with the ease of a man long accustomed to riding.

"I thought you said you didn't want to talk about it."

Grady tossed his foreman a furious look, but Wiley responded with a knowing chuckle. The old man knew he could get away with saying what he damn well pleased, and an angry glower wouldn't change that.

"He let drop a few bits of information on the way into town," Wiley admitted as he, too, remounted. "He's been workin' on the Triple C over in Williamsburg for the past couple years."

Grady had heard of the ranch, which was one of the larger spreads in the Texas hill country. He'd spoken to Earl Chesterton, the owner, a time or two at the district cattlemen meetings, but they were little more than nodding acquaintances. Compared to the Triple C, the Yellow Rose was small stuff.

"You gonna check on him?" Wiley asked in a tone that said he disapproved of the idea.

Grady snorted. "Why would I do something like that? He doesn't work for me, remember?"

"You're the one with all the questions," Wiley pointed out.

"I was curious. You can't blame me for that, especially when all I'm doing is looking out for Savannah." He didn't want to say it out loud, but he was worried about his younger sister. Not once in all these years had she openly crossed him. Not that she didn't have any opinions, and not that she was meek or passive, like some people assumed.

Savannah had ways of making her wishes known. Subtle ways. The fact was, he'd come to recognize that when she baked his favorite peach cobbler, she had something on her mind. She'd wait until after dinner; when he was enjoying dessert, she'd sit down with him, sweetness personified, and ask a few harmless—but pertinent—questions. Slowly she'd lead up to what she really wanted, making her point casually and without fanfare.

Grady always listened, and often her nonconfrontational style worked and he'd change his mind. He considered himself a fair man; if he felt her concern was valid, he acted on it.

Then Laredo Smith arrived, and suddenly his sister's behavior had undergone a drastic change. She'd actually raised her voice to him, and all because of this worthless drifter. Well, she was welcome to Laredo Smith. If she wanted to walk around with her heart dangling from her sleeve, acting like a lovelorn fifteen-year-old, he wasn't going to stop her. By the same token, he wouldn't offer sympathy when a month or two down the road Laredo left her high and dry.

"How old is Savannah now?" Wiley asked. "She's over twenty-one, right?"

"You know damn well how old she is."

Wiley set his Stetson farther back on his head and grinned. "You're right, I do. I was just wondering if *you* did."

Grady frowned. "She's old enough to know better."

"Old enough to know her own heart, too, I'd say."

Grady nudged his gelding, Starlight, into a trot and turned toward the house, following the fence line. He wanted to check that it was secure and ascertain the condition of the windmill and water tank before he headed in for the night.

"Like I said earlier," he announced stiffly, "I don't want to talk about it."

"Then you aren't interested in hearin' what else Smith said."

What Grady wasn't interested in was playing games. He reined in Starlight and turned to look back at the foreman. "You got something to say, then I suggest you say it."

"He's a wrangler."

Grady wasn't impressed. Wranglers are a dime a dozen in Texas.

"We could use a good wrangler. Payin' someone

to come in and care for the horses can get downright costly."

"I can take care of them myself."

"Sure, the same way you can deliver calves, plant alfalfa, move herds and everything else all by your lonesome. Hey," he said with a shrug, "it was just a suggestion."

Despite his dour mood, Grady threw back his head and laughed. "Wiley, why do you think I'm paying you the big bucks? Since you're so concerned about my welfare, *you* can be my wrangler from now on. You think we need to take one on full-time? Then I'm naming you the Yellow Rose's official wrangler. You can feed, water, groom and worm the horses from this day forward. Don't forget to take care of the tack, too, while you're at it."

"Quit foolin' around."

"Do I look like I'm fooling?" Grady asked with a broad grin. The expression on Wiley's face was worth a thousand bucks. For the first time in longer than he cared to remember, Grady threw back his head and laughed until his throat felt raw.

Savannah set the platter of chicken-fried steak on the oven rack and turned the saucepan of thick cream gravy to simmer. The green beans were tender, and she'd sliced fresh tomatoes from her kitchen garden. An apple pie cooled on the counter. All she needed to do now was stir up a pitcher of lemonade, and dinner would be ready when Grady and Wiley returned.

With a few extra moments on her hands, she decided to step outside. Laredo had been working all afternoon in the hot sun, and knowing he was probably thirsty, she poured him a glass of iced tea. As she walked into the sunshine, she was honest enough to admit that the tea was only an excuse to be with him.

Her gardens had never looked better, but she couldn't find Laredo. He'd been there no more than five minutes ago. Disappointed, she was about to return to the house when she spotted him in the goat pen with Samson and Delilah, her two kids. They were a thank-you gift for the roses she'd given a friend for an anniversary party. Seeing Laredo, she felt her heart go still, and she smiled with pleasure.

Grady had delighted in teasing her about her pets. He called it a silly woman thing, viewing her goats the same way he did her roses. He didn't care one whit about something she dearly loved. Roses were her heart, her joy, her passion. Sometimes Savannah wondered if they could truly be brother and sister, their differences seemed so profound.

Laredo knelt in the grass with the two young goats, petting them, talking to them. Samson, in particular, didn't normally take to strangers, but apparently Laredo was a special case.

Savannah wasn't sure how long she stood there watching. Several minutes, anyway, because the cold glass in her hand had numbed her fingers. Not wanting Laredo to know she'd been spying on him, she returned to the house. She set the glass aside and raised her cold hands to her face, to cool her flushed cheeks.

Incredibly the urge to cry came over her, and she didn't know why. She'd barely exchanged a word with Laredo all day; they'd both been busy with their own chores. And yet Savannah had never felt closer to anyone than she did to him for those few moments, watching him with her goats.

This stranger, this man she barely knew, possessed the ability to touch her soul. Savannah wondered if she'd ever be the same.

Three

Savannah enjoyed listening to Wade McMillen preach. His messages, simple and direct, cut straight to the heart. He was the most unlikely preacher she'd ever seen. A large man, tall and muscular, he looked as though he'd be more comfortable at home herding cattle than delivering sermons. Perhaps that was what made him so popular.

It might have been her imagination, but Savannah felt the curious stares of those around her. The word about her and Laredo was out, she was sure of it. Now everyone in the town knew she—and not Grady—had hired him.

Soon she'd be the subject of speculative comments and whispered questions—if she wasn't already. She felt mortified, but pride helped her hold her head high and look straight ahead. Her mind wandered throughout Wade's sermon, though, something that didn't usually happen. When her thoughts weren't focused on the consequences of her actions, they zoomed with startling ease to Laredo.

She'd wanted to invite him to church and had tried

to broach the subject a number of times, but had lost her nerve. Even an invitation to Sunday-morning worship had seemed rather brash. In light of the interest she'd generated, Savannah would be forever grateful that Laredo *wasn't* with her. His presence would've set tongues wagging for sure.

Laredo had worked all day Saturday building trellises, even though she'd insisted she didn't require him to work weekends. He'd brushed aside her protests and pounded and sawed from dawn to dusk. By the end of the day, a long row of freshly painted trellises stood drying in the late March sun.

After dinner he sat on the porch with her until Grady arrived. Her brother's disapproval was evident in everything he said and did. She wanted to plead with Laredo to ignore him, wanted to insist she was her own woman, but again she remained silent.

A coward, that was what she was. Savannah would've given just about anything to find the courage to tell him what was on her mind and in her heart.

Actually, as Caroline had said, she'd done one thing that made her proud. She'd stood up to Grady, and because she had, Laredo was still at the ranch. Challenging Grady was no easy task. His strong personality had quelled braver souls than hers.

The congregation stood, and Savannah reached for the hymnal and opened it to the appropriate page. Her soft voice lifted with those in the choir. She glanced over at Caroline, standing in the front row of the choir in her long white robe. Her friend must have noticed because she acknowledged Savannah with an almost imperceptible wink. Savannah relaxed for the first time since she'd entered the church that morning.

After a closing prayer organ music once again filled the church and the service ended.

Savannah followed Nell Bishop and her two children out of the pew. Jake Bishop had been killed in a freak tractor accident three and a half years ago. They'd always seemed the perfect couple, so deeply in love—a great team, everyone said. Savannah knew life had been difficult for Nell without Jake and she admired the other woman's strength. Nell had refused to leave the ranch, working it herself. When asked why she hadn't sold off the spread and moved into town, Nell had simply explained that keeping the ranch was what Jake would have wanted. Walking with Nell, Savannah felt safe from gossip. The widow was a private person, as she was herself, and would never pry into her affairs.

Louise Powell stood in the vestibule, craning her neck. Savannah strongly suspected the woman wanted to grill her about Laredo.

Savannah wished there was some way she could just vanish.

"Savannah! Savannah, over here!" Louise raised one gloved hand and waved frantically.

It would do no good to avoid her, Savannah decided miserably. If there was one thing she hated more than gossip, it was being the center of attention.

As soon as she reached the vestibule, Louise was at her side. Louise had celebrated her fiftieth birthday in January and hated the thought of being a half a century old. In the weeks since, she'd changed her hairstyle and purchased a new wardrobe, trying for a younger look. Unfortunately she came across as a woman who was obviously fifty and dressed like twenty-five.

"I met your new friend!" Louise exclaimed. Savannah suspected this was Tammy Lee's influence on her. Tammy Lee—Louise's new friend—was a middle-aged divorcée whose reputation could charitably be described as colorful. "What a nice young man." She paused, waiting for Savannah's comment, but when none was forthcoming, she plowed ahead, wrapping her arm around Savannah's waist. "I understand he's working for you." An annoying giggle followed. "Savannah, I wonder if we really know you, after all. I've always thought of you as shy and retiring, but you know what they say about still waters." The girlish giggle returned.

"There's someone I have to see," Savannah said in an effort to escape.

"Laredo?" Louise asked. This was accompanied with a squeeze tight enough to make Savannah wince. "If you run out of work for him, you send him my way, understand?"

"If you'll excuse me, please…" Savannah said a little desperately.

The Moorhouse sisters, Edwina and Lily, stepped into the vestibule, distracting Louise. Both were retired schoolteachers. Miss Edwina had been Savannah's first-grade teacher and Miss Lily her third. The two were inseparable and Savannah loved them dearly.

"Good morning," Savannah mumbled as she slipped past the elderly pair.

By the time she walked outside, she felt like gasping for air. Reverend McMillen stood just outside the large double doors and greeted each parishioner by name. Wade had a way of looking at a person and seeing more than the obvious. "Are you okay, Savannah?" he asked, holding her hand between both of his. "You're looking flushed."

"I'm fine. Just a little warm." Her discomfort had more to do with attracting unwelcome attention. All she wanted was to hurry home before someone else had the chance to corner her.

"Savannah! Savannah!" Maggie Daniels, Caroline's five-year-old daughter, raced to her side and proudly offered her a crayon drawing she'd made in Sunday-school class.

"Hi there, Maggie-may. What's this?" Savannah asked, studying the paper. Maggie was her joy, the child of her heart. It had been a shock when Caroline Daniels announced she was pregnant her senior year in college. From the beginning there'd been plenty of speculation about the father of Caroline's child, but Caroline had never said, and no one had ever asked. Caroline's mother, Florence, had served as postmistress in Promise for years, and when she died last spring, Caroline had taken over her duties.

Maggie had apparently transferred her love for her grandmother to Savannah. It made Savannah feel privileged, and she reciprocated the child's feelings a hundred percent. Recently Caroline had relied more and more on Savannah to babysit, but she never minded. It was a delight to spend time with the little girl.

"That's Joseph," Maggie explained now, pointing to a lumpish figure in her drawing.

"Ah, I see," Savannah said. "He's wearing his coat of many colors. Look what a good job you've done!"

Maggie glowed with pleasure. She tucked her small hand in Savannah's. "Where's Mommy?"

Savannah was about to ask the same thing. The

question was answered soon enough when Caroline exited the side door with the other members of the choir. It generally took her a few moments to hang up her robe and put away the music sheets.

"Mommy, Mommy, look!" Maggie cried, rushing toward her mother, pigtails bouncing. The youngster threw her arms around Caroline as if it'd been a year since they'd seen each other.

"Would you like to join us for brunch?" Caroline asked, lifting Maggie into her arms.

Savannah declined with a quick shake of her head. "I put a roast in the oven before I left."

"Did Louise corner you?" Caroline lowered her voice.

"She tried."

"Hey, give the old biddy something to talk about."

"Caroline!"

"She's jealous, that's all."

"Jealous of what?" Savannah wanted to know.

"Of you. For being young and pretty and having a good-looking man in your life."

"Laredo's not in my life—at least not in the personal sense," Savannah felt obliged to protest—although she wished it wasn't true. She'd like him to kiss her or hold her hand—anything so she'd know he felt the same things she did. Once she'd caught him looking at her and she thought he seemed…interested, but she couldn't be sure. If she'd had more experience, she'd know.

"Well, more's the pity," Caroline said with a laugh. "A little romance would do you a world of good."

"What about you?" Caroline was a fine one to talk.

Savannah couldn't remember the last time her friend had gone out on a date.

"Me? Romance?" Caroline shook her head. "No, thanks. I've had enough romance to last me a lifetime."

"Oh, Caroline, don't allow one negative experience to sour you forever."

Sadness dimmed her eyes, although Caroline made an effort to hide it. "Some people are meant to fall in love, and then there are people like me…" Her words faded and she looked away.

Savannah's heart went out to her, but she didn't know what else to say.

Laredo heard Wiley whistling in the back of the bunkhouse. The old coot was certainly in a good mood. By nature the foreman appeared to be an easygoing sort, but this afternoon he was downright cheerful.

Stitching a stirrup, Laredo inserted the needle into the worn leather. No one had asked him to repair the saddle, but he had time on his hands, and keeping himself occupied was better than sitting around doing nothing. He wasn't a man who could remain idle long.

Although it was none of his concern, he'd visited the barn and inspected the horses. They were well cared for and in good health. Widowmaker, the stallion kept for breeding purposes, reminded Laredo of Grady. Man and beast shared the same temperament— although he figured he'd have a better relationship with Widowmaker than he ever would with Grady. Horses instinctively recognized Laredo as a friend. He shared an affinity with them that was the key to his success as a wrangler. From the time he was a toddler he'd enjoyed working with his father and their horses.

One of his fondest childhood memories was of his father holding him high enough to pet and talk to Midnight, a beautiful roan gelding. Memories of his father were few and far between. Laredo had been six when word came that Russell Aaron Smith had been killed in a country with a name he couldn't pronounce. He'd bled to death in a rice field six thousand miles from home. Shortly afterward Laredo's mother had moved back with her parents, into the very house where she'd been born, and had never remarried. His grandfather was a good man, patient and caring, but he'd owned an office-supply store and didn't understand Laredo's love of the country or his passion for horses.

As a teenager Laredo had started working summers on local ranches. His talent was soon recognized. To please his mother he'd graduated from high school, but the instant that diploma had been placed in his hand he was gone. She'd dated Clyde Schneider for years and Laredo had always assumed that once he was out of the picture they'd finally get married, but it hadn't happened.

His mother would love Savannah, Laredo thought, but he hesitated to say anything in his next letter home for fear she'd give the relationship more importance than it warranted. Laura Smith wanted grandchildren and brought up the subject at every opportunity, reminding him that it was time he settled down, started a family. He'd dismissed her heavy hints; he didn't consider himself the marrying kind. Not now, anyway, when he had nothing to offer a woman other than a few hundred dusty acres he'd bought in Oklahoma and a stallion he'd recently spent his life savings to acquire. Laredo was on his way to pick him up. Renegade—the horse he'd pinned his dreams on. The horse he hoped would sire a dynasty of quarter horses. But right now that was all he had—and Savannah Weston deserved a damn sight more. If he was ever in a position to entertain marriage, he hoped he found a woman like her. No, he couldn't mention Savannah to his mother; if he did he'd never hear the end of it.

Wiley broke into song and Laredo gave an involuntary shudder at the off-key rendition of an old Kenny Rogers hit. He couldn't recall the title, but it was some ballad about a woman not taking her love to town. In Wiley's version the words were barely distinguishable, the tune not at all.

When Wiley appeared, his hair was wet and slicked back, his boots polished. He wore a tan suede jacket and string tie with a turquoise piece the size of a silver dollar. He reeked of cologne so strong, Laredo's eyes watered.

"You're lookin' right pretty," Laredo teased the foreman.

Wiley laughed. "I'm off to visit the Widow Johnson in Brewster. Grady can work himself into an early grave if he wants, but I've got places to go, people to see. Don't be concerned if I'm a bit late this evening." He winked and all but danced out the door.

If Laredo remembered correctly, Brewster was at least a hundred miles east of Promise. Wiley's cheer was contagious, though, and he couldn't keep from smiling at the older man's pleasure. His task finished, Laredo carried the saddle back into the barn and returned his tools. He'd watched Savannah walk out to the car this morning, a Bible in her hand, and knew she was headed for church.

He couldn't remember the last time he'd darkened the door of a house of worship.

As twelve-thirty approached he found himself listening and watching for Savannah. He would have enjoyed spending more time with her, but her watchdog of a brother made that difficult. Every time they were alone for more than a few minutes, Grady showed up. Rather than place Savannah in the awkward position of having to defend her actions, widening the rift that already existed between brother and sister, Laredo made his excuses and left. He'd dined with them only once, the night of his arrival, preferring to eat by himself in the bunkhouse ever since.

When he left the barn, Laredo saw the car, which meant Savannah was back. He must have stood in the same spot for five minutes trying to decide what to do. Grady was out checking the herd, so he'd probably be away for several hours. This was the perfect opportunity to seek out Savannah's company. A tempting thought.

On the other hand he wasn't doing her any favors by leading her on. He had nothing to offer her other than a few stolen kisses. Besides, he'd already decided that once he'd earned enough to pay for the truck repairs he'd be on his way. And yet...

He shook his head. He barely knew the woman, and even if a relationship developed between them, it would do no good. He'd be living in a small secondhand trailer while he built his business from the ground up. It'd be years of blood and sweat before he had anything to show for his efforts. One day in the distant future his stock would be legendary; he was certain of it. But until then...

When he left Promise, he wanted to go without regrets. Savannah was sweet and gentle, and he'd rather cut off his right arm than hurt her. He wasn't stupid; he saw the look in her eyes. Even though she tried to hide it, she was interested. Damn it all, so was he!

She was the type of woman a man introduced to his mother. Savannah deserved more than a flirtation. He should go back to the bunkhouse now before he started something he couldn't stop. Something he had no *right* to start.

The decision was taken from him when Savannah stepped onto the back porch. When she saw him standing there, staring at the house like...like a stunned steer, she paused. A look of pure joy lit up her face.

"I was just about to ask you to join me for lunch," she said.

He knew he should politely decline, but he hadn't the heart to disappoint her—or deny himself the pleasure of her company. "I'll wash up and be inside in a minute."

On his way toward the house he started whistling; when he realized what he was doing, he stopped. He shouldn't be this happy. Damn it all, he was looking at trouble with his eyes wide open and grinning like a schoolboy.

The scent of roast beef greeted him as soon as he entered the kitchen. Savannah was bent over the stove, pulling a tray of biscuits from the oven. The scene was a homey one. After years of meals on the run, it was a rare treat to sit down at a real table, to have lunch with a woman, to eat in a civilized and leisurely fashion.

"When did you have time to make those?" he asked. She couldn't have been home more than ten minutes.

"Early this morning," she said, scooping the biscuits from the tray and placing them in a breadbasket. Everything else was already on the table.

He seated her and bowed his head while she said grace, then reached for a biscuit. It was too hot to hold, and he tossed it between his hands, making Savannah laugh. A man could get used to hearing this woman's laugh, he mused. Warning signs flashed in every direction, and again Laredo ignored them.

"They're buttermilk biscuits," she said. "The recipe was my mother's." She waited for him to take his first bite.

The biscuit was incredible. The best he'd ever tasted. He told her so and watched her eyes light up at the compliment.

"It'll just be the two of us. Grady's busy just now." She didn't meet his eyes.

Laredo already knew as much. "Would you rather I ate in the bunkhouse?" he asked.

"Oh, no! I like being with you."

"Me, too." He supposed he shouldn't tell her that but found it impossible to keep to himself.

Savannah started passing him serving dishes. "How was your morning?" she asked, handing him the platter of sliced roast beef.

He wanted to tell her he'd missed her; instead, he helped himself to the carrots and potatoes. "I wrote a couple of letters," he said as he set the bowl aside.

Their conversation felt stilted and awkward in the beginning as if they were unsure of each other, afraid of saying too much or too little. But gradually he grew comfortable speaking with her again. There was a naturalness about Savannah. When she asked him questions, her interest was so obviously sincere that he couldn't help responding with equal sincerity.

Following the meal, they sat and lingered over coffee. Savannah asked about his family and perhaps because he'd written to his mother earlier, he described his early years in Texas before his father had gone off to war.

She was such a good listener that Laredo continued, recounting his father's death and the move to Oklahoma to live with his mother's parents, both dead now. He told it all as casually as if he was discussing the weather. In an unemotional voice, he talked about the painful details of those early unhappy years, things he'd rarely shared with anyone.

He sensed that Savannah intuitively understood the significance of the memories he confided in her. She understood and appreciated that he was sharing a piece of his soul, although he made light of it, even joked. But he suspected that the pain revealed itself in the pauses, the unspoken words, and that she was attuned to it.

Her questions were thoughtful and perceptive. After a time he thought he should reciprocate. "What about you, Savannah?" he asked. "Tell me about your family."

She left the table so fast he wondered if his question had offended her. She stood with her back to him, supporting herself on the kitchen counter. He longed to place his hand on her shoulder. Apologize.

He of all people should know enough to respect the privacy of another's pain. After talking about himself nonstop for more than an hour, with her constant encouragement, he'd felt a certain right to ask. It was a right he didn't have. Savannah owed him nothing. Nothing. He was the one in her debt.

"Savannah, I'm sorry," he whispered. He raised his hands to touch her and dropped them just as quickly.

She was still turned away from him, her head still lowered. "Did you know I have two brothers? Grady and Richard."

"No, I didn't know that."

"Richard's younger than me. He's twenty-nine." She turned then, to face him.

"Does he live close by?" he asked gently.

She shook her head. "I don't know where he is. Neither Grady nor I have seen Richard in six years— since the day we buried Mom and Dad."

Laredo didn't know how to respond. He continued to fight the urge to put his arms around her and found it more and more difficult to resist. Speaking of her younger brother clearly upset her.

"He…disappeared." Her voice was shaking with emotion.

"Savannah, listen, you don't need to say any more. I shouldn't have asked." Her pain was right there, and so real it was agony to see. He felt helpless, unable to console her.

"No…please, I want to tell you."

He nodded.

She took a moment to compose herself. "Apparently Dad told Grady that if anything were ever to happen to him, Grady should go to the safe-deposit box at the bank in Brewster." She paused and bit her lower lip. "The day before the funeral Grady and Richard visited the bank together. You can imagine how shocked they were to discover that the safe-deposit box was full of cash. Grady estimated there must have been close to forty thousand dollars there, along with a letter.

"Dad wrote that he'd seen what had happened to people who put their faith in life-insurance companies and after the savings-and-loan fiasco, he didn't trust banks much, either. He didn't want Mom and us three kids to worry about finances, so he'd been putting the money aside little by little for years. His plan was that there'd be enough money to pay the inheritance taxes on the ranch, plus keep the place going. I don't even think my mother knew.

"The next day we buried my parents," Savannah whispered, and her voice quavered with remembered pain. "I recall almost nothing about that day. Again and again I've gone over the details in my mind and it's all a blank. I remember the people—so many friends and family came. I remember how kind and generous everyone was. That part I have no problem with. What I can't recall is the last time I saw Richard. He vanished without a word to anyone. At…at first we assumed that something terrible had happened to him. That in his pain and grief he'd done something crazy. I was worried sick. Grady, too."

Slowly Savannah raised her eyes and Laredo could see that they'd filled with tears. When she spoke again, her voice was small and weak. "He took the money— every dime. As best as we can figure, he left the funeral and went straight to the bank, forged Grady's signature and cleaned out the safe-deposit box. He took what belonged to all three of us. He left us with nothing. We'd just lost Mom and Dad. Our grief was unbearable, and he made it worse with his betrayal. Neither Grady nor I have heard from him since." Some of her tears spilled over. "Grady's never been the same. He's practically killed himself trying to hold on to the ranch, and I think he hates Richard.

"I can't hate him—he's my brother. You see, Laredo, in one day I lost my parents, and I lost both my brothers, too."

Nothing could have kept Laredo from reaching for her then. When he did, she came to him as though he'd held her a thousand times. It felt so...*right* to press her against his heart. Her body was warm and pliant, molding to his as naturally as if they'd been designed for each other.

Laredo had no idea how long they stood there. Not nearly long enough, of that he was sure. Savannah's arms were around his middle, her face buried in his chest. His hands were in her hair, his eyes closed, savoring the wonder of being close to someone this beautiful and this good.

He didn't hear the door open, but he should have realized it was bound to happen.

The screen door slammed and Laredo's eyes shot open. Instinctively his arms tightened around Savannah before he reluctantly released her and faced her brother. Eye to eye. Man-to-man.

"What the hell do you think you're doing with my sister?" Grady Weston shouted.

Grady mulled over what he had to say before he confronted Savannah. Pacing the living-room floor, he carefully weighed each word.

Okay, so maybe he'd been out of line earlier when

he'd found her and Smith clinging to each other like lovers. The sight had distressed him and before he could stop himself he'd exploded.

He didn't want to fight with Savannah. She was his sister, but damn it all! Her infatuation with Laredo Smith—or whatever his name might be—had deprived her of all reason. It was more than he could bear, watching her make a fool of herself over this useless drifter.

Unfortunately his methods of convincing her hadn't worked so far, and Grady realized he needed to change his tactics. To this point, all that his anger and frustration had netted him was the silent treatment. He'd never known a woman who could say more without uttering a word.

Okay, okay, he was willing to admit he'd made mistakes, too. Earlier in the week Savannah had cooked him his favorite dinner as a peace offering, but he'd been so angry he'd chosen to overlook the gesture. He'd been wrong to ignore her outstretched hand, but he was man enough to admit it. He hoped to make peace with her now—hoped he could persuade her to see reason.

Savannah had given him the cold shoulder since he'd walked in on her and Smith in the kitchen. For the rest of the day she'd conveniently disappeared and had retired to her room as soon as it was dark. She wasn't asleep; he could hear her moving about upstairs, as restless as he was here below.

He continued pacing, then decided to talk to her now, before the opportunity was lost. Before he changed his mind. He headed up the stairs, taking them two at a time, paused outside her bedroom, inhaled deeply and knocked. Loudly.

"Yes?" his sister said through the door. Her voice was anything but warm, and the door stayed closed.

"Savannah, I'd appreciate the opportunity to discuss the matter of Laredo Smith with you," he said. It'd taken him ten minutes to come up with those words, to strike the proper tone. He thought he sounded formal, calm, even lawyerly.

The door opened and she stood stiffly in the doorway, blocking the entrance. "Downstairs might be more comfortable," he suggested, gesturing down the narrow staircase.

She hesitated, then reluctantly nodded.

Grady relaxed slightly and wondered how much this peace was going to cost him. Being on the outs with his only sister distressed him more than he cared to reveal.

Savannah followed him down the stairs and took a seat on the sofa. "You owe me an apology, Grady."

"All right, all right," he said, raising both arms in surrender. "I apologize."

"How about apologizing to Laredo?"

That was going too far, but Grady was smart enough to see that arguing the point wouldn't serve his purpose. "I want to discuss Laredo," he said again, and because it was impossible to hold still, he stood up and resumed his pacing. This next part was the most difficult. "I'm worried about you," he said.

"I'm thirty-one years old and I don't need my brother treating me like a child. You're not my guardian. I was mortified today, Grady. Simply mortified."

His behavior had embarrassed him, too, but he

hadn't been able to prevent it. Walking into the house and finding Savannah in a man's arms had been a shock.

"I apologize," he muttered again. He walked the full length of the room and turned back.

"Then why did you act like...like a bull on the rampage?"

Grady didn't know what to tell her other than the truth. "I'm afraid you're going to be hurt."

"My life is none of your concern."

On the contrary, he thought, what happened to her was very much his concern. He was her brother. She was naive about men—especially con artists like Laredo Smith—and whether she realized it or not, she needed him. At least he could be counted on to keep a level head. "Savannah, you're setting yourself up for heartache, getting involved with a drifter."

She sighed as if to say he clearly had no concept of how she felt. Perhaps he didn't, but that didn't change the facts.

"Laredo's been the perfect gentleman," she explained calmly. "I was crying and he comforted me."

"He made you cry?"

"No." The word was filled with exasperation. "I told him about Richard, and I always cry when I talk about Richard."

Grady's jaw tightened at the mention of his younger brother, but he didn't want to discuss him now. He crossed to Savannah and squatted down in front of her. "Savannah, look at me."

"I like Laredo."

"I know you do, and that's what troubles me."

"But why? Haven't you seen how hard he's worked

in my garden? He's done nothing but show me kindness."

Grady ground his teeth in frustration. "There are things about him you don't know," he said as gently as he could.

"Grady, look at me, really look. My youth is slipping through my fingers and I've been given this... this precious gift, this blessing, a chance to love and be loved. I'm not going to let you or anyone else ruin it for me."

"Love." The word felt like acid on his tongue. "You *love* him? You hardly know him!"

She lowered her gaze to her clenched hands. "I *could* love him, I know I could, and he could love me, too. He understands me and I understand him."

"You've known him what? Three days? Four? Savannah, for crying out loud, what's happened to you?"

She looked at him then, and to his amazement she smiled. "Something wonderful, Grady, something really wonderful." She touched his arm and nearly blinded him with the brilliance of her smile. "I feel alive, truly alive for the first time in years. I'd forgotten how good it felt."

"Savannah, Savannah," he moaned. She made this so damned difficult.

"Grady, please be happy for me."

"I can't."

"Then don't ruin it for me, please. That's all I ask."

He stood, feeling the pain of what he had to tell her until the words felt like bricks loaded on his back. "You can't trust him."

"How can you say that?" Her face wore a look of

pure puzzlement. "Laredo's been nothing but trust-worthy."

"You can't trust him," Grady repeated.

"I'd trust him with my life. Do you honestly think I'm such a bad judge of character? He's patient and generous, and for you to say otherwise proves you don't really know him."

"You're naive. He'll use you, and when he's finished, he'll leave you to face the consequences alone."

His words were followed by a shocked angry silence. Then she said, "That comment was unworthy of you."

Well, she'd wait a long time before he'd apologize. He hated what he had to tell her next. Hated to be the one to destroy the fairy tale she'd built around this cast-off cowboy. "Ask me where I was this afternoon," he demanded.

Savannah blinked. "Where were you?"

"I stopped off at Cal Patterson's to make a phone call."

"You couldn't do it here?"

"No. Cal's got the names and phone numbers of all the district members in the Cattlemen's Association." He waited until the information sank in.

"You tried to find out about Laredo," she said, and her voice dropped to a whisper.

"Savannah, listen to me. It gives me no joy to tell you this, but your precious Laredo Smith was fired from his last job."

She remained outwardly calm, but Grady noticed her clenched hands in her lap. "I talked to Earl Chesterton myself," he continued. "Smith was fired and for a damn good reason." If that didn't convince her of the truth about this man, nothing would.

A moment of shocked silence followed, or what he mistook for shock. To his amazement, Savannah slowly smiled. "Oh, Grady, how worried you must have been, but there was no need. I already knew all about that."

Four

Grady wasn't looking forward to talking to Frank Hennessey, but he'd delayed his visit to the sheriff long enough. His fingers tightened on the steering wheel as he drove toward town, and his thoughts darkened with his fears. It bothered him that his sensible intelligent sister had been taken in by a lowlife like Smith.

One thing Grady couldn't tolerate was a thief. As far as he was concerned, stealing what belonged to another was about as low as a man could go. His feelings, no doubt, were influenced by what Richard had done. From the time his younger brother was an infant, he'd been spoiled and coddled by their parents. Savannah was guilty of catering to him, as well—along with everyone else. Even in high school, when Richard should have been maturing and accepting adult responsibilities, he'd made it an art form to pawn off his obligations on others. From early childhood Richard had charmed his way through life. How that boy could talk, Grady recalled cynically. He'd often watched in astonishment as Richard, so glib and smooth, managed to get out of one scrape after another. Nothing had been his fault. Someone else was always to blame. His brother had continually found ways to shift the responsibility for his failures and problems onto other people.

Richard was a charmer, a ladies' man and a smooth talker, but Grady had never suspected his brother was a thief. Then he'd learned the truth. After the shock of the theft had worn off, Grady had been left to face the reality of their dire financial circumstances. He'd even blamed himself. He should never have taken Richard to the Brewster bank or let him know where he kept the key to the safe-deposit box. But Grady had trusted him. And learned the hard way that it had been a mistake.

He wasn't willing to make a second mistake, especially not where his sister was concerned. Savannah was all the family he had left, and he wasn't going to lose her.

In the beginning Grady's opinion of this outsider had been tainted by Savannah's attitude. For the first time in more years than he could remember, she'd challenged his judgment. So Grady's natural inclination was to dislike the man she'd favored against his advice. But he *had* tolerated Laredo Smith's presence. He'd even taken some good-natured ribbing from Wiley and Caroline Daniels about being unreasonable. Given time, he might have put the drifter on the payroll himself. As Wiley and Savannah had reminded him often enough, they needed extra help.

He wouldn't hire Smith now, though. Not after what he'd learned. No way in hell would he offer a job to a known thief.

Grady had discovered everything he needed to

know about Laredo Smith in his short conversation with Earl Chesterton. He wanted Smith off his land as soon as possible and as far way from Savannah as could be arranged. Frank would understand, and because the sheriff was fond of Savannah, he'd be eager to help Grady send him packing.

His sister's words—*Don't ruin this for me*—echoed in Grady's head, and although he believed he was making the right choice, he felt a sense of guilt. The last thing he wanted was to see Savannah hurt. He wanted to get rid of this drifter, but he had to manage it in such a way that Savannah would agree it was the only prudent course of action.

For that he needed Frank Hennessey's help.

Grady considered it his duty to protect his sister. She claimed she knew everything necessary about Laredo; Grady doubted that. A thief was a thief, and if Smith had stolen once, he'd steal again. Grady strongly suspected this cowboy had tangled with the authorities on more than one occasion. That was what he intended to find out from Frank Hennessey. Faced with the raw truth, Savannah would have no qualms about sending Smith on his way.

Grady found Frank Hennessey relaxing at his oak desk, feet propped on the edge and hat lowered over his eyes as he enjoyed a midafternoon snooze. Frank had represented the law in Promise for as long as Grady could remember, and while an able lawman, he took business in his stride.

Grady closed the door a little harder than necessary and Frank used his index finger to lift his Stetson off his forehead just enough to let him take a peek at his visitor.

"Howdy." Frank greeted him lazily with the familiarity that years of friendship allowed. "What can I do for you, Grady?"

Grady hesitated, unsure how to begin. At last he blurted, "I've got trouble."

The older man's smile faded and he slowly straightened. "What kind of trouble?"

Grady removed his hat and rubbed a hand across his brow. "I need to ask a favor of you, Frank. Now, I know you wouldn't normally do this sort of thing, but it's the only way I can think of to save Savannah."

"What's wrong with Savannah?" Frank asked abruptly, gesturing toward the hard wooden chair that sat alongside his desk.

It gave Grady no pleasure to drag family business into the open; however, he had no choice but to involve Frank. "You've heard about Savannah hiring a drifter to work in her rose garden?"

Frank's mouth angled into a half smile. "The story's been all around town twice by now, and Dovie was full of the news." He paused to chuckle appreciatively. "Apparently Dovie didn't think Savannah had it in her to stand up to you."

Grady hated the thought of folks talking about Savannah behind her back and let Frank know his feelings on the matter with a dark scowl.

Apparently Frank got the message because he cleared his throat and looked apologetic. "You know how women love to gossip," he said with a disapproving frown—although it was well-known that the sheriff wasn't opposed to indulging in the habit himself.

The fact that the news had spread all over town complicated things. Grady figured all he could do now was get to the point and leave the problem in Frank's capable hands.

"I don't trust him. First off, I've got to think Smith's a phony name."

"He might have picked something more original than Smith if that's the case, don't you think?" Frank asked, rubbing his chin thoughtfully.

"Why he chose that name isn't the point," Grady argued. "'Laredo Smith' sounds about as real as a three-dollar bill."

"Other than not liking his name, have you got a reason not to trust him?" Frank asked next.

"Plenty." Surely Frank didn't think he'd come to him over something trivial! "Smith mentioned that he last worked for Earl Chesterton on the Triple C over in Williamsburg, so I called Earl and talked to him myself. Found out Earl fired Laredo Smith for stealing." He spit out the last word. Even saying it left a bad taste in his mouth.

Frank's eyebrows lifted. "Why didn't Earl press charges?"

"I asked him that myself." The other rancher would have saved Grady a great deal of trouble if he had. "Apparently it was one man's word against another's and no way to prove who was telling the truth and who wasn't. Earl fired them both."

"I see," Frank murmured. "Seems to me that if Smith had something to hide, he wouldn't have mentioned working on the Triple C."

Grady sighed and wondered why no one else viewed the situation with the same concern he did. "I'm asking you to do a background check on Smith," he said and realized he was expecting a great deal of their friendship. Frank had every right to turn him down, but Grady hoped he wouldn't.

The sheriff frowned and his chair creaked noisily as he leaned back and considered Grady's request. "I understand you're worried about Savannah and I can't say I blame you. Your sister is one of the most kind-hearted people I know, and if this saddle bum hurts her, he'll have me and half the town to deal with."

"You'll do it, then?" Grady said with relief.

"I'll check him out," Frank said reluctantly.

The two exchanged handshakes and Grady left. On his way out of town, he decided to stop off at the post office and talk to Caroline. If he couldn't get through to his sister, maybe her best friend could. Reversing direction, he headed down Maple, then sat in the parking lot, debating the wisdom of his decision. In the past year or so he'd begun to notice Caroline Daniels. She was younger than Savannah, and while they'd been friends for several years, he'd always thought of her as a kid. For some time now it'd become difficult to view Caroline as anything but an attractive woman.

However, Caroline was also opinionated and head-strong. More often than not, her views clashed with his own, and as a result they argued frequently. Another problem existed, as well.

Maggie.

Grady enjoyed the five-year-old, but for reasons he didn't understand, the little girl was terrified of him. Savannah babysat her on Monday nights while Caroline did volunteer work, and it had reached the point that Grady stayed out of sight rather than intimidate the little girl.

Things being what they were, it was a risk to ask

for Caroline's help, but one he was willing to take. More than anything, asking Caroline to join forces with him proved how desperate he'd grown to get Savannah to see reason.

Thankfully Caroline was alone when he approached the front counter.

"Hello, Grady," she said, glancing up from the mail she was sorting.

"Have you had lunch yet?" he asked.

Her eyes widened—but she was no more surprised by his invitation than he was himself.

"It's three-thirty."

"Coffee, then," he suggested gruffly, feeling gauche for not looking at the time. No wonder his stomach growled; he'd missed lunch entirely. Which also went to show how desperate he'd become.

"I don't suppose it'd hurt if I took a few minutes off," she said and set the mail aside.

Definitely curious, Caroline invited him behind the counter. She located a clean mug for him in the back room and filled his cup and her own. "What's on your mind?" she asked.

"Savannah." Grady couldn't see any need to beat around the bush. "I'm worried about her and that drifter."

"He has a name," Caroline said, stirring a spoonful of sugar into her coffee.

"Sure. *Smith.*"

"Laredo Smith."

"All right, Laredo Smith," he said impatiently. Grady didn't know what it was about Caroline that attracted and irritated him at the same time. Lately he found it difficult to carry on a decent conversation with the woman, although he did actually like her.

"What's the problem?" Caroline asked, her eyes meeting his above the rim of her mug.

"I'm afraid he's going to abuse her generosity." In Grady's opinion, the wrangler was already guilty of that and more.

"Don't you trust your sister's judgment?"

"Of course," he flared. "It's just that she's naive and vulnerable. Savannah doesn't have a lot of experience with men, especially smooth talkers like Laredo Smith."

"Laredo's a smooth talker?" Caroline echoed. "I hadn't noticed." The mug was at her lips again, and it seemed to him she purposely held it there to hide a smile. Apparently his concern for Savannah amused her.

"Is something funny?" he challenged, disliking the way she made him the target of her humor.

"Of course not." The amusement left her eyes, replaced by a mock seriousness that infuriated him even more.

"I can see coming here was a mistake," he said, putting the mug down with a clatter. "I should have known you'd find this all a joke." He turned away, but she stopped him.

"Grady."

He hesitated.

"Listen, I doubt there's as much to worry about as you think. Savannah's the most levelheaded person I know."

Grady used to believe the same thing. "She's not herself. He's changed her."

"Yes, he has," Caroline admitted.

At last they could agree on something. "Then you know what I'm saying?"

"Grady," she said, her look gentle, "Laredo *has* changed Savannah, but he's changed her for the better. Don't you see how happy she is? You can't be around her and not feel it. I might not be the best judge of character, but I don't think Laredo is evil incarnate the way you seem to. Maggie was full of stories about him Monday night after I picked her up. She thought he was great. It isn't every man who'd sit and read to a five-year-old until she fell asleep. Savannah said the three of them spent an hour in the calving barn, showing Maggie the newborn calves."

"In other words she likes Smith," Grady muttered. Maggie liked Smith but not him. Caroline apparently didn't realize the insult she'd delivered.

"It's much more than that."

"Really?" He didn't even try to hide his sarcasm.

"What is it you're really afraid of?" she asked.

For the first time Caroline sounded concerned. He held her gaze a long time, then finally said, "I don't want anyone to take advantage of her."

"She's old enough to know her own mind."

"She's too damn trusting."

"Is that bad?"

"Yes," he stormed. "I'm afraid he's going to take advantage of her. I'm afraid Savannah's going to end up alone and pregnant."

The eyes that had just a moment ago revealed the first shred of understanding and compassion flickered with a jolt of unanticipated pain. It took Grady only an instant to realize what he'd said.

"In other words you're afraid your sister will end up like me?"

Grady struggled for the words to apologize. They didn't come easy to a man like him. "I didn't mean that the way it sounded," he said.

"Of course you did."

He probably should have left well enough alone, but he was desperate and he knew Savannah would listen to Caroline before she would him. "Will you talk to her?" he asked hopefully. At her absent look he continued, "About getting rid of Smith before he can hurt her."

"No," she said flat out.

"No?"

"You heard me. If I was going to talk to anyone about this, it'd be you." Caroline's voice gained strength. "And what I'd say, Grady, is leave Savannah to live her own life."

"And make a fool of herself?"

"Yes, if that's what it takes. She's not a child to be chastised and ridiculed. She's a woman with a woman's heart. Grady, I swear if you do anything to spoil her chance of finding happiness, I'll never forgive you."

"Happiness with a saddle bum like Smith?" He might have laughed if there'd been any humor in the suggestion.

"Yes," Caroline responded without hesitation.

Furious, more with himself than with Caroline, Grady stalked out of the office. He should have known better than try to reason with Savannah's best friend. She was as stubborn as his sister. And less tactful about it, too.

* * *

"Good afternoon, Laredo," Savannah said shyly as she joined him in her rose garden. She carried out a tray and two tall glasses of iced tea. Rocket was at her side, so old now that he found it difficult to move. Generally he stayed in the house, but he appeared to be a little more energetic than usual just now and had followed her outside and into the warm sunshine.

Laredo's efforts were in evidence in every corner of her small paradise. Never had her garden looked more beautiful. The beds were meticulously groomed. Even the roses themselves had responded to his care. They'd burst into flower days earlier than anticipated. Some would claim it was due to the unusually warm spring, but Savannah chose to believe it was because of the love and care she and Laredo had given them.

"Afternoon," he said, leaning on the hoe.

It never failed. Her heart—like her beautiful roses—bloomed with excitement and joy whenever she saw him. He was tall and strong and lovely. She realized that *lovely* wasn't a word often associated with men, but she could find none more appropriate. Beyond everything else Laredo had given her, the most precious was the way she felt around him. Savannah had never considered herself beautiful, but that was how he made her feel. Beautiful. Feminine. Desirable.

"Would you like some iced tea?" she asked.

"That'd be great." He set the hoe aside, removed the tray from her hands and led the way to the small wrought-iron table in the farthest corner of the garden. She'd purposely placed it there amidst the old roses in order to enjoy their fragrance and special beauty.

Rocket followed them there and with a groan sank down in the table's shade.

"I'm about finished with the hoeing," Laredo said, bending down to stroke the dog's ears.

This was a problem. He completed each task with speed, skill and determination. She longed to urge him to slow down, to linger over each small assignment so that the work would last, but he never did. From the first he'd set out to prove his worth and he'd done so, many times over.

Another day, two at the most, and he'd have completed her list. Everything thereafter would be a make-work project. Not that she couldn't come up with some.

"Wiley stopped by earlier," he said, and downed half the tea in a series of deep swallows. He wiped the back of his hand across his mouth, then leaned forward and stroked Rocket's ears again. Savannah's gaze rested on the dog who'd once belonged to her father and she smiled as he snored softly, already asleep.

"He told me about Roanie's sore leg and he asked me to look at it. You don't mind, do you?"

If anything, Savannah was relieved. All three realized it'd be best if Grady didn't know about Laredo doctoring one of the horses. Nevertheless it'd be a shame to let the old roan suffer. Especially when Laredo could help—save them the expense of calling the vet.

"Of course I don't mind," she assured him.

"I'll probably need to rub in some ointment and wrap up the leg."

She nodded. "I'm grateful." If Grady wouldn't say it, she would, but her appreciation extended far beyond any expertise Laredo offered in the area of horses.

He'd blessed her life in the week since his arrival. One week. Seven fleeting days, and yet it felt as though he'd always been part of her life. People would say it was fanciful or ridiculous, but in an odd way, Savannah felt as if her life had been on hold while she waited for Laredo to find her.

She smiled to herself, amused that Grady was making such a fool of himself, all the while calling *her* the fool. Considering the fuss her older brother had made, anyone would think she'd become Laredo's lover when in reality he hadn't so much as kissed her.

But she wished he would.... She'd dreamed of it endlessly, hungering for his touch. Grady had chastised her for claiming to love Laredo on such short acquaintance, and for the first time in recent memory she'd lied to her brother. She'd told him she didn't love Laredo but that she could.

The truth was she *did* love him. She loved him for the gentle care he gave her roses. For his loving way with animals. For his honesty. For his tender patience with Maggie, and most important, for the joy he'd brought into her life. Each day she awoke happy and excited, knowing he'd be in the kitchen to greet her. Each night she laid her head on her pillow, her mind full of dreams she'd never dared to believe possible, never believed were meant for a woman like her.

So, while it was true he hadn't touched her except for that one time he'd held her in the kitchen, she knew instinctively that he shared her feelings. She felt his love in a thousand ways. Unspoken, but real. As intense as her own for him.

Yes, Grady had called her a fool, and perhaps she

was. But if being considered a fool meant she was this happy, then he could call her whatever name he liked.

"Is there anything more I can do for you this afternoon?" Laredo asked.

She shook her head. "I'll be leaving soon."

"If you're going into town, would you mind checking on my truck at Powell's Garage?"

"I... I can do that for you later in the week, if you want, but I wasn't planning on going into town." Savannah had hoped to avoid any questions about her destination. She'd hoped to slip quietly away and return to the ghost town. It had taken her a full week to gather the courage to go back, but despite her reservations, she'd decided to do it. She was sure there were more old roses to be found.

"Savannah," Laredo said, touching her hand. "You're headed back to Bitter End, aren't you?"

She lowered her eyes and nodded, knowing that, like Grady, he'd disapprove. "I want to look for more roses. If the plants in the cemetery survived, there're bound to be others." In the days since her last visit Savannah had managed to convince herself that the darkness, the sense of oppression, had come from her own imagination. It'd been nerves and excitement, that was all. Grady had warned her about the ghost town so often that her head had been filled with nonsense. After a while she'd come to believe it. And even if what she'd experienced was real, she'd managed the first time and would again.

"Your brother—"

"Grady disapproves of a great deal in my life just now. I'm going back to Bitter End, Laredo, with or without Grady's approval."

The strength of her objection appeared to catch him unawares. "Surely your brother has a reason for not wanting you there?"

"You know Grady," she answered. "He's overprotective."

"I don't know your brother," Laredo told her quietly, "but everything he says and does is because he loves you and is concerned about you. It might be best to heed his advice."

If Savannah hadn't fallen in love with Laredo already, she would have lost her heart right then and there. He'd defended Grady, when Grady had done nothing but cause him problems.

"He doesn't understand," she murmured.

"Where is this place?" Laredo asked. "I haven't heard anyone else talk about a ghost town in this area."

"I don't think many people know about it." Grady had located the town as a teenager and promised he'd take her there himself. It was the only time she could remember her brother breaking his word. "Grady was there once, but he refused to talk about it afterward. No matter how much I pleaded, he refused to give in. All he'd say was that he was never going back and he certainly wasn't going to take his little sister there."

"Then how'd you find the place?"

She laughed lightly. "It wasn't easy. It took me weeks."

"Why now? Because of the old roses?"

Savannah smiled. "I read an article in one of my gardening magazines about a man who found a huge number of old roses in a ghost-town cemetery. I'd nearly forgotten about Bitter End, but once I remembered, I couldn't stop thinking about it. I asked Grady as much as I could without arousing his suspicions, but eventually he caught on and wouldn't give me any more information."

Laredo frowned. "Savannah," he pleaded, "if your brother's that worried about it, then so am I. Don't go."

Her heart sank. Not Laredo, too. "Please don't ask that of me," she whispered.

He got up and walked around the table to stand in front of her. "Then don't do it alone," he said urgently.

"But there isn't anyone—"

"There's me."

Savannah leaned back to see him more clearly. "You'd do that for me?"

He nodded and knelt in front of her, his expression earnest. "Promise me, Savannah."

"I promise." She needed to touch him. She couldn't have explained why, but the yearning inside her was too strong to ignore. Hesitantly she pressed one hand to his cheek, her palm curving around his jaw. The skin was stubbled with his beard, and yet she'd never felt anything more sensual.

Laredo closed his eyes and gripped her wrist with a strength she hadn't expected. "You make it damn near impossible," he said from between clenched teeth.

"Impossible?" she whispered. She found it difficult to breathe or swallow. Her heart beat at an alarming rate, and she feared he would guess how his closeness unnerved her.

"Don't you know?" His words were half groan, half speech, as if her touching him, even in the most innocent way, caused him pain. She felt the urgency in him and the restraint. She honored him for that restraint—but she didn't need it anymore.

"I want you to kiss me, Laredo. I've dreamed about you every night." Her raspy voice was barely audible.

"Savannah, please."

"Please what? Ignore my heart? I can't! I tried, Laredo, I really did."

He cradled her face, and their eyes met. In his she read determination and a kind of desperation. "Grady's made it difficult enough for you," he said. "I can't, I won't make it—"

"I don't care what my brother thinks," she choked out, stopping him by placing her fingertips to his lips. "I know my heart, Laredo, and my heart wants you very much."

His hands slid from the sides of her face and into her hair. Then slowly, inch by thrilling inch, he brought her mouth to his.

The instant their lips touched, Savannah felt her heart leap with a burst of joy. It overtook her, drove everything else from her mind.

His mouth was warm and moist, and he tasted of iced tea and fresh mint. He moved his lips hungrily against hers, molding her mouth to his with a heat that seared her senses. Although her experience with love-making had been limited, she'd had her share of kisses. But never like this. Never with this kind of heat, this degree of passion. Had it happened with anyone else, it would have frightened her.

Soon their arms were wrapped completely around each other in a struggle to get closer. She realized the fierceness with which they clung must be hurting his ribs. She tried to say something, to shift her hands, but he wouldn't allow it, his movements urging her to hold him closer, hold him tighter.

The kiss grew hotter and hotter as they each sought to give more, take more, be more. Laredo's breath came hard and fast. Her own echoed his.

With a moan, Laredo finally broke away, his shoulders heaving. "That shouldn't have happened," he said in a tortured voice. "I don't want to hurt you."

"You could never hurt me," she assured him, her face against his chest. In all her days she'd never been more brazen with a man, asking him outright to kiss her, to hold her. But hard as she tried, Savannah couldn't make herself regret what she'd done. If anything she wondered why it had taken her so long. She'd had no idea kissing could be this…incredible. Her friends should have told her!

"Say something," she pleaded. "I need to know you're feeling it, too."

"I think I knew the minute you stopped to offer me a ride." He got to his feet and walked away from her.

"Laredo?"

"I promised Wiley I'd check on Roanie. Remember?"

In other words their discussion was over; he had nothing more to say. Nor did he wish to hear what *she* might say. "All right," she said, hanging her head in defeat.

He got as far as the garden gate, then turned back. "You won't go to the ghost town without me?"

"No," she promised.

He nodded. He seemed about to speak again but hesitated. If he dared apologize for kissing her, she didn't know what she'd do. Probably scream in frustration. That would be an unprecedented event—

Savannah Weston screaming! She gave an involuntary giggle.

Savannah watched him leave, then carried the tray of empty glasses back into the house. Despite his withdrawal, his abrupt departure, she felt like dancing around her kitchen. He'd kissed her! And it had been wonderful.

Not only had Laredo kissed her, he'd said he'd been thinking about it for days. The same as she had. That was enough to make her heart wild with joy. But there was more. He'd as much as said he loved her.

"Oh, please," she prayed, closing her eyes and clasping her hands, "let it be true. Don't let this be a cruel joke." But she knew otherwise; she'd felt it in the wonder of his kiss.

With the afternoon free, Savannah baked chocolate-chip cookies, one of her many specialties. She tucked a dozen inside the freezer to save for Maggie's visits and filled the cookie jar with the rest.

Because the kitchen door was open, she heard Grady's truck pull into the yard, followed by his near-frantic shout.

"Savannah!"

It wasn't her name that shook her, but the way he yelled it. Rushing to the door, she found him stalking toward the house.

"Grady, for heaven's sake, what's wrong?"

"You're not to talk to him!"

"Grady," she said, her patience gone. "We've already had this discussion. Laredo—"

"Not *Laredo*," he barked as if she were slow-witted or being purposely obtuse.

"Who?"

"Richard."

"Richard?" She saw him then, her younger brother. Her "big boy," the baby she'd loved and cared for and spoiled. He walked slowly down the long driveway, hefting his suitcase, eyes focused on the house as if the sight of it was the only thing that kept him on his feet.

"Richard," she cried and pressed her hands to her mouth. "Grady, how could you drive past him like that?"

"He's not welcome here, Savannah."

"Grady, he's our *brother*." Not caring what he thought, she flew out the door and raced down the stairs. Richard. He was here at last. Now they'd learn the truth, the real truth, and everything would be right with their world again.

Richard had come home.

Five

Richard had changed, Savannah mused. Although dusty from the road and weary to the bone, he'd acquired a look of sophistication she hadn't seen six years ago. This was Richard, her brother, but at the same time he was someone she no longer knew. None of that mattered, however, the instant he wrapped his arms around her and joyously hugged her close. Her tears mingled with laughter and pleas that he put her down.

"Savannah, oh, it's so good to see you." His face brightened with excitement. "You're even more beautiful than I remembered."

Wiping the tears from her cheeks, she smiled up at him. "I can't believe it's you."

"I'm home. You have no idea how good this old place looks." He gazed longingly toward the house.

Her heart warmed in that moment, and she was almost willing to forgive him the agony his betrayal had cost them.

"Don't get comfortable, little brother." Grady's eyes were savage. He stood on the top step, feet apart, arms akimbo, barring the door.

Slowly Richard set Savannah away from him and faced his brother.

"Grady," she said in warning. Despite his faults, Richard *was* their brother and the least they could do was hear him out. "Give him a chance to explain."

Richard looked from brother to sister. He advanced slowly toward Grady, then paused. "I don't blame you, Grady. You have every right to be angry."

"You've got that straight."

"What I did was despicable." Richard stretched out his arm to Savannah as if he needed her to stand with him. She stepped to his side, wanting to right the past and thrust all the ugliness behind them. They were a family, and if they couldn't forgive one another, then they'd be hypocrites to sit in church every Sunday. The Good Book was full of the power of forgiveness. Only this wasn't what Grady wanted to hear. Not now. Not yet. He demanded his pound of flesh first, and while Savannah understood his anger, she wanted him to give Richard the opportunity to set things straight.

"Despicable is only one in a long list of words that come to mind when I think of you." Grady's face was hard and unyielding. He'd braced his feet apart in a way that said it would take the strength of ten men to budge him from that porch. Nothing Richard could say would change his mind. Savannah had bumped against that pride of his often enough to know. Unless something drastic happened, Grady wouldn't let Richard set foot in the home where he was born and raised.

Her younger brother hung his head in shame. "I don't blame you for hating me."

"Oh, Richard, you don't know how difficult it was

for us," Savannah said, despite her determination to hold her tongue.

Richard's face crumpled with regret. "I'm so sorry. I was young and stupid, and then once I owned up to what I'd done... I couldn't face you and Grady. I was too ashamed."

"You stole that money from your own flesh and blood!" Grady spit out.

"I was crazy with grief," Richard pleaded, sounding the same way he had as a child when he knew he'd done something wrong. "I didn't think. All I knew was that Mom and Dad were gone."

"And Dad had stored away a hunk of cash," Grady said.

Richard gestured weakly. "I was never cut out to be a cowboy, even you have to admit that," he said and glanced up at Grady for confirmation. "I could read the writing on the wall. With Dad gone you'd expect me to help around the place, and it just wasn't in me. Still isn't. Cows and me never saw eye to eye. You said it more than once yourself." He gave a crooked half smile, enticing Grady to agree with him.

Grady remained cold and silent, his eyes as hard as flint.

"I know it was wrong to take that money. A thousand times since, I've cursed myself for being so stupid, so greedy."

"You should have phoned," Savannah chastised. "You could have let us know where you were. Grady and I were worried sick." She looked to her brother to continue, to explain what they'd endured because of Richard.

Once again Grady's cool silence was answer enough.

"I thought about coming home," Richard said in a small pleading voice. "You don't know how many times I've thought of it. You're right, Savannah," he said, rushing his words. "I should've called. I know that now, but I was afraid of what you'd say. I didn't have the courage to face you."

"What happened to the money?" Grady threw the question at his brother with a vengeance.

"The money," Richard repeated, and the sigh that followed said it all.

"You blew it," Grady said with disgust.

"I put it up as capital in a business venture. My plan," he said, glancing desperately at Savannah and then Grady, "was to triple it and share the profits with you two. I thought if I did that, you'd forgive me and let me come home. Then we could go on the way we always have. But—" he paused and looked away "—the venture went sour."

"In other words you lost everything."

Richard nodded slowly. "The investment wasn't as solid as I was led to believe. It was a bitter lesson. But you have to understand," he added, motioning toward Grady, "I was desperate to come home." His voice shook as though the memory was as painful to him as it was to Savannah and Grady. "By this time I missed you both so much I would have done anything to find a way home."

"You could have written," Savannah said. "Even if you weren't ready to talk to us…." For months she'd prayed for a letter, a phone call, anything that would explain what had happened. She'd refused to give up hope, refused to believe Richard would steal from them and then just disappear. After six months she stopped making excuses, and when they hadn't heard from him after a year, his name was dropped from their conversations.

"I *wanted* to write," Richard said, leaping on her words. "I tried. As God is my witness, I tried, but I was never good with words. How could I possibly explain everything in a letter?"

Grady snickered loudly. "Seems to me you're about as slick with words as a snake-oil salesman."

A flash of pain appeared in Richard's eyes. "You really hate me, don't you, Grady?"

"How could we hate you?" Savannah answered in Grady's stead, fearing his response. "You're our brother."

At her words Richard rallied somewhat and gazed around the yard. "You've obviously done all right by yourselves. The ranch looks great."

"No thanks to you."

"Think about it, Grady," Richard challenged. "What good would I have been to you if I'd stuck around? As far as I'm concerned, cows smell bad, have a negative disposition and are always needing something done to them. If I'd stayed, I wouldn't have been any help. Okay, I admit taking the money was pretty underhand, but all I really did was lay claim to part of my inheritance a little early."

"We almost lost the ranch," Savannah felt obliged to tell him. Surely he must have realized that? "Richard, I don't think you have a clue how hard it's been for Grady and me," she said.

"I'm sorry," he repeated with what sounded like genuine regret. "How many times do I need to say it?"

"Sorry?" Grady said the word as though it were the foulest obscenity.

Richard ignored the outburst. "I'll admit that what I did was rotten, but would it really have been such a bad thing if you'd been forced to sell the land?"

"What do you *mean?*" Savannah asked, certain she wasn't hearing him correctly. This land had been in the Weston family for generations. Their ancestors had settled here, worked the land, raised cattle. Generations of Westons had been buried here in a small cemetery plot overlooking the main pasture. This land was their heritage, their birthright. Their future. That Richard could suggest selling it revealed how little he understood or appreciated the legacy.

"These days everyone knows it's not a good idea to eat a lot of red meat," he explained when it became apparent that his words had upset her. "The beef industry's been declining steadily for some time, or so I hear. Actually I'm surprised you've held on to the old place this long."

Savannah's heart sank. It seemed impossible that Richard shared the same blood that flowed through Grady's veins and hers. But he was her brother and she refused to turn her back on him, despite his shortcomings. Despite his betrayal.

"You think because you say you're sorry it makes everything right?" Grady asked, his voice shaking with such rage Savannah feared he was near exploding. "Do you honestly believe you can walk back into our lives as if you'd done nothing wrong? I'm here to tell you it's not going to happen."

Confused and uncertain, Richard looked to his sister for support. "But I'm willing to do whatever's necessary to make it up to you."

"Give me back six years of constant hard work," Grady shouted. "Days that stretched fifteen hours without rest. Days in which I did the work of two men. Backbreaking work. Can you do *that*, little brother?"

Richard stood still and silent.

"For six long years I fought off the wolf at the door. For six years I dealt with grief and stress and worry so bad I couldn't sleep." He climbed down the steps, one step for each statement. Anger seethed below the surface unlike anything she'd ever seen in Grady. Not the explosive kind common with him, but the deep bitter anger that gnawed at a man's soul.

"I can't change the past," Richard muttered, his shoulders hunched, "but I'd hoped we could put all this behind us and start fresh."

"Not on your life," Grady said. He stood face-to-face with Richard now, glaring at him. "You haven't shown any true regret. Not once have you asked Savannah and me to forgive you. As far as I'm concerned, you got your inheritance, and you wasted it. Now get off *our* land."

"You want me to leave?" Richard sounded incredulous. He looked at Savannah but she turned away. "You're my family!" he cried. "The only family I've got. You don't mean this. Okay, okay, you're right, I should have asked you to forgive me. I meant to—that was the real reason I returned. Like I said, I want to make it up to both of you."

Savannah wavered, ambivalent.

"You should have thought of that sooner," Grady replied, his voice clipped.

She'd hoped they could resolve their differences and make Richard a part of their lives again, but Grady was right. Richard hadn't revealed any sincere sorrow for the agony he'd caused them. But then he'd always been weak and easily influenced. Nevertheless he was their brother; it came down to that. If for no other reason than to honor the memory of their parents, she wanted there to be no ill will between them.

"You're serious?" Richard's face clouded with disbelief. "You want me off the ranch?"

"I've never been more serious in my life."

Brother stared down brother.

"I… I'm without a job. I was working at…at a sales job, and they downsized. I don't have anywhere to go. I left instructions for the check from my severance package to be mailed here." He glanced hopefully at Savannah and then at Grady.

Savannah silently pleaded with Grady, but he refused to look in her direction. It was hell staying quiet, especially when Richard begged for her help.

"You, too, Savannah?" he whispered in the hurt voice that tugged at her heart. "Do you want me to leave, too?"

Savannah was in torment, not knowing how to respond. Of course she wanted him to stay, wanted their lives to return to the way they'd been before. But she didn't know if that was possible.

"I'm ruined," he whispered brokenly. "The money's gone. I lost my job and I have no savings. All I could think about was getting back to you and Grady. Making things right again."

Tears filled her eyes and she bit her lip, trapped as she was between the strong wills of her two brothers.

Not waiting for her reply, Richard leaned down and reached for his suitcase. Apparently he was weaker than they realized because he staggered, but caught himself in time to keep from collapsing.

Savannah could hold her tongue no longer. "Grady, please! He's about to faint. One night," she begged, sliding her arm around Richard's waist. "Let him stay one night."

For a moment she didn't think Grady would relent. "All right," he gave in, his reluctance clear, "but he sleeps in the bunkhouse. First thing in the morning he's out of here. Understand?"

"Thank you, brother," Richard said softly. "You won't be sorry, I promise you that. I'll find a way to make it up to you and Savannah. I didn't know, didn't realize… I'll do whatever you want if you'll just let me stay. You're the only family I've got."

Laredo hadn't meant to listen in on the scene outside the house. But he'd been in the garden at the time, and it had been impossible to ignore. He wasn't sure what had finally occurred between Savannah and her two brothers, but the three had apparently come to some kind of understanding. He didn't see Savannah again until dinnertime, and when he entered the house, she was all aflutter. He smelled biscuits baking, their aroma more enticing to him than the world's most expensive perfume. An apple pie cooled on the kitchen counter beside a standing rib roast, recently taken from the oven.

When she saw him, her beautiful face brightened with a shy smile of welcome. "Richard's here."

"So I understand." Laredo had tried to put the events of the early afternoon behind him and had hoped she had, as well. Kissing her had been a mistake, one he regretted. His weakness for her complicated an already difficult situation.

The last thing he wanted was to let her believe in something that could never be. His property—three hundred acres in Oklahoma—was waiting for him. That and his horse. They were all he had. And they were almost nothing compared to the Westons' huge spread. Compared to what Savannah had now. It would be cruel to mislead her into thinking she could be part of his future. But if the kissing continued, it'd be as hard for him to walk away as it would be for her to let him go.

"He hasn't eaten in two days," she said, explaining the frenzy of cooking that had taken place that afternoon. "I baked his favorites just the way Mom would have."

"How's Grady dealing with this?"

A sadness came over her and some of the excitement drained from her voice. "Not very well, unfortunately. He won't let Richard stay more than the night. He's forcing him to sleep in the bunkhouse. Richard said he was willing to work for his keep, and I think if I reason with him, Grady might let him stay on until his severance check arrives. I'm hoping he will, but it's hard to tell with Grady."

"Savannah!" Footsteps echoed as Richard Weston bounded down the stairs from the upstairs bedroom and burst into the kitchen. "I found my old guitar." He slid the strap over his shoulder and ran the pick over the tight strings, laughing with childish delight.

"I couldn't make myself throw away your things," Savannah admitted.

Walking about in his stocking feet, Richard circled the kitchen playing a mellow country hit Laredo recognized from the early nineties. A song of Reba's, if memory served him.

The family resemblance was strong, Laredo noticed. Richard was a younger, slimmer, blonder version of Grady, good-looking and suave. Apparently he'd inherited a double portion of charm, as well. He serenaded his sister, causing Savannah to blush unmercifully. Laredo knew he should leave, but he found himself enjoying the scene.

When Richard finished the song, he set the guitar aside and glanced in Laredo's direction, his eyes questioning.

Savannah's gaze followed her brother's. "This is Laredo Smith," she said. She reached for Laredo's hand, tucking it in both of hers. "He works for me."

"Really, Savannah," Richard joked. "I never suspected my older sister would have her own boy toy." He laughed then as if he found the comment hilarious.

Any goodwill Laredo had felt toward the other man vanished with the ugly suggestiveness of his remark. Savannah's face turned a deep shade of scarlet, and it was all Laredo could do to keep his mouth shut.

"It's n-not that way with us," she stammered.

"Whatever you say, big sister," Richard responded. "Hey, when's dinner? I could eat the entire roast myself." He gripped Savannah by the shoulder and noisily kissed her cheek. "I can't tell you how good it is to be home. I've missed you, Savannah, almost as much as I've missed your melt-in-the-mouth buttermilk biscuits."

"I need to be getting back," Laredo said, eager to

check on Roanie. "I just stopped by to tell you I won't be here for dinner."

"You won't?" Savannah's eyes pleaded with him, and he realized she'd been counting on his support. She appeared to have forgotten that Grady had no particular fondness for him, either. He wished he could help her, but feared he'd do her cause more harm than good.

"Wiley invited me to play poker with him and his friends tonight," he explained to justify his absence. "The game's over at the Double Z bunkhouse."

She forgave him with a brave smile. "Have fun."

"Will everything be all right here?" He watched Richard walk past Rocket and give the old dog a vicious shove with his foot. His anger flared again, but he said nothing.

"Everything's going to be just fine," Richard answered on her behalf. "Grady can be downright stubborn at times, but he'll come around. Don't worry, I'll make sure big brother doesn't hassle her." He placed his arm around his sister's shoulders and squeezed hard. Savannah winced and Laredo battled the urge to grab the man by the shirtfront and jerk him away.

Although Laredo didn't see Savannah again that evening, it didn't mean she wasn't on his mind. He worried about her dinner with her brothers, which burdened his concentration to the point that he lost at poker. Twenty bucks was more than he could afford to throw away in a poker game. By the end of the evening he regretted accepting Wiley's invitation.

He and Wiley returned to find Richard in the bunkhouse, sitting on the edge of his bed, strumming his guitar and singing drunkenly at the top of his lungs.

Wiley snorted in contempt and headed immediately for his small room. Richard didn't seem to notice. He interrupted his song every so often to reach for a whiskey bottle and gulp down a swig. He held it up in silent invitation when he saw Laredo.

"Care to join me?" he asked. "I broke into Grady's private stock. By the time he misses it, we'll both be long gone." He laughed as if stealing liquor from his brother was some kind of triumph.

"No, thanks," Laredo muttered in disgust.

"I should've been a country singer," Richard announced at the end of a barely recognizable Garth Brooks tune. Not that his singing voice was all that unpleasant, but the words were badly slurred.

"I've got talent, you know?" He lifted the bottle to his mouth, gulped down another swallow and threw back his head. "Ahh." He gave an exaggerated shudder. "Powerful stuff. My big brother only buys the best." He set the guitar down on the floor, holding it carelessly by the neck.

Laredo was tired; he'd put in a full day and his thoughts were heavy. In addition, he was worried about Savannah and how the animosity between the two brothers would affect her. She was the one stuck in the middle between two angry men, struggling to maintain the peace. One brother was stubborn and unyielding, the other manipulative and demanding.

He wished there was some way he could protect her.

Twice Laredo had to ask Richard to turn out the light. "Give me five minutes," was the response both times. The light Laredo could handle; it was a small matter to turn on his side and put his back to the harsh glare. But the drunken singing and guitar strumming weren't as easily ignored.

By midnight he'd had enough. He threw back the covers, walked over to the wall and flicked off the switch himself. "You got a problem with that?" he challenged. His day had started at five that morning and he desperately needed to sleep.

A tense silence followed. "Whatever," Richard muttered. He dropped or shoved something onto the floor, and the crash echoed through the room. Frankly, Laredo didn't care. He was through with the niceties as far as Richard Weston was concerned.

Laredo awoke at dawn, showered, shaved and was preparing for his day when he happened to notice Richard. He stopped, squinting as he took a closer look. He'd heard movie stars and the like used such devices, but he'd never personally seen one.

Richard Weston lay sprawled across the bed, his arms and legs dangling over the edge of the small mattress. He wore silk pajamas, and of all things, a black satin sleep mask to protect his eyes against the sunlight. Never in all his life had Laredo seen a more incongruous sight in a bunkhouse.

Shaking his head, he stopped in the barn to check on Roanie before he made his way to the kitchen for coffee. Squatting down, he gently tested the roan's leg, working with practiced hands, exploring the damage to the delicate muscle. The swelling was down and the pain had apparently lessened.

After coffee and a solitary breakfast, Laredo worked in the rose garden; he installed the trellises he'd built earlier in the week and transplanted some shrubs Savannah wanted him to move. She hadn't come outside and he guessed she was still busy in the house. Actually he hoped she'd treat herself and sleep in. She must have been exhausted yesterday, cooking for her ungrateful brother. He gritted his teeth just thinking about the other man.

Shortly after noon Richard wandered out of the bunkhouse, looking as if he hadn't been awake more than a few minutes. His hair was mussed and he yawned as he strolled across the yard, his shirt unbuttoned. He wore canvas shoes without socks.

Before going to the house for lunch, Laredo decided to rewrap Roanie's leg and apply the ointment again. He was half-finished when he felt someone's presence. He turned around and found Grady standing outside the stall watching him.

"I understand I'm in your debt," he said with the pride of a man who preferred to owe no one. He looked tired and drawn, as if he hadn't slept much. For the first time since making Grady's acquaintance, Laredo felt sorry for him.

"No problem," he said, straightening. He rubbed his hand down Roanie's back, reassuring the gelding that all was well.

Grady lingered. Apparently there was something else on his mind. "Savannah told you about the ghost town, didn't she?"

"She mentioned it," Laredo said stiffly.

"I thought she might have." Grady leaned against the stall door. "Listen, I haven't made my feelings any secret. I don't like you, Smith. Nor do I trust you. A man who steals gets no respect from me."

"For what it's worth, I didn't do it," Laredo said, although he doubted Grady would believe him.

"I have even less respect for a liar."

Laredo tensed. If it wasn't for Savannah, he'd have had his fist down the other man's throat. He'd worked hard to prove himself, but apparently a good day's labor wasn't enough for Grady Weston.

"You should know I've asked Sheriff Hennessey to do a background check on you, although I suspect Smith is probably an alias."

Laredo's hackles were already raised, but defending himself again would be a useless waste of breath. He exhaled sharply. "Fine. To be fair, if Savannah was my sister, I'd do the same thing. You're looking to protect her. I can't blame a man for that."

If Grady was surprised, he didn't show it.

"I'm pleased to hear you say that, because she needs protecting."

Savannah's brother had Laredo's attention now. "What do you mean?"

"Unfortunately she mentioned finding Bitter End to Richard and he seemed far too interested. I heard the bastard when I was washing up for dinner. He was hinting that she should take him there." He paused. "I don't want it to happen."

Laredo agreed with Grady. "She's already promised me she wouldn't return alone. I hope she doesn't go with Richard, either."

Surprise flickered in Grady's intensely blue eyes. "So she did plan to go back." He scratched the side of his head. "Why on earth would she do such a thing?" He looked to Laredo for the answer.

"The roses," he said, amazed Grady hadn't figured it out.

"She's already got more roses than she knows what

to do with. How could she possibly want more? What's wrong with that woman? Why would she risk her fool neck over a few flowers?"

"She's after old roses," Laredo explained.

"Old roses." The two words were part of a deep sigh. Grady seemed lost in thought for a minute and then his gaze found Laredo's again. "I don't want her going there with Richard or anyone else, for that matter. It's not safe. Regardless of my feelings toward you, I care about my sister and I'd appreciate your help."

"You might find this hard to believe, Grady, but I care about Savannah's well-being, too."

"Then keep her away from Bitter End."

Laredo wasn't sure he could do that. "I'm not making any promises, but I'll do what I can."

Grady nodded wearily. "That's all I ask." He hesitated, glanced over at Roanie's leg and then back to Laredo. "We could use a wrangler this time of year. Are you interested in the job?"

"I'd need to square it with Savannah."

"That isn't what I asked," Grady said, his words sharp.

"I'm interested," Laredo answered.

"Fine," he said. "You can start after lunch."

Damn, but the old town looked good. It was midafternoon as Richard slowly drove Grady's battered pickup down Main Street. He'd barely been back twenty-four hours, and it felt as if he'd never left. Well, not quite, but close enough. He'd thought about returning to Promise more than once—but not driving his brother's clunky truck.

Despite the town's familiarity, a lot had changed

over the years. The savings-and-loan had a sign that alternately flashed the time and the temperature. Damn if that didn't beat all. Next thing he knew the town would have its own Dairy Queen.

Luck was with him. Slowly but surely he'd manage to wriggle his way back into Grady's good graces—enough, at any rate, to convince his big brother to let him stay for a while. It wouldn't take long to win Savannah back, but then his sister had always been a soft touch. Grady, however, wasn't nearly as easy. So far, it was Richard two, Grady zilch.

Because not only was Richard staying at the ranch, he had the truck. Okay, Savannah had been the one to give him the keys, but what Grady didn't know wasn't going to hurt him.

His brother was a fool. Grady could have sold that ranch ten times over and lived off the profits for years. Instead he'd half killed himself holding on to twenty thousand smelly cattle-filled acres. Richard had listened to the spiel about their forefathers struggling against impossible odds and all that garbage. So what? He wasn't about to let the ranch or anything else tie him down. He had better ideas than following a bunch of senseless cattle around all that godforsaken land.

Richard pulled into the first available parking spot and hopped out of the cab. Six years away, and he still knew this town inside out, recognized every street and practically every building. On the other hand, no one was going to recognize *him* dressed as he was. What he needed, Richard decided, was new clothes.

His first stop was Jordan's Town and Country. Max Jordan who owned the place would be close to retirement by now.

"Max," Richard said as he walked into the Western-wear store. He greeted Max as if they'd been the best of friends, slapping the older man jovially on the back. "Don't you know me?" he asked. "Richard. Richard Weston."

"Richard." The other man's eyes brightened with recognition. "When did you get back?"

"Yesterday. Listen, does Grady still have an open account with you?" He fingered the pearl buttons on a polished-cotton shirt and checked the cost, raising his brows at the price.

"That's one of our designer shirts," Max said, and steered him toward another less pricey rack of clothes.

Richard returned to the original shirt. "Do you have it in a forty-two?"

"I think I just might," Max said with some surprise. He shifted hangers as he searched out sizes. "Yup, got one right here."

"Great. Grady said I should buy what I need."

"Not a problem," Max assured him, grinning at the prospect of a big sale. "How's Grady doing these days? I don't see much of him."

"He works too hard," Richard said. And it was true. His brother needed to relax and not take everything so seriously.

"It's good to see you, my boy," Max said, watching Richard try on a pair of three-hundred-dollar snake-skin boots. They fit perfectly as if they were just waiting for him. "I'll take these, as well."

"Good choice."

Grady wouldn't think so, but Richard would pay him back. Eventually.

"I've got to say I still miss your parents," Max continued. "They were good people. My, but your mother knew how to cook, and your pa, why, he was the life of the party."

The word *party* struck a pleasant chord with Richard. He didn't imagine there'd been much celebrating around the Yellow Rose since he'd been away. Not with Grady being such a tightwad. He doubted his brother even knew how to laugh anymore, and Savannah ran and hid from her own shadow.

"Funny you should mention a party," Richard said as the owner tallied the bill. "Grady's throwing a bash to welcome me home on Sunday. You're welcome to come. Bring the missus, too."

"Who else'll be there?"

"The whole town's invited. Spread the word, will you?"

"Sure. It'll be great for everyone to get together. Haven't had a real party all spring, and it's weeks yet until the big summer dance."

Richard left soon after signing his name to the yellow slip. On the sidewalk outside Jordan's he ran into Ellie Frasier. "Ellie," he said and did a double take. "Little Ellie?" Only she wasn't so little anymore. She'd been in junior high when he was a high-school senior, and he remembered thinking then that she was going to be a looker. He'd been right.

She stared at him blankly.

"Richard!" he cried and spread his arms wide. He was surprised she didn't recognize him in his new shirt, hat and boots. His gaze lowered to her full breasts. He always had been partial to a well-endowed woman. Yup, he could see he'd come home in the nick of time.

No ring on her finger, either. Not that it mattered. Often, forbidden fruit was all the sweeter.

"Richard Weston?"

"The one and only."

She asked the same questions as Max—when he'd arrived, what he'd been doing, how long he planned to stay and so on. He was vague until he mentioned the party.

"Bring whoever you want, but be sure to save me a dance, all right?" He winked, letting her know he was interested.

"I don't know… My dad's been sick and—"

"Come, anyway," he urged. "You need the break, and what better way to put your troubles behind you than to kick up your heels and party?"

Dancing. That meant music. They were going to need a band, and on short notice. That'd cost a few extra bucks, but hey, no problem. Grady was tight with a penny, but he probably had plenty of cash stored away. His older brother was too much like their father to cut it close to the bone.

"Who's playing at the Chili Pepper these days?" he asked, referring to the best barbecue pit in town.

Ellie named a band he hadn't heard of. He nodded and headed in that direction. While he was there, he'd arrange to have Adam Braunfels set up a barbecue. They were going to need lots of food. Naturally Savannah would want to cook up most of it herself, make salads and such; she'd insist on that the same way Mom would if she were alive.

He remembered his parents with fondness. Their deaths had put an unexpected crimp in his life, but Richard was a survivor. The years had proved that.

He'd weathered his current troubles, hadn't he? He was home and as safe as a babe in arms.

By the time Richard drove back to the ranch, he'd made a number of arrangements for the party. He'd ordered a dozen cases of beer and he'd made sure there was going to be plenty of soda pop for the youngsters. Millie over at the flower shop had suggested Chinese lanterns and agreed to set them up early in the afternoon. For a price, naturally, but she'd been reasonable about it.

Savannah was working in her garden when he arrived. She wore one of those long dresses of hers with an oversize straw hat and looked more like a nun than the big sister he remembered. Briefly he wondered what was up between her and that prickly hired hand.

"My, don't you look beautiful this afternoon," Richard said as he waltzed through the gate. "As pretty as one of your roses."

She blushed and Richard was struck by how truly pretty she was. It surprised him.

"Listen, sis, I probably shouldn't have done this, but I ran into some friends in town."

Savannah straightened and dabbed the sweat from her brow. "I imagine everyone was glad to see you."

"They were, but there just wasn't enough time to visit with everyone the way I wanted. I hope you don't mind, but I invited a few people over for dinner Sunday evening. You wouldn't mind cooking up some of your prize-winning potato salad, now, would you?"

"For how many?"

Richard laughed and hugged her close. "Enough for about 150."

Six

Grady swore Richard must have invited the entire population of Promise to this so-called party. Neighbors and friends whirled around the makeshift dance floor, while others sat in the sunshine and exchanged gossip. Grady didn't want anything to do with it.

The first he'd heard of Richard's party was when he found Savannah in the kitchen this morning cooking her heart out. The next thing he knew, Millie Greenville from the local flower shop was stringing Chinese lanterns around the backyard and asking him when he intended to set up the tables. According to Millie, he was going to need at least twenty to accommodate everyone.

Before he fully comprehended what was happening, people started to arrive. The lead singer of the Hoss Cartrights asked him questions he couldn't answer. Apparently they didn't need his help because the next time he stepped out of the barn, they'd set up a stage, plugged in their sound equipment and spread a bale of straw across the lawn for a dance floor.

Richard, dressed in his fancy new duds, was in his

element. Grady didn't know what had possessed him
to give in to Savannah's pleadings to let their worthless brother stay on until his severance check showed
up. Grady wasn't entirely convinced there *was* a check.
Furthermore he wondered where the hell Richard was
getting the money to pay for his new clothes, not to
mention this party. The guy was supposed to be broke.
Well, maybe he had a charge card he hadn't told them
about.

As for Richard's staying on, Savannah insisted it'd
only be a few days. Richard needed to recuperate, rest
up. To hear her tell it, you'd think he'd been working
on a chain gang for the past six years and was practically at death's door. Judging by the energy his kid
brother displayed on the dance floor, he'd recovered
quickly, Grady thought.

The beer flowed free and easy. Grady was on his
second bottle himself: the Chili Pepper's spicy barbecue sauce sizzled on the large tin-drum grills, filling the air with a spicy smoky aroma. The dinner line
extended halfway around the house.

Those who weren't eating or dancing mingled in the
yard, making themselves at home. Grady had origi-
nally decided not to participate in Richard's party, but
his standoffishness hadn't lasted long.

Cal and Glen Patterson, neighboring ranchers and
friends, arrived then. They sat with him on the porch
steps. Grady couldn't remember the last time he'd shot
the breeze with the brothers. The three of them had
grown up together and remained close to this day. As
close as Grady allowed anyone to get.

"I didn't think you'd ever welcome Richard back,"
Cal said, leaning back, a beer in one hand. Cal and the

sheriff were the only two who knew about Richard's theft. It wasn't the kind of information you shared about family.

"I didn't welcome him back." Grady wanted that understood right then and there. This party wasn't his idea.

Grady noticed Sheriff Hennessey twirling Dovie Boyd around the dance floor. His opinion of the lawman had fallen several degrees when he'd failed to turn up anything on Smith. If the man was doing his job, he grumbled to himself, Frank would be down at the office right this minute, instead of partying.

"If you aren't responsible for this welcoming, then whose idea was it?" Cal asked. "Savannah's?"

"Nope. Richard organized it himself." Grady took another swallow of beer. The cold brew helped relieve his growing sense of frustration. Again he wondered how Richard intended to pay for all this. Surely he wasn't expecting *him* to foot the bill. That would be too brazen even for Richard.

His mistake, Grady realized, was giving in and allowing Richard to stay that first night. Now his younger brother had manipulated him once again—made it look as if Grady had welcomed him back with open arms. As far as he was concerned, Richard couldn't leave soon enough.

Savannah had been slaving in the kitchen since before dawn. Neighbors he hadn't seen in months had brought over pies, cakes and an assortment of side dishes; they'd delivered picnic tables and dozens of lawn chairs. And now Grady was indebted to each and every one of them. His neighbors would be looking for return favors, too. Especially of the social kind. It wouldn't take long for the invites to arrive, and he'd be expected to accept. Damn it all. He'd never been a partygoer and didn't intend to start now.

"What I'd like to know," Grady muttered to his friends, "is how the hell he's paying for all this."

"Did you ask him?" Glen, the younger of the Patterson brothers, inquired.

"I didn't have a chance." The party was happening before Grady even knew there was going to be one. If he'd had a clue what his brother was up to, he would have put a stop to it. The last time he'd seen this many people had been the day he buried his parents. Leave it to Richard to dredge up the most pain-filled memory of his life.

"Who's that?" Glen asked, directing their attention to a blond woman walking in from the driveway. The row of cars stretched all the way to the road. Fifty at last count.

Grady didn't recognize the newcomer, either. She was young and pretty, if such attributes mattered to him, which they didn't. She didn't seem to know many people because she stood at the edge of the crowd, looking self-conscious in a pin-striped power suit. Whoever she was, she'd completely overdressed for the party.

Cal sat up and gave her a long stare. "Isn't that the new doc? Jane something-or-other."

"She's a doctor?" Glen asked with disbelief. "Promise has a lady doctor? When did all this happen?"

"Last week." Cal nudged his brother with an elbow. "Don't you two read the paper?"

"Who has time?" Grady wanted to know.

"Cal keeps the weekly edition by the john, don't you, big brother?" Glen teased.

"Well, it gets read, doesn't it?" Cal chided. "Her picture was on the front page. She's here on one of those government programs."

"What government program?"

"I don't know the name of it, but the paper said she agreed to work off her medical-school loans by volunteering her skill in a deprived area."

"Promise is a deprived area?" This was news to Grady.

"Must be," Cal muttered, sounding as surprised as Grady.

"Hey, we got a doctor who didn't fight in the battle for the Alamo?"

Doc Cummings had retired at the first of the year at the age of seventy. At least he admitted to being seventy, but in Grady's opinion, he was on the shady side of that figure. He'd delivered Grady and just about everyone else in town under forty. Rumor had it that Doc Cummings was lazing his days away on the Gulf coast now, eating shrimp and soaking up the sunshine. Grady wished the old coot well.

Caroline Daniels strolled past, carrying a bowl of potato salad. She returned a minute or so later with an empty one. Straining, Grady glanced into the kitchen and caught a glimpse of Savannah feverishly making another batch of salad. Smith was there with her, sitting at the table and dutifully peeling potatoes. Those two were as thick as thieves, despite all his warnings. His talk with Laredo Smith hadn't made any difference; he suspected Savannah was still planning a return visit to Bitter End. It hadn't been easy swallowing his pride and asking for Smith's help. The wrangler appeared to have gotten the wrong message, too, because he spent every available minute with Savannah, just as if Grady had given the pair his blessing. He hadn't. Despite his job offer, he wanted the other man off the ranch and the sooner the better.

"Are you going to dance with me or not?" Breathlessly Ellie Frasier plopped herself down next to Glen. They were good friends and had been for years. Grady had never understood how a man could be friends with a woman and not get romantically involved. But that seemed to be the way it was with Glen and Ellie. They were friends and nothing more.

Ellie needed a confidant these days, according to Cal. Her father was terminally ill and had been transferred to a hospital in San Antonio. Her mother was spending all her time there while Ellie ran the family store. Grady sympathized; he knew all too well the pain of losing a parent. Ellie was young to be taking on such heavy responsibility, but from what he heard, she was up to the task. She spent as much time as possible visiting her father, and between driving to San Antonio and managing the business, she was running herself ragged. It surprised him a little that Ellie was at the party, and he guessed Glen had something to do with that. Getting away from all the emotional pressures was probably the best thing for her.

"So what about that dance, Patterson?"

"Seems to me you've already got yourself a dance partner," Glen said. He stared pointedly in Richard's direction. Grady's brother was at his most charming, teasing and laughing with the women, exchanging jokes with the men. Outgoing, personable, the life of the party—and self-appointed guest of honor, to boot.

"I gotta say," Ellie said, speaking to Grady, "your brother's mighty light on his feet."

Yeah, in more ways than one. Grady was tempted to say it but didn't. He frowned, instead. Richard had been on the dance floor for hours without revealing any signs of slowing down. Grady suspected his brother had danced with every woman in town at least once, and the pretty ones twice. He'd taken a liking to Ellie, that was for sure. Grady had seen the two of them dancing three or four times already. He wanted to issue a word of caution, seeing how vulnerable Ellie must be feeling, but he bit his tongue. She'd find out soon enough what kind of man his brother was.

"I'd forgotten how much fun Richard could be," Ellie said.

"He's a regular laugh fest," Grady agreed sarcastically; he couldn't help it. Ellie studied him for a moment and he hoped she'd gotten the message.

"Don't mind Grady," Glen said, looping his arm around Ellie's shoulders. "He's just sore because he doesn't have anyone to dance with."

Grady's frown deepened. He wasn't about to make a fool of himself in front of the entire town. While Richard might know his way around a dance floor, Grady had been cursed with two left feet. The last time he'd attempted to dance he'd been in his teens and forced to wear a suit and boutonniere.

"I haven't seen this many people since the Willie Nelson Fourth of July picnic," Cal said. Like Grady, his friend wasn't much of a social animal. Glen was by far the most outgoing of the three men. He'd tried to drag Grady off to the town's biggest function—next to the cattlemen's dance and the rodeo—for the past six years. Every Fourth of July Promise threw a Willie Nelson picnic, hoping the popular entertainer would agree to visit. Willie had politely declined each year, but the town councillors hadn't let that deter them from holding the affair in the singer's honor.

"Come on," Ellie urged, tugging at Glen's hand. "I want to dance." With a show of reluctance, Glen untangled his feet and stood.

The pair was out of earshot when Cal spoke. "We won't see him the rest of the night. Once he's out on the floor, he won't quit."

"Go ahead if you feel like it," Grady told his friend. "No need to keep me company."

"No thanks. I'm happy to sit here for a while."

Cal lingered an hour or so, not that they said much. This was what Grady enjoyed most about his friend. They didn't have to fill every silence with idle chatter. A couple of times he was on the verge of mentioning Savannah's recent trek to the ghost town, but he held his tongue. The last time either one of them had talked about Bitter End, they'd been in their teens. Anyway, there wasn't anything Cal could tell him he didn't already know. Besides, Savannah was his concern, not his neighbor's. After a time Cal drifted away to get himself some barbecue.

Laughter and music abounded. It disgusted Grady to watch his brother. Richard continued to be sociable and entertaining, the focus of the party. It certainly hadn't taken him long to put the good people of Promise under his spell. Once again Grady wondered how his brother intended to pay for all this, but it wasn't his concern, and he wasn't going to worry about it.

The kitchen door opened and Caroline stepped outside. Her gaze caught Grady's; she waved, then walked over to where Adam Braunfels was handing out beer. She collected two.

Grady was somewhat surprised when she brought the extra bottle over to him. "You look like you could use this," she said and sat down on the step beside him. She tucked one knee under her chin while her foot tapped to the beat of the music.

Grady saluted her with the bottle and took a long swallow of beer. Neither spoke for a few minutes; both of them just stared at the dance floor. Finally Caroline said, "He's really something, isn't he?"

"If you came over here to sing Richard's praises, I don't want to hear them."

"This might surprise you, Grady, but I'm not a fan of your brother's."

It *was* news to Grady, and he found himself grateful that at least one other person hadn't been blinded by Richard's charm. "I get the impression you aren't particularly fond of me, either," he said wryly.

She grinned. "I don't dislike you. I don't always agree with you, but you're not half-bad."

It wasn't much of a compliment, but Grady would take what he could get. "Hey, careful. Sweet talk just might turn my head."

Caroline burst into laughter.

Grady smiled for probably the first time that day. "So you're not one of Richard's adoring fans." Funny how that one bit of information encouraged him.

"If it was up to me, I'd string Richard up by his

thumbs. Savannah's been stuck in the kitchen for hours. I don't think she had any idea what to expect. Richard had told her to plan for about 150 people—she assumed he was joking."

Right then and there Grady decided that, come morning, Richard was off the Yellow Rose. He didn't care how many arguments Savannah made in their brother's defense. They should've run him off the property the minute he set foot on their land. Grady shook his head. Surely Savannah would agree with him now.

"Maggie certainly seems to be taken with him," he noted, frowning as he brought the beer bottle to his lips. His younger brother danced with the five-year-old, twirling her about the floor. The youngster's shrieks of delight could be heard over the music. Richard's success with Maggie rankled, especially since the child ran away in terror whenever she laid eyes on Grady. Somehow or other, without realizing what he'd done, Grady had frightened the kid. For the life of him, he didn't know how it'd happened, and despite his efforts, he hadn't been able to repair the damage.

Caroline kept a close watch on her daughter. "She's easily swayed by charm, it seems."

"She isn't the only one."

"Are you jealous, Grady?"

"Hell, no," he protested before he had a chance to fully consider the question. On second thought, he had to admit there was a grain of truth in Caroline's words.

It was bad enough that Richard had implied—or outright said—that Grady and Savannah were throwing him this party. The fact that he had just about every woman in town fawning over him and almost every man eager for his company only added insult to injury.

"I don't suppose I could convince you to take a spin," Caroline said, motioning with her head toward the dance floor.

"Not on your life."

Caroline sighed as though disappointed. "That's what I thought."

"Hey, you don't need me." He gestured toward a group of single men standing under a live oak tree. "Any one of them would be happy to dance with you."

"I suppose." But she didn't budge, and truth be known, he was glad she didn't. He thought of inviting her to go bowling with him—that would be more to his liking—but hesitated. It'd been so damn long since he'd gone out on a date he wasn't sure how to go about asking.

Then it dawned on Grady that maybe Caroline was interested in him. "Are you saying you want to dance with *me?*" In other circumstances he probably wouldn't have asked, but he'd downed three beers on an almost empty stomach and his inhibitions were definitely lowered.

"I might be," she responded.

He mulled over her answer. He liked Caroline, admired her for the good friend she was to Savannah, and while he'd certainly noticed her, found her attractive, he'd never thought to make anything of it.

"You should get married," he said, and for the life of him, Grady didn't know what had prompted him to suggest such a thing. Horrified, he stared down at his empty beer bottle.

"Do you have anyone in mind?" Caroline asked.

"Not me." He wanted that understood.

"Don't worry, Grady, you aren't in the running."

He'd asked for that, but he didn't like hearing it. Then, thinking he should resolve this before things got out of hand, he decided to explain. "Maggie needs a father."

Caroline was on her feet so fast it made his head spin. "Don't tell me what my daughter needs or doesn't need, Grady."

"Fine, I won't."

"Good," she declared and stomped away.

Women! They had to have the last word. But after Caroline left, Grady regretted the conversation. Worse, he knew he was one hundred percent at fault. He should never had said the things he had. It wasn't his place to suggest Maggie needed a father. It had made him sound judgmental and disapproving when that wasn't his intent at all. He respected Caroline; he just thought her life as a working single mother was too hard. And he hated the way little Maggie seemed so susceptible to any man's charm. Any *con* man's charm. Well, nothing he could do about it now.

The sun set and after a while someone lit the Chinese lanterns. The lights swayed in a soft breeze, casting shadows that danced about the yard. The band switched from lively melodies and line dances to slower, more mellow songs. Couples, wrapped in each other's arms, slowly circled the floor.

Families with young children packed up their youngsters and started home, prompted by thoughts of work and school in the morning. Playing the role of gracious host to a T, Richard escorted them to their cars, then stood in the driveway and waved them off.

"Nice party," Adam Braunfels said as Grady headed toward the house, around nine o'clock.

"Not *my* party," he was quick to tell the owner of Chili Pepper.

"I hope everything was satisfactory," Adam said next.

Grady tucked his hands in his back pockets. "Great. I certainly didn't hear any complaints."

"Good. I want you to know I was as fair as I could be with the tally."

Grady didn't know what Adam was talking about, or rather, why Adam was telling *him,* but he nodded his head, which had started to pound. He hadn't eaten since breakfast and his mind continued to dwell on his disastrous conversation with Caroline.

Adam pulled a slip of paper from his hip pocket and handed it to Grady. "I'd appreciate if you could write me a check now, Grady, before I go back to town."

"What?" He was sure there'd been some mistake.

"For the barbecue," Adam explained as if he were dense. Grady knew why he wanted to be paid; what he didn't understand was why Adam expected *him* to do it.

"I already said this wasn't my party."

Adam's mouth thinned. "I don't care whose party it is, I need my money."

"And you expect me to pay?"

"Yes."

"This is Richard's business." Grady was about to walk off when Richard raced to their side.

"I need my money," Adam repeated, looking from one brother to the other.

Richard's feet shifted nervously. "Would you mind

paying him, Grady?" he asked. "I honestly thought my check would be here before now." He looked down at his boots. "I... I feel horrible about this."

Arms folded, Adam stared at Grady, ignoring Richard completely.

Grady felt as though the top of his head was about to explode. He had no choice but to pay up. His brother had done it to him again. Either he wrote Adam a check now or he came off looking like the bad guy.

Laredo was elbow-deep in the kitchen sink when Frank Hennessey walked into the room. The sheriff nodded politely at Savannah, who sat with her feet propped up on a chair. It was the first time all day Laredo could get her to take a break. He knew she was exhausted. Hell, he was himself, and he hadn't worked near as hard as she had.

While he hadn't been particularly fond of Richard before, Laredo actively disliked him now. He'd been around men like the younger Weston in his time. Fast talkers. Users. Selfish and thoughtless. Richard certainly knew which buttons to push when it came to his sister, Laredo had noticed. All he had to do was mention their mother, and Savannah crumbled. It infuriated him to watch the jerk take advantage of her that way.

Laredo knew Grady was onto Richard, but he suspected Savannah wasn't. Even if she did find out what kind of man her brother was, she was perfectly capable of overlooking it, and that worried Laredo.

"If you don't mind, Mr. Smith, I've got a few questions I'd like to ask you," the sheriff said.

A little confused, Laredo lifted his hands from the

dishwater and reached for a towel. He didn't like the idea of the sheriff singling him out, but he didn't want to make a fuss in front of Savannah, either.

"Is there a problem, Sheriff?" Savannah asked, looking concerned.

"No, no." Hennessey caught Laredo's glance. "Perhaps you'd like to step outside, Mr. Smith."

"Sure." Laredo dried his hands and squelched his growing sense of irritation. Grady had put the lawman up to this; he'd admitted it earlier himself. Not that Laredo had anything to hide, but he hated the way it made him look to Savannah.

He waited until they were in the cool night air before he spoke. "I don't have any kind of record."

"Wrong," the lawman was quick to correct him. "You ran a red light back in 1995."

Stuffing his hands in his back hip pockets, Laredo glared at the sheriff. "I stand corrected."

Hennessey ignored the sarcasm. "I got a couple of questions for you."

"Fire away." Laredo clamped his teeth together, anger simmering.

"How long do you plan to say in Promise?"

"As long as I damn well please." His tolerance for this kind of treatment was gone.

"Listen, Smith, it won't do you any good to get smart-mouthed with me. If you want trouble, you don't need to look any farther than right here. I can make enough trouble to last you a lifetime. Now I suggest you check your attitude." He gave him a moment to let the warning take hold, then repeated the question.

"I plan on heading out as soon as I can pay for the

repairs to my truck." Laredo kept his voice a mono-
tone and trained his gaze on the barn door.

The lawman's crisp voice mellowed when he next
spoke. "Miss Savannah's a mighty fine woman."

Laredo's eyes clashed with the sheriff's. "You think
I don't know that?"

"No one wants to see her hurt."

"I don't, either," Laredo said. He didn't understand
why everyone assumed he'd purposely do anything to
hurt Savannah.

"For reasons I can't quite grasp, she seems to have
taken a liking to you. But if you're leaving soon, I
figure you'll be gone before there's any real damage
done."

Laredo kept his mouth shut, knowing the lawman
would use anything he said against him.

"Look, I know I'm speaking out of turn here, Smith.
It's none of my affair when you come or go. All I'm
saying is that a lot of folks around here think highly of
Savannah. No one wants to see her used, especially by
a drifter who'll desert her without a second thought.
You get what I'm saying?"

Laredo pressed his lips tightly closed in order to
hold his tongue.

"Good. Like I said, Savannah's the sweetest gen-
tlest soul in these parts, and if you or anyone else de-
cides to take advantage of her, you'll answer directly
to me. You got that, boy?"

Laredo's shoulders ached because of the stiff way
he held his back. It'd been a lot of years since anyone
had called him "boy." Laredo hadn't liked it then and
liked it even less now.

"You heard me?" Sheriff Hennessey asked, more forcefully this time.

"Loud and clear."

The lawman nodded and slapped Laredo amiably on the shoulder. "I'm glad we had this little talk. Now you go back to whatever you were doing, and I'll give Miss Dovie one last spin around the dance floor."

Laredo didn't comment. He stood rigid and angry while the sheriff strolled away.

"Laredo?" Savannah said his name softly as she joined him. "Is there a problem?" The distress in her voice melted away his anger. Hennessey was only speaking his mind, prompted, of course, by Grady. The long hours he'd spent working with Roanie hadn't been enough to prove himself to Savannah's brother. But Laredo didn't imagine Grady was ever going to accept him, no matter what he did. Not that it was necessary, other than to ease Savannah's mind. The situation weighed heavily on her, and for that reason alone, it bothered Laredo.

"Everything's fine," he told her.

"You sure?"

"Positive." He took her hand and led her to the porch swing, then sat down beside her. After a few moments he slipped his arm around her shoulders and she rested her head against his chest. To hell with Grady Weston, Laredo decided. He was holding Savannah and he didn't give a damn *what* her older brother thought.

Despite his defiant attitude, Laredo had taken the sheriff at his word. Hennessey could easily make trouble for him. He wasn't looking to cause problems, but he wasn't going to run off with his tail dragging between his legs, either.

Savannah was quiet, and after a moment he assumed she'd gone to sleep. Content to hold her, Laredo entertained himself by watching the party, which was still in progress, although the numbers had dwindled considerably. He figured things must be winding down.

When the band took a break before their final set, Richard brought out his guitar. Taking advantage of the more or less captive audience, he started playing. A dozen people gathered around him. A few children, including Maggie, camped at his feet. A sing-along ensued, and Richard performed several of the songs he'd massacred a few nights earlier in the bunkhouse. Only this time he managed to do a respectable job of carrying a tune, and the words were recognizable.

Twenty minutes later the band returned, and the lead singer encouraged all the men to bring their sweethearts onto the floor. Laredo watched as Richard chose Ellie Frasier—and even managed to steal a kiss when he thought no one was looking. He didn't dance with Ellie long, though, changing partners and dancing with several elderly ladies and then with Maggie and a few of the other children still at the party. The little girls' delight at having the guest of honor pay them such attention sounded in their excited shrieks. The guy was smooth, Laredo gave him that.

"Is this the sweetheart dance?" Savannah asked him, lifting her head from his shoulder.

"That's what he said."

She sighed deeply. Laredo had never been much of a ladies' man, but he knew what that sigh meant. Savannah wanted to dance the sweetheart dance with him, but she wouldn't ask. He had to be the one to invite her.

Damn, he wasn't any good at this romance stuff, but he hated to disappoint Savannah. Nor was he good at dancing. It always made him feel awkward and uncomfortable. Especially in front of an audience. And especially when it was this slow music.

But rather than let her down, Laredo stood and extended his hand in a courtly fashion. "May I have the honor of this dance?"

Her responding smile was worth any embarrassment he might bring on himself, Laredo decided. Savannah's beautiful blue eyes filled with happiness. "Does this mean I'm your sweetheart, Laredo Smith?" she asked softly.

Hennessey's words of warning echoed in his ears. But hell, the man could arrest him for all he cared just then. "It must."

Savannah placed her hand in his and stood.

"Be warned, I might step on your foot," he muttered under his breath as they approached the dance floor.

"I suggest you watch your own feet. It's been a long time since I did anything like this."

Laredo should have known Savannah would find a way to put him at ease. Being with her always made him feel...special. As though he alone, of all men, was worthy of this good and beautiful woman. Right this minute he could almost believe it....

Several couples swayed to the romantic music, holding each other close. One couple was deeply involved in a kiss.

Laredo drew her into his arms and concentrated on moving his feet in a box step, mentally counting to four. One step back, one step to the right, one step forward and then to the left.

"Laredo," she whispered in his ear, wrapping her arms around his neck. "Relax, okay?"

"But—"

"All I really wanted was for you to hold me."

That was all he wanted, too. He shut his eyes and pulled her into the shadows. He kissed her ear, smiling when he felt her shiver.

"Like that, do you?"

"Oh, yes."

He rubbed her back.

"I like that, too."

Laredo was just beginning to feel that he had the hang of this when she captured his earlobe between her lips and gently sucked on it. His eyes flew open and his blood went hot. He slowly let the breath drain from his lungs, then locked his hands at the small of her back. Soon she was flush against him. With her softness touching him like that, in the most intimate places, Laredo lost count of the steps. Not long afterward, he discontinued dancing altogether, other than to shuffle his feet a little.

"Laredo," she whispered. "I'm glad Grady asked you to stay. I'm glad for a lot of reasons."

"Me, too," he whispered. "So glad…"

The song continued and he closed his eyes again, wanting to savor these moments. His heart felt so full it actually hurt. Until now, with Savannah in his embrace, Laredo hadn't thought such a possibility existed. But his heart ached. Not with grief or pain but with love.

Of all the memories that could have come to him at

a time like this, the one that did was of his father. The last memory he had of his father still alive.

Laredo had been a young boy when his father left for Vietnam. He didn't understand about war; all he knew was that the man he adored was going away. He'd hidden in the barn, thinking if no one could find him, maybe his father wouldn't have to leave. Naturally his childish plan hadn't worked, and he'd been found in short order.

Then his dad had taken him on his lap and held him for a long time without saying a word. When he did speak, he'd promised Laredo that, no matter what happened while he was away, nothing—not distance, not time, not even death—would separate Laredo from his father's love.

Months later, when Laredo had stood in front of a cold casket and watched his father's body lowered into the ground, he'd recalled those words. At the memorial service he'd stood proud and tall. His mother and grandparents had wept, overcome with grief, but Laredo's eyes had remained dry.

Emotion welled up inside him now and he understood, perhaps for the first time, the intensity of the love his parents had shared. The depth of it. With this revelation came the knowledge that he felt the same way about Savannah. His mother had never remarried, and Laredo finally understood why.

A gruff voice broke into his thoughts and he lifted his head from Savannah's to see her older brother standing by the side of the dance floor.

"I don't like the way you're holding my sister."

Laredo released Savannah. Grady Weston's face was flushed and angry.

"Grady, please!" Savannah reluctantly moved away from Laredo. "You're making a scene and embarrassing me."

"Leave us alone," Laredo warned. Their eyes met, challenged, clashed. His willingness to make peace with Grady had vanished after that talk with the sheriff.

Before he realized exactly how it had happened, he and Grady were facing off, their fists raised.

"Grady, stop!" Savannah cried, and when it did no good, she turned to Laredo. "If you care for me, you won't do this."

Laredo did care, so damn much it terrified him. But this was one fight he wasn't walking away from.

"Please," Savannah said, stepping directly in front of him.

Laredo felt himself weakening.

Caroline Daniels arrived then and slid her arm through Grady's. "It seems to me that what you need is a nice hot cup of coffee," she announced, steering him toward the kitchen.

Laredo watched the two of them walk toward the house.

Savannah slipped her arms back around Laredo's neck. "I believe this dance was mine," she said, nestling close to him once more.

A lot more than this dance belonged to Savannah Weston, Laredo realized. She also owned his heart.

Seven

The early-morning sun shone cheerfully on the Yellow Rose. Savannah had been much too tired the night before to worry about cleanup, but in the revealing light of day, the entire front yard was a disaster. The Chinese lanterns sagged. Paper plates and napkins littered the once-flawless grass amid a welter of abandoned tables and chairs. The straw from the dance area stretched like a spider web from one end of the lawn to the other.

While the coffee brewed, Savannah dragged a garbage can into the yard. She'd only been working ten or fifteen minutes when Grady joined her. Wiley and Laredo followed, yawning. Savannah quickly distributed plastic garbage bags, since there was far too much trash for one container.

"Where's Richard?" Grady demanded.

"Sleeping," Wiley said with a chuckle. "What did you expect?" He began picking up litter and stuffing it into a bag.

"Then drag his sorry ass out here. It was his party. The least he can do is clean up the mess he created."

"Why should he start now?" Again the question came from Wiley.

"I got better things to do than this," Grady grumbled, stuffing his own armload of garbage into a bag.

"I didn't hire on to do housekeeping, either," the foreman put in.

Savannah had heard enough. "Stop it—both of you!" she shouted, unable to bear the bickering. It was rare for her to raise her voice, let alone yell, and she immediately got everyone's attention. Grady and Wiley stopped and stared at her; even Rocket lifted his head, as if shocked by her outburst.

A frown creasing his brow, Laredo paused in his raking and waited.

"I didn't ask for your help," she said. "If you're going to complain, then leave. I'd rather tend to the cleanup myself than be subjected to your foul moods." The comment was directed at Grady. Her good feeling about her brother—the fact that he'd hired Laredo—was rapidly fading.

"I'm in one hell of a fine mood," Grady barked, grimacing in a parody of a smile. "I'm as happy as can be." Savannah thought he looked like he was posing for the cover of *Mad* magazine, but restrained herself from saying so.

"You're happy?" Wiley asked, his words drenched with sarcasm. "You look about as happy as when you wrote out that check to Adam Braunfels for the barbecue."

This was the first Savannah had heard about it. "Why'd you pay Adam?"

"I didn't have any choice," Grady snapped. "He wanted his money and Sleeping Beauty in there—"

he gestured at the bunkhouse "—didn't have it. What the hell else could I do?"

Savannah wished she hadn't asked, since the money was obviously a sore spot with Grady. Not that she blamed him, but surely Richard expected his check soon, otherwise he wouldn't have thrown himself this party.

"It was good of you to pay Adam," she said, wanting Grady to know she appreciated his dilemma. "Money's tight just now."

"My money got even tighter with the party," Grady muttered. "I hope to hell he doesn't expect me to pay for everything, because I won't do it." He sounded as though he wasn't sure who he was trying to convince, her or himself.

"Richard will make good on it," Savannah felt obliged to say. Her younger brother had made plenty of mistakes, but he'd learned his lesson. At least that was what he claimed—and what she desperately wanted to believe.

Although the party had drained her physically and emotionally, she'd enjoyed watching Richard with their neighbors. He'd been a gracious host, warm and welcoming, and it gave her a sense of pride. He was like their father in that way—although admittedly not in others.

Mel Weston had always been the life of the party. Friendly, charming, universally loved. Her world had gone dark without him there—to call her his princess, to give her encouragement and approval and unconditional love. Having Richard home again produced a flood of happy memories and she didn't want those destroyed. Not if she could help it. So she was willing to give him the benefit of the doubt.

Everyone had mentioned what fun Richard was and how the children had adored him, especially Maggie. Seeing them together had done Savannah's heart good. The five-year-old tended to shy away from men, but she'd taken to Richard at first meeting, and he'd been wonderful with her, paying her lots of attention.

"I kissed that money goodbye the minute I signed the check," Grady grumbled, telling her in no uncertain terms that he continued to distrust Richard.

"He'll pay you back," Savannah insisted.

Grady stared at her long enough to make her uncomfortable. "When are you going to learn, Savannah? What's it going to take? Richard's a user. He'll never amount to anything because he's never been made accountable. I want him off this ranch, understand?"

"You're wrong, Grady. Richard might have a few bad habits—we all do—but he has a good heart. I refuse to believe otherwise."

"Don't kid yourself. As soon as he's awake, I want him to pack up and leave. I've paid his debts for the last time."

"You don't mean that!" Savannah couldn't believe her brother could be so hard.

"I want him gone by noon."

"Grady…please." Her voice cracked with emotion. "Don't do this."

"I'm not giving in to you this time," Grady said, stuffing more garbage deep into the plastic bag.

Savannah jumped at the fierce anger she heard in him.

"Don't talk to her like that," Laredo demanded,

walking over to Savannah. The animosity between him and Grady was worse than ever, Savannah knew. She had no idea what had possessed her brother to cause a scene on the dance floor.

In a replay of last night Laredo and Grady glared at each other with mutual dislike.

"What do you suggest we do?" Wiley asked her, apparently finding the men's behavior amusing. "Get a hose and cool 'em both down?"

"That doesn't sound like a bad idea," Savannah responded, grateful for his sense of humor in this tense situation.

"Okay." Wiley took charge. "We're done here," he said, stepping directly in front of Laredo.

Savannah thought Laredo might challenge the foreman, but after a short hesitation he nodded and set aside the rake. As he turned to head for the barn, he caught her watching him and winked.

Savannah blushed with pleasure, remembering the dance they'd shared. After spending all day and most of the evening in the kitchen, her hair damp with sweat and her clothes spattered with mustard and mayonnaise, she must have looked a sight. Yet he'd called her his sweetheart and looked at her as if she were beautiful. Savannah had always known she was no beauty. She'd never been one to turn men's heads, and being shy had made it worse.

Over time she'd given up hope she'd ever find love. She'd never felt real attraction for a man, and as far as she knew, had never inspired it, either. All these years she'd been certain that a husband and family were for others and not for her. Her roses and her pets had become like her children. Grady constantly complained about the way she spoiled Rocket, but the dog was old, and if he was more comfortable in the house, she had no objection to letting him inside. And although Grady complained, she noticed that he was as guilty as she was about sneaking him leftovers.

Her musings returned to Laredo, and her heart softened at the thought of him. In less than two weeks he'd changed her life, given her reason to dream, given her the most precious of human emotions—hope.

She loved him. It was that simple. That profound.

"I suppose you're waiting for me to apologize for making an ass of myself last night," Grady said, breaking into her thoughts. She'd almost forgotten he was there.

"You owe Laredo and me an apology."

He paused, then to her amazement, agreed with her. "I suppose I do. My only excuse is that I was furious with Richard and took it out on Laredo. I realize I acted like an idiot. I don't have any excuse other than I'd been drinking on an empty stomach."

The irony of it, Savannah mused, was that Grady had ended up paying for a dinner he hadn't bothered to taste.

"I'd be obliged if we could put the incident behind us," he said stiffly.

"On one condition."

He held up his hand to stop her. "I already know. You want me to apologize to Laredo."

"You didn't start this morning any better than you left off last night."

"I know." He wiped a hand down his face and she noticed that his eyes were tired and sad, and she wondered if he'd gotten any sleep whatsoever. "I'll talk to him later."

"What do you have against him?" she asked, genuinely curious. "Laredo isn't anything like you think. He's thoughtful and hardworking and—"

"Do you mind if I listen to you sing his praises some other time?" Grady asked from between clenched teeth.

"Oh, Grady." It was then she realized her brother was suffering from a hangover. After his confrontation with Laredo, he'd apparently continued drinking—and probably not beer, either. The first moment she could Savannah had escaped to her room, taken a quick shower and fallen into bed. She'd fallen asleep immediately but woke periodically throughout the night. At least tired was all she felt—not hungover, like Grady.

"Yeah," he groaned. "I had a few drinks after everyone went home. Figured it'd calm me down. It didn't. But guess what? I found there was booze missing—my good single-malt Scotch. Where do you think it went?"

Savannah shook her head.

"Starts with *R*."

"Oh, no. Are you *sure?*"

Grady gave her a cynical look and returned to his garbage collecting.

When the cleanup was finished, Grady grabbed a cup of coffee and headed about his day; Savannah went back to the house. It was almost eleven before Richard bothered to make an appearance.

"Good morning, my beautiful Savannah!" He kissed her noisily on the cheek, then hopped onto the kitchen counter, bare feet dangling while he nursed a mug of coffee. "What's for breakfast?"

"It's almost time for lunch."

He didn't react. "I was looking forward to sampling some of those fluffy scrambled eggs of yours. I woke up dreaming about eggs all gooey with melted cheese and toasted homemade bread."

"Richard," she said, angry with him and needing to let him know, "how could you have left Grady to pay Mr. Braunfels for the barbecue?"

"I feel really bad about that. I explained the situation to Adam earlier, and he seemed okay with me paying when I could. I wonder what happened to make him change his mind."

She wanted so much to believe Richard, but it was becoming more and more difficult.

He must have realized that, because he leaped down off the counter, crossed the room and reached for her hand. "Savannah," he said, holding her gaze, "I promise you by everything I hold dear that I'll reimburse Grady the minute my check arrives. You've got to trust me."

She wanted to, but the doubts refused to go away.

"You're the only one who believes in me," Richard said in obvious distress. "If it wasn't for you, Grady would have kicked me off the ranch that first day. Give me this opportunity to prove myself, that's all I'm asking."

Savannah studied her brother, hoping against hope that he'd fulfill his promises.

The beginnings of a smile lit up his eyes. "I can hardly wait to see the look on Grady's face when I give him the money. Won't he be shocked?" He laughed as if viewing the scene that very moment.

Savannah relaxed. Richard was her brother. He'd made mistakes, painful ones, but he was older now, mature. He couldn't help his impulsive sociable nature—couldn't resist throwing that party. However, he wouldn't take advantage of her and Grady a second time, she was sure of it.

"Do you believe me?" The color of his eyes intensified as his gaze implored her to give him the benefit of the doubt.

Savannah couldn't refuse him. "I believe you," she whispered and silently prayed he wouldn't let her down.

Richard squeezed her hand. "You won't be sorry, Savannah, I promise you. I'm going to prove Grady all wrong, just you wait and see. Then you can say 'I told you so' to our high-and-mighty brother. You trusted me when no one else would, and someday you'll be able to laugh in Grady's face."

"I'd never do that." Her older brother might be strong-willed and opinionated, but his intentions were good.

"Are you going to scramble me up some of my favorite cheese eggs?" he asked in a cajoling voice.

She'd finished washing the breakfast dishes fifteen minutes earlier. "All right," she conceded. Richard gave her a hug, then climbed back onto the counter while she took the eggs, cheese and milk from the refrigerator.

"I was looking around your garden and noticed some of those roses you were telling me about. Where'd you find those pretty white ones?"

"Oh, this place and that," she said, and while she was pleased by his interest, the less he knew about her venture into Bitter End the better.

"You went there, didn't you?" he asked, lowering his voice.

"There?"

"Don't play games with me, Savannah. You're no good at it."

Her cheeks flushed hot pink. Richard was right, she'd never been any good at games. He was curious about the ghost town and this wasn't the first time he'd bombarded her with questions. Some about roses, others about the town itself.

"Did you go inside any of the buildings?" Richard asked. "They're still standing, right? Imagine that after all these years. What stories those walls could tell! It amazes me, you know, that Bitter End could be sleeping in those hills with only a handful of people even knowing about its existence."

"It is rather remarkable," Savannah agreed.

"I bet the buildings were in sad shape?"

"I didn't investigate the town itself," she said. The cemetery was as far as she got. Whatever was there had driven her back before she'd set foot in the actual town. But she'd know the answer to her brother's questions soon enough. Today was it, she'd decided. She was going back for a second visit, despite all Grady's efforts to keep her away.

"So where exactly is it?" Richard asked.

"Oh, sort of east of here," she said vaguely. "I had a hard time finding it." That was all she planned to say on the matter.

"Weren't you afraid?" he teased.

She wasn't sure how to describe her wariness. "Not really," she said, downplaying the eerie sensation she'd experienced on her first visit. She added the beaten eggs to the small skillet as the butter sizzled.

"I really don't think visiting the place again is a good idea," Richard surprised her by saying. Not that *she* wanted him there, but a few days ago, he'd certainly been dropping hints to that effect. He buttered the toast when it popped up and sat down at the table, awaiting his breakfast.

"I *have* to go back," she said, surprised she had to fight Richard on this, too. Grady and Laredo had formed an uneasy partnership in their efforts to keep her from returning. "There're bound to be other roses," she explained, although it wasn't necessary. All three men knew her reasons. "I might find an even rarer form. I can't tell you how thrilled I was with my original discovery."

"Think carefully before you go back," Richard said, smiling gratefully when she set the plate of steaming eggs in front of him. "You'd be wise to heed Grady's advice, Savannah. A ghost town isn't any place for you to go exploring alone."

"Earlier you said you wanted to come along. You—"

"I said that?" He flattened his hand against his chest. "Not me. I'm as chicken as they come. You won't catch me anywhere close to Bitter End. I have a healthy respect for the supernatural."

Savannah refused to be dissuaded, but she didn't intend to discuss it further. She'd do what she did the last time—steal away before anyone knew she was gone.

* * *

Grady sat in his office and pinched the bridge of his nose, hoping that would help him focus on the long row of ledger numbers. He hadn't slept more than a couple of hours the entire night. Instead, he'd been leaning over the toilet, examining parts of it that were never meant to be viewed from this perspective.

Hard liquor had never agreed with him. Especially in quantity. After he'd embarrassed himself and Savannah, he'd holed up in his office with a bottle of cheap whiskey. The good stuff had disappeared, as he'd told his sister—but he hadn't been in any mood to appreciate the difference.

This morning his head throbbed with a vengeance. He couldn't think, couldn't work. Richard had been back less than a week, and already Grady was reduced to a useless piece of... He didn't finish the thought.

The phone pealed and he slammed his eyes closed as the sound pierced his brain, shattering what little serenity he'd managed to recover. He waited for Savannah to answer.

No one knew he was in his office, and that was the way he wanted it.

The phone rang a second time and then a third. Where the hell was Savannah? If not her, Richard? Rather than suffer the agony of a fourth ring, Grady grabbed the receiver.

"Who the hell is it?" he snarled.

A shocked silence greeted him, followed by a sob, then tears and "Mommy, Mommy."

Damn. It'd been Maggie for Savannah, and he'd frightened the poor kid half out of her wits.

"Maggie," he shouted, wanting to apologize for his

outburst. Apologize was all he seemed to do these days. He felt faint stirrings of hope when he heard someone pick up the receiver.

"Maggie, listen—"

"It's Caroline," she interrupted coolly. "And this must be Grady." She didn't give him a chance to respond before she added, "What exactly did you say to Maggie to upset her like this?"

"I didn't know. I thought…" Even his tongue refused to work properly.

"Obviously you *didn't* think."

He could hear Maggie softly weeping in the background.

"I'm sorry, Caroline," he said. "Hell, I didn't know it was Maggie. I certainly didn't mean to frighten her."

"What's gotten into you, Grady?"

He braced his forehead against his hand. If the answer was that simple, he would've saved himself a great deal of embarrassment. The truth was he didn't know anymore.

"You made an ass of yourself last night."

"Nice of you to remind me." Leave it to a woman to kick a man when he was down.

"You had too much to drink."

"You brought me one of those beers," he felt obliged to remind her.

"So this is all *my* fault?"

Grady closed his eyes at her outrage. "No," he admitted, feeling about as low as a man could get. "I accept full responsibility."

The silence stretched between them until Caroline slowly released a deep breath and asked, "Where's Savannah?"

"I don't know. I expected her to pick up the phone." Clearly so had Maggie, who continued to weep noisily in the background.

"Is she all right?" Caroline asked.

"She was this morning." And not afraid to set him down a peg or two, although he knew he'd asked for it.

Maggie's cries subsided into soft muffled sounds.

"What are you doing home?" he asked Caroline. She should be at the post office, but then, he wasn't the one to talk, seeing as he should be out on the range with Wiley. Or working in the barn with Laredo Smith.

"Maggie wasn't feeling well this morning, so I took the day off."

"How's she doing?"

"She's feeling better—or she was," Caroline said pointedly.

"I'd like to talk to her if you'd let me, so I can apologize." He wasn't sure he knew *how* to talk to a five-year-old, but he didn't want her cringing in terror every time she was out at the ranch. She was a sweet little girl and Savannah was deeply attached to her.

"I don't know if she'll talk to you."

"Ask her, will you?" His hand tightened around the receiver while he waited. In the background he could hear Caroline reasoning with the child. He was somewhat amused when he heard her compare him to the beast in *Beauty and the Beast*. He made a lot of loud noises and sounded mean, Caroline said, but deep down he was really a prince who'd been put under a spell.

Caroline returned to the phone a couple of minutes later. "I'm sorry, Grady, but I can't convince her to give you a second chance."

"I can't say I blame her," Grady said with a sigh. "I was pretty rough when I answered."

"She called to tell Savannah she had a tummy ache."

"My kind of sympathy wasn't what she was looking for, was it."

The sound of Caroline's half chuckle did more to lift his spirits than anything had that day.

"I guess you could say that," she said softly.

"I have been a beast, haven't I?"

"You could say that, too."

"Since she won't let me talk to her, will you tell Maggie I'm sorry? I promise I won't shout at her again." He didn't know if it would do any good, but it was the best he could manage. The next time Maggie visited the ranch, he'd try to square things with her.

"I'll let Savannah know you phoned," he said, reaching for a pen. If he didn't write it down, he'd forget, and he didn't think Caroline would be willing to forgive him that on top of everything else.

They exchanged goodbyes and he replaced the receiver.

With an effort he glanced down at the ledger and reached for the calculator, determined to make good use of his time. He couldn't laze in bed until noon like his worthless brother.

Laredo assumed he'd find Savannah in the rose garden, but she was nowhere in sight. Nor was she in the house. He'd done everything short of knocking on her bedroom door.

Grady had disappeared, as well, but that was more a blessing than a matter of concern.

Unsure where to search next, Laredo headed back to the barn. It was one of the last places he expected to find Savannah. A niggling sense of fear refused to leave him. She'd looked pale that morning, and although he hadn't been eager to clash with Grady so soon after their last confrontation, he wasn't about to let him harass Savannah.

The barn door creaked as he pushed it open. Light spilled into the interior and Savannah spun around. Her eyes instantly widened with guilt.

Laredo had no idea what she'd been doing, but clearly it was something she didn't want anyone knowing.

"Savannah?"

"Hi." Her smile was a bit sheepish.

"What are you doing in here?"

"Nothing. I was—"

"Savannah," he said and held out his arms, needing to reassure her. She didn't hesitate, not so much as a second. He brought her into his embrace and hugged her. "Don't ever play poker, sweetheart. Your expression's a dead giveaway."

Her arms circled his waist and she pressed her face to his shoulder. "I'm so sorry about what happened last night," she said.

This was the first chance they'd had to discuss the incident, but Laredo preferred to drop the entire thing. He'd been at fault, too, eager to put her brother in his place for embarrassing Savannah. And he'd been angry after his chat with Hennessey, knowing Grady had instigated the sheriff's questioning.

"Let's put it behind us, okay?"

He felt her deep sigh. "Is that what you want?" she asked in a solemn voice.

"Yeah."

"I'm willing to forget it—except for one thing." She tilted her head back and gazed at him with wide adoring eyes.

"What's that?" Laredo didn't know what he'd done to deserve having such a beautiful woman look at him that way.

"I could put the…incident behind me if Grady hadn't cheated me out of my sweetheart dance."

"Not all of it."

"I begrudge every second he stole from me."

Laredo kissed the top of her head and reached behind him to take hold of her hands. "Don't you hear the music?" he asked.

"Music?" Her eyes narrowed as if she was straining to hear before she realized what he was doing. She smiled then, and it was all he could do not to cover her mouth with his.

"I believe there *is* music in here," she said, her face alight with happiness.

"There must be."

Laredo danced her about the barn floor, making turns so wide that her skirt flared straight out as they whirled around. Savannah threw back her head and laughed with such pure joy Laredo was soon smiling himself.

They whirled faster and faster until they were both winded and ready to collapse with laughter. Savannah pressed her hand to her throat as she drew in a deep breath.

"Okay, confess," he said once he'd caught his own

breath. He leaned against the wall and watched as the amusement left her.

"Confess?"

"What were you up to earlier?"

He watched as she shifted her feet a couple of times before she lowered her head. "You'll be angry with me."

Laredo didn't think that was possible. "Why?"

"I was about to break the promise I made you. I—I'm sorry...."

Then it dawned on him. She'd been gathering equipment to sneak away to that damned ghost town. He exhaled sharply, grateful he'd found her when he had. He was disappointed, too. He'd expected Savannah to be a woman of her word.

"I'm sorry," she said again, with such genuine regret that he couldn't help forgiving her. "Richard and I were talking about Bitter End this morning, and I felt this urge to go there again. Now. Today. I have to, Laredo. Because of the roses." She glanced down at her feet. "And I didn't want Richard to know. Or Grady. I wasn't sure where you were...and I've got to leave quickly." She raised her head to look at him. "Can you come with me?" she asked, her expressive eyes filled with hope. "It won't take much time. I'll leave Grady a note and explain."

Grady might owe him a favor, but Laredo didn't feel ready to collect it quite this soon. Then he changed his mind.

"All right," he said, "we'll do it."

She clapped her hands, then forgetting herself, leaped forward and kissed him on the mouth. "I'll pack up a lunch and afterward we can have a picnic."

He hadn't the heart to disappoint her, but his idea of how he wanted to spend the day wasn't sitting in some field full of bluebonnets, lingering over sandwiches. Not even with Savannah.... He thought of all the chores that awaited him. Chores Grady counted on him to do.

"How long will we be?"

"Not too long," she promised. "All I want to do is walk around and see if there are any other roses. We won't stay."

He nodded.

"There's a lovely spot a few miles down the road where the river bends. We can have lunch there." She wasn't about to drop this picnic idea of hers, and really, he supposed, it was a small thing to ask.

With their plans set, Laredo loaded the shovels and other tools into the back of the pickup. As he did, an uneasiness settled over him. Apparently what Grady had told him about the place had made a stronger impact than he'd realized. His uneasiness grew into dread and refused to leave him.

They weren't even off the ranch yet, and already he was convinced they shouldn't go.

Eight

The truck pitched and heaved, first left and then right, as they neared Bitter End. Savannah hung on as best she could, but her shoulders continued to slam against Laredo's, jarring them both. Thankfully they were able to follow the tire tracks from her last visit, otherwise she wasn't sure she could have located it a second time.

"I can't believe you found this place on your own," Laredo said, his hands gripping the steering wheel tightly.

"It wasn't easy—took me weeks of searching."

More than once she'd been tempted to forsake the idea, but the thought of finding old roses had spurred her onward. Her patience had been richly rewarded. Not only had she discovered the White Lady Banks, her most valuable find to date, but on that same day she'd come across Laredo.

The truck pitched sharply and Laredo cursed under his breath.

"We're pretty close now," she assured him. His face was tense with concentration, and although he drove cautiously, he couldn't avoid jolting the truck on the rough ground. There was barely even a track.

Savannah was grateful Laredo had agreed to escort her back to the ghost town, but what she looked forward to even more was their picnic. They were rarely alone. This stolen time was bound to be special.

Laredo eased the truck to a stop when they could go no farther.

"It's only a short walk from here," she promised.

The trek was difficult, through brush and dense cedars, and they were both breathless before the town came into view.

"So this is Bitter End," Laredo muttered as he climbed over rocks to a limestone ledge that overlooked the town. He offered Savannah his hand.

She took it and stepped up. From the outskirts Bitter End resembled any other ghost town. A row of forsaken buildings lined the main street, four or five on each side, in various states of disrepair, various stages of dying. Paintless shutters hung crookedly by empty windows. The stillness and lack of sound gave it an eerie unreal feeling. Wind-tossed tumbleweeds had wedged in the corners and along the boardwalk. A quick inspection didn't reveal any visible plant life, but there had to be some roses. The ones in the cemetery had survived. Others would've, too.

The largest building in town was the church, which sat on a hill at the far end of town, next to the cemetery. Time had left it remarkably untouched. It'd remained white and unblemished except for the charred steeple, which had apparently been struck by lightning. At the other end of town was a corral.

They clambered down a rocky embankment into

the town itself. Then it happened just as it had on her first visit. The feeling of sadness and pain. Whatever possessed Bitter End wasn't ghosts or spirits, of that she was fairly certain, but a sorrow so strong even the years hadn't dimmed it.

She looked at Laredo, who faced the town squarely, feet slightly apart, ready, it seemed, for anything. He stood there silently as if he was listening and yet heard nothing.

"Do you feel it?" she whispered. Normal tones didn't seem right. On her previous visit she hadn't murmured a word. She'd been in and out of the town within ten minutes. Just long enough to dig up the roses and replace them with a bush from her own garden.

"Are you sure you want to go ahead with this?" Laredo asked. He, too, spoke in a whisper, unwilling to disturb whatever it was that awaited them.

Savannah slipped her arm through his. "I'm positive."

"Then let's get it over with and get the hell out."

"There aren't any ghosts here," she told him, still in a whisper.

"Whatever you say." He smiled for the first time since their arrival.

"It won't take long to look for more roses," she said. The presence of another person—someone she trusted—made the town seem a little less frightening.

If Laredo wasn't in such an all-fired hurry to leave, it might have been fun to explore the interior of some of the buildings. But then again, Savannah had the distinct impression they were trespassing as it was.

"Where do you want to start?" Laredo asked as they neared the main street.

"Anyplace is fine. I was in the cemetery earlier." She motioned toward the church and the graveyard behind it. They walked side by side, holding hands. His warm grasp lent her reassurance.

The farther they went into town, the stronger the sense of sorrow became. With each step down the narrow street, the feeling grew darker. During her last visit she'd hurried through Bitter End as quickly as possible on her way to the cemetery, trying to shake off the sense of misery and unease.

She'd actually enjoyed visiting the graveyard. The sensation hadn't been nearly as powerful there, and she'd been fascinated by the headstones. Most of the names and dates on the simple markers were no longer legible, but that hadn't stopped her from picturing the kind of life the people of Bitter End had lived. It would have been a harsh existence, battling hunger, disease and the elements.

Savannah recalled the stories she'd read about the frontier days when Texas had been wild and unforgiving. Stories she would one day read to her own children.

Her own children.

The thought caught her unprepared. All these years Savannah had assumed she'd never marry. Since meeting Laredo she'd begun to believe that all things were possible for her. A husband and a family of her own. Despite the eeriness of the place, Savannah's heart gladdened.

After a few minutes exploring the town's streets, Savannah realized that the trip had been a waste of time and energy. Whatever flowers, roses or otherwise, once bloomed in Bitter End had long since died. Nothing grew inside the town. Nothing. Everything was dead, including the land itself.

The lone tree, an oak with gnarled limbs, was hollow and lifeless. It stood in silent testimony to a time and place long forgotten.

"Don't you think it's a bit bizarre that there's nothing alive here? Not even a weed?" Laredo commented.

She nodded. The only plants that had survived one-hundred-plus years were the roses she'd discovered at the cemetery. "I want to go back," she said.

"I couldn't agree with you more," Laredo murmured.

"I mean, to the cemetery," she said.

He hesitated. "Are you sure that's wise?"

"I don't know, but I'm curious about the grave site where I found the roses." It didn't add up in Savannah's mind. If those roses had survived, then it made sense that other plants would have, too.

"In my humble opinion," Laredo said, his words barely audible, "we shouldn't tempt fate. Let's leave while the leaving's good. All right?"

His hand gripped Savannah's with such force that her fingers throbbed. He wasn't intentionally hurting her, she knew, but reacting to the tension inside him.

"All right," she agreed. "We'll go. I'll look some other time."

"No." The force behind the single word brought her up short.

"I don't want you coming back here," he said with an urgency that baffled her. "Not for anything. Understand? This place gives me the creeps."

Despite her love for him, she couldn't make that kind of promise. "No. Someday there might be a very good reason for me to return."

Clearly, he wanted to argue the point, but right then, leaving appeared to be a higher priority. Frequently looking over his shoulder, Laredo led her back toward the faint path that would take them to the truck.

As they walked, the sensation gradually lifted from her shoulders. Savannah could feel it slipping away. Like a silk scarf dragged across a palm, the sensation faded until it was completely gone.

Once they reached the pickup, Laredo helped Savannah inside, then climbed in himself. He couldn't seem to start the engine fast enough. His anxiety, even greater than her own, was contagious.

Savannah didn't want to know what had created the feeling that pervaded Bitter End. There was nothing good in that town and maybe there never had been.

Life was filled with mysteries, Laredo told himself. The answers weren't always meant to be known. That was the way he felt about this ghost town. Grady hadn't said much about it, only that it wasn't a safe place for Savannah. Her brother couldn't trust her not to return on her own, so he'd put aside his dislike and distrust of Laredo and sought his help.

For the first time Laredo appreciated Grady's fears. He didn't know what the hell had happened in that town. But he didn't need to know. As far as he was concerned, Bitter End could continue as it had for more than a hundred years without interruption from him.

He leaned against the tree trunk and watched Savannah unpack the picnic basket. He still wasn't keen on lazing away the afternoon under a flowering pecan, but his objection to the wasted time felt much less urgent now.

The spot she'd chosen for their picnic was as lovely as she'd promised. The river flowed swiftly nearby, the clean sound of water a sharp contrast to what he'd experienced a short time before.

Savannah finished unloading the wicker basket and quickly assembled them each a plate—roast-beef sandwiches, yesterday's potato salad, homemade pickles. They ate in companionable silence for a while, then both spoke at once.

"You felt it, too, didn't you?" she asked.

"Was it the same as before?" he asked.

They paused and grinned, then Laredo took the lead. "I'll tell you what," he said. "Let's not talk about the town."

"Why not?"

He wasn't sure if she was disappointed or relieved. "I want to talk about you."

"Me?" She shook her head. "You already know everything."

"No, I'm sure I don't. For instance, who taught you to cook like this?" He couldn't remember a time he'd eaten better. Not in years. Not since he was a child, when he'd been too young to appreciate a home-cooked meal.

"My mother loved cooking. Baking, too. Mealtime was a matter of pride to her. I guess we're more alike than I realized." Her eyes grew wide. "You would have liked her, Laredo—she was a wonderful woman."

He didn't doubt that, not with the way he felt about

Savannah. Relaxed as he was, the sun behind him, the sound of the river singing nearby, Laredo yawned, lulled by the serenity of the spot. "You'd like my mother, too."

He hadn't meant to talk about himself, but once he'd mentioned his mother, she wouldn't let the subject drop. Before long he was answering her questions, talking about his mother in Tulsa. About her being widowed in 1972. And how she'd moved back to the same house where she'd been born and raised, the house where she still lived. How she'd been dating the same man for twenty years without any plan to marry him.

"I know I'd like her," Savannah said wistfully. Then she lowered her gaze until her long lashes grazed the high arch of her cheek. "Would you... Never mind." Savannah reached for a blade of grass and nervously twisted it around her finger.

"Would I what?" he prodded, enjoying her discomfort. Little did she realize that he'd do just about anything for her. All she had to do was ask.

Her eyes fleetingly held his before she glanced away. "Would you like to put your head in my lap?" she asked.

This was what dreams were made of, he decided as he rested his neck against her thigh. It didn't take long for her fingers to weave their way into his hair, her touch soft and gentle. A memory rushed forward, one of his father and mother. His mother cutting his father's hair in the kitchen. Laredo couldn't have been more than four at the time, but he recalled the loving way his mother's hands had smoothed back the hair from his father's brow. His father had reached for her hand and kissed her palm.

Without realizing it, Laredo caught Savannah's fingers and brought them to his lips. His heart constricted with the strength of emotion that coursed through him.

He didn't intend to kiss her, but that was a natural progression. As natural as drawing his next breath. He lifted his head from the sanctuary of her lap and gently met her mouth with his. The hunger that surged to fire in his blood stunned him. The strength of his desire would have frightened her had he acted on it, Laredo thought. Instead, he involved himself in the kiss, his lips lingering on hers.

One kiss, he promised himself. But it soon became obvious that a single kiss wasn't enough for either of them. They exchanged one after another, each more intense than the last. Laredo had to call on every ounce of willpower he possessed to stop.

"I like it when you kiss me," Savannah whispered. She kept her eyes closed as she spoke.

"I like it, too," he confessed.

"Don't stop," she pleaded.

Once again Laredo found himself in the position of being unable to refuse her.

The kiss was even better than the others; he'd assumed that was impossible. Savannah lay on the blanket, smiling up at him and he leaned over her.

"You taste so good I don't want you to ever stop," she whispered when he hesitated.

"Sweetheart, you don't know what you're asking."

"I do," she murmured, her mouth moist and slightly swollen from his kisses. "I want you to kiss me forever."

That didn't sound like a bad plan to Laredo, but sooner or later, kissing wouldn't be enough to satisfy either one of them. They were fast approaching that point now.

"Savannah," he whispered, wondering how he could explain why it wasn't a good idea to continue.

He didn't get a chance. She locked her arms around his neck and drew his mouth down to hers again. He tried to show her without words what she did to him. This kiss was fierce, as fierce as his growing need.

He urged her lips apart and swept her mouth with his tongue, fully expecting— Hell, he didn't know *what* he was expecting. Certainly not this acceptance, this welcoming. His breath jammed in his lungs as the kiss deepened. While he waged war with his needs, she returned his lovemaking with an eagerness that destroyed his restraint. Her nails dug into his shoulders as if to bring him closer, become part of him. Laredo was convinced she didn't really grasp the overwhelming physical intensity of his reaction, didn't realize what she was doing to him.

Above all, he didn't want her ending up in a sexual situation she wasn't ready for.

When he could endure no more, he abruptly broke off the kiss and rolled away. His shoulders heaved with the strength of will it had taken to leave her.

"Did I do something wrong?" she asked after a moment.

He waited until he'd caught his breath before he answered. "I wouldn't say that."

"Then why did you stop?"

He closed his eyes. "I don't think you understand—"

"Don't treat me like a child, Laredo. I know exactly what was happening."

He felt depleted; he hadn't the energy to argue with her. She made him vulnerable. Much more of this kissing would have sent him over the edge. He knew his limits and they'd been reached.

He sat up and smiled. Or at least made the effort to smile. In an attempt to clear his head, he took several deep breaths.

"I called about the repairs to the truck," he said, not looking at her. He focused on the tree limbs overhead, hoping she realized why he'd abruptly changed the subject.

His announcement was greeted with silence.

"Paul said the parts were in and all he needed was the go-ahead from me." Laredo paused and waited for a response.

More silence.

Finally she said, "I know what you're doing, Laredo."

"Do you?" He doubted it.

"You're telling me that you're leaving Promise as soon as you can."

So she did know, and if she was that smart, she'd probably figure out the rest. "I don't want to hurt you, Savannah."

"You couldn't," she said, her voice small. "You've already brought me such incredible happiness. When you do…leave—" she appeared to have trouble saying the word "—don't worry that I'll do anything to stop you. I'm grateful for each day we can be together. Grateful for each moment…each kiss."

He didn't see it that way. After all, he was the one

in *her* debt. "I think we should get back before anyone misses us." He was strongly tempted to resume their lovemaking, and he couldn't be sure he possessed the determination to resist.

"Not yet," she pleaded softly. "I left a note in the kitchen so no one'll worry."

He didn't know what would happen if they kissed again—and didn't think he could afford to find out. He stood, removing himself from temptation.

"Just a few more moments." She regarded him with such longing he found it impossible to refuse her.

"All right," he said and sat back down on the blanket. "But only a few minutes longer. Okay? And no kissing."

She nodded and thanked him with the sweetest of smiles.

A few minutes soon became two hours. Savannah closed her eyes and was immediately asleep. Laredo wondered if she'd gotten much rest the night before. He knew *he* hadn't. He suspected that the only one who'd enjoyed the luxury of a night's uninterrupted sleep was Richard.

He knew how Savannah felt about her brother and feared it was only a matter of time before Richard disappointed her. Laredo didn't want to see that happen, but he was helpless to protect her.

Uncomfortable with his thoughts, Laredo sat against the tree and watched Savannah, appreciating her gentle beauty. Each minute was a gift; she'd been the one to express that thought, and he, too, had discovered the truth of it.

The world, his mother once told him, had a way of making all things equal. A divine order. *We receive*

back what we give, or something along those lines. He
hadn't paid close attention at the time and now wished
he had. But it seemed to him that meeting Savannah
made up for everything that had ever gone wrong in
his life. Every broken promise. Every unmet expectation, every unfair act.

But why did he have to meet her *now?* He snapped
off a blade of grass and chewed on the end. Why would
he meet this woman—and fall in love with her—when
he had nothing to offer but hardship?

Laredo loved Savannah; he'd admitted that early
on. He loved her enough to leave her, rather than ask
her to scrimp and sacrifice with him. She deserved
far better. He refused to cheat her of the comfort and
certitude that were her right.

Ellie Frasier was busy in the back room dealing
with a shipment from one of her main suppliers when
Richard Weston strolled in. He wore a crisp pair of
jeans, his fancy boots and brand-new Stetson, and
looked more like a country singer than a rancher.

"So this is where you've been hiding yourself," he
said. He gazed at her boldly, eyes roaming from her
hair to her booted feet, letting her know without words
that he liked what he saw. Ellie wasn't opposed to a
bit of flattery now and again. Lord knew Glen and the
other men in her life were damned stingy with their
appreciation.

It had come as a shock to see Richard again after all
these years. At first she hadn't recognized him. As a
schoolgirl she'd had a crush on him. Richard Weston
had been an "older" man, both handsome and charming. That much hadn't changed.

"I thought I'd let you take me to lunch," he said, glancing over her shoulder to read the clipboard.

"I don't have time today." She wouldn't have minded spending her lunch break with him, but she was simply too busy. She'd taken on her father's responsibilities, as well as handling her own. Glen had suggested she hire someone to look after the books, and while she knew he was right, she'd delayed.

"You could use some time off," Richard said, evidently disappointed she'd refused him. "And I'd love the company."

"I wish I could."

"Come on," he said. "It'll do you good." He sent her an appealing boyish grin. "I can be a fun guy, you know."

"I noticed." Ellie didn't bother to disguise her smile. The welcome-home party had been just the tonic her sinking spirits needed. The pressures of holding down the feed store and the worries over her father's health had exhausted her.

Glen stopped off a couple of times a week to offer moral support. He was her best friend, and his down-to-earth humor had gone a long way to bolster her courage and resolve. At Richard's party she'd relaxed and enjoyed herself for the first time in weeks. She'd danced with Glen and with Richard—and Richard had even kissed her. It was the closest thing to a date she'd had in months.

"Maybe I will escape for an hour or so," she said, surprising herself. "The world won't come to an end without me."

"Great." A smile lit up his handsome face.

Not too often was a woman given the opportunity

to realize her schoolgirl dreams, Ellie mused. Okay, so she'd been fifteen and impressionable, but Richard Weston had been by far the most attractive boy in Promise. There hadn't been a girl in school who wouldn't have given...whatever for the chance to go out with him. Richard had played it cool, though. He'd never dated one girl for any length of time. In that sense he hadn't changed; he must be close to thirty now and had yet to settle down.

"Where do you want to go?" he asked.

Seeing as there were very few restaurants in town, Ellie didn't figure there were many options. "You choose."

"How about your house?" He leaned close enough for her to catch a whiff of his musk-scented aftershave.

"My house?"

"Sure, we can rustle up something for lunch and then snuggle on the sofa for a while and talk about old times."

He had a smile that would charm a snake. "What old times?" Ellie asked.

"We can make that part up as we go along." His voice fell, heavy with suggestion.

"Richard!" The man was a blatant flirt.

"Why not?"

"First, I'm the world's worst cook. Trust me, you wouldn't want to eat anything I've made myself. Second, snuggling up on the sofa, tempting as it sounds, is the last thing I have time for."

"I bet I could convince you otherwise."

"Really?" This guy was too much. She shook her head and tossed the clipboard on a shelf facedown. "And just how do you intend to do that?"

He grinned that boyish grin again and reached for her hand, tugging her after him.

"Hey, where are we going?"

"Someplace private—where I can show you what I mean." He looked furtively around, then pulled her inside the office and closed the door.

"Richard?"

The next thing she knew he had her pinned against the wall. He'd kissed her at the party; she'd enjoyed the attention—and the kiss hadn't been bad, either. Maybe it was just what she'd needed to revive her energy and enthusiasm. All work and no play had dulled her senses, but Richard Weston had brought them back to life.

His kiss now was deep and sultry. By the time he lifted his head from hers, Ellie's knees felt weak.

"How was that?" he asked.

"Not bad." Her reply was breathless, despite her effort to sound casual. Her hands were flattened against the wall behind her, as if to prop her up. She took a deep breath. Her emotions must be in a sorry state, indeed. In fact, everything in her life seemed to be in a constant state of upheaval.

"There's a lot more where that came from," he promised. He ran the tip of his index finger down the V of her shirt, trailing it lower, close to the curve of her breast.

"Unfortunately," she said, slapping his hand away, "I can't squeeze an affair into my busy schedule."

"Where there's a will there's a way."

"Richard, please, I'm flattered but—"

He interrupted her with a second kiss. This one wet and seductive and a little too rough.

Ellie couldn't believe she was allowing this to continue. What she'd said was true—she was flattered, but she wasn't one to indulge in casual sex. Or casual anything.

"I've got responsibilities."

"Don't we all?"

"Richard!"

"That's my name and I certainly like to hear you say it, but not quite like that." His hands massaged her tired shoulders. Against every dictate of her will, Ellie closed her eyes.

"I want you to whisper my name when we're in bed…"

She gasped. "I can't believe you're actually serious!"

"I've never been more serious. I thought about you when I was away…and I wondered if you were married. I'm glad you're not."

"You didn't even know who I was!"

"Are you kidding? Believe me, I knew, but a guy can get arrested for thinking the way I did about you back then."

Ellie recognized a lie when she heard one. "I appreciate the offer, I truly do, and if I have a vacancy anytime soon, I'll give you a call."

"Hey, don't be hasty here. We were going to lunch, remember?"

A loud knock sounded on the office door. "Ellie, are you in there?"

Glen Patterson. Arriving like the cavalry the minute she needed rescuing. His timing couldn't have been better.

"Come on in," she called, moving toward the door.

Glen let himself inside and frowned when he saw Richard.

"I was trying to talk Ellie into getting away for an hour or so. To have lunch," Richard explained, his smile as friendly as if they'd been involved in harmless conversation instead of a kiss.

It might have helped if Glen had displayed a shred of jealousy, but he didn't. "Good idea," he said, glancing at Ellie. "You need to get out more."

"I can't today. Maybe some other time," she said and scampered past the two men.

Ten minutes later Glen found her in the storeroom going through the order. "Richard's gone?" she asked.

"Yeah. He hasn't changed much, has he?"

"How do you mean?"

Glen didn't answer until she glanced up from the clipboard.

"He's a wheeler-dealer."

"So I noticed," she said with a chuckle. She fanned her face and deliberately expelled a breath.

"Hey, what does that mean?"

"What do you *think* it means?"

Glen thought about that for a moment, and either didn't get it or wasn't willing to say it out loud.

"Let's put it like this," Ellie said. "Richard Weston was interested in a whole lot more than lunch."

Glen's eyes widened considerably.

"Why does that shock you? Does it surprise you to realize other men might look on me as more than one of the guys?"

Again he took his time responding. "Not really. You're about the best damn friend I've ever had. And you're game for just about anything."

"Within limits," she said, thinking of Richard's proposal.

"Within limits," Glen agreed, then laughed. "Hell, maybe it isn't such a bad idea, after all."

"You and me?"

He looked stunned. "Hell, no. You and Richard."

Nine

Sunday morning Maggie slipped into Savannah's pew and leaned against her just as Wade McMillen approached the pulpit. Slipping an arm around the child, Savannah pulled her close, acknowledging just how much she'd come to love her friend's daughter. They'd formed a special bond, and it wasn't unusual for Maggie to sit with Savannah during church services.

A talented speaker, Wade often used humor in his sermons. The theme of this morning's talk revolved around the opportunities God presented. Savannah found herself laughing along with the rest of the congregation as Wade relayed the story of a man stuck on a rooftop in a flash flood.

Three times a rescue team had come for him, and each time the man insisted that God would provide. The man died and went to heaven and confronted the Lord, demanding to know why his faith had gone unanswered.

"I sent the Red Cross, a boat and a helicopter," God told him. "What more could I have done?"

Wade had a way of communicating truth without

being obtrusive, dogmatic or self-righteous. Savannah often wondered why he remained unmarried when any number of eligible young women in Promise would have been thrilled to be his wife. It was a frequent source of interest, gossip and speculation at any gathering of church members.

Maggie squirmed as the sermon drew to a close. She smiled up at Savannah and silently turned the pages of her hymnal, waiting until the choir stood to sing and she could see her mother.

The love she felt for this child poured through Savannah's heart, and with it a desire so deep and so long denied that it bordered on pain. Until she'd met Laredo, she'd relinquished the dream of ever becoming a bride—and, of course, along with that, a mother.

The yearning to bear a child of her own burned in her heart now. She closed her eyes and her mind instantly filled with the image of a young boy of five or six. He was dressed in jeans, a shirt, hat and boots, a miniature version of Laredo. The child trailed after him as they headed toward the corral. Father and son. Their child, hers and Laredo's. The thought moved her so strongly, she battled back a sudden urge to weep. Savannah felt a thrill of pure happiness at the sheer wonder of having found Laredo.

What a wonderful husband and father he'd be. Laredo had been patient and gentle with Maggie from the first, while Grady groped clumsily in his effort to make friends with the little girl. Laredo was a natural with children, and it was easy to imagine him surrounded by a whole brood of them.

Most important of all Laredo loved her. She was confident of that. Not that he openly confessed his feelings. But Savannah didn't need a formal declaration or flowery words to know how he felt. A hundred times, more, he'd shown her his feelings.

Laredo was protective of her, his manner traditional in the very best way. He was thoughtful and considerate, sensitive to her moods and needs. As far as Savannah was concerned, his actions spoke far more eloquently than anything he could ever say. Last week, for instance, while she was working on the design for her catalog, he'd brought in a cup of coffee, set it on the desk beside her, kissed her cheek and silently left the room. Another day he'd seen her carrying a heavy load of laundry outside to hang on the clothesline, and he'd rushed to her side and carried it for her.

Wiley had teased Laredo unmercifully that day, pretending he was in dire need of assistance, mincing around and flapping his hands in a ridiculous imitation of a woman in distress. Laredo had paid no attention to his antics.

After the Sunday service was dismissed, Caroline met Savannah in the front of the church. "I thought you said Richard was coming with you this morning," her friend said.

"I thought he would." Savannah was deeply disappointed in her younger brother. Grady was barely speaking to her, which was nothing new, and all because she continued to champion her brother's cause. Despite Richard's reprehensible actions, he *was* their brother. No matter what he'd done, she wouldn't allow Grady to throw him off the ranch. He had nowhere else to go. He'd told her he was still waiting for the money that was supposed to be in the mail; he seemed so sure it would be arriving any day. Because she

believed him—*had* to believe him—she'd lent him
money herself, although she didn't let Grady or Laredo know that.

"Do you think he's ever going to change?" Caroline
asked. "I'm just so afraid that if you trust him, you
might be setting yourself up for heartache."

"He's my brother," Savannah said simply. She
was convinced that their mother, had she been alive,
wouldn't have allowed Grady to kick Richard out, either.

"There's something different about you," Caroline
said when she reached her car.

"Different?" Although she formed the word as a
question, Savannah knew what Caroline meant. And
it was true. She wasn't the same woman she'd been as
little as a month ago. "I'm happy," she said, blushing
profusely. "Really truly happy."

"Laredo?" Caroline asked.

Savannah lowered her eyes and nodded.

"I like Laredo," Maggie announced. "And Richard."

"What about Grady?" Caroline coaxed her daughter.

Maggie pinched her lips together tightly. "Grady's…
okay, I guess, but he yells too much."

"I don't think she's forgiven him for shouting at
her over the phone. I've tried to explain that he's—"

"A beast like from *Beauty and the Beast,*" Maggie supplied. "I don't care if he *is* a handsome prince.
When he yells I have to cover my ears."

"Oh, Maggie," Savannah whispered, feeling
wretched. "Grady likes you very much and wants to
be your friend, too."

"Then he shouldn't shout at me on the phone," she said in an eminently reasonable tone.

Savannah wanted to shake Grady. She didn't know what had possessed him to explode at Maggie. His only excuse, weak as it was, had something to do with not knowing who was on the other end of the line.

It was getting to the point that she barely knew what to think of her own brother. She wasn't sure who'd changed the most in the past few weeks, Grady or her. She knew having Richard around troubled him, and while Grady talked about throwing Richard out, she sensed that he struggled with what was right the same way she did. Richard was a charmer, but of the two men, Grady was the one with heart.

"Would you like to join us for dinner?" Savannah asked her friends, thinking it might help Maggie feel more comfortable with Grady. "I've got a huge roast in the oven, and fresh strawberry shortcake."

"Mmm." Maggie licked her lips. "Strawberries are my favorite." Wide-eyed, she looked up at her mother.

"Not today, Savannah, I'll take a rain check."

"But, Mommy…"

Maggie's disappointment was a soothing balm to Savannah's own. Since the phone incident Caroline hadn't been out to the ranch. Whenever Savannah suggested she visit, her friend came up with a convenient excuse, or in this instance, just a polite refusal. It bothered Savannah and she hoped the uneasiness between Grady and Maggie would soon resolve itself.

When Savannah arrived back at the ranch, she discovered Richard sitting on the porch, strumming his guitar and singing softly. He stopped and waved when she pulled into the yard, then strolled over to the truck.

"Where were you all morning?" he asked as if her disappearance had worried him.

"Church. I thought you said you were coming with me."

"I would've if you'd woken me up."

"You're an adult, Richard."

His fingers stilled, the pick poised above the guitar strings. "You're not angry with me, are you?"

She sighed. "No."

He grinned boyishly and continued his song while Savannah went into the house. She set her Bible aside and checked the oven. The noonday meal was the primary one on Sundays. In the evening they all fended for themselves, giving Savannah time to pursue her own interests.

An hour later Savannah served the roast and dished up hot-from-the-oven buttermilk biscuits, mashed potatoes and gravy, corn, a large green salad and strawberry shortcake for dessert. The meal vanished in minutes with lavish compliments from Richard and quiet appreciation from Laredo, Wiley and Grady.

Everyone disappeared afterward, leaving Savannah to herself. The afternoon was lovely, the sky blue and bright, the sun warm without the intense heat of summer. Spring was Savannah's favorite time of year. After spending an hour in her garden, she arranged a vase of roses and set them in the kitchen, allowing their fragrance to fill the room.

When she'd finished, she picked up her knitting and sat on the porch, Rocket stretched out beside her. There was silence all around her, except for the soughing of wind in the greening trees and the occasional distant sound of traffic from the highway. Without informing anyone of his plans, Richard had disappeared. Grady had vanished into his office to catch up on some reading and Wiley was visiting his widow friend in Brewster. She didn't know where Laredo had gone, but she hoped he'd join her, as he often did.

Enjoying the Sunday-afternoon tranquility, Savannah lazily worked the yarn and needles. It didn't take long for Wade McMillen's message to make its way into her thoughts. *God-given opportunities*. She mulled over the opportunities that had recently come her way. Quickly, inevitably, Laredo sprang to her mind.

Deeply absorbed in her thoughts, she wasn't aware of his approach until he stepped onto the porch.

"It's a lovely afternoon, isn't it?" she said, delighted when he claimed the empty rocker beside hers. For as long as she could remember, her parents had sat in these very chairs, side by side, lifelong companions, lovers and friends.

Laredo watched her hands moving the needles and the yarn. "My mother knits, too," he said.

"My grandmother was the one who taught me." She reached for the pattern book and showed him the cardigan she was making for Maggie. The needles clicked gently as she returned to her task.

"Church this morning was great," she went on. "I enjoy Wade's sermons." She told him about the man in the flood, and Laredo laughed at the punch line, just as she knew he would. Someday she hoped Laredo would attend services with her, but she hadn't had the courage to ask him. Not yet.

Courage. She'd missed opportunity after opportunity in her life because she was afraid. Afraid of what, exactly, she didn't know. No more, she decided then and there.

"Wade got me to thinking," she said. If she didn't tell Laredo what was in her heart now, she'd always regret letting this opportunity slip by. She used her knitting as an excuse to avoid eye contact.

"Thinking?"

"About the opportunities that have come into my life...lately."

Laredo leaned back in the rocker and relaxed, closing his eyes.

"I've never dated much," she said. "I suppose it shows, doesn't it?"

He lifted his hat brim enough to look at her. "It's not a disadvantage, if that's what you're asking."

She *felt* at a disadvantage, though, talking to him about such things, but forged ahead, anyway. "It's a bit of a detriment," she said, trying to disguise the trembling in her voice. Her heart beat so fast she felt nearly breathless.

"I wouldn't want to change anything about you, Savannah."

"Thank you," she whispered, encouraged by his response.

He apparently thought their conversation was over, because he sat back in the chair once more, stretched out his legs and lowered the brim of his hat.

"There's something I need to say and I'm not sure how to go about it." Her fingers felt clammy and stiff, and she let the knitting lie idle in her lap as she composed her thoughts.

"You can tell me anything, you know that."

Despite the turbulent pounding of her heart, Savannah felt a sense of calm. "Since I don't have much experience in this kind of situation, I hope you'll forgive me for speaking frankly."

She had his attention now, and he lifted the brim of his Stetson with one finger. "Situation?"

Gripping the knitting needles tightly, she continued, "I need to know if there's a proper way for a lady to speak of certain…matters with a gentleman. Matters of the heart," she added nervously.

Laredo's position didn't alter, but she thought she saw him stiffen. "That part I wouldn't know."

"I see." Her mouth grew dry with anxiety.

An awkward silence followed while she carefully weighed her words. "Considering that you seem to be as much at a loss as I am, perhaps the best way to discuss this would be in a straightforward manner. My mother used to say, 'Nothing works better than the truth.'"

"Savannah…"

He tried to stop her, but she wouldn't let him, not while she had the courage to go on. Inhaling deeply, she began to speak. "I love you, Laredo. My heart's so full, some days I don't think I can contain all this joy. I want to thank you, to let you know how grateful I am to have met you."

Her words appeared to stun him. Slowly Laredo sat upright and stared straight ahead, not responding to her words at all. If they'd brought him any pleasure, he wasn't letting it show.

She waited, her hands trembling now at the bold thing she'd said. "Perhaps I've spoken out of turn, but it seems that when a woman loves a man she—"

"Savannah," he interrupted quietly. "Don't say any more. Please."

The color of acute embarrassment erupted in her cheeks. "Is saying I love you improper?"

"There's nothing improper about you. It's me."

"You?" She was utterly confused, completely on edge. She feared what would happen next.

"I'm not the right man for you."

The relief was so great she nearly laughed aloud. "Oh, Laredo, how can you say such a thing? Nobody's ever been more right for me in my entire life."

"Savannah, I have nothing…"

"Do you think that matters?"

"Yes," he said quietly. Intensely. "It does."

She waited a moment, then told him with gentle insistence, "For most of my life my parents and then Grady were sure they knew what was right for me. The amazing part of all this is that no one ever bothered to ask my opinion. I'm thirty-one years old, and believe it or not, I know what I want. I want you. I love you."

He leaned forward and pressed his elbows to his knees as though her words had brought him pain, instead of joy.

Her back went rigid. "I apologize if I've embarrassed you."

"It's not that. Savannah, listen to me. I'm truly honored that you love me, but it won't work. It just won't work." His voice sagged with regret, with defeat.

"Is it— Don't you care for me?" It seemed impossible he didn't share her feelings. She'd been so sure. And she'd hoped that revealing *her* love would free him to acknowledge his.

He hesitated. "I…"

"If you tell me you don't return my affection, then I'll apologize and never mention it again." Although she made the offer, Savannah had no doubts. Laredo couldn't have held her or kissed her with such gentle passion if he didn't care for her.

He waited so long to answer she feared he was about to lie. "You already know what I feel."

She closed her eyes in gratitude. "I do know." Now that he'd admitted the truth, she felt confident enough to continue. "Once we're married—"

"Married?" He half rose from his seat, his voice harsh with shock.

His reaction jolted her. When two people loved each other, marriage seemed to be the next step. And really, given she was already over thirty, there was no reason to wait. Especially if they intended to start a family, which she sincerely hoped they would. The sooner the better.

"I assumed... I hoped," she faltered, then blushed when she realized he might not consider marriage necessary. "I'm afraid that if we don't legally marry, my brother will object. I... I would, however, defy him, if that were...necessary." But she prayed with all her heart it wouldn't be.

Laredo stood up and walked over to the railing, holding on to it, his back ramrod-straight with tension. "I won't marry you, Savannah."

Her heart sank as she absorbed the firm conviction in his statement. "I see," she said, struggling to hide her disappointment. "As I said earlier, while marriage would offer certain advantages, I'm willing to forgo the...legalities."

He whirled around. "Savannah, dear God in heaven,

don't you understand what I'm saying?" He knelt in front of her, his eyes wide with pain. "It isn't that I *won't* marry you. I can't."

"Can't?" The awful possibility dawned. "Are you... do you already have a wife?"

"No."

She brought both hands to her heart in a gesture of relief.

"Look at me!" he demanded. "I don't have a pot to piss in. I don't have one damn thing to give you. Do you honestly think I'd take you away from your home, your family and friends, your roses and everything else to live in a *trailer?* Because that's all I've got—a lousy trailer."

Feeling his pain, his inadequacy, she touched his cheek lovingly. "Do you think it matters to me where we live? As for my garden, I can start another. You're all I need, all I'll ever need."

He closed his eyes. "Savannah, I can't. I'm sorry, but I can't." His hands squeezed hers with enough strength to make her fingers ache.

"I'm offering you my heart, my love, my life," she said, her voice barely audible.

He claimed both her hands with his own, then turned them over and pressed his lips to her palms. When he raised his head, his eyes held hers. "You'd give all this up for me?"

"I wouldn't be giving up anything, Laredo. I'd be gaining so much more."

That night Laredo sat up in his bunk, his back against the wall, his mind whirling. Savannah had almost made him believe it was possible for the two of them. He was well aware that she'd be the one to make all the sacrifices; while that didn't seem right or fair, she'd assured him of her willingness to do it. To do whatever was necessary for them to be together.

Laredo rested his head between his hands and dreamed with his eyes open. A growing sense of excitement, of possibility, grew within him. *He loved her.*

Richard strolled into the bunkhouse and threw himself down on the cot where he'd slept that first time. Some nights he slept in the house; Laredo wished this was one of them. He supposed it depended on whether or not Grady was in the house and likely to notice. Despite her older brother's insistence, Laredo knew Savannah would never make Richard leave. She'd even let him stay in his boyhood room, perhaps allowing herself to believe that everything was all right again. Other nights, Richard slept in the bunkhouse. Grady must be around this evening.

"Hey, what're ya doing?" Richard asked.

"Thinking," Laredo answered shortly, hoping Weston would take the hint.

"So you're trying to steal Savannah away from us."

How did Richard know? "Do you have a problem with that?" Laredo demanded, suspicious of the other man's intentions.

"None whatsoever." Richard's hands flew up and he grinned broadly. "As long as you love her," he added in melodramatic tones.

"I do." Not until the words escaped his lips did Laredo realize he had no problem telling Richard how he felt, although he'd never once told Savannah he loved her, not in so many words, at least.

"Ain't love grand," Richard said with an exaggerated sigh. He flopped back on the cot and gazed up at the ceiling. "At least in the beginning."

Laredo let the comment slide, although it hit its mark. Bull's-eye. What started out beautiful could often end up a disaster.

"Savannah's a real sweetheart," Richard continued. "Did you notice how hard she worked cooking for the party? Actually, if I know my sister, she was grateful to stay in the kitchen. It's always been difficult for her to deal with crowds, even people she's familiar with and known most of her life. I don't know why she's so damn shy. Take her out of her element and she wilts like a flower without water."

Laredo frowned, wondering if Richard was actually delivering a subtle message, one he would deny if asked, but would gleefully recount as an I-told-you-so if it came to pass.

"If you have something to say, then just say it," Laredo muttered.

"Me?" Richard's voice echoed in surprise. "I'm not saying anything other than how pleased I am for the two of you."

"Nothing's been decided." Laredo wanted to correct that impression right off.

Richard rolled his head to one side to get a better look at Laredo. "Really?"

"Really."

"Well, if everything goes as planned, it'll be wonderful. I know she'll make you happy, and once the kids start coming…"

"Kids?" The word exploded from Laredo's lips before he thought to censor it. They wouldn't be able to afford kids for years, although he knew Savannah was eager for a family. He was, too, but it just wasn't going to be possible, not until he'd established himself, had some income he could count on.

"I wouldn't advise you to wait too long," Richard was saying. "Savannah's already over thirty. Apparently the older the woman the more likely the chance of complications." He shook his head wisely and sounded as if he knew what he was talking about.

"I hope you've got good health insurance," he added. "From what I've heard, having a baby costs thousands of bucks these days."

Health insurance? Laredo could barely afford to put food on the table, let alone worry about extras. He knew Savannah, too. If there were problems, she wouldn't let him know because she wouldn't want him to worry.

"What about her rose garden?" Richard asked next. "We both know how important that is to her."

"She's talked about moving part of it," Laredo responded, but his mind was still stuck on the possibility of something happening to Savannah, miles from town, with few friends or neighbors. The reality of what he was asking hit him hard. It sounded romantic and exciting—the two of them building a home together, breeding quarter horses—until he thought about the risks.

"Moving part of the garden," Richard repeated. "Great idea." He sat up, tapping one foot on the floor. "You be real good to my big sister now, you hear?" Clapping his hands together, Richard laughed. "Hey! I'll bet you want me to keep my mouth shut about this in front of Grady. Right?"

Laredo didn't answer. The next time he looked up Richard was gone, which was just as well. Savannah's brother had opened his eyes to a few home truths. While it was fine to dream about making Savannah his bride, a dream was all it would ever be. He couldn't take her away from everything she knew and loved, couldn't put her health and happiness at risk. One of them had to keep a level head, and it looked like the responsibility had fallen to him.

He loved her, but he couldn't marry her. *Wouldn't* marry her. As soon as it could be arranged, he'd get out of her life. For her own good, as well as his own.

A week later, as Grady sat on Starlight and watched over the grazing herd, his thoughts grew dark and oppressive. Sometimes he could cast off these moods when they threatened. More often, like now, he couldn't. He worried more and more about Savannah; he wasn't sure what had happened to his sister, but she hadn't been herself. Not for days. Outwardly nothing seemed wrong; she was as pleasant and cordial as always. Still, the difference was there. It seemed as if the light had gone out of her eyes somehow. The joy he'd seen in her of late had vanished.

He was no expert when it came to romance, but the answer was obvious. Something had happened between her and Laredo, who seemed equally miserable. Clearly they'd suffered some sort of falling-out. It was bound to happen, Grady realized.

He hated to see his sister hurt, and it made him feel helpless. He had no idea what to do, what to say. He'd even considered talking to Caroline, this being a woman thing and all. Savannah's best friend might be able to see her through this disappointment.

If only he could talk to someone about Richard. He supposed Cal Patterson, as his closest friend, would be that person. And yet he felt embarrassed. Ashamed. He hardly knew how it had happened, but Richard had managed to sweet-talk his way back into the family. It hadn't taken long for Savannah to pick up where their parents had left off, Grady thought with some bitterness. She spoiled him, indulged his every whim, pandered to his wishes as if he deserved a hero's welcome.

Grady still wanted Richard off the ranch, but every time he got to the point of ordering him to leave, he found he couldn't. Either because of Savannah's pleading or his own sense of...what? Obligation? Family loyalty? Pity? The one thing Grady had insisted on was that Richard sleep in the bunkhouse, but his worthless brother had found a way to thwart even that.

It had started innocently enough, with Richard cleaning out his old bedroom, sorting through his things. Before long he'd started sleeping up there. Some nights, anyway; Grady never knew for sure. It was another way Richard kept him off balance.

Grady shifted his weight in the saddle, tired after a long day. Just when he was about to head back to the ranch, he noticed another rider approaching at a gallop.

Laredo Smith. He waited for the man to join him.

"Problems?" Grady inquired.

"Not really."

From the way he'd ridden out here Grady wondered if the house was on fire. "There's a reason you came to see me, isn't there?"

"There is."

Apparently Smith was having a difficult time spitting out the words. He looked even worse than Savannah, pale and lifeless.

"You were right, Grady," he said without emotion. "Have been from the first."

Grady liked the way this conversation had started. With Richard pulling the wool over everyone's eyes, it felt good to be told he was right about something. "How do you mean?"

"About me."

Grady's smile faded. This wasn't what he wanted to hear, wasn't what he'd expected, either. "In other words, you're the thief Earl Chesterton suspected?"

"No." His denial was quick. "Not that."

Grady would have been disappointed had it been the truth. Smith had proved himself a hardworking and talented horseman, probably the best he'd ever hired. He still didn't trust him, though, especially where his sister was concerned, and because of that, Grady had made a point of being difficult, demanding, even unreasonable. Laredo hadn't responded in kind, not once, and in the process had earned Grady's respect.

"You claimed I wasn't good enough for Savannah," Laredo said bluntly.

Grady frowned. He really didn't like the turn this conversation had taken. "What's going on between you two?" he asked, eyes narrowed.

Laredo ignored the question. "I need a favor."

"You got it."

His immediate response appeared to surprise Smith. "You might not be so fast to agree once you hear it involves money."

Grady sobered; the wrangler was right. "How much?"

"I need a loan. Enough to pay for the repairs on my truck and get me to Oklahoma."

"Any particular reason you're anxious to be on your way now?"

Smith rested his hands on the saddle horn and averted his face. "I've got my reasons."

"I don't suppose those reasons have anything to do with my sister?"

"They might."

"You hurt her, Smith, and you'll regret it." Grady was torn. On the one hand, Savannah's happiness seemed to depend on this man; on the other, he'd prefer to see Smith leave, get clear away from her. Grady suspected Smith's departure would come too late, that Savannah was already in too deep, emotionally committed to a drifter.

"Why the hell do you think I need that money so damned bad?" Laredo asked savagely. "The sooner I'm out of her life the better. Listen, I don't expect you to give me that loan without collateral. I'll leave the title to my truck with you until I can pay you back. Agreed?"

Grady mulled it over, not the decision to lend Laredo money—he had no problem with that—but why, exactly, Laredo seemed so anxious to leave. He sighed. He wasn't sure if he should interfere in the man's private affairs; he certainly wouldn't have appreciated anyone meddling in his.

"Agreed?" Laredo said again.

"There's another way," Grady said thoughtfully. Laredo stared at him long and hard before Grady continued. "You could stay here. I'll make you an offer that'll make it worth your while. A partnership—you and me and Savannah. I understand you're interested in breeding quarter horses. You could do that here on the Yellow Rose just as well as Oklahoma."

Either Laredo was speechless at the offer or he was shocked that Grady knew this much about him and his plans. Grady credited Wiley for the information. His foreman had a loose tongue.

"If you're trying to bribe me into staying, all I can say is you've insulted the finest woman I know."

"It isn't a bribe," Grady insisted, damning himself for his inability to say things the way he wanted. "All I'm trying to do is give you another option." He stopped and boldly met the other man's eyes. "You love my sister, don't you?"

"Loving Savannah doesn't have anything to do with the loan," Laredo said stiffly. "Look, I have almost nothing to bring to a marriage. Nothing that's *mine,* that I worked for. I can't give her the things she's used to and deserves to have. I won't ask her to give up what she's got here. And a partnership...well, there's no way I could buy into the Yellow Rose, so a partnership is charity, pure and simple. I work for what I get—I don't accept charity."

Laredo's anger seemed to burn itself out and he said, "That loan. Are you willing to give it to me or not?"

"It's yours if you want it, but—"

"I want it."

"All right," Grady said and thrust out his hand. For the very first time he believed in Laredo's sincerity. For the first time he fully accepted that his sister had chosen a man who deserved her love. A man he respected. A man he'd misjudged.

Laredo gripped his hand, and not for the first time Grady noted the intense sadness in his eyes. Grady refused to let go, demanding Laredo's full attention. "Are you sure this is what you want?"

Laredo nodded. "I'm sure."

He rode off with the same urgency with which he'd approached.

Grady frowned, wishing there was something he could do. But he knew that neither Savannah nor Laredo would appreciate his intrusion in their lives. This was between them; they had to work it out themselves—or not.

Bad as he felt for both of them, he could do nothing.

Laredo noted the number on the small single-story dwelling in a quiet neighborhood and glanced down at the address on the slip of paper. He was about to commit perhaps the most cowardly act of his life. But what else could he do?

He stepped out of the truck and walked down the narrow path to the front door, a long narrow box tucked under his arm. He hesitated briefly, then rang the doorbell. It didn't take long for someone to answer. Maggie Daniels's eyes lit up in delight when she saw who it was.

"Hi, Laredo!"

Caroline revealed no such pleasure. "What are you doing here?"

He removed his hat. "I need you to do something for me if you would."

Savannah's friend didn't invite him inside, and it

was just as well. He wanted to leave now, immediately. As he'd told Grady, the sooner he was able to put some distance between Savannah and him, the better.

"Come in," Caroline finally said, unlocking the screen door.

Laredo declined. "Thanks, but this should only take a moment." He handed her the box. "Would you mind giving this to Savannah for me?"

"You can't do it yourself?"

"No, ma'am."

She didn't accept the box. "Why not?"

"I don't plan on seeing her again." Saying the words created a terrible sense of loss. He might be convinced that leaving was for the best, but that didn't make it any easier. He'd gotten the loan from Grady, and after supper Wiley had driven him into town to pick up his truck. He'd said his goodbyes to everyone.

Everyone except Savannah.

Although he called himself every name in the book, he couldn't make himself do it. He couldn't look her in the eye and pretend he didn't love her, and that was the price she'd demand before he left. She'd insist he say it to her face and he wouldn't be able to.

It occurred to him as he drove away from Powell's Garage that this feeling of grief and fear and loss must be similar to what his father had experienced when he left for Vietnam all those years ago.

"Well, if you won't come in, I'll join you on the porch." Caroline opened the screen door and stepped outside. Maggie, dressed in purple pajamas, followed her mother.

"I'd be much obliged if you'd give this to Savannah for me." He repeated his request.

Caroline's smile was knowing. "You love her, don't you?"

Laredo couldn't have denied it if he'd tried. "Sometimes love isn't enough."

"Really." She crossed her arms and walked to the porch railing and stared into the night sky. "Don't you think Savannah deserves to have you give her that gift yourself?"

"She deserves a great deal more than I can ever give her."

Caroline turned and faced him, leaning against the railing.

"What's in the package, Mommy?" Maggie asked.

"A gift for Savannah," her mother answered.

"Can I see?"

Laredo opened the box. As a parting gift and a token of love, it wasn't much, but it was all he could afford. "It's a shawl." He brought it out to show the little girl.

When Caroline saw the antique white silk threaded with gold strands, she sighed in appreciation. "It's perfect for her."

He was tempted to smile. He'd realized the same thing when he noticed it in the window of Dovie's shop. Instantly, he'd pictured Savannah sitting on the porch, the shawl wrapped around her shoulders. He'd never thought of himself as romantic, but in some small way he hoped that when she wore it, she'd feel his love. He hoped she'd understand that even though he'd left her, he would always love her.

"I know I'm asking a lot of you," Laredo said to Caroline.

"No," she replied. "The one you're asking a lot of is Savannah."

He recognized the truth of that immediately.

"Like I said," Caroline went on, "she deserves to have you give her this gift."

He shook his head. "I can't. Either you do it or I'll mail it."

Caroline hesitated. "Is there any message to go with it?"

He shook his head. He'd already said more than he'd intended.

"Nothing, Laredo?" Her eyes begged him not to be so cruel.

"Tell her…" His throat felt thick.

"Yes?"

"Tell her thank you." He set his hat back on his head and hurried down the walkway.

Maggie tugged at her mother's sleeve. "Where's Laredo going?"

"I don't know, sweetheart. Laredo!" Caroline called to him.

He looked back.

"How'd you manage to pay for the repairs to your truck?"

He stood silent, refusing to answer her.

It didn't take Caroline long to figure it out. "Grady. He lent you the money, didn't he?" She leaped down the porch steps and planted her hands on her hips. "That son of a—" She bit off the last word.

Laredo climbed into his truck and started the engine, desperate to leave before he found an excuse to stay.

Ten

"What do you mean Laredo's gone?" Savannah didn't understand what Caroline was telling her. He'd been on the ranch earlier that day; she'd seen him herself. They'd both made an effort in the past week to pretend their discussion had never taken place. But it had, and her declaration of love stood between them. It was something they could neither forget nor ignore.

Every time Savannah thought about the foolish way she'd exposed her heart, she grew weary with self-recriminations and regret. Her rash behavior had embarrassed them both, yet she realized she probably couldn't have kept silent any longer. She loved Laredo, and hiding her feelings had become increasingly more difficult.

"He asked me to give you this," Caroline said with a regretful sigh, handing her a rectangular box.

"It's really pretty!" Maggie added enthusiastically.

"You've talked to him?" Savannah said. The pain was immediate. Laredo had left, and instead of coming to her, he'd gone to Caroline. He'd talked to Caroline, but not to her. He'd left without even a goodbye.

"He was on his way out of town when he stopped by and asked if I'd give you this."

Savannah felt an overwhelming need to sit down. Slowly sinking onto a kitchen chair, she brought her fingers to her mouth to suppress a cry. *Laredo isn't coming back.*

"Do you want me to open the box for you, Savannah?" Maggie volunteered, eagerly lifting a corner of the box as she spoke. "It's so pretty and you're going to like it. Mommy did and so did I."

Caroline restrained her daughter by placing her hand on Maggie's shoulder. "Let Savannah open it when she's ready, okay, sweetheart?"

The child looked disappointed, but she nodded.

Savannah slid her fingers over the top of the box, but lacked the courage to look inside. All her strength went into holding back the tears that burned her eyes.

Laredo was gone. Without a word of farewell, without a note. Nothing. The pain of his leaving had devastated her. But in some odd inexplicable way she understood why he'd left so abruptly.

Laredo Smith *couldn't* say goodbye. He loved her too much to hurt her more. Loved her too much to refuse if she'd asked him to stay. And so he'd done the only thing he could. He'd slipped away like a thief in the night; he'd stolen her heart and taken it with him.

"Savannah, are you all right?"

She nodded even as she felt swallowed up in the emptiness.

Caroline's fingers gripped hers tightly. "I'm so sorry," she whispered.

Somehow Savannah managed to look at her friend. She could lie and offer reassurances, but she hadn't the strength to maintain a facade. It would be easy enough to fool Grady and Richard, but not Caroline.

"It's a shawl," Maggie blurted, unable to hold back any longer. "A pretty white one with gold—"

"Maggie," Caroline snapped.

The little girl lowered her head and bit her lip.

"A shawl... How nice," Savannah said, struggling. Knowing Maggie was impatient for her to open the gift, she pulled off the lid. The child was right; the shawl was quite possibly the loveliest she'd ever seen. Lifting it from the tissue paper, she let the delicate fabric slide across her fingers. "Was there...did he give you any message for me?"

Caroline hesitated, then said gently, "He wanted me to thank you."

Her heart was breaking, the pain raw and real, and yet—despite the emotional intensity of the moment— Savannah smiled.

"Thank you." She repeated his message. This, too, she understood. The simple words held a wealth of meaning and in some ways were more valuable to her than the gift he'd asked Caroline to deliver.

Despite his desertion, Laredo had thanked her for loving him. Even though he'd walked out of her life with the same suddenness with which he'd entered it, he'd wanted Savannah to know her love had touched him. He couldn't say it himself, so he let someone else say it for him.

Caroline's eyes flashed with anger. "I don't understand why he'd do such a thing! He admitted he loved you—he said as much."

"I know."

"But when I asked why he was leaving, all he'd say

was that sometimes love wasn't enough—whatever the hell that means." Caroline sat down, then got to her feet again and started pacing.

Savannah didn't try to explain. What Laredo apparently didn't grasp, and what she'd been unable to make him believe, was that his love was the one thing she'd ever need.

He seemed to think a prosperous ranch would make her happy, or a million head of cattle. A luxurious ranch house. A rose garden. Those things gave her security and contentment, true. But Laredo's love gave her happiness, and it gave meaning to everything else in her life. She'd tried to convince him that she'd happily work at his side, that their love would allow them to create a new security and contentment of their own. Why couldn't he believe her?

"Can I go sit on the swing outside?" Maggie asked.

Caroline nodded. "Stay on the porch."

Maggie assured Caroline she would, and the screen door slammed behind her. Caroline brewed Savannah a cup of strong coffee, then brought it over to the table. "Drink this," she ordered. "You look pale as a sheet."

Savannah raised the cup to her lips. Surprisingly the coffee revived her.

Caroline poured herself a cup and sat down next to Savannah. "I know you probably don't want to hear this at the moment, but I'm going to say it, anyway." She paused long enough to inhale deeply. "Right now, you're hurting too much to believe that everything happens for a reason. I don't know why, but that's the way it seems to work.

"When I discovered I was pregnant with Maggie, I felt as if the world had caved in on me. I was young and stupid and determined not to let a mistake ruin my life. First I thought the father would marry me, but…well, that was impossible. I'd already decided I wanted to have this baby, so I was left to deal with the pregnancy alone."

In all the years they'd been friends, this was the first time Caroline had discussed anything to do with Maggie's birth. Or Maggie's father.

"When I couldn't hide that I was pregnant any longer, I had to tell my mother. I expected her to be furious, to call me all the names I'd called myself. Instead, Mom asked me a few questions and then held me. We both cried.

"It was what I'd needed most—her love. She talked about how difficult it must have been for me to keep this pain bottled up inside me all those weeks. I didn't want to tell her about Maggie's father, but I did, and how stupid I'd been to think he actually loved me…" Her voice wavered and it was a moment before she could continue. "You see, Savannah," she whispered with emotion shining in her eyes, "this mistake was really a gift. I made a mistake, but *Maggie's* not a mistake. She's my heart and my joy. I can't imagine life without her."

The screen door opened just then, and Maggie flew into the room and raced across the kitchen. Breathless, she wrapped her arms around Caroline's leg, hiding her face against her mother's jeans.

Grady followed her inside, looking frustrated and confused.

"What'd you do this time?" Caroline demanded.

"Not a damn thing," Grady said. "I saw Maggie

outside and thought it was time the two of us talked, but it seems she's not ready."

Maggie clung to her mother's leg all the harder.

"It'd help if you hadn't yelled at her on the phone," Caroline suggested calmly.

"How was I supposed to know it was Maggie?" he shouted in return.

"He's yelling again," Maggie surfaced long enough to announce.

"Explain to her that it was all a mistake, would you?" Grady said in a strained voice, gesturing at Maggie. "She's right, I was a beast. But I'm willing to be a prince, too, if she'll give me the chance."

"You're too mean to be a prince," Maggie said next. Breaking away from her mother, she climbed into Savannah's lap and locked both arms around her neck. "I don't like Grady 'cause he yells."

"He's not one of my favorite people, either," Caroline said, glaring at Savannah's brother.

"What'd I do *now?*" he groaned. "Damn, but it's hard to understand women. I haven't talked to you in days—what could I possibly have done to offend you?"

"You know very well what you've done."

Clearly perplexed, he shrugged. "I'm afraid you're going to have to tell me because I haven't got a clue."

"You're lower than a...a worm," Caroline said.

"So what else is new?" Grady sounded bored.

"Caroline?" Savannah said her friend's name softly, confused by the display of anger. "What did Grady do?"

Still glaring at him, Caroline crossed her long legs. Her foot swung with a furious rhythm. "I wasn't going to tell you," Caroline said, speaking to Savannah, "but you'll figure it out soon enough. Grady gave Laredo the money so he could pay off the repairs on his truck."

Savannah felt as if she'd been punched, as if the air had been forced from her lungs. She looked at her brother in shock and pain and disbelief. The abruptness of Laredo's leaving was almost more than she could bear, but knowing that her own *brother,* her own flesh and blood, had made it possible—had no doubt *encouraged* it—was like a knife in the back. She gasped. "Grady?"

"I didn't *give* him the money," Grady said, and his gaze darted between her and Caroline as if he didn't understand what he'd done that was so wrong. "I *lent* him the money."

He'd betrayed her.

There was nothing more to say.

Barely aware of what she was doing, Savannah stood and slowly placed one foot in front of the other. Hardly knowing how she'd managed it, she climbed the stairs to her room, dragging herself one step at a time.

"What'd I do that was so terrible?" her brother shouted after her. "Tell me, Savannah! I want to know!"

"Leave her alone," Caroline said angrily, her voice drifting toward Savannah as she climbed the stairs. "If you can't figure it out, trust me, I'll be happy to fill in the blanks. And you know what? I'll use small words so you'll be sure to understand."

Grady delayed speaking to Caroline about Laredo for ten days. He knew he needed to say something— to explain, to talk about Savannah, to ask her advice.

He saw her enter the Winn-Dixie one evening and followed her inside. He didn't want Caroline to assume he'd sought her out; he intended her to believe their meeting was accidental.

Taking a cart and maintaining a safe distance behind her, he trailed her into the produce section. Savannah was the one who did all the grocery shopping, and other than picking up a necessary item now and again, he was rarely in the supermarket.

He paused in front of a pyramid display of bright juicy-looking oranges, and with one eye on Caroline and the other on the task at hand, he reached for an orange. To his horror, the entire display collapsed.

Grady saw it happen as if in slow motion. He attempted to catch as many as possible before they tumbled to the floor, his arms moving frantically in every which direction. In the end he abandoned the effort, kneeling on the linoleum floor surrounded by fruit.

Everyone in the produce department stopped and stared at him. Even small children pointed and snickered. Grady smiled weakly and searched for a witty remark, but like everything else these past few weeks, his wit failed him.

He was about to turn tail and run when Caroline squatted down beside him. "This is another fine mess you've created, Grady Weston."

He didn't need Caroline to tell him that. If he wanted to make a fool of himself, he wouldn't choose to do it in front of half the store. Nope, he preferred to manage that with just one or two onlookers. Like Caroline. And his sister.

Together they gathered the spilled oranges and set

them back on the display case. "Is there a reason you followed me in here?" she asked bluntly.

"Was I that obvious?"

"Don't apply to the Secret Service, all right?"

Since it was entirely obvious that running into her hadn't been an accident, he got straight to the point.

"Do you have time for coffee?" he asked, and then because he was afraid she might think he was asking her out, he added, "I'm worried about Savannah. I'd feel better if I talked about this with someone."

She checked her watch, and Grady had the feeling time wasn't her major concern. "Talked about this with just anyone?" she asked.

"With you," he amended, burying his pride. He owed Caroline this much.

"Let me phone the day care," she said, "and then I'll meet you at the bowling alley."

"Okay. See you there in a few minutes." He was eager to make his escape before he toppled a display of something *really* embarrassing—like feminine hygiene products.

The café in the bowling alley served some of the best food in town. It was certainly the most reasonably priced, with coffee only a quarter a cup. They served decent coffee, too. There was always a special; according to the reader board outside, today's was T-bone steak and a baked potato. And the place stayed open all night on weekends. In Grady's opinion, it was a damn good deal. Although he wasn't interested in a steak at the moment.... Even if he'd been hungry, he couldn't have choked it down.

Arriving first, he found an empty booth and turned over two mugs. The waitress brought him a couple of menus and smiled. "Haven't seen you in a while, Grady."

"Hello, Denise. How're Art and the kids?" Grady had attended high school with Denise a hundred years ago. While he was out chasing cattle, his classmate had married, had three kids and started working here part-time.

"I can't complain. Billy's in junior high this year."

Hard to believe, Grady thought. Art and Denise's oldest boy was reaching his teens and *he* wasn't even married yet.

Denise filled his mug with coffee. "Are you going to order something to eat?"

"Not me, but Caroline might."

"Caroline Daniels?" Denise filled the second mug.

He nodded, disliking the flicker of interest in her eyes.

"Are you two seeing each other now?" she asked, her interest far too avid.

Grady opened his mouth to deny everything. He didn't have to.

"No way," Caroline answered for him as she slipped into the booth. She handed Denise the menu, effectively dismissing her, and reached for the sugar dispenser. "You had something you wanted to say about Savannah."

"Yeah." This was more difficult than he'd imagined.

"Is she all right?" Caroline leaned back against the patched red vinyl upholstery, and he noted for the first time how pale she was. He didn't comment because sure as hell she'd make something of it—something he'd never intended. His only chance to have a peaceful conversation was to stick to the matter at hand and ignore everything else. Still, he wondered.

"How come you haven't been out to the ranch?" he blurted. His sister needed a friend, and he'd expected Caroline to be there for her, especially now.

"I stopped by a couple of times when you weren't around."

"On purpose?" he asked, thinking she'd taken to avoiding him because of Maggie.

"No, it just happened to work out that way. I haven't gone anywhere in a couple of days. I've been dealing with postal inspectors all week. I had my own crisis to handle, but fortunately that's behind me now." She cradled the mug between her hands. "I've phoned Savannah every day." Her eyes held his. "Is something going on with her that I don't know about?"

"Not with Savannah, exactly," he said, then looked away, finding her scrutiny uncomfortable. "First off, I was wrong about Laredo Smith."

That captured her attention, he could tell. She raised her eyebrows but said nothing. Not yet, anyway. Naturally she'd delight in hearing how wrong he'd been.

"I should have accepted Savannah's assessment of his character," Grady said, embarrassed that he'd allowed his fears to get in the way. Admitting he'd made a mistake had never come easy. "I...came to some, well, erroneous conclusions about Smith. The result was that he and I got started on the wrong foot."

"You should tell Savannah this, not me."

"I have!" he snapped, then took a deep breath in an effort to control his impatience. When he spoke again, he lowered his voice. "I did tell her, but I wanted you to know, as well."

"Should I be grateful?"

Grady decided to ignore the sarcasm. "Laredo came to me and asked for a loan. Despite what you think, I'm not blind. I knew something wasn't right. I didn't want him to leave and I told him so."

This appeared to surprise Caroline. Her eyebrows rose again. "You did?"

"Yes—not that it did any good. In the end I agreed to lend him the money and he insisted on giving me the title to his truck. The day he left I apologized for the scene at Richard's party and we shook hands." He stared into the steaming mug. "I took my aggravation with Richard out on Laredo and made a complete ass of myself."

Caroline didn't disagree with him. Not that he expected she would.

"Although it's none of my business," he said, "Laredo as much as admitted he loved Savannah."

"He told me that, too." Caroline shook her head in dismay. "What I can't fathom is why he felt he had to leave. What is it about men? I don't understand it. Laredo Smith is loved by the sweetest, kindest, most wonderful woman he's likely to meet in ten lifetimes and what does he do? He walks out on her without a word. It doesn't make sense." She tossed her hands in the air as if to say she'd never understand the male of the species.

"A man has his pride, especially a man like Smith, but my guess is Richard had something to do with it." It was the first time he'd suggested this to anyone, and he was curious to see how Caroline would react. He half expected her to jump all over him and insist he quit trying to blame Richard for everything, including the national debt. She said nothing for several moments.

"I wouldn't put it past him," she murmured at last.

Grady was so damn grateful that she agreed with him it was all he could do not to hug her right then and there. If Denise was going to spread rumors about him and Caroline, *that* would give her something to talk about.

"Did you ask Laredo if Richard said anything to him?"

"No," he told her reluctantly.

"Why the hell not?"

"Well, because… I was trying to get him to stay." Grady didn't know what Caroline had thought he could do. It wasn't like he could hog-tie the wrangler until he agreed to marry his sister. Grady hadn't intended to tell Caroline this, but suddenly he wanted her to know. "I offered Laredo a partnership in the ranch. I realize now it must have come as quite a surprise to him. Hell, I surprised myself."

He'd already known Savannah was in love with Laredo; that day he'd learned about Smith's love for Savannah, too. This man was important to her happiness; if it was in Grady's power to make her happy, he was willing to do whatever it took.

He noticed how Caroline's face tightened as she considered this information. "What'd he say to that?"

Glancing away, Grady relived the terse conversation. "That he didn't accept charity and I'd insulted Savannah and him. Hell, everything I do these days is wrong. I was only trying to help." He reached for his coffee. "At first I thought Laredo didn't love Savannah, but now I think he loves her too much."

Caroline gave a hard shake of her head. "As far as I'm concerned, he'd better not show his face around here, because I swear I'll wring his neck if he does."

Grady was a little taken aback by the vehemence of her response.

"All this crap about pride and honor—it's asinine, that's what it is." Her lips thinned. "Never mind him. How's Savannah doing?"

"You said you haven't seen her in the past couple of days, didn't you?"

Caroline nodded. "Why? What's up?"

"Something's happened—she's changed."

"Of course she's changed! She's hurt and angry. And I can't blame her."

"It's more than that."

Caroline leaned closer. "What do you mean?"

"Like you said, she's hurt—but I can't imagine how that would lead to…this." He didn't know how to say it without sounding demented, so he just plunged in. "Hell, I don't know what's happened to her, but two days ago she cut her hair."

"Savannah?"

"It's been long for so many years I didn't recognize her. It's shoulder-length now and in a—" he made a circular motion with his finger "—page boy, I think is what you call it. The ends tuck under sort of nice and neat."

This left Caroline speechless.

"Then yesterday I found her in jeans."

"Savannah?"

"Yeah. I didn't know she even owned any."

"But why?" Caroline asked, clearly puzzled. "Why'd she do these things?"

"I have my suspicions and I'll tell you right now, it makes my blood run cold."

"Really," Caroline said thoughtfully, "when you think about it, what's so terrible about Savannah cutting her hair and updating her wardrobe?"

"I'm worried." Grady didn't mind admitting it, either. "This morning I saw her standing on the porch looking down the driveway as if she expected Laredo to come back. Personally I wish to hell he would, but I don't think it's going to happen."

"I hope you didn't tell her that!"

"Of course not!" What kind of idiot did Caroline think he was, anyway? "Then she told me Laredo Smith was a fool," he added.

"I couldn't agree with her more," Caroline muttered.

"You know what I think? I think Savannah's decided to look for a husband." He spoke quickly, finding the subject of marriage an uncomfortable one with Caroline.

Caroline gave an elaborate shrug. "There's nothing wrong with marriage, although neither of *us* seems interested in it."

"I agree—nothing wrong with it. But I'm afraid that in Savannah's current frame of mind any man will do."

"Did she have someone in mind?"

"Not that I'm aware of." But Grady knew his sister, and while he wasn't an expert, he recognized the look. Savannah was on the prowl. And when a woman set her mind on marriage, he believed, there was damn little a man could do but run for shelter.

"You're sure about this?" Caroline frowned.

"Not a hundred percent, but it's fairly obvious."

Then to his consternation, Caroline burst out laughing.

Grady didn't take kindly to being the butt of a joke. "What's so damned funny?" he demanded.

"You! I don't think Savannah's on the prowl, as you put it, but if she does find a decent man to marry, more power to her. There's too much love in her heart to waste. If Laredo doesn't want to marry her, then so be it. Eventually she'll find a man who does."

"In some tavern?"

"Savannah's not into that scene."

"That's what I thought, but then Richard…" Grady hesitated, uncertain he should tell her this, but if Caroline could help…

"What about Richard?" she asked, her laughter draining away quickly.

It helped that his no-good brother hadn't fooled Caroline, that she recognized the kind of man he was. "Richard offered to take her barhopping and introduce her around."

"Terrific," Caroline said sarcastically. "All the best men hang around bars. Is she going to do it?"

"I don't know," Grady said. "I just don't know."

Glen Patterson sat down in front of the television with a cold can of soda. He was supposed to meet Ellie for dinner, but she'd phoned and said she'd be hung up until after seven. This was a difficult time for his friend. Twice this week he'd made excuses to drive into town and check up on her. The last report he'd heard on her father wasn't good. The doctors seemed to think John Frasier wouldn't last more than another week or two.

"You're frowning," Cal said as he stepped into the

living room. It wasn't as neat and orderly as when their mother had done the housekeeping, but it wasn't as bad as it might've been, either. The two brothers had hired a woman to come in once a week to clean ever since their parents had retired and moved into town to open a bed-and-breakfast.

"I was just thinking," Glen said.

"Worried about Ellie?"

"Not really." He downplayed his concern rather than admit it to his brother.

"Maybe you *should* be worried," Cal said as he claimed the recliner. He sat down and stretched out his long legs.

"Do you know something I don't?"

Cal didn't look at him when he spoke. "I hear Richard Weston's got his eye on her."

"Richard? He's harmless. Okay, so he likes to flirt, but Ellie knows that."

"You jealous?"

If anyone understood his relationship with Ellie, it should be his own brother. "Why would I be jealous? Ellie and I are friends. Nothing more. Nothing less."

Friends. It shouldn't be a difficult concept to understand. Cal and Grady Weston had been good friends for years. It just so happened that *his* best friend was a member of the opposite sex. People had been trying to make something of it for years.

Cal regarded him skeptically.

"What?" Glen asked in annoyance.

"Men and women can't be friends."

Glen had his older brother on that one. "Wrong. Ellie's like one of the guys. She always has been—you know that."

Cal folded his hands over his trim stomach. "In other words, it doesn't bother you she's been seeing Richard."

"Not in the least." It did a little, but not enough to really concern him—and not for the reasons Cal might suggest. Glen was afraid that Ellie was especially vulnerable just then, and he didn't want Richard Weston to take advantage of her.

"You know how Grady feels about him," Cal said.

"Yeah, so what? Richard wasn't cut out to be a rancher—we both know that. He has a right to come home now and then, don't you think?"

Cal was silent for a moment. Then he said, "If I were you, I'd keep an eye on Ellie."

Glen found himself frowning again. Cal had a suspicious nature but he hadn't always been this cynical or distrusting. Glen traced it back to Jennifer Healy— Cal had been engaged to her a couple of years ago, and Jennifer had dumped him. Afterward Cal's disposition had soured, particularly toward women. It bothered Glen and he'd tried a number of times to steer his older brother into a new relationship, but Cal didn't seem interested.

"Well, I know for a fact that Richard can be a real bastard," Cal added. "If you're Ellie's friend, like you say, you'd better warn her."

"Warn?" Obviously Cal hadn't been around her often enough. Ellie had a mind of her own and wouldn't take kindly to his interference.

Anyway, he just couldn't take Richard seriously as a threat. An annoyance, yes, but not a threat.

Eleven

As Savannah drove toward Bitter End, she considered the unmistakable fact that her family was worried about her. She'd shocked everyone by cutting her hair, no one more than herself. The decision had come on the spur of the moment, without warning or forethought.

She'd been washing her face as she did each morning and happened to catch her reflection in the bathroom mirror. For a long moment, she'd stood there staring.

How plain she looked. How ordinary. Carefully, critically, she examined her image and didn't like what she saw. That was when she decided something had to be done. Anything. Not until she reached for the brush did she consider cutting her waist-length blond hair. One minute she was staring in the mirror, the next she had a pair of scissors in her hands.

Savannah knew she'd shocked Grady and Wiley that first morning. They'd come into the kitchen for breakfast and stopped cold, unable to keep their mouths from sagging open. Her brother squinted and looked at her as if she were a stranger. Not that Savannah blamed him. She *felt* like a stranger.

Naturally Grady, being Grady, had simply ignored the change after that and didn't say a word. Frowning, he sat down at the table and dished up his breakfast as though there was nothing out of the ordinary. And Wiley, being Wiley, couldn't resist commenting. He approved of the change and said so, forcing Grady to agree with him.

Savannah began to like her new look. Everything that followed after she'd cut her hair was a natural progression of this first action. She'd worn the ankle-length dresses for comfort and out of habit. The jeans were leftovers from her high-school days, and surprisingly, still fit.

Of the three men Richard had been the most complimentary about the new Savannah. Her younger brother had done his best to flatter and charm her. To his credit his efforts had made her laugh, something she hadn't done in quite a while. She worried about Richard and his finances, but again and again he assured her the check would be coming soon. The one who surprised her most was Grady. It was as if he'd forgotten about Richard, but her younger brother was smart enough to avoid him. He spent his evenings in town, and while Grady was out working, Richard practiced his guitar or serenaded her. The past few afternoons he'd joined her on the porch to keep her company. It helped distract her from thoughts of Laredo, and Savannah was grateful. A couple of times he'd attempted to talk her into going to town with him to, as he put it, live it up a little. He seemed to believe that all she needed was a new love interest. Another man, who'd take her mind off Laredo.

What Richard didn't understand was that she couldn't turn her feelings on and off at will. He prodded her, claiming it would lift her spirits to get out and circulate. While she appreciated his efforts, she wasn't ready. In truth she didn't know if she would ever be. Not that she intended to mourn the loss of her one and only love for the remainder of her days. She'd given herself time to accept that Laredo was out of her life; after that, she was determined to continue on as she had before.

Easier said than done.

Savannah's hands clenched the steering wheel as she came to a particularly bumpy stretch of road. Although she knew Grady highly disapproved of her going back to the ghost town, she'd decided to do it, anyway.

Not because of the roses, either. She'd already discovered the day Laredo had come with her that no other flowers were to be found there, old roses or otherwise. The land was completely barren. Nevertheless, she felt compelled to return for one last visit.

Her reason was nebulous, hard to analyze or explain. But Savannah didn't care. The *why* of it no longer concerned her. She felt drawn in some indefinable way to this lifeless empty town.

She was pitched and jolted around as she drove slowly toward Bitter End. Oddly, the truck seemed to remember each turn, and she followed without question, parking in the same spot and hiking the rest of the way.

As she neared the place, the memories of her last

visit with Laredo immediately came to mind. For weeks now she'd managed to curtail her thoughts of him, telling herself it did no good to brood on might-have-beens; he was gone and nothing she said or did would bring him back. She had no choice but to accept his decision.

At least that was the sane and sensible approach. In reality it just hurt too damned much to linger over the memories.

Every time she stepped into her garden the first thing she saw were the trellises he'd built for her. The roses he'd fertilized and cared for had exploded with fresh blooms. She would cut and arrange them, knowing that his hands had touched these very stems.

It hadn't been easy. None of it.

Caroline worried about her, too, and phoned frequently to check on her. Rather than come right out and tell her she was concerned, her friend manufactured excuses for her calls. She still wasn't coming out to the ranch very often, but Savannah blamed Grady and his talent for frightening Maggie.

As she climbed onto the rocky ledge, Bitter End came into view. She stared at the church at the outskirts of town. The whole place looked peaceful and serene from here, and she wondered about the sadness and oppression she'd experienced on her last visit. Maybe it was her imagination, after all. Laredo's, too. He'd shared her uneasiness and hadn't been able to get her away fast enough.

But as she walked past the church and down the main street, the sensation returned. The feeling seemed to wrap itself around her, but Savannah refused to be intimidated. She wasn't going to run away.

Not this time.

She moved forward carefully and deliberately. The sidewalks had been built a good two to three feet off the ground and were lined with railings. A water trough, baked for a hundred years in the unyielding sun, sat by the hitching post. Savannah advanced toward it, thinking that, instead of walking down the center of the street as she had with Laredo, she'd take the sidewalk and explore a couple of buildings along the way.

Just then she heard a bird's mournful cry reverberating in the stillness. The wind whistled, a keening sound, as though someone was grieving some great loss. Sagebrush tumbled down the hard dirt street. She stopped, looking around, and realized there was something different.

"The rocking chair," she said aloud. She was certain no chair had been there before. But now one stood outside the mercantile store, creaking in the wind, and her heart lodged in her throat.

Determined not to give in to the fear that sent goose bumps skittering up her arms, she strolled fearlessly ahead. Her bravado didn't help. The feeling of dread persisted.

In that instant she understood. It was an emotional understanding and it told her why she'd come, what had driven her back to the ghost town. Standing in the middle of town, she looked up and down the barren street and saw nothing but tumbleweeds and dust.

The street was stark. Empty. Bare. Even the land refused to nurture growth.

This town, this lifeless unproductive street, was like her life. She lived holed up on the ranch with her unmarried brothers. Her entire life revolved around their needs, their wants, their demands.

Her roses and her mail-order business were tolerated, but no one had offered her one word of encouragement. Except Laredo. Grady cared about her; she didn't mean to belittle his concern. But he hadn't the time or energy to invest in understanding her or her needs. As for Richard, although she loved him, she knew he'd never been able to look past his own interests.

Until Laredo, her existence had been empty. Outwardly focused, with no regard for her own happiness, her own growth. *Before Laredo. After Laredo.* Savannah smiled to herself. It seemed her entire life would now be divided into two parts. Before he'd come and after he'd left.

How odd that she'd find herself smiling like that. Just when she'd recognized her life for what it was. Shallow. Without a center.

The restlessness she'd held at bay all this time felt as though it would crush her. Ignoring the unhappiness had done no good. Repressing it hadn't worked. For weeks she'd been fighting headaches and listlessness. For weeks her body had tried to tell her what standing alone in the ghost town had finally made her understand.

She saw a small corral across from the hotel, a large rock beside it. Savannah walked over and sat there, trying to assimilate what she'd learned about herself.

A memory came to her. One she'd long forgotten. She'd been barely ten when her father had been tossed from his horse. He'd badly broken his leg but had

Get Up To 4 Free Books!

Dear Reader,

IT'S A FACT: if you answer 4 quick questions, we'll send you 4 FREE REWARDS from each series you try!

Try **Essential Suspense** featuring spine-tingling suspense and psychological thrillers with many written by today's best-selling authors.

Try **Essential Romance** featuring compelling romance stories with many written by today's best-selling authors.

Or **TRY BOTH!**

I'm not kidding you. As a leading publisher of women's fiction, we value your opinions... and your time. That's why we are prepared to reward you handsomely for completing our mini-survey. In fact, we have 4 Free Rewards for you, including 2 free books and 2 free gifts from each series you try!

Thank you for participating in our survey,

Pam Powers

To get your 4 FREE REWARDS:

Complete the survey below and return the insert today to receive up to 4 FREE BOOKS and FREE GIFTS guaranteed!

"4 for 4" MINI-SURVEY

1 Is reading one of your favorite hobbies?
☐ YES ☐ NO

2 Do you prefer to read instead of watch TV?
☐ YES ☐ NO

3 Do you read newspapers and magazines?
☐ YES ☐ NO

4 Do you enjoy trying new book series with FREE BOOKS?
☐ YES ☐ NO

Please send me my Free Rewards, consisting of **2 Free Books from each series I select** and **Free Mystery Gifts**. I understand that I am under no obligation to buy anything, as explained on the back of this card.

☐ **Essential Suspense** (191/391 MDL GNQK)
☐ **Essential Romance** (194/394 MDL GNQK)
☐ **Try Both** (191/391/194/394 MDL GNQV)

FIRST NAME	LAST NAME

ADDRESS

APT.#	CITY

STATE/PROV.   ZIP/POSTAL CODE

READER SERVICE—Here's how it works:

somehow managed to crawl to safety and avoid further injury.

Savannah remembered how her mother, frightened and ashen-faced, had run to his side and held his hand while she drove him to the clinic. Mel Weston had smiled, and between deep breaths, assured his wife that the pain told him he was still alive.

That was what this pain told Savannah. She was alive. She could still feel and love and be. Laredo had taught her that, and so much more. For the first time in her adult life, she recognized how much love her heart could hold.

No matter how much it hurt, she'd do it all again.

She bowed her head against the wind as it blew sagebrush about her feet. Tears filled her eyes, but they weren't the same tears that had burned her face in weeks past.

Savannah had made peace with herself.

Grady noticed a difference in Savannah the minute she got out of the truck. Her face radiated a serenity, an acceptance, one that had clearly been hard-won.

His sister hadn't told him where she was going, but Grady could guess and he hadn't liked it. Not one damn bit. How she'd come away from Bitter End with any kind of tranquility was beyond him. Half a dozen times he'd considered going after her and talked himself out of it, knowing Savannah wouldn't appreciate his interference.

She joined him in the kitchen and put on water for a pot of tea. "I'm going to be all right now," she told him.

Grady wasn't sure what to say. He'd wanted to talk to her about the last conversation he'd had with Laredo, wanted to comfort her, but he feared he'd do more harm than good.

"I won't be going back," she said next as she took the china teapot from the shelf above the stove. She didn't say where and he didn't ask.

"Good," was all Grady said, at a loss for words.

"Would you care for a cup of tea?" she asked, sounding almost like her old self.

Grady preferred dark strong coffee and Savannah knew it. The offer was more a gesture of reconciliation, an outstretched hand. "Tea sounds wonderful," he said.

Savannah smiled and brought down an extra cup and saucer.

In the days that followed, the transformation in his sister became more apparent. Color returned to her pale cheeks and a radiance to her face. She started to sing and hum once again and baked his favorite chocolate-chip cookies. Savannah was back, and yet it wasn't quite the same Savannah as before. These changes were very subtle.

His sister had always been a fearless advocate for people she believed in. Now she believed in herself, too. Her fledgling mail-order business took off like gangbusters once she finished her catalog. Orders poured in from across the country—surprising even Savannah, who'd barely got her catalog mailed out when the responses started to arrive, at a fast and furious pace. The fax machine was in constant use. She soon became known as an expert on old roses and two awards came in quick succession. First she was honored with the grand prize by the Texas Rose Society for one of her premier roses, which she'd named

Laredo's Legacy. The following day, she was asked to speak at next year's Rose Festival in Tyler, Texas, known as the rose capital of the world. Public speaking terrified Savannah, and Grady suspected she'd politely decline. To his amazement she accepted.

Grady wasn't the only one who noticed the changes in Savannah. Caroline did, too. Even Richard, self-centered as he was, commented on her new attitude. Grady was proud of her, exceptionally proud, and he wanted to let her know. He could think of only one way. He ordered her prize-winning rose, Laredo's Legacy, and together with Savannah, planted it at their parents' grave. Savannah had thanked him with tears shining in her eyes.

His sister, Grady realized, was quite possibly the most incredible woman he'd ever known. How odd that it had taken him so long to realize it.

Twelve

Humming softly to herself, Savannah checked the living room one last time to be sure everything was in place. Laredo had been gone more than six weeks now, and she'd stopped waiting for him, stopped dreaming he'd return. Her life had settled back into a comfortable groove, and the happiness she'd found with him would forever be part of her. That happiness, that sense of possibility, was what she chose to remember rather than the emptiness she'd felt at his leaving.

It was Savannah's turn to host the women's group from church, and her nerves were fluttering. Within a couple of hours twenty women would crowd into the living room to plan a church dinner.

Earlier in the day she'd baked apple pies, and because Grady had been such a good sport about everything lately, she'd made a lemon meringue pie for him, too. The scent that lingered in the house was an enticing mixture of cinnamon, nutmeg and lemon.

"Is Caroline coming?" Grady asked, walking into the kitchen. Just as he was about to stick his finger into the lemon pie, she slapped his hand.

"You can have a piece later," she told him. "And, yes, Caroline's coming."

"What about Maggie?"

Savannah carried the pie to safety. "She'll be with Dovie Boyd."

"Dovie?" He sounded almost disappointed. "She's old enough to be Maggie's…"

"Grandmother," Savannah supplied. "Caroline's mother and Dovie were good friends, and Dovie likes to fill in as Grandma every now and again. Why are you so curious?"

He shrugged and strolled out of the kitchen. Savannah didn't have time to wonder about it. As soon as she finished the last of the dishes, she needed to shower and change clothes.

Two hours later the living room was filled with the chatter and laughter of women. Savannah handed out copies of her apple-pie recipe and refilled coffee cups from her mother's silver pot. She was joking with Millie Greenville from the flower shop when the room went strangely quiet. Everyone had turned to look behind Savannah. Certain Richard was up to one of his tricks, she turned around, too, ready to chastise him.

She froze.

Laredo stood in the doorway, his Stetson in his hand. He looked about as uncomfortable as a man could get—as though it was all he could do not to turn tail and run.

"Hello, Savannah," he said.

She couldn't have responded had her life depended on it. He looked travel-weary. His jacket was dusty and his face pale beneath his tan, but Savannah had never seen anyone more beautiful.

He seemed to be thinking the same thing about her because for that long, unbroken moment he didn't take his eyes off her.

"I can see I've come at a bad time," he said, glancing away from Savannah long enough to scan the room. All the women were openly curious about him; Savannah had never heard anything louder than this silence.

"You couldn't have come at a better time," Caroline insisted, leaping to her feet. "It looks to me like you'd appreciate a slice of Savannah's apple pie. Sit down and make yourself at home while I dish it up for you. Savannah'll see to your coffee."

A space magically appeared between two women sitting on the sofa. Savannah remained frozen, unable to breathe or think. This was unfair. Just when she'd forged a new path for herself, accepted his absence, he was back.

Unable to hide his discomfort, Laredo settled down between Nell Bishop and Ellie Frasier, looking as out of place as a junkyard dog sitting between toy poodles.

Caroline served him a huge slice of apple pie. "Perhaps you'd like to tell Savannah why you're here?" the postmistress asked pointedly.

The room fell silent again, awaiting Laredo's response. Every eye was on him. Including Savannah's. His gaze darted about the room and he swallowed noticeably. "I've come to ask Savannah to be my wife."

The silver coffeepot in Savannah's hands suddenly weighed a hundred pounds, and she set it down on the silver platter with a clank. The buzz of voices surrounded her. Her heart raced and everything felt unreal.

At that precise moment Grady burst into the room. "Is that Laredo's truck parked in the yard with the horse trail—?" He came to an abrupt halt when he realized he'd walked into the middle of the church group.

"I believe it is," Caroline answered, gesturing toward Laredo.

The wrangler sprang to his feet, looking at Grady with unmistakable relief.

"What are you doing here?" Grady demanded.

Savannah wanted to stop him, to explain that Laredo had already been through one inquisition and that was enough, but she wasn't given the chance.

"I've come to ask your sister to marry me," Laredo answered as he had earlier, only this time there was a hint of challenge in his voice, as though he expected Grady to argue with him.

Again a murmur arose.

Edwina Moorhouse's old bones creaked as she stood and motioned at Laredo. "All right, young man, tell me what makes you think Savannah should marry you."

Color surged into Laredo's neck and crept upward. "I love her," he answered simply.

"So does everyone else in this room," Lily put in, following her sister's lead and standing up.

"And we're not about to let some stranger steal her away." This from Millie Greenville.

"That…that was one of the reasons I left," Laredo explained haltingly. "I didn't want to take Savannah from her home and family."

"How has that changed?"

Laredo motioned with his head toward Grady. "I decided to take her brother up on his offer."

"What offer?" Savannah asked, turning to regard her brother.

Grady had started to ease his way toward the kitchen. "Ah, perhaps we should talk about all this later. In private," he added pointedly.

"It's time for us to go," Caroline suggested. The ladies began to gather their purses, but Edwina called a stop to it.

"Now just a minute. I'm seventy-five and too old to go without my sleep. I can tell I'm not going to rest until I hear Savannah's answer. Do you love this man?" she asked, pointing at Laredo.

Savannah nodded.

"You're willing to marry him?"

Again she nodded, more forcefully this time.

"It's been a while since Wade performed a wedding ceremony," Nell Bishop piped up. Her mother-in-law agreed, trying to remember whose wedding that was.

"I always did love a summer wedding," Lily Moorhouse said, glancing from Laredo to Savannah.

"A wedding's just what this town needs," Louise Powell declared as though that should be the last word on the subject.

But it wasn't. The group of delighted women became engaged in the conversation, exchanging ideas, offering suggestions. The level of noise and excitement rose perceptibly and wedding plans flew in all directions. Millie suggested white and pink roses for the bridal bouquet, but white calla lilies for the arrangement on the altar. Louise had strong opinions on the meal that should be served. Edwina recommended some musical selections.

Through all this Laredo's eyes remained locked

with Savannah's, and it seemed that only the two of them were present. She felt his love; it warmed her, even from halfway across the room. His expression told her how miserable he'd been without her, how lonely. She knew that, like her, he'd struggled with the pain. He'd also struggled with pride. But in the end his love, *their* love, was stronger. Laredo Smith needed her as badly as she needed him.

"I do think we should leave now, don't you, ladies?" Caroline tried again, gathering up empty plates and cups.

A chorus of agreement followed this time, and everyone stood.

"Well, that's that," said Edwina. "Come on, Lily, if we hurry home we'll be in time for a game of cribbage before *Jeopardy* comes on."

The room emptied more quickly than Savannah would have thought possible. She happily forgave Caroline for abandoning the stack of dishes. In less than a minute the crowd was out the door, and the sound of cars starting replaced the chatter of twenty women.

"You cut your hair," Laredo said now that they were alone. He stood half a room away from her, his hat in his hands.

Savannah raised her fingers to touch it.

"It looks wonderful." His voice dipped. "*You* look wonderful. You're more beautiful now than ever. I didn't think that was possible."

"You look wonderful, too." She smiled. "What happened?" she asked suddenly, the words rushing from her lips. "Why'd you go?"

"For all the wrong reasons. My pride, mainly, and my fear."

"Fear?"

"My mother told me I was a fool to have listened to…my doubts. I sold my land in Oklahoma," he said, "and brought Renegade with me. If you're agreeable, I'll accept Grady's offer to become a partner in the ranch. Renegade will be my stake, and in time the Yellow Rose will have the finest quarter horses in the country. I promise you that. I don't have a lot to offer you, not nearly as much as you deserve, but I love you, Savannah." He took a step closer. "I didn't realize how much until I reached Oklahoma. My land was there, my dream, and it meant nothing if you couldn't share it with me."

"I thought my life was over when you left," she whispered. "You didn't even say goodbye."

"I couldn't—but I swear I won't leave you again. Mom's right—I'm too much like her. I'll only love once in my life, and if I let you go, there won't be a second chance. I couldn't ask you to wait, but I realize now that I couldn't wait, either. I love you too much."

"I love you, too, so much… Why are you standing way over there when I'm right here?"

Laredo covered the space between them in three strides. None too soon she was in his arms. It was heaven to feel his lips on hers, warm, moist, hungry. His kiss told her everything. How much he wanted her, needed her. How much he loved her.

Savannah felt the steady beat of his heart beneath her palm and returned his kiss in full measure, clinging to him. Her heart was full enough to burst.

"Children?" She managed the question between kisses.

"As many as you want. Oh, Savannah, I can't wait

for you to meet my mother. She loves you already." His arms tightened about her.

From behind them Grady cleared his throat loudly. "I take it everything's been decided?"

Laredo tucked his arm around Savannah's waist and held her close. "We're getting married as soon as it can be arranged."

"Good. I assume that's Renegade in the trailer?"

Laredo nodded. "I'm taking you up on your offer, Grady, but I want it understood right now that I'll pay my own way. I'm here because of Savannah, not because of anything you offered. Understand?"

Grady held up both his hands and grinned widely. "Understood."

"Hot damn," Richard said as he sauntered into the room, guitar slung over his shoulder. "You mean there's going to be a wedding in the family? Well, all I can say is better late than never!"

* * * * *

TEXAS TWO-STEP

One

A month ago this had been her family home.

Ellie Frasier stood on the tree-lined sidewalk in Promise, Texas, staring up at the traditional two-story house with its white picket fence. The Sold sign stared back at her, telling her that nothing would ever be the same again. Her father was dead, and her mother gone.

This was the house where she'd been born and raised. Where she'd raced across the front lawn, climbed the pecan tree and hung upside down from its branches. On that very porch she'd been kissed for the first time.

Oh, how she'd miss that porch. Countless pictures had been taken of her on these steps. Her mother holding an infant Ellie in her arms the day she brought her home from the hospital in Brewster. Every Easter in a frilly new dress and every Halloween in a costume her mother had sewn for her.

The day Ellie turned thirteen and wore panty hose for the first time, her dad had insisted she have her picture taken on the porch. Then at eighteen, when she was a rodeo princess for the Brewster Labor Day

Festival, her father had posed her on the front steps again. At the time he'd told her he'd be taking her picture there in her wedding dress before she left for the church.

Only, her father would never escort her down the aisle.

The rush of pain came as no surprise. She'd been dealing with it for weeks now. And before that, too, while he was in the hospital, desperately ill. But Ellie couldn't believe he would actually die; death was something that happened to other people's fathers, not her own. Not yet. He was too young, too vital, too *special*, and because she'd refused to accept the inevitable, his passing had hit her hard, throwing her emotionally off balance.

Even then, she'd been forced to hold her grief inside. Her mother had needed her to be strong. Ellie's personality was like her father's—forceful, independent and stubborn. Her mother, on the other hand, was fragile and rather impractical, relying on her husband to look after things. She'd been unable to deal with the funeral arrangements or any of the other tasks that accompany death, so they'd fallen on Ellie's shoulders.

The weeks that followed were like an earthquake, and the aftershocks continued to jolt Ellie, often when she least expected it.

Her mother had given her the worst shock. Within a week of the burial service, Pam Frasier announced she was moving to Chicago to live with her sister. Almost immediately the only home Ellie had ever known was put up for sale. By the end of the first week they'd had an offer.

Once the deal was finalized, her mother packed up

all her belongings, hired a moving company, and before Ellie could fully appreciate what was happening, she was gone. Whatever she'd left behind, Pam told her daughter, was Ellie's to keep. The family business, too. Pam wanted nothing from the feed store. John had always intended it to go to Ellie.

Squaring her shoulders, Ellie realized there was no use delaying the inevitable. The key seemed to burn her hand as she approached the house for the last time and walked slowly up the five wooden steps. She stood there for a moment, then forced herself to unlock the front door.

A large stack of boxes awaited her. Ellie had a fair idea of what was inside. Memories. Years and years of memories.

No point in worrying about it now. Once she'd loaded everything up and carted it to her rented house, she had to get to the feed store. While her customers had been understanding, she couldn't expect unlimited patience. George Tucker, her assistant—he'd been her father's assistant, too—was trustworthy and reliable. But responsibility for Frasier Feed was Ellie's, and she couldn't forget that.

Which meant she couldn't take the time to grieve properly. Not when she was short-staffed during the busiest season of the year. June brought with it a flurry of activity on the neighboring cattle ranches, and many of those ranchers would be looking to her for their feed and supplies.

By the third trip out to her truck Ellie regretted turning down Glen's offer of help. Glen Patterson was quite possibly the best friend she'd ever had. Although she'd always known who Glen was—in a town the size of Promise, everyone knew everyone else, at least by sight—there was just enough difference in their ages to keep them in separate social circles during their school years.

The Pattersons had been buying their feed from Frasier's for years. Her father and Glen's dad had played high-school football together. For the past few years Glen had been the one coming to town for supplies. When Ellie began to work full-time with her dad, she'd quickly developed a chatty teasing relationship with Glen.

She was lighthearted and quick-witted, and Glen shared her sense of humor. Before long she'd found herself looking forward to their verbal exchanges. These days whenever he stopped by, Ellie joined him for a cup of coffee. They usually sat on the bench in front of her store, idling away fifteen or twenty minutes, depending on how busy she was. When the weather discouraged outdoor breaks, they sat in her office to enjoy a few minutes' respite.

It got to be that they could talk about anything. She appreciated his wry good sense, his down-to-earth approach to life. Ellie tended to obsess about problems, but Glen took them in stride. While she ranted and raved, he'd lean his chair against the building wall and tuck his hands behind his head, quietly listening. Then he'd point out some error in her thinking, some incorrect assumption or faulty conclusion. Generally he was right. His favorite expression was, "Don't confuse activity with progress." She could almost hear him saying it now.

It'd been a week or more since his last visit and Ellie missed him. She could count on Glen to distract her, make her smile. Perhaps even ease this gnawing pain. But when he'd offered to help her sort through the boxes, she'd declined, moving everything on her own. Knowing she'd have to face these memories sooner or later and preferring to do it alone.

Within minutes of her arrival at the feed store, the place was bustling. Naturally she was grateful for the business, but she would have liked a few moments to herself. Then again, perhaps it was best to be hurled into the thick of things, with no chance to dwell on her grief and all the changes taking place in her life.

It was almost two before Ellie could dash into her office for ten minutes, to collect her thoughts and have lunch. Although her appetite was nonexistent, she forced herself to eat half a sandwich and an apple. At her desk, she sifted through the phone messages and found one from Glen. It was unusual for him to call during the day, especially in early summer when he spent most of his time working with the herd. Just knowing she'd been in his thoughts buoyed her spirits.

Since his parents had moved into town and opened the local bed-and-breakfast, Glen and his older brother, Cal, had taken over management of the ranch. Thus far they'd kept the spread operating in the black, doing whatever work they could themselves and hiring seasonal help when necessary. In the past few years, they'd begun crossbreeding their cattle with Grady Weston's stock.

The phone rang, and thinking it might be Glen, Ellie reached eagerly for the receiver. "Frasier Feed."

"Ellie, I'm glad you answered. It's Richard Weston."

If it couldn't be Glen, then Ellie felt pleased it was Richard. He'd recently returned to Promise after a six-year absence, and they'd gone out on a couple of dates before her father's condition worsened.

"How are you?" Richard asked in a concerned voice.

"Fine," she responded automatically, which was easier than confessing the truth. She just couldn't talk about her grief, her deep sense of loss. Maybe Glen was the only person she could share that with, Ellie reflected. But not yet. It was too soon. For now, she needed to forge ahead and do what was necessary to get through the day.

"You've been on my mind a lot, Elle."

"I appreciate your thoughtfulness, Richard, I really do." Ellie was sincere about that. She'd been a schoolgirl when he left Promise, and like every other female in her class, she'd had a major crush on him. Richard was still the best-looking man in town. The years away had refined his features, and he was suave in ways ranchers could never be. City-suave. She liked him well enough but didn't expect anything from their friendship. To be frank, she was flattered that he sought her out. The huge flower arrangement he'd sent for her father's funeral had touched her, it was the largest one there and stood out among the other smaller arrangements. A number of the townsfolk had commented on it.

"I received the thank-you card," he said. "The flowers were the least I could do."

"I wanted you to know how much Mom and I appreciated it." She paused. "It was nice of you to do that for us."

"I'd like to do more, if you'd let me," he said softly. "If there's anything you need, make sure you phone."

"I will." But it was unlikely she'd take him up on his offer. Not even Glen, her best friend, knew how emotionally shaky she was. The pain was still so new, so raw, that she had to deal with it herself before she could lean on anyone else. Her father had been like that, too, and she was, after all, her father's daughter.

"You know, Ellie," Richard said next, "I think it'd do you a world of good to get out."

A date? Now? No way. Ellie wasn't ready, and besides, she had a million things to do before she gave a thought to her social life. She was about to tell him that when he spoke again.

"Nell Bishop called to tell us she's having a birthday bash for Ruth this Friday night. Sounds like she's going all out. How would you feel about tagging along with me?"

Ellie hesitated.

"You need to relax a little. Have a few laughs," he added with the same empathy he'd shown earlier. "Let me help you through this."

Ellie had received an invitation herself. Attending a party was the last thing she felt like doing, but Nell was a good friend and a good customer. She needed to make at least a token appearance.

"I probably wouldn't stay long," she qualified, thinking it would be best if Richard went without her. They could meet there.

"No problem," Richard quickly assured her. "I'm not much into this birthday thing myself. The only reason I told Nell I'd come was so I could ask you."

"Oh, Richard, that's so sweet."

"Hey, that's just the kind of guy I am."

"If you're sure you don't mind leaving early, I'd be

happy to go with you." Ellie had always been fond of Ruth Bishop. She knew that Ruth and Nell had supported each other through the trauma of Jake's death. Nell had lost the love of her life; Ruth had lost her son. Nell had struggled to hold on to the ranch despite numerous hardships, financial and otherwise. Ruth had been a wonderful help, and Ellie was sure Nell had planned this party as a means of thanking her mother-in-law.

"I'll swing by your place around six," Richard suggested.

"Six would be perfect." They chatted a couple of minutes longer, and as she hung up the phone, Ellie realized she was actually looking forward to an evening out. It would feel good to laugh again, and Richard was always entertaining.

The sun beat down on Glen Patterson. He and his brother were on horseback, driving almost four hundred head of cattle to one of the far pastures. With two hired hands, seasonal help, they'd shuffled all the cattle through narrow chutes, vaccinating them.

Removing his Stetson, he wiped his brow, then glanced quickly at his watch. Ellie had been in his thoughts most of the day. He shouldn't have listened to her protests; he should've stopped at her parents' house that morning despite everything. Ellie could use a helping hand, whether she was willing to admit it or not. The woman was just too damn stubborn.

In his view she'd declined his offer mostly out of pride. He wondered if she felt mourning should be done in private, and he wanted to tell her she didn't have to hide her grief, that it was okay to accept an offer of help. She didn't have to do everything herself. He knew it had all been a brave front, but he didn't have much choice other than to accept her decision.

Vaccinating the herd was not Glen's favorite task. Still, it was better than checking the cows and heifers for signs of pregnancy, although he strongly suspected the animals weren't any keener on the practice than he was himself. Glen wished to hell someone would invent a urine test for cows.

"I think I'll head on back," Glen told his brother. They'd reached the pasture, and the cattle began to spread out.

Cal's attention didn't waver from the last stragglers. "Going into town?" he asked.

Glen raised his hat a bit. "I was thinking about it," he said with some reluctance. His brother's ability to read his mind was uncanny at times. And damned irritating.

A telltale quiver at the edges of Cal's mouth signaled the beginnings of a smile. "You're going off to see Ellie, right?"

"So what?" Glen didn't care for that tone of voice. His brother never had understood how he and Ellie could be friends and nothing else. But then, Cal had an attitude when it came to women, no matter who they were. Not that Glen blamed him. If a woman had publicly humiliated *him* the way Jennifer Healy had humiliated his brother, Glen supposed his own feelings toward the opposite sex would be tainted, too. At times, however, Cal's lack of perspective annoyed him.

"You two should own up to a few truths," Cal announced as though being two years older gave him some kind of wisdom—or authority.

"Truths?"

"You and Ellie have something going."

"You're right," Glen admitted, and he could see that agreeing with Cal had taken his brother aback. "We're friends. Is that so difficult to understand?" Glen couldn't figure out what it was with his brother, and a few others, too. Even Grady Weston, his lifelong friend and fellow rancher, obviously believed there was more between him and Ellie than friendship.

The fact was that in four years they'd never so much as held hands—which should say something. He simply enjoyed Ellie's company, and she enjoyed his. Anything romantic would ruin one of the best damn friendships he'd ever had. Ellie felt the same way. Okay, so they'd never openly discussed it, but then there was no reason they should. They understood each other. An unspoken agreement.

Yes, that was it; he felt better for having analyzed the situation. "Ellie and I have an understanding," he explained with a sense of satisfaction. Cal wouldn't argue with that. "It's like the way you and I never talk about Bitter End."

Cal's eyes narrowed. Only a small number of families in Promise knew about the ghost town hidden in the Texas hills. Few ever mentioned it. Once, as teenagers, Grady, Cal and Glen had decided to look for the town themselves. It was supposed to be a summertime adventure. Something they could brag about to their friends. It'd taken them weeks to find the place, but eventually they'd stumbled on it. The town, with its abandoned buildings and eerie silence, had terrified them so much they'd never gone back. Not only hadn't they returned, they rarely spoke of their experience.

"What's Bitter End got to do with Ellie?" Cal demanded.

"Nothing. What I mean is, you and I don't discuss Bitter End, and Ellie and I don't talk about our relationship because it's understood that neither of us is interested in a romance. Why's that so hard to accept?"

"Fine," Cal said with a snort of disbelief. "You believe what you want and I'll pretend not to notice the truth."

Glen was fast losing patience. "You do that, big brother." He didn't know what made Cal think he was such an expert on women. He was tempted to say so, but restrained himself. "I'll see you tonight sometime," he said, eager to set off. Ellie might act as if clearing out her childhood home was no big deal; Glen knew otherwise.

"Whenever," Cal said without apparent interest.

Glen eased Moonshine into an easy canter and headed toward the ranch house. One of these days Cal would find the right woman and that would shut him up. Glen had never been too impressed with Jennifer Healy; as far as he was concerned, Cal had made a lucky escape. Unfortunately his older brother didn't see it that way. Being ditched by his fiancée had made him cynical about women.

Switching his thoughts to Ellie, Glen smiled. He could almost see the quizzical smile she sometimes wore, could almost hear the sound of her laughter. That was what Ellie needed now—a reason to laugh. Laughter was a great emotional release, and she'd kept her feelings hidden inside for far too long.

He'd shower first, Glen decided, make himself

something to eat and be on his way. Cal could sit in front of the tube if he wanted, but Glen had other plans. Much better ones.

Grady Weston's throat felt parched as a dried-up creek bed. He walked into the ranch house and straight to the refrigerator. His sister, Savannah, made a tall pitcher of iced tea for him and Laredo every afternoon. Not bothering with the niceties, he reached for the glass pitcher and drank directly from that.

"Grady!" Savannah admonished him, coming into the room. Grady's old dog, Rocket, followed her, his movements slow and awkward. She carried an armful of fresh-cut old roses, their pungent scent filling the kitchen.

He finished one last swallow and set the pitcher down on the counter, then wiped his mouth with the back of his hand. "Where's Richard?" he demanded, not wanting to hear about his lack of manners.

Okay, he should've taken the time to grab a glass, but damn it all, he was tired and thirsty. He added *irritated* to the list the moment he glanced out at the drive and saw that his pickup was missing. If it turned out that his no-good brother had absconded with his truck, his irritation would quickly turn to fury.

"I...don't know where Richard is," Savannah answered and lowered her gaze. The way she avoided meeting his eyes was a sure sign that she had her suspicions but wasn't willing to share them.

"He took the truck, didn't he?"

Savannah shrugged, then nodded.

"I figured as much," Grady growled, his anger mounting. Six years earlier Richard had stolen all the family's money and promptly disappeared. Savannah and Grady had been left to deal with the aftermath of their parents' deaths, the inheritance taxes and all the legal problems, while Richard was busy squandering every dime on God only knew what. Then, this past spring, he'd shown up, down on his luck and needing a place to live until the severance check from his last job arrived. Or so he'd told them. Savannah chose to believe Richard's story, but Grady wasn't going to trust him again. Not by a long shot.

Should've kicked him off the ranch the first day. He would have, in fact, if it hadn't been for his soft-hearted sister. In the weeks since, Grady had called himself every kind of fool. Opportunity after opportunity had presented itself to send Richard packing, but he hadn't taken advantage of a single one.

Grady had tried to reason it out in his own mind, especially after Richard had thrown himself a welcome-home party and stuck Grady with the bill. Deep down, Grady recognized that he *wanted* to believe Richard had changed. Even when every bit of evidence claimed otherwise. As the oldest he felt a responsibility to make everything right. He looked for ways to honor the memory of his parents. Ways to hold on to the ranch.

Their mother had spoiled Richard; her youngest son had been her favorite. She might be partly to blame for his self-centered behavior, but regardless of what he'd done, she'd have expected Grady to give him shelter. Even now, six years after her death, Grady found himself seeking her approval.

"Where'd he go this time?" Grady asked, disgusted more with himself than with his brother. Richard was a master when it came to manipulating people. He was charming and a clever conversationalist, unlike Grady who was often loud and brusque. He wished he'd inherited some of Richard's success with the ladies, but he was too old and too stubborn to change now.

Savannah slowly shook her head.

"Does that mean you don't know where Richard went or you don't want to tell me?"

"A little of both," she confessed.

Despite his anger, Grady smiled and sat down at the table. "I probably would've given him the keys if he'd asked," he admitted with a certain reluctance.

"I…didn't actually give him the keys, but I told him where they were."

Savannah sat down across from him. It struck Grady how beautiful his sister was. As little as six months ago he would never have thought of her that way. She was just Savannah, his kindhearted younger sister. A woman who rarely raised her voice, rarely disagreed. A picture of calm serenity, while he struggled to contain his explosive temper. A woman who'd always been happy with her quiet low-key life.

Then one day, out of the blue, his sister had changed. No, he corrected himself, she'd always been strong in ways that made others seem weak, but he'd failed to recognize or appreciate those qualities in her. It had been quite a lesson she'd given him. She'd begun to assert her own needs; she'd made him aware that she wanted more from life than he'd realized or been willing to acknowledge. These changes came about because of Laredo Smith, a drifter who'd stumbled into their lives. A cowboy. A godsend. Grady and Laredo were partners now. The wedding had taken place a few weeks earlier in her rose garden, with only a few close friends as guests. In time the newlyweds would be building their own home and starting a family. Grady looked forward to having children on the ranch.

Falling in love had transformed his sister into a woman of true beauty. It was as if all the goodness inside her had become outwardly visible. He wasn't the only one who'd noticed, either. A couple of months ago she'd cut her hair—formerly waist-length—and begun wearing jeans instead of those long loose dresses. All at once other men had started to take heed. Too late, however, because her heart belonged to Laredo.

"What time did he leave?" Grady asked, rubbing his face tiredly. The problems with Richard just seemed to multiply. The money he'd claimed was coming had yet to arrive, although he'd managed to reimburse Grady five hundred dollars.

Grady had serious doubts about any so-called severance pay owed to Richard. He suspected the money was just the beginning of a long list of lies his brother had been feeding them.

To Grady's relief, Savannah no longer actively championed Richard's cause, and he knew she felt as troubled as he did about their younger brother. Neither was comfortable at the thought of kicking him off the ranch entirely. Besides, Richard occasionally made himself useful, running errands in town and making token efforts to help around the ranch.

"He left about three this afternoon."

"He didn't go into town, did he?"

Savannah hesitated. "I don't think so, but then, he didn't tell me where he was headed."

"I could have used an extra hand this afternoon," Grady murmured.

But they both knew Richard's answer to that. He was never cut out to be a rancher, which was the reason he'd given for fleeing with the family money—his share of the inheritance he'd called it, since he wanted no part of the ranch. The excuse stuck in Grady's craw every time he thought about it.

"He's been keeping himself busy," Savannah said and held his gaze a moment longer than usual. Neither one of them was entirely sure what he did with his time. He disappeared for hours at a stretch without telling anyone where he went or who he was with. Normally Grady wouldn't care, but considering Richard's history, it was worrisome.

"I heard him talking to Ellie on the phone earlier," Savannah told him. "He invited her to Ruth's birthday party."

This didn't give Grady any cause for celebration. He'd noticed his younger brother's growing interest in Ellie Frasier. The fact that she'd recently inherited the family business hadn't escaped Richard's notice, and Grady worried that his brother's interest might be leaning more toward that feed store than to Ellie. She'd dealt with enough grief to have anyone exploit her now.

"She doesn't know, does she?" Savannah asked.

Grady shook his head. Few people in Promise were aware of Richard's crime. It was something Grady preferred not to share. No one wanted his friends and neighbors to learn that his only brother had robbed him blind. Only a handful of folks knew Richard had run off with every penny in the family coffers the day they buried their parents. Vanished for six years until he'd needed help himself.

Grady cursed under his breath and waited for Savannah to chastise him.

She didn't, and Grady soon realized why. The screen door opened and Laredo walked into the kitchen. The wrangler's gaze immediately met Savannah's and they exchanged a tender look.

They fascinated Grady. His sister and her husband were so deeply in love he doubted either one remembered he was in the room. Savannah stood and poured Laredo a glass of iced tea, which the man accepted gratefully. After downing the contents in four or five gulps, Laredo set the glass aside and hugged her close.

Grady watched his brother-in-law's eyes drift shut as he savored holding Savannah. In all this thirty-five years, Grady had never seen any two people more in love. Watching them lost in each other's embrace was almost painful, reminding him how alone he was. He realized he wasn't an easy man to love—he knew that—and he doubted any woman would put up with him for long. Yet he couldn't watch Savannah and Laredo and not wish for that kind of contentment himself.

Grady had never felt lonely before, never given much thought to marriage. *Someday* was about as close as he'd gotten to thinking about any future romance and then only if he could find a woman willing to look past his very noticeable flaws.

There hadn't been *time* to give any consideration to his marital status and romantic hopes—such as they were. It'd taken him six years of backbreaking labor to dig the ranch out of debt. If all went well with this year's herd, they'd be completely in the black once again.

"Caroline's coming over later," Savannah murmured.

Grady wasn't sure who the comment was meant for. Probably him. Nor was he sure whether she intended this as a warning or as…something else. Caroline Daniels was Savannah's best friend and the town's postmistress; he couldn't seem to get along with her, but he was afraid Savannah still had matchmaking ambitions concerning them. A completely hopeless and wrongheaded idea. Lately his sister and Caroline had spent a lot of time discussing and designing house plans, and while that didn't affect Grady one way or another, he often found himself in the company of Caroline's five-year-old daughter, Maggie. He'd been gruff and impatient with the girl not long ago, and she would barely look at him now. Grady felt bad about that.

And it irritated him no end that Maggie had taken to Richard, and being the smooth-talking charmer he was, his younger brother soon had the kid eating out of his hand.

Grady considered his squabbles with Caroline more her fault than his. He admired people who spoke their minds, but Caroline did it a little too often for his liking.

"Are you going to Ruth's birthday party?" Savannah asked.

Grady hesitated, but only for a moment. "Probably not."

His sister's eyes flared briefly and he knew that wasn't the response she'd wanted.

"Why not?"

He wasn't accustomed to explaining his decisions, but Savannah had that look about her, and he knew it was better to deal with the subject now than postpone it.

"Do I need a reason?"

"Laredo and I are going," she said, wrapping her arm around her husband's waist. "Ruth's a sweetheart, and it means a great deal to Nell that there be a nice turnout."

"Cal's not going." Grady couldn't resist pointing this out, although he didn't feel he should have to.

"That's exactly my point," Savannah returned. "If you're not careful, you're going to end up just like Cal."

"And what's wrong with Cal?" Although he asked the question, Grady knew what she meant. Ever since Jennifer had more or less left him at the altar, Cal Patterson had little that was good to say about women. His cynical attitude got to be a bit much, even for Grady, but now wasn't the time to admit it.

"There's nothing wrong with Cal that a good woman wouldn't cure."

"Savannah would like you to ask Caroline to the party," Laredo inserted. He wasn't much of a talker, but when he did speak, he cut to the chase. No beating around the bush with Savannah's husband.

"What? You want me to *what?*" Grady pretended his hearing was impaired and stuck his finger in his ear. He thought he was pretty comical.

Savannah didn't. "Is there a problem with Caroline?" she demanded. Her eyes flashed with spirit and

Grady could see it wasn't going to be easy to mollify her.

"Nope."

"You'd be fortunate if she accepted!"

"Of course I would," he agreed with more than a touch of sarcasm.

"Grady!"

Chuckling, he held up his hands in surrender. "Caroline's all right," he said. "It's just that we don't see eye to eye about a lot of things. You know that, Savannah. I like her, don't get me wrong, but I can't see the two of us dating."

"Because of Maggie?" Savannah asked.

"Not at all," Grady assured her, knowing how close Savannah and the little girl were.

"Savannah thought it'd be a good idea if the four of us went to Ruth's party together." Again it was Laredo who spelled out Savannah's intentions.

"Me and Caroline?" Grady burst out. He bent forward and slapped his hands on his knees in exaggerated hilarity. "Caroline and me with you two?" Even more amusing. The lovebirds and him…with the postmistress. Yeah, good idea, all right. Great idea. He and Caroline could barely manage a civil word to each other. "You've got to be kidding. Tell me this is a joke."

"Apparently not." The cool voice came from the back door.

Grady's blood turned cold. Caroline Daniels and Maggie stood just inside the kitchen, and a single glance told him she'd seen his whole performance, heard every derogatory word.

Two

The boxes awaited Ellie as she unlocked her front door and stepped inside the small rented house. Stacked against the far living-room wall, they represented what felt like an insurmountable task. She paused, her eyes drawn to the piled-up cartons. If she was smart, she'd move them out of sight and deal with the emotional nightmare of sorting through her father's things when she was better able to handle it.

But she wouldn't put this off. Again she was her father's daughter, and he'd taught her never to procrastinate. The thought of those boxes would hound her until she'd gone through every last one of them.

A number of delaying tactics occurred to her. There were letters to write, phone calls to make, people to thank; nevertheless, she recognized them for the excuses they were. The remains of her father's life would still be there, demanding her attention. Occupying her mind.

It would be easy to focus her anger on her mother, but Ellie was mature enough to recognize and accept that Pam Frasier had been pampered all her life. She'd been indulged and shielded from all unpleasantness from the time she was a child. First by her family and then by her husband. John Frasier had treated his wife like a delicate Southern blossom and protected her like the gentle knight he was.

His lengthy illness had taken a toll on Ellie's mother. To her credit Pam had done the best she could, sitting by his side for long periods at the hospital. But unfortunately she had required almost as much care and attention as her husband; she had trouble dealing with any form of illness and was horrified by the thought of death. And so, comforting John had mostly fallen to Ellie.

Dealing with John's effects, coping with the memories, was just one more obligation her mother couldn't manage. Heaving a sigh, Ellie rolled up her sleeves and tackled the first box.

Clothes. Work clothes the movers had packed. Ellie lovingly ran her hand over his favorite sweater, the elbows patched with leather. Pam had wanted him to throw it out—too old and shabby, she'd said. It astonished Ellie that her parents had ever married, as different as they were. They'd met while her father was in the service, and although no one had said as much, Ellie was convinced her mother had fallen in love with the uniform. Their courtship was far too short, and all too soon they were married and John was out of the army. He'd returned to Promise with his bride and joined his father at the family feed store. Ellie had been born two years later, after a difficult pregnancy. John had assured his wife he was perfectly content with one child and there was no need for more. Even as a young girl Ellie had realized her father intended to groom her to take over the store. Not once had she thought of doing anything else. She'd majored in business at the University of Texas at Austin, and although she'd dated several young men, she'd never allowed any relationship to grow serious. She couldn't, not when it was understood she'd be returning to Promise and the feed store. After graduation, she'd found a small house to rent a few blocks from her parents and started working with her dad.

Ellie kept the sweater, but rather than unpack the rest of the clothes, she set the box aside, along with the next two, all of which contained items from his closet. The local charities were always in need of good clothes, and it would be an easy matter to drop them off.

When she opened the fourth box, Ellie paused. The old family Bible rested on top of a photo album. Carefully, using both hands, she lifted the fragile book from its cardboard shelter. The Bible had been in her father's family for a hundred-plus years, handed down from one generation to the next. Ellie had known about it; she'd read the names listed in the front for a high-school report years before, but hadn't opened it since. In fact, she wasn't sure where her mother had stored it.

Curious, she sat down on the sofa and set the book on the coffee table. Leaning forward, she opened it. Once again she read the names listed, reacquainting herself with each one, recalling what her father had told her about her ancestors.

Her great-great-grandparents, Jeremiah and Esther Frasier—good Biblical names, Ellie mused—together with their three sons, whose births were also noted, had placed all their worldly possessions in a covered wagon. Then with courage and faith they'd ventured west, risking all for the promise of land in Texas.

Ellie ran her index finger down the names of the three children, pausing over the youngest, Edward Abraham. His birthday was recorded and then the date of his death only five years later. No reason was listed, only a tear-smudged Bible reference. *Matthew 28:46.* Not recognizing it, Ellie flipped the pages until she located the verse. *"My God, my God, why have you forsaken me."*

The agony of Esther's loss seemed to vibrate from the page. With her own heart still fragile from the pain of her father's death, Ellie was keenly aware of this young mother's anguish over the loss of her son. Unable to read more, she closed the Bible and put it aside.

As she did, a single piece of cloth slipped from between the pages and drifted onto the coffee table. Ellie reached for it and frowned. The muslin square had yellowed with age; each side was no bigger than six inches. In the middle of the block was an embroidered bug that resembled a giant grasshopper. The detail was exquisite, each infinitesimally small stitch perfectly positioned. Nevertheless, it was an odd thing to place inside a Bible. What could possibly have been important enough about an embroidered grasshopper to save it all these years, tucked between the pages of a family Bible? But these were questions for another time, another day.

Her stomach growled, and glancing at her watch, Ellie realized it'd been almost six hours since she'd last eaten. She carried the Bible into her bedroom and placed it on her dresser top, then rummaged around her kitchen until she found the ingredients for a tuna salad.

An hour later a half-eaten salad and an empty milk glass on the carpet beside her, Ellie happened upon the box of John Wayne videos. Her father had loved the Duke. In the worst days of his illness, it was the one thing that was sure to calm him. These movies were as much a part of his heritage as the family Bible. She placed them in the cabinet below her television and on impulse inserted one into the VCR.

McLintock! with Maureen O'Hara was one of Ellie's favorites. Soon she found herself involved in the movie, the boxes forgotten. She didn't have to unpack *every* box that night, she decided.

With the lights dimmed she sat cross-legged on the sofa, watching the television screen. This particular John Wayne classic had been a favorite of her father's, as well. Only a few months earlier, he'd suggested that when Ellie decided to look for a husband, she wouldn't go wrong if she found a man like the kind John Wayne usually portrayed.

Where the tears came from, Ellie didn't know. One moment she was laughing at the very place she laughed every time she saw the movie, and the next her cheeks were wet with tears.

Chastising herself for being too sentimental, she dried her eyes with a napkin. A minute later, the tears started again. Soon they flowed with such vigor she required a box of tissues.

It didn't take Ellie long to realize that the movie had triggered the release she'd needed all these weeks. Stopping the flow of tears was impossible, so she gave up trying, sobbing openly now. With a tissue pressed to each eye, she sniffed, then paused, holding her breath, thinking she'd heard a noise unrelated to the movie.

The sound was repeated and Ellie groaned.

The doorbell.

She yearned to ignore it, but anyone who knew her would recognize her car parked out front.

With a reluctant sigh, she walked slowly toward the door. She glanced through the peephole, but whoever was there had moved out of her range of vision.

"Who's there?" she demanded.

"The big bad wolf."

Glen.

"Damn," she muttered under her breath, frantically rubbing at the tears on her face. "Go away," she called out. "I'm not decent." Which wasn't far from the truth. He was her friend and a good one but she didn't want him or anyone else to see her like this.

"Come on, Ellie, open up."

"Not by the hair of your chinny, chin, chin," she called back.

"Then I'll huff and I'll puff and I'll blow your house down."

She hesitated, unsure what to do.

"Ellie, for heaven's sake, grab a towel or whatever and let me in."

He twisted the knob and she realized he was going to enter with or without her permission. This was what she got for not keeping her front door locked, but it was a habit she'd never developed. No need to in a town like Promise.

"Come on in," she said, finally opening the door.

"You're dressed," he said with some surprise. "I

thought you said—" Apparently he noticed her tear-blotched face because he stopped short.

She squared her shoulders, not knowing what he'd do or say. They'd laughed together, disagreed, teased and joked, but she'd never allowed Glen or anyone else to see her cry.

His hand rested gently on her shoulder. "I thought as much," he whispered.

It would have been better if he'd made a joke of it, Ellie mused. She might have been able to laugh off her embarrassment if he had.

"It's the movie," she said, pointing to the television set behind her. "I...started watching it and..." To her utter humiliation, the tears came back in force.

"Ellie?"

She turned her back to him. "I'm not fit company just now," she managed to whisper.

"Do you want me to leave?" he asked from behind.

Did she? Ellie didn't know. Wrapping her arms around her middle, she couldn't remember a time she'd felt more alone. Her beloved father was gone and her mother had all but abandoned her. It wasn't supposed to happen like this. Her father had been everything to her.

"Ellie?" Glen questioned again.

"You'd better go."

A long moment passed. Anyone else would have left by now, but Glen hesitated as though he couldn't make himself do it. That was when Ellie knew she wanted him to stay.

"Would...would you mind sticking around for a while?" she choked out.

"Of course." With his arm loosely about her shoulders, he steered her back to the sofa. "Sit here and I'll get you something to drink."

She nodded, grateful once again that Glen Patterson was her friend. A good stiff drink was exactly what she needed. Something strong enough to dull the pain.

Within a couple of minutes Glen returned with a tall glass. Ice clinked against the sides when he handed it to her.

She appreciated his tact and understanding and accepted the glass. Tentatively tasting the drink, she tried to remember what she had stored in the liquor cabinet above the refrigerator. Vodka? Gin?

Almost immediately she started to cough and choke.

Glen slapped her hard on the back.

She needed a moment to catch her breath. When she did she glared at him with narrowed eyes. "You brought me *ice water?*" she cried. The man had no sense of what she was suffering. None whatsoever, or he'd realize that a time like this required liquor.

"What's wrong with water?" he asked with a look of such genuine innocence that Ellie knew it would do no good to explain.

She dismissed his question with a wave of her hand and gestured for him to sit down.

Glen claimed the empty space next to her on the sofa. "Do you want to talk about it?" he asked.

"No," she said and for emphasis shook her head. "Just watch the movie."

"All right." He leaned back and stretched his arms along the back of the couch. With one foot resting on the other knee, he seemed perfectly at ease.

Ellie did her best to focus on the movie, but it was

pointless. So was any attempt to hold back the tears that pooled in her eyes, then leaked from the corners, making wet tracks down the sides of her face. At first she tried to blink them away. That didn't help. Neither did holding her breath or staring up at the ceiling. She drank the glass of water, and when she could disguise the need no longer, made a frantic grab for the box of tissue.

"I thought as much," Glen said for the second time. He placed his arm around her shoulders and pulled her against him. "It isn't the movie, is it?"

"What makes you ask that?" she sobbed.

"Because I know you."

Men always assumed they knew a woman when they didn't have a clue. And Glen Patterson was as clueless as any man she'd ever known, friend or not.

"As I said earlier, I'm not very good company at the moment." She blotted her eyes with a fresh tissue. In an effort to distract her thoughts, she showed him the old Bible with the names of family who'd lived and died over a hundred years ago. When she talked about Edward Abraham's death, the tears began again.

"Hey, if I'd been looking for scintillating company, I would've stayed home with Cal," Glen said, then laughed at his little joke.

They both knew Cal was about as much fun as a rampaging bull these days.

"Come on," he urged with real tenderness. "Let it all out."

She swallowed a sob. It would have been better, she thought now, if he hadn't stayed, after all. But it felt good to lean on someone. So good. Ellie feared that once she lowered her guard and gave way to her emotions, it would be like a river overflowing its banks. All semblance of control would vanish. As close a friend as Glen was, she preferred to shed her tears alone.

"Relax," he instructed, sounding like the older brother she'd never had. He squeezed her shoulder and rested his chin against her hair. "It's okay to cry. You have the right."

"I couldn't make myself believe it," she sobbed into his chest. The doctors had explained soon after he was diagnosed that his condition was terminal. No hope.

"Believe what?" Glen asked softly.

"That he was dying. I should have been prepared for it, but I wasn't."

"He was your father, Ellie. How could you prepare to lose your father? How could anyone?"

"I—I don't know." Her whole body shook; she couldn't control the tremors.

"Quit being so hard on yourself, okay?"

"I wanted to celebrate his life," she added. "Not... not act like this." She felt as though she were walking around with a giant hole inside her. Grief overwhelmed her. She missed him in a thousand different ways. Every minute, every hour, she found reasons to think of him. Everything she said and did reminded her of how close they'd always been. She couldn't walk into the store without confronting evidence of him—his work, his personality, his plans for the future. If that wasn't bad enough, every time she looked in the mirror it was his deep blue eyes that stared back.

"You *are* celebrating his life," Glen murmured, and his lips brushed the top of her head.

"I am?" Easing herself from his embrace, she raised her face to look up at him.

"You were the apple of your father's eye," Glen reminded her. "He couldn't keep the buttons of his shirt fastened, he was so proud of you."

While Ellie knew that was true, it felt good to hear Glen say it. "He was a wonderful father." She bit her lower lip to keep it from trembling.

"The best." Glen gazed down at her and with his thumb caught a tear as it rolled from her bottom lashes and onto her cheek.

He paused with his finger halfway across her face and when her vision cleared, Ellie noted Glen's look of surprise. Their eyes met, widened. They couldn't seem to stop gazing at each other's faces. Ellie suddenly felt herself frowning, but before she had a chance to analyze what was happening, she realized something else.

Glen was going to kiss her.

She could have moved, avoided his kiss and the embarrassment that was sure to follow, but curiosity got the better of her. As his mouth slowly lowered toward hers, her eyes drifted shut. She half expected him to draw back at the last second, but he didn't—and she was glad.

His lips were moist and warm as they settled gently on hers. The gentleness lasted only a moment, and then he thrust his fingers into her short hair and increased the pressure of his mouth. Ellie felt the heat in him, the unaccustomed desire. And she felt his tension. She understood it because she was feeling the same thing. A sense of discomfort, even guilt. This was Glen, her friend. And they were kissing like lovers, like a couple well beyond the range of friendship.

Ellie slipped her hands up his chest and anchored her fingers at his shoulders. The kiss took on another dimension. The hunger that had been held in check was replaced by heady excitement. Ellie opened to Glen without restraint, reserving nothing. He deepened the kiss until they both trembled. When he abruptly broke it off, his breathing was heavy and labored. So was hers.

Slowly Ellie opened her eyes. Glen was staring at her, his forehead creased in a deep frown.

"What was that?" she asked, her voice barely above a whisper.

"A kiss," he said, sounding almost angry.

"I know that. What I'm asking is…why?"

"Why?" he repeated, sounding as uncertain as she was. "Because…because you were crying."

"So?"

"It was shock therapy," he said, easing himself away from her, gently at first and then as if he couldn't move fast enough. He scooted unceremoniously to the side of the sofa.

Not knowing what to think, much less say, she blinked.

"It worked," he said as if this entire incident had been carefully planned. "You're not crying, are you?"

Ellie raised her fingertips to her face. He was right.

"I had to do *something*," he said, sounding more like himself now—confident, amused, down-to-earth.

"Something," she repeated, trying not to press her fingers against her slightly swollen lips.

"Anything," he added. "I was getting desperate. You feel better, don't you?"

She had to consider that for a moment. But it was true.

"Hey, I didn't mean…" He hesitated as if not sure how to continue.

Ellie wasn't sure she wanted him to. "Me neither," she told him quickly, far more comfortable dropping the matter than exploring it further. Glen was a damn good friend and she didn't want one stupid kiss to ruin this friendship.

He relaxed visibly. "Good."

She smiled and nodded. "I gotta admit, though," she said, eagerly falling back on the comfortable banter they'd always enjoyed, "you're one fine kisser."

"Damn fine," he agreed and puffed out his chest in a parody of male pride. "You aren't the first one to tell me that."

Ellie rolled her eyes toward the ceiling.

"You aren't so bad yourself."

"Don't I know it." Standing, she hooked her thumbs in the belt loops of her jeans and rocked on her heels. "Plenty of other guys have told me I'm hot stuff."

"I can see why."

They laughed then, both of them, but Ellie noticed that their laughter had a decidedly shaky sound to it.

"Shaky" pretty well described how Glen felt. An hour later he pulled into the long driveway that led from the highway to the Lonesome Coyote Ranch. He trembled every time he thought about kissing Ellie.

Fool that he was, he'd given in to a crazy impulse and damn near made the biggest mistake of his life.

Glen blamed Cal for this. His brother was the one who'd planted the idea, claiming Glen's relationship with Ellie was far more than friendship. Cal had just said it a few too many times and hell—Glen shook his head—one minute he was looking down at Ellie and the next thing he knew they were kissing. What scared the living daylights out of him was how incredibly good the kiss had been. It wasn't *supposed* to be that good, but it had shot straight off the Richter scale.

Oh, yeah, Ellie had shaken him up plenty.

Thank goodness he'd been able to make light of the incident, brush it off. Ellie had seemed just as eager to put it behind them. For the first time in years he'd been uncomfortable with his best friend. With Ellie. All because of an impulsive kiss, something that never should've happened.

He parked the truck and sat in the stillness of the night to gather his wits about him. He recalled how the kiss had ended and she'd looked up at him, her striking blue eyes wide with shock. Damn if it hadn't taken every ounce of willpower he possessed not to kiss her again.

Thank God he hadn't. Gratitude welled up inside him. Had they continued much longer they would've ruined everything. Knowing he was being less than subtle about it, he'd gotten the hell out of that house. Again Ellie had obviously felt relieved to be rid of him. With any luck they'd both forget the entire incident. For his part he never intended to mention it again, and he sincerely hoped Ellie didn't, either.

Once he felt sufficiently calm, he climbed out of the truck and walked into the house. Cal sat in the kitchen with ledgers spread out across the table. He glanced up when Glen entered the room and did a double take.

"You okay?'

"Why shouldn't I be?" Glen demanded sharply.

"No need to bite my head off," his brother snapped back. "What happened? You have a spat with Ellie?"

"No."

"I see." Cal returned, not bothering to suppress a smile.

"I'm going to bed," Glen announced.

"Good idea," Cal called after him. "Sleep might improve your disposition."

Glen stomped up the stairs and was breathless by the time he entered his bedroom. He closed the door and sagged onto the edge of the mattress. With his elbows resting on his knees, he inhaled deeply several times. No wonder he was shaking. He'd had a narrow escape.

The night was alive with sound. The intoxicating aroma of old roses filled the air. Katydids chirped and the porch swing creaked as Savannah and Laredo swayed back and forth, back and forth. The stars were generous with their glittering bounty that night. It all said *romance,* the romance of song and story, and it suited Savannah's mood perfectly.

She leaned her head against Laredo's shoulder and his arm held her close. Even now, resting in her husband's strong embrace, she found it difficult to believe this wonderful man loved her.

"What's on your mind?" he whispered.

Savannah's lips eased into a ready smile. "I was just thinking how fortunate I am that you love me."

Laredo went still, and she knew his thoughts; he didn't need to voice them. It was that way sometimes when people were deeply in love. Their marriage was like a miracle, an unexpected gift—and it had come when they were least prepared for it. Because of that, they'd come close to losing it all.

"I loved you when I left you," Laredo said, his voice hoarse with the intensity of his feelings. "I worry sometimes that you don't know how difficult it was to walk away from you."

"I did know, and that's what made it so hard," she confided. She would never fully comprehend it, but Laredo had believed that she deserved someone who could give her more than he could. It was one of life's cruel ironies—without him, money, land and possessions meant very little. But with his love she was rich beyond measure. It was the most precious thing she'd ever had.

The kitchen door creaked open and Savannah's older brother stepped onto the porch. She wasn't too pleased with Grady's poor timing, but decided to overlook it. Not for the first time, either. Look what he'd done just the other day, when he'd made those comments about Caroline at the worst possible moment.

Grady walked to the porch steps and stared into the night sky. "I decided to attend the birthday bash for Ruth," he said without glancing in their direction.

Savannah heard the reluctance in his voice and realized the decision hadn't been an easy one.

"With Caroline?" she asked, trying not to sound eager.

He hesitated before answering. "I thought about asking her, then decided against it."

Savannah knew that if he let himself Grady would enjoy Caroline's company. Unfortunately he bungled all her efforts at playing matchmaker. What she'd hoped was that he'd become comfortable enough with

Caroline at the birthday party to invite her to the Cattlemen's Association Dance later in the month. The dance marked the beginning of summer and was the most anticipated event of the year.

"Why *don't* you ask Caroline?" She was losing patience with him.

"Because I didn't think she'd want to after the way... Hell, you should know the answer to that. I made a fool of myself."

"Caroline was more amused than angry," Savannah assured her brother.

"Yeah, well, that's not how I saw it. I thought I'd invite someone else."

"Like who?"

"I don't know..."

"How about the new doctor?" Savannah suggested. Dr. Jane Dickinson had replaced Doc Cummings at the Health Clinic when he retired. She'd read in the local newspaper that Dr. Dickinson had agreed to stay on for three years as a means of repaying her medical-school loans. If Grady wasn't going to ask Caroline, then this new doctor was a good choice.

"No, thanks."

"What's wrong with *her*?"

"Nothing...everything." Grady didn't elaborate.

The problem with her brother, Savannah realized, was a complete lack of confidence in himself when it came to women. Grady failed to recognize his own masculine appeal. His *considerable* appeal. She suspected that Richard's presence made it worse. Richard was handsome and sociable, a smooth talker who had no difficulty attracting female companionship. Grady, on the other hand, was awkward around women and constantly seemed to say the wrong thing.

Savannah edged closer to her husband. "Um, Grady, I don't think it's a good idea to wait until the last minute."

"You don't?"

Both Savannah and Laredo shook their heads.

Grady rubbed the back of his neck. "The hell with it," he muttered. "Nell didn't say anything about bringing a date. If Cal shows up you can bet he'll be without a woman. Nothing says I need one, either."

Savannah resisted the urge to box his ears. "Do you intend to live the rest of your life alone, Grady?"

Her brother didn't answer her for a moment. "I don't know anymore. It just seems to be the way things are headed." With that, he went back inside.

"I almost feel sorry for him," Laredo said.

"It's his own fault," Savannah didn't mean to sound unkind, but her brother was too stubborn for his own good. "If he'd open his eyes, he'd realize Caroline's perfect for him."

"You can't push him into a relationship with your friend, love."

Savannah realized that. "But…"

"It'll happen for Grady when the time is right."

"How can you be so sure?"

"It did with us."

Sighing, Savannah dropped her head against his shoulder once again. This was her favorite time of day, sitting in the moonlight with Laredo, feeling his love enclose her.

They kissed then, and the sweetness of it was enough to bring tears to Savannah's eyes. She savored the contentment of being in his arms, wishing every-one could experience this kind of love. Grady and the embittered Cal Patterson and Caroline and…

"Ellie Frasier needs someone, too," she said wist-fully.

"Are you the resident matchmaker now?" Laredo teased.

"Yes—even if it *is* self-appointed." She nudged him with her elbow. "Now—a man for Ellie."

"Not Richard."

"Not Richard," Savannah agreed. "Glen Patterson."

Laredo laughed lightly. "You're way off base with that one, Savannah. I can't see it. They make much better friends than they ever would lovers."

The evening was much too fine to argue. She didn't need Laredo to agree with her to know she was right.

Three

Nell Bishop flipped the braid off her shoulder and surveyed the yard. Everything was ready for Ruth's surprise party. The Moorhouse sisters, both retired schoolteachers, were keeping her mother-in-law occupied in town. Knowing Edwina and Lily, they'd take their assignment seriously. The last Nell heard, they'd planned a visit to the library, followed by a little birthday celebration at Dovie Boyd's antique shop. Dovie had recently added the Victorian Tea Room, and each afternoon at three, she served tea and scones. Sometimes she added cucumber sandwiches and a small glass—or two—of the Moorhouse sisters' special cordial, which she made from a recipe handed down by their maternal grandfather.

Nell gathered that the sandwiches tended to be dry but the cordial was well worth the price of admission. The Moorhouse sisters would bring her back at the start of the festivities. All three would probably be a little tipsy and in a fine party mood.

It was time the Bishop family did a bit of celebrating. Jake wouldn't have wanted them to spend the rest of their lives grieving. Things had been difficult for Nell since her husband's death, but with Ruth's help she'd managed to hold on to the ranch.

"Mom, where do you want me to put the potato chips?" Jeremy called from the back porch steps. Her eleven-year-old son stood with a huge bowl in his hands, awaiting her instructions.

"Set it on the first picnic table," she answered, pointing at the line of five covered tables that stretched across the freshly groomed yard. She'd spent half the day spiffing up the flower beds and mowing the grass and the other half cooking. Fried chicken, her special recipe for chili, a smorgasbord of salads, plus a huge homemade birthday cake.

Jeremy carried the bowl to the table, then promptly helped himself to a handful. Nell bit her tongue to keep from admonishing him not to spoil his dinner. This was a celebration and she wasn't going to ruin it by scolding her children. Both Jeremy and nine-year-old Emma had been helpful and cooperative, as excited about the party as she was herself.

Jeremy's hand stopped midway to his mouth and he cast a guilty look at his mother.

"All I ask is that you save some for the guests."

He nodded, smiling hugely. "We got plenty."

How like Jake her son was. She couldn't look at him and not be reminded of the only man she'd ever loved. They'd grown up together, she and Jake, and Nell knew from the time she'd first started thinking about boys that one day she'd marry Jake Bishop. It had taken him several years to reach the same conclusion, but men were often slower when it came to figuring out these things.

Both Nell and Jake were tall and big-boned. Nell was nearly six feet by the time she stopped growing. She had the kind of looks that were usually described as handsome, not pretty. And certainly not cute. The only man she'd ever known who hadn't been intimidated by her size—or treated her like one of the boys—had been Jake, and that was because he was six feet four inches himself.

Jake had taught her the wonders of being feminine. They'd had almost ten years together, and she'd treasured every one of them. Some folks expected her to remarry, but she'd yet to meet the man who could match the husband she'd lost. Nell wasn't willing to accept second best, not after loving Jake.

For the first year after Jake's death in a tractor accident she'd felt cheated and angry. It had taken her another year to accept his death and to reshape her life now that her husband was gone. With his mother's love and support she'd been able to keep the ranch, raise her kids, plan for the future.

She was a good cook, an able manager, and thanks to Jake, knew a great deal about ranching. More than she'd ever wanted to learn, in fact. The time had come to put all that knowledge to good use.

The party was to serve a dual purpose. To celebrate Ruth's birthday of course. And also to announce that she was opening her doors and turning Twin Canyons into a dude ranch. By the end of next year she hoped to be giving a group of greenhorns a taste of the real Texas.

Her research had shown that the cowboy era was alive and well in the minds of adventurous Americans. The travel agents she'd spoken with had assured her they could fill the bunkhouse with tourists eager to spend their vacation dollars learning about life in the Old West.

And Nell was just the one to teach them. She'd feed them her chili, get them on the back of a horse and demonstrate how to herd a few head of cattle. Take them on a trail drive—like in the movie *City Slickers*. And after all that, she'd gladly accept their credit cards.

"Mom!" Emma called, her freckled face smeared with frosting from the birthday cake. "Should I put the candles in now?"

"Not yet."

"Hey!" Jeremy hollered. "*I* was supposed to lick the beaters!" He grabbed a fresh supply of potato chips, apparently to compensate for the frosting he'd missed.

"Wash your face," Nell instructed her daughter. "I need your help out here."

"Yeah," Jeremy said with an air of superiority. "Help Mom."

"I am," Emma insisted. "I tasted the frosting to make sure it was good."

Despite herself, Nell laughed. "Come on, you two. The party's going to start soon and I want all the food on the tables, ready for the buffet." She headed for the house to collect paper plates and napkins.

"Will Grandma be surprised?" Emma asked.

Nell knew how hard it had been for her daughter to keep the birthday party a secret. "Very," she promised. "And Grandma's going to have a wonderful time. We all are."

She was sure of it.

* * *

The birthday party was already in full swing when Ellie and Richard arrived. People clustered about the yard, talking in small groups. There was an air of joy and festivity that Ellie found infectious. Party sounds—laughter, animated conversation and music— were everywhere. Ellie began to hope she might actually enjoy herself the way she used to.

She glanced around and realized she was looking for Glen. Although she'd agreed to attend the party with Richard Weston, she wished now that she'd turned him down.

She hadn't seen Glen in three days. Not since he'd kissed her. Hadn't heard from him, either. While it wasn't unusual for them to go a week or longer without talking to each other, for some reason this three-day stretch felt more like three months.

She had no intention of mentioning the kiss, but that didn't mean she hadn't been thinking about it. As a matter of fact, she'd thought of little else, and she wondered if the incident weighed as heavily on Glen's mind as it did hers.

Probably not.

"I should have brought my guitar," Richard said, pressing his hand against her back as he steered her into the yard.

Richard had a fairly good singing voice and he'd entertained a crowd at his welcome-home party a few months earlier. He seemed quite impressed with his musical talent— excessively so, in Ellie's opinion. Although his voice was pleasant, it would assure him a position in the church choir but nowhere else.

"Did I tell you how beautiful you look this evening?" he asked.

"Twice," she murmured. One thing about Richard, he was a charmer. His remarks were nice to hear, but she didn't take them seriously.

"I'm pleased to see you're keeping track of how often I say it," he muttered with a tinge of sarcasm.

Ellie gave him a sharp look. She was well aware of the kind of man Richard Weston was. She'd seen him in action and had to admire his skill. He issued his compliments with just enough wonder in his voice to sound sincere. Some women might believe him, but she wouldn't allow herself to be deluded. She also suspected that Richard didn't like her perceptiveness.

Ellie was delighted to see that Nell had gotten the big turnout she'd wanted. No one ever came right out and said it, but the town was proud of Nell Bishop. They were attending this party as much for her as for Ruth. Folks wanted Nell to know they respected the way she'd managed to keep the ranch in operation. The way she'd stood against popular opinion and refused to sell. At the first sign of financial difficulty, a lot of well-meaning friends had suggested she get rid of the ranch. Ellie wasn't sure she would have advised otherwise, but Nell had insisted on keeping the small spread. It had been her husband's heritage; now it was her children's. More than that, Ellie realized, the ranch was part of Jake, and Nell had deeply loved her husband.

"Help yourself to a plate," Richard urged as they neared the picnic tables. Ellie surveyed the wide assortment of hot dishes and salads. From the look of it, Nell had cooked everything herself.

A card table was stacked with brightly wrapped birthday presents, and Ellie added hers to the pile. Busy seeing to some other guests, Nell waved a hand in greeting and Ellie waved back. Ruth sat in the seat of honor, a rocking chair, with her friends circled around her. The older woman, who was normally quiet and reserved, appeared to relish being the center of attention. Jeremy and Emma raced about the yard with several other children in hot pursuit.

"You ready to eat?" Richard asked, sounding as if it'd been at least a year since he'd last sat down to a decent meal.

"Sure." Ellie reached for a paper plate and suddenly, out of the corner of her eye, caught sight of Glen. She turned slightly and noticed that he sat under the shade of an oak tree chatting with Grady Weston. He seemed to see her at the same time, and their eyes locked and held for an embarrassingly long moment. Any other time she would've waved and gestured for him to save her a place. But not now. Instead, she pretended she hadn't seen him and proceeded down the buffet line.

Apparently Richard was aware of the moment and staked his claim by sliding his arm about her waist and nuzzling her neck. Ellie didn't dare look in Glen's direction for fear of what he'd think.

"Richard," she murmured under her breath. "Stop it."

"Stop what?" he asked. "I can't help it if I find you irresistible."

"Yeah, right." What he found her, Ellie surmised, was a trophy. The victor's spoils, to wave beneath Glen's nose. Although close in age, Richard and Glen had never been friendly, and while they weren't openly hostile to each other, there was no love lost, either.

Ellie filled her plate and tried to ignore Richard as he added a spoonful of this and that, insisting she sample every dish. Considering all the attention he paid her, anyone might have assumed they were a longtime couple. All this solicitude embarrassed her.

"Would you kindly stop?" she said, and despite her displeasure she laughed at the woebegone look he wore.

"I can't help myself," he said. "You're the most beautiful woman here." Ellie just shook her head.

They found an empty space on the grass, shaded by the house. The scent of freshly mowed lawn and a row of blooming roses mingled with the sights and sounds of the party.

Far more aware of Glen than she wanted to be, Ellie talked nervously, telling Richard about her week. He didn't pay much attention until she mentioned the old family Bible she'd found among her father's things.

"How old did you say it was?"

"More than a hundred years," Ellie answered. Although there were a number of dates entered in the Bible, she wasn't sure when it had first been purchased.

"Your ancestors were part of the original group that settled in Bitter End?"

"From what I understand they were."

"Have you ever been there?" Richard surprised her by asking next.

The question was ridiculous. No one had, no one she knew, anyway. Bitter End was a mysterious almost mythical town people whispered about. Its location remained a secret, and despite her childhood curiosity, her father had told her very little. But as far as she could figure, there simply wasn't that much to tell. The town had been settled shortly after the Civil War and for unknown reasons was later abandoned. A scattering of the original settlers—Ellie's ancestors among them—then founded Promise.

Richard's eyes darted around as if to gauge whether anyone was listening in on their conversation. "I've been to Bitter End," he whispered dramatically. "Not that long ago, either."

"Get out of here!" It was all a joke and she wasn't going to fall for it. If she did, he'd laugh at her for believing him, and she didn't want to be the brunt of his teasing remarks.

His eyes narrowed and he bent toward her. "I'm serious, Ellie."

If Bitter End was anywhere in the vicinity, people would be flocking to it—ghost towns were fascinating, this one particularly so because of the mystery surrounding the original settlers' departure.

"Have you noticed that people don't talk about it much?" he asked, lowering his voice again. He made it sound as though the residents of Promise had conspired to keep the town a secret—to which *he* held the key.

Ellie frowned, unwilling to play his nonsensical game.

"It isn't called a ghost town for nothing." Richard shivered as if a sudden chill had raced up his spine.

"Richard," she snapped, "if this is a joke, I'm not amused."

His expression was earnest as he shook his head. "I swear to you on my parents' grave I'm serious."

"You've seen Bitter End yourself?" Even now she wasn't sure she should believe him.

"Yes," he insisted. "So have others."

"Who?" She didn't know anyone who'd been to the ghost town, and she'd spent her entire life in Promise.

"Glen Patterson for one."

Now she *knew* he was joking. Glen was her best friend, and he would certainly have mentioned this if it was true.

Richard must have read the doubt in her eyes because he added, "He found it, along with my brother and Cal, when he was a kid. If you don't believe me, ask him yourself."

Ellie intended on doing exactly that.

"When were you last there?" she asked, still feeling suspicious.

"Recently."

"How recently?"

"This week."

Ellie's curiosity went into overdrive. "You'd better not be razzing me, Richard."

"I swear it's the truth."

"Will you take me there?"

He hesitated.

"Richard, you can't tell me about Bitter End and then refuse to show it to me! What's it like? Where is it? Are any of the old buildings still standing? And how in heaven's name did you find it?"

Chuckling, he held up his hand to stop her. "Whoa! One question at a time."

"All right," she said, her heart pounding with excitement. She wanted to see this place. Her father's great-grandparents had settled there. It was in Bitter End that they'd buried their five-year-old son, the child whose name was in the old Bible.

"How'd you ever find it?" she asked again.

"It wasn't easy," he said, licking his fingertips and seeming to savor her attention as much as he did Nell's fried chicken. "I knew it was real because I'd heard... the others talked about it years ago—and I found it."

"Why wouldn't they tell you?"

"For the same reason I'm not telling you."

"Oh, no, you don't!" She wasn't going to let him pull that on her.

"Ellie," he murmured, his gaze pinning hers, "it's haunted."

"'I ain't afraid of no ghosts,'" she teased, quoting the popular movie *Ghostbusters.*

Always quick with a laugh or a smile, Richard revealed neither. "I'm not joking."

"I'm not, either. I want you to take me there."

He shook his head, obviously regretting that he'd ever brought up the subject. "That's not a good idea."

"Then I'll have Glen take me."

Richard's face hardened. "It's dangerous there, Ellie. Anything can happen. I wouldn't feel right about taking you to someplace like Bitter End."

"I don't care. I want to see it. Just once," she pleaded.

Again he hesitated.

"Please?" she asked softly.

Richard sighed, and Ellie's gaze drifted to Glen, partly because she was curious about what he was doing, but also as a subtle message. If Richard wouldn't take her, odds were she could convince Glen to.

"All right, all right," he muttered irritably.

"When?"

"Soon."

"Tomorrow?"

Richard looked decidedly uncomfortable. "I... I don't know."

"We'll make a day of it," she coaxed, eager to explore the old town. Besides, Richard might change his mind if she didn't act quickly.

"You can't tell *anyone*."

"Why not?"

"Ellie, you don't seem to understand how serious this is. It was a mistake to mention it in the first place."

"Okay," she said, knowing that if she didn't agree he'd never take her there. "I won't tell anyone else."

"I want your word of honor," Richard insisted. "I'm not kidding, Ellie. The place is dangerous, and I don't want some fool kid to break his neck because you let word out. The minute kids around here know about it, you can bet someone's going to get hurt. I don't want that on my conscience."

Ellie didn't want it on hers, either. "You have my word, Richard."

He nodded, apparently accepting her promise. "I'll take you tomorrow afternoon, then. Be ready by two."

Despite his best intentions, Glen couldn't keep his eyes off Ellie and Richard. They sat huddled together, their heads close, deep in conversation. He would've sworn Ellie was too smart to be taken in by a charlatan like Richard Weston. Okay, so maybe Richard was on the level—Glen didn't really know, for Grady was as reluctant to talk about his brother as he was about everything else.

"Looks like Ellie and Richard might have more in common than I realized," Glen muttered. He noted the concerned expression on Grady's face.

"I'd say she's pretty vulnerable right now," Grady commented. He seemed to be asking Glen to keep an eye on Ellie. "Someone needs to watch out for her."

Glen's own concerns mounted. He didn't like the way those two were gazing at each other—as though nobody else was around. In fact, it bothered him. *Really* bothered him.

"How good a friend are you?" Grady asked.

"Good." Good enough for him to kiss her, Glen mused. Not just any kiss, either. But one that had damn near knocked his socks off. He'd thought of little else for three days and three sleepless nights. Every time he closed his eyes she was there in his mind, and damn it all, he found himself wanting to kiss her again.

He worried that he'd ruined their friendship, and from her reaction when she arrived at the party, that looked all too likely. As for the way things were developing between her and Richard—well, he didn't trust Grady's younger brother, not one bit. The guy was too glib, too smooth. And that was only the half of it.

Glen had heard from Cal how Grady got stuck with the bill for Richard's welcome-home party. It was all a misunderstanding, Richard claimed, but Glen would bet his last dollar Grady'd never see that money again.

Some time later, when the opportunity presented itself, Glen made his way over to Ellie. Richard was preoccupied singing a jazzed-up version of "Happy

Birthday" to Ruth. Glen never did trust a man who craved being the center of attention. Anyone else would have asked Ruth to stand up, would have made *her* the focus. Not Richard. He had everyone gather around him, and it seemed to Glen he treated Ruth's birthday like an afterthought, like a mere pretext for his own performance. Typical. Richard sure hadn't changed.

"Nice party," he said, strolling casually to Ellie's side.

She stood at the edge of the group and Glen was grateful she hadn't taken a front-row seat to Richard's antics. Grady's brother had plenty of other admirers at the moment and seemed to have forgotten his date. Glen, however, resisted pointing this out to Ellie. "Good news about Nell and her dude ranch," he said, instead.

"Sure is," Ellie responded. "I really think she can make it work."

"Yeah. Nell can do it if anyone can."

Ellie nodded. "I haven't seen you in a few days."

"I've been busy."

"Me, too."

"I noticed," he said, thinking about the way she'd cozied up to Richard.

Ellie laughed. "You sound jealous."

"Not me." He raised both hands in a dismissive gesture, then realized she was making an effort to put their relationship back on its previous footing. "But I could be," he said, falling into the easy banter they'd so often exchanged.

"I'm glad to hear it." Her smile was like a splash of sunshine, and Glen felt a rush of relief. She was as determined as he was to forget that stupid kiss. "You're a good friend, Ellie."

"Not as good as I'd hoped."

His heart went still. "What do you mean?"

"You didn't tell me about Bitter End," she accused him, turning to meet his eyes.

"What?" He hadn't been to the ghost town since he was a teenager, and once was enough. There was something dangerous about that place—and he wasn't thinking about the abandoned wells, either.

"Who told you?" he demanded, although the answer was obvious.

"Richard."

"Listen, Ellie," he said, gripping her elbow. He longed to take her by the shoulders and shake some sense into her, but he knew she wouldn't listen and he'd hurt his cause more than help it. "I'd forget about Bitter End if I were you."

"Why should I? This is the most exciting thing I've heard in ages. My father's great-grandparents belonged to the first group of settlers, you know." She paused and studied him. "Glen, what's so bad about this town? Why doesn't anyone talk about it? If you know where it is and other people do, too, why is it a deep dark secret?"

Glen wasn't sure how to explain it to her, especially since he didn't fully understand it himself. All he could remember was the eerie sense of danger and oppressiveness he'd experienced the one and only time he'd been there. He couldn't have been more than fourteen at the time. Cal, Grady and he had inadvertently overheard their parents discussing the old town and decided to locate it on their own. It'd taken them weeks to find it, but instead of feeling a sense of triumph and elation after their first visit, they'd been terrified. They'd hardly spoken of it since.

"I don't want you going there," he ordered, rather than answer her questions. The second those words left his lips, Glen recognized his mistake. Ellie wasn't going to take kindly to anyone telling her what she could or couldn't do.

"Too late. Richard's driving me there tomorrow afternoon."

"No, he's not." Even knowing he was digging himself in deeper didn't prevent Glen from blurting it out.

"You don't have any right to tell me that."

"Ellie, listen to me—"

"I've heard everything I care to hear. I thought we were friends."

"We are," he said, his mind spinning. He realized that the thought of Ellie in that deserted town frightened him. All his protective instincts snapped into place—instincts he'd never associated with Ellie. "I don't want you going there."

"You're being ridiculous. You found it, and now I want to see it, too. It was okay for you, but not for me? I don't accept that, Glen."

"If you value our friendship, you won't go."

Ellie looked at him as though she'd never seen him before, and once again Glen realized he'd said it all wrong. "If you value my opinion..." he altered hurriedly, but he could see it was already too late.

"I don't think I know you any longer," she whispered. It wasn't her words as much as the way she said them, in a hurt voice that vibrated with doubts.

He'd known it was going to happen, had worried

about it for days. He just hadn't thought it'd be so soon. That kiss really had ruined everything. Every shred of closeness they'd once shared was gone. They seemed incapable of even the most basic communication.

"Fine," he said, furious with himself and taking it out on her. "Go ahead and do as you like. Just don't say I didn't warn you." Having botched the entire conversation, he whirled around and walked away. Ellie would discover everything she needed to know about Bitter End soon enough. But she wouldn't have him standing guard over her when she did.

"You ready?" Richard asked, entering the feed store fifteen minutes past the time they'd agreed to meet.

"As ready as I'll ever be." The argument with Glen weighed heavily on her mind. She'd considered phoning Richard to beg off, but she refused to allow Glen to tell her what to do. She had as much right as anyone else to visit Bitter End.

Richard laughed. "Just remember you're the one who insisted on going." He sang a few bars of the theme song from *Ghostbusters,* and Ellie laughed, too. He certainly seemed to be in high spirits, which helped to reassure her.

Glen, on the other hand, had made it sound as if going to Bitter End meant risking life and limb. While she might have been willing to listen to reason, she'd deeply resented the way he'd spoken to her. He'd given her *orders,* for heaven's sake.

Everything about their short exchange rankled. Ellie felt bad about it herself, wanting their relationship to return to the way it had been before the kiss. She should have stopped him, should have known anything physical between them would lead to problems. The only reason she'd let it happen was that she'd been so upset. Glen had regretted it, too; he'd as much as told her.

Richard helped her into the truck, which Ellie realized was Grady's. His spirits remained high as he drove out of town, down the two-lane highway.

Suddenly he veered off the road into a rocky meadow with cedar shrubs and knee-high weeds.

"So this is the way?"

"No," he said. "I just want you to think it is." The pickup pitched sharply right, one of the front tires slamming against a rock. Ellie was shoved into the door, hitting her shoulder hard. She yelped in pain.

"Sorry," Richard said, slowing the vehicle. "You okay?"

"Fine. What about the truck?" She assumed he was stopping to survey any damage to the wheels, but she was wrong.

He leaned toward her and opened the glove compartment, removing a black handkerchief.

"What's that?" she asked.

"A blindfold."

"A what?" she exploded.

"Blindfold," he repeated calmly. "I thought about this carefully and it's the only way I'll agree to take you to Bitter End."

"You're joking, right?"

"I'm taking you against my better judgment. If Grady ever found out, he'd have my hide."

"Glen wasn't too pleased about it, either."

"You told him?" Richard's eyes flared with anger.

"Yes, we…we exchanged a few words and left it at that."

"Tell him you changed your mind."

Ellie stared at Richard in shock. "You want me to lie?"

"Well, not lie…exactly. Just let him assume you followed his advice. Understand?"

"A lie by omission is still a lie."

"Whatever. Just do it." He held up the blindfold.

"I'm not wearing that."

"Then I'm not taking you to Bitter End." The way he said it made her realize he wasn't kidding. The facade vanished, and she viewed a side of Richard she'd never seen before. A side that wasn't cordial or friendly but dark and rather menacing.

"I have to wear the blindfold?"

He nodded, then his face relaxed into a boyish grin. "Think of it as a game."

"All right." But she didn't like it, and her dislike intensified when he placed the handkerchief around her eyes, tying it securely at the back of her head.

"Can you see anything?"

"No."

"You're sure?"

"Positive." His repeated questions irritated her.

He started the truck again and pulled back onto the highway. He seemed to be driving around in circles. When he finally did leave the road, she was completely confused and had no idea what direction he'd taken. On the rough off-road terrain, the truck bounced and heaved in every direction.

Ellie lost track of time. It might have been fifteen

minutes or an hour, she didn't know. All she knew was that they'd stopped.

"Richard?"

He didn't answer. But she knew immediately that they were close to Bitter End. She *felt* it. A heavy uncomfortable sensation descended on her, a feeling that was completely at odds with the sun's warmth pouring through the windows.

"We're here, aren't we?" she asked.

Silence.

"Richard?"

Silence again.

She heard a soft eerie sound, a creaking that could have been the truck door opening. Or was it something else? Something sinister.

"This is ridiculous," she said and lifted the blindfold from her eyes. Richard wasn't beside her, nor was he visible from where she sat. Squinting into the sunlight, she climbed out of the truck.

The first thing she saw was a faint footpath leading away from the truck. Not knowing what else to do, she followed it, clambering over rocks and forcing her way through the undergrowth. Soon the town came into sight; she could see it clearly from a limestone outcropping just above. She stopped and stared.

Bitter End was surprisingly intact. A number of buildings, some of them stone, some wood, stood along a main street, which was bordered by a plank walk. A church steeple showed in the distance, charred by fire. She saw a hotel and livery stable with a small corral. Even a building that had apparently been a saloon.

She still couldn't see Richard anywhere.

"Richard!" she called again. "Where are you? If this is a joke I'm not laughing."

She half slid, half ran down the incline to the town.

She felt a sudden chill on her bare arms. Although the day was warm and windless, the town was decidedly cold.

"Richard!" she shouted again.

Nothing.

Cautiously she ventured onto the street, but her companion was nowhere to be seen. Panic clawed at her stomach as she spun around. "Richard! For the love of God, where are you?"

Four

Caroline was busy sorting mail when she heard a customer at the front counter. Because the post office was open only two hours on Saturdays, she often did a brisk business then.

Setting aside the stack of letters, she stepped out to the customer-service area. When she recognized Grady Weston, her posture immediately became defensive; she could feel it. Generally Savannah—and now occasionally Richard—collected the mail for the Yellow Rose Ranch. Grady hadn't been into the post office since last May and he'd come only because he was seeking her help. But then, he'd been worried about Savannah's relationship with Laredo Smith. A relationship he'd tried to destroy. He hadn't trusted Laredo, and he hadn't understood Savannah. In fact, Grady had seriously underestimated both of them.

"Morning, Grady," she said warily. The last time she'd seen him, he'd been laughing hysterically at the prospect of attending Ruth's birthday party with her.

"Caroline." He nodded, looking about uncomfortably. He removed his Stetson and held the brim with both hands.

"Can I help you?" she asked.

He blinked as though someone had lifted him off his horse and hurled him straight into the middle of town. He shook his head in a puzzled way, apparently wondering how he happened to be there in the post office, talking to her.

"Do you need stamps?" she asked.

"No." He shifted his weight from left to right. "I, uh, came for another reason."

She waited patiently for him to continue. Grady had never been a smooth talker like his brother, but Caroline suspected his hesitation had something to do with their last unfortunate meeting.

"It's about what I said the other day—or what I said that you heard. What I mean to say…" He snapped his jaw closed and she noticed the color creeping up his neck. "Savannah said you weren't really offended, but I can't help feeling that—"

"Don't worry about it," she said, rather than have him endure this embarrassment any longer. "Let's put it behind us."

He relaxed visibly. "That's kind of you. I didn't mean anything by it."

"I know. Savannah shouldn't play matchmaker— she has no talent for it." Caroline was all too aware that her best friend was in love with love. Savannah wanted Caroline to know the same happiness herself but unfortunately was convinced Grady was the man she'd find it with.

Caroline knew she was at fault, too. She should have discouraged Savannah from the first, but deep down part of her had *wanted* Grady to notice her. She liked Grady, perhaps more than she should, seeing that they couldn't even carry on a conversation without arguing about *something*.

"I wouldn't have minded going to Ruth's party with you. I realize I must have sounded like I'd rather pluck chickens, but that isn't so."

Despite his apology, his attitude tweaked her pride.

"You have to admit it was a crazy idea," he said, holding her gaze. "You and me going out together." He seemed to expect some response from her.

"Let's drop it, all right?" She slapped the mail down on the counter and glared at him, not completely understanding her own anger.

He flinched at the sound. "Now what'd I say?" he demanded.

"Nothing."

"Then why are you looking at me like you're madder than hops?"

Caroline shook her head. "You're the only man I know who can apologize with an insult."

"I insulted you?" His jaw went slack with astonishment.

Caroline drew a deep calming breath and held up her right hand. "Let's just say we'll agree to disagree."

He frowned and twisted the rim of his Stetson. "I need to know what we're agreeing to disagree about."

She gave an impatient sigh. The man was completely and utterly obtuse. "You and I both love Savannah," she said with exaggerated slowness. "But when it comes to each other, we don't see eye to eye, which is fine. We don't really need to. I have my life and you have yours. You don't want to go out with me and that's fine, too. Because frankly I'm not all that interested in you, either."

His eyes narrowed. "In other words you're turning me down before I even get a chance to ask you to the Cattlemen's Dance."

He was asking her to the dance? So *that* was what this was all about.

Now he was the one who seemed agitated. He gestured with his hand as if he wasn't sure how to continue. "I take the better part of the morning driving into town," he finally managed to say. "I've got an entire herd of cattle that need tending, but instead, I waste a good part of my day just so I can invite you to a stupid dance. Then before I can even get the words out, you're telling me you'd rather go out with a polecat than with me. Well, if that doesn't beat all." He slammed his hat back on his head with enough force to make her recoil.

"You wanted to invite me to the dance?" she asked, recovering in record time, "and I'm supposed to be grateful?"

"No...yes." He faltered, then ignored the question. "Why else would I drive into town on a Saturday?" Not giving her time to respond, he added, "Cal's right. A woman's nothing but trouble."

Caroline's heart sank. She would have enjoyed attending the biggest dance of the year with him. Instead, she'd ruined any chance she had of stepping onto the dance floor with Grady Weston.

"I told Savannah this wouldn't work," he said with the self-righteous attitude of a man who thinks he's been right all along. "As far as I'm concerned, this is the last time I'm inviting you to any social function in this town. If you want a date you're going to have to ask *me*."

The insinuation that he was the only man who'd ask her out infuriated Caroline. "I don't need you in order to get a date."

"Oh, sure, I suppose you're interested in Richard, too."

"Richard? What's he got to do with anything?"

Grady opened and closed his jaw, but apparently decided against explaining. "Never mind. I'm out of here."

Caroline stretched out her hand to stop him, but it was too late. Grady had already turned and was storming out of the post office, leaving the door to slam in his wake.

"My, oh my, what's gotten into that young man?"

For the first time Caroline noticed Edwina and Lily Moorhouse standing in the post-office foyer. Both women continued to dress as if they still spent their days at the front of a classroom. Caroline couldn't remember ever seeing either one in anything but well-pressed shirtwaist dresses. On Sunday mornings and at important social functions, they wore dainty hats with matching purses and spotless white gloves.

Lily, the younger and less talkative of the two, clutched her mail to her breast as if in mortal fear of having Grady rip it from her.

Edwina, who'd never had a problem sharing what was on her mind, was sputtering about "that young man."

"I apologize, ladies," Caroline said. "Grady and I were having a...difference of opinion."

"So it seems." Edwina pinched her lips together, clenching her purse tightly with both hands.

"Are you all right?" Lily asked.

Caroline shook her head, dismissing the older woman's concern. But the encounter had left her more shaken than she cared to admit.

"You like him, don't you?" Lily asked in a soft voice and reached across the counter to pat Caroline's hand.

Caroline nodded. Yes, she did like Grady—even if they didn't get along—and it was well past time she admitted it. But then, her judgment in men wouldn't exactly earn her any awards. Maggie's father had left her pregnant, and every other romantic relationship in her adult life had ended badly. "I guess some women are better judges of character than me," she said.

"Grady's a fine young man," Lily insisted, apparently over her shock.

"He's got a heart of gold," Edwina agreed. "But if you want my opinion, I think that young man's constipated."

"You think so, sister?" Lily frowned thoughtfully.

"Indeed I do. You be patient with him, Caroline, and he'll come around. Mark my words."

"I couldn't agree with Edwina more," Lily said, brightening somewhat. "There's nothing wrong with that young man that a large bowl of stewed prunes wouldn't cure."

"Or Grandpa's cordial."

"Indeed!"

Ellie's heart hammered in her ears as she stepped backward, slowly edging her way onto the path toward the truck. Richard was still nowhere to be seen.

Glen's warnings about the ghost town echoed in her mind. Even Richard had advised her not to come. She'd been the one to insist on making the trip, certain that Glen, at least, was being overprotective.

What was worse—far worse—was this…sensation, this feeling. It was as though she was being watched. And judged. And…disliked. Her pulse still thundered in her head, gaining volume and intensity. Her feet dragged heavily as she walked. It almost felt as if someone had bound her arms and legs and was slowly tightening the rope, binding her.

All she could think about was escape. But she couldn't leave, couldn't just turn and run. Somehow, someway she had to find out what had happened to Richard. Although every dictate of her heart and mind urged her to get out of there, she couldn't abandon him.

Besides, she hadn't a clue how to find her way back to Promise. She'd have to search this place and—

"Boo!"

Ellie screamed and leaped a good three feet off the ground. Richard threw back his head and laughed hilariously, as if her terror was the funniest thing he'd seen in years.

Furious, Ellie clenched her hands into fists and glared at him.

"Hey," he said, continuing to chuckle, "you're the one who claimed not to be afraid of ghosts."

"Where'd you go?" she demanded, gripping his arm and clinging tightly. She was too frightened to stay angry for long.

"Hey," he repeated softly, "you're really scared, aren't you?"

"You know I am!"

"Sweetheart, it was a joke."

"A stupid one."

"Okay, okay, it probably wasn't the best thing to do, but you were so sure nothing was going to frighten you. Sorry," he said with a casual shrug. "The real danger is letting your imagination run away with you."

Her fingers tensed on his arm. "I don't like this place."

"I told you." He sounded cool and unaffected.

"Don't you feel it?" she asked, studying him.

"Feel what?"

"The...sense of oppression."

He looked at her as if she needed a psychiatrist. "I don't feel anything. Come on, let me show you around. Old as it is, there's still lots to see."

Even though she was curious, Ellie shook her head. "I think we should head back."

"We just got here. Don't you want to check out the mercantile? I actually found some bloated canned goods left on the shelf. Can you believe it? The cash register is there, too. I looked, but there wasn't any money inside."

Did he actually expect there to be cash for his taking? Ellie wondered.

"What happened to the church?" she asked, gesturing toward the small hill at the far end of the main street.

"I didn't go in. Doesn't interest me. Outside looks like it got hit by lightning."

Ellie stared, fascinated despite her fears.

"Come on," Richard urged again, "let's explore."

Ellie realized it wasn't likely she'd come back for

a second visit. "Okay, show me the mercantile," she said, uncertain even now that it was a wise thing to do.

"Sure." He took her hand and led her up the two steps to the raised wooden sidewalk. The old boards creaked with their weight, making an eerie inhuman sound. It looked as though the town had been fairly prosperous at one time. A hotel and saloon, a livery stable, a small corral. The sun-bleached planks of the boardwalk were bleached and splintered with age, and several sections had rotted through.

"Watch your step," Richard said and slipped his arm around her waist, holding her unnecessarily close.

"Maybe we should go to the hotel," he whispered suggestively. "Find a room with a bed."

"No, thanks," she murmured.

"Hey, don't be so quick to turn down a good thing. We could have a lot of fun."

"No, thanks," she said again, her tone reinforcing the message.

"Pity. We could be good together."

Ellie sincerely doubted that.

As Richard opened the door to the mercantile, the hinges squeaked loudly and Ellie shivered. The sensation persisted, the feeling that she was being watched.

The inside of the old store was like something out of a museum. The counter stretched the length of the room, with shelves built behind it. What Richard had said was true; there were several tin cans scattered about. The cans themselves were swollen, their labels faded.

"What happened to make people move fast enough to leave goods behind?" Life was hard in the Old West, and food was often in short supply.

"Who knows?" Apparently Richard didn't find her question of any interest.

The cash register was there, too, the till open. Bramble weeds littered the floor. Ellie saw a couple of old barrels and a table, but no chairs.

"Okay, we've seen it," she said. "I'm ready to go back."

"You don't want to see anything else?"

"No." Her curiosity was gone and all she wanted now was to escape. Even knowing that her father's great-grandparents had walked these very streets and stepped inside this store wasn't enough to keep her.

"Come on, let's go look at the hotel," Richard urged again. "There's quite a fancy staircase—if you ignore the occasional broken step."

"Richard!" The hotel had to be riddled with danger. If the staircase collapsed or they fell through a damaged floor, heaven only knew how long it'd be before someone found them.

Glen would come. Ellie was genuinely relieved that she'd told at least one other person where she was headed, even if he disapproved. If she did turn up missing, Glen would leave no stone unturned. He'd look for the town until he located it again. Then he'd mount a search-and-rescue effort, enlist everyone's help. He wouldn't rest until he knew exactly what had happened and why. He was that kind of man. That kind of friend.

"I want to check the cemetery," she decided as they left the mercantile.

"The cemetery? As jittery as you are?" Richard said. "Why?"

"I want to look for a grave. A little boy by the

name of Edward Abraham Frasier." Since the Bible
had given no information about what had caused his
death, perhaps a grave marker would.

"All right," Richard agreed, but she could see he
wasn't enthusiastic.

The sensation of someone following them grew less
intense as they walked toward the outskirts of town.
The gate to the cemetery hung by one hinge.

"Someone's been here recently," Ellie said, stopping
just inside the fenced area. The dirt had been churned
recently to plant a rosebush.

"Savannah," Richard said. "She was after some old
roses and replaced the ones she took."

"Savannah's been here?" Ellie wasn't completely
surprised. Savannah scoured the highways and byways
for old roses, hoping to find unfamiliar and unusual
species. And replacing the roses she'd removed? Savannah never took without giving; it was her nature.

"What was the name again?" Richard asked.

"Edward Abraham Frasier." Some of the graves
were marked with wooden crosses that had badly de-
teriorated with age. And only a few names were legible on the stone markers. After a couple of minutes
she gave up the effort.

"You done yet?" Richard asked, sounding bored.

"Yeah." While she wished she'd found the grave,
she didn't want to linger in town any longer.

Richard held her hand as they scrambled up the
incline, then followed the rocky path that led to the
truck. He helped her into the cab—obviously charm
died hard—and climbed inside himself. "Put on the
blindfold," he instructed her, turning the ignition key.

Ellie complained under her breath. He had nothing

to worry about; she had no intention of returning to Bitter End. She didn't know what had made her ancestors leave the town; all she could say was that she didn't blame them.

Once the blindfold was securely in place, Richard put the truck into gear.

The ride back to Promise was accomplished in half the time it had taken to drive out. Once again the truck pitched and bucked over the uneven terrain, leaving Ellie to wonder how he'd found Bitter End on his own. Of one thing she was sure—neither Glen nor Cal would have taken him there. Nor would Grady or Savannah. No one she knew would purposely return to Bitter End. She wouldn't. Never again. Glen was right; once was more than enough.

Richard dropped her at the feed store. "Thanks," she said and was about to open the door and climb out when he stopped her.

"Hey, there's no need to rush, is there?"

She did have work to do. "Well—"

"Don't you want to thank me?" he asked.

"I thought I already had."

"A kiss wouldn't hurt." Without giving her a chance to respond he reached for her shoulders and brought his mouth to hers. Technically it was a kiss, but Ellie experienced none of the warmth or gentleness she had with Glen. None of the surging passion. What Richard classified as a kiss was little more than the touching of lips.

Apparently he wasn't satisfied, either, because he opened his mouth and twisted it over hers. Ellie still felt nothing. Which surprised her, considering how attractive the man was.

Richard released her and smiled. "I'll give you a call soon," he said as though nothing was amiss. "We could have something good together, Ellie. Think about it, all right?"

She stared at him, at a total loss for anything to say. The kiss that had left her cold had somehow convinced him they could become romantically involved.

"You're coming to the Cattlemen's Dance with me, right?" he asked when she finally climbed down from the truck.

"Ah…" She stood with one hand on the door, ready to close it. "I'll let you know for sure, but I don't think so."

Richard's eyes widened with surprise. "But I'll see you there?"

"I… I don't know." She wasn't in the mood for much partying. "Perhaps," she said vaguely.

"In any case I'll see you soon," Richard said cheerfully and with a jaunty wave drove off.

Ellie walked into the store and George Tucker handed her a pile of pink slips. "Glen Patterson called three times," he muttered in a way that told her he wasn't keen on being her secretary. George's expertise didn't extend to the office.

"Glen phoned?" Her heart reacted immediately.

"Would you kindly put that young man out of his misery?" George asked. "I've got better things to do than answer his questions about you."

Smiling to herself, Ellie headed for her office in the back of the store. Maybe, just maybe, there was some hope that she and Glen could resurrect their friendship, after all.

* * *

Glen hadn't been worth a plugged nickel all day. Glen and Cal had been out at Cayuse Pasture, which was approximately twelve miles square in size. They were grazing about 400 cows and yearlings there. Even the dogs didn't want anything to do with him, and Glen saw their point. His mood had been murderous all day. Three times he'd left Cal and the other hands to race back to the house so he could call Ellie. His frustration rose each time he was forced to leave a message with George. Now that he was back at the ranch house, he discovered his disposition hadn't improved. The answering machine showed that Ellie hadn't tried to call him back, which meant she was still with Richard in Bitter End. He didn't like it, not one damn bit.

"If you're so concerned about Ellie," Cal said, "why don't you drive into town and find out what happened to her?" Cal himself would be driving into town later for his weekly visit to Billy D's, the local watering hole. Most single ranchers met at Billy D's for a cold beer on Friday and Saturday nights. Then some of them would wander over to the café in the bowling alley or the Chili Pepper for a barbecued steak. Adam Braunfels served up one of the best T-bones in the state. Glen would probably join his brother and friends—after he'd talked to Ellie.

"You're letting a woman mess with your mind, little brother," Cal said with the voice of one who'd been disillusioned by love. He opened the refrigerator and reached for a can of soda. "Take my advice or leave it—that's up to you. But the way I see it, Ellie's already got a ring through your nose."

"The hell she does," Glen argued. Sure, she'd been

on his mind, but *only* because he was worried about her and Richard visiting Bitter End.

"I was thinking about moseying into town early," Glen admitted, making light of it.

"Yeah, fine," Cal said with a decided lack of interest. "Why don't you just marry Ellie and be done with it?"

Glen frowned at his brother, but rather than become involved in a pointless argument he tore up the stairs to shower and change.

By the time Glen reached the outskirts of Promise, anger simmered just below the surface. He intended to check in with his friends at Billy D's in a while, but he wouldn't rest easy until he'd spoken to Ellie. He needed to see for himself that she was all right.

When he arrived at the feed store, George Tucker took one look at him and pointed him toward the business office. So Ellie was back, but she hadn't bothered to return his calls.

The door was half-open and Glen saw Ellie sitting at the desk, her fingers flying over calculator buttons. She glanced up when he walked into the room. Under normal circumstances he would have poured himself some coffee. Not this afternoon. At least not yet. He wanted to find out what her mood was like first.

"You went to Bitter End, didn't you," he said quietly. Although he wished she'd taken his advice, his relief that she was safely home overrode any real anger.

"Did you honestly expect me not to?"

"No," he said, knowing his actions the night of Ruth's party had made that impossible.

"I... I wasn't overly impressed with the town," she admitted.

Well, he thought, that was a start in the right direction.

"Why didn't you ever mention it before?" she asked, and he noticed a hurt tone in her voice.

"I never talked about it with anyone." He walked across the room and reached for the coffeepot. "If I'd told you, you would've wanted to see it for yourself—which you did."

"To tell you the truth, I understand why you didn't want me there."

That was what he'd figured. "I was worried about you," he said.

"I know. I talked to Cal a few minutes ago."

Glen frowned. He could just imagine what his brother had said. On second thought he didn't want to know.

"You plan on making a return visit?" he asked, instead, keeping the question light.

"Go back? Not on your life."

"Good." He raised the mug to his lips and took a sip of coffee.

"I think we should talk," Ellie surprised him by saying.

"Talk?" He froze, not sure he liked the sound of this.

She laughed softly, and Glen realized how much he'd missed hearing that. She had a deep rich laugh, unlike a lot of women he knew who had delicate laughs. Ellie's was robust and confident, as if she didn't need to prove her femininity by being reserved. He found her unique in any number of other ways.

"We can try to ignore it, pretend we've forgotten

it, but the best way to deal with…what happened is to discuss it."

His eyes held hers. "Are you talking about…" He was having as much trouble saying the word as she was.

"The…kiss." There, she'd said it.

"The kiss," he repeated in low tones, as though this were something dark and dangerous. He was beginning to think it was.

Ellie laughed, and soon he did, too.

"We should acknowledge that we were caught up in a momentary impulse," she suggested primly. "And… Oh, hell, let's just forget it."

Leaning against the edge of her desk, Glen cradled his coffee mug in both hands. "I don't think that'll work."

"Why not?" Ellie stood and replenished her own coffee.

Because they'd been friends all these years, Glen knew exactly what she was doing. What had prompted her sudden burst of activity wasn't a craving for more coffee but an effort not to let him see what was in her eyes.

He set his mug aside and touched her shoulder. She jerked around as though he'd burned her.

"I don't want to forget the kiss," he said with blinding honesty. He didn't recognize it as the truth until the words left his lips.

"You don't?" She sounded startled.

"Do you?" He was a fool to ask, but he couldn't have held back the question for anything.

"I… I don't know."

"Yes, you do." If he could hang out his pride to

dry, then she'd damn well better be prepared to do the same thing.

She blinked twice. "All I want is for us to be friends."

"We are. That hasn't changed."

"But it *has!*" she cried, gesturing wildly with her hands. "That kiss changed everything. I used to be able to talk to you."

"You still can."

"No, I can't."

"Try me," he challenged.

She threw back her head and laughed, but this time her amusement lacked sincerity. "We can talk about anything, can we?" she flung at him. "Fine, then we'll talk about how Richard's kisses leave me cold and how all I could do was compare the way I felt when I was in your arms."

Glen didn't hear anything beyond the first few words. "So you're kissing Richard now. Is there anyone else I don't know about?"

"See?" she cried, tossing her arms in the air. "My point exactly."

"What point?"

"We can't talk."

"We're already talking! What do you mean?" This was the kind of convoluted conversation women suckered a man into—giving him just enough rope to hang himself. Glen had seen it happen often enough and had always managed to avoid it with Ellie. Until now.

"You said there wasn't anything I couldn't discuss with you, and already we're at each other's throats."

"I am not at your throat!" he shouted, his patience gone. The entire day had been a waste. First he'd fretted about her with Richard in Bitter End. Then he'd attempted to revive their friendship, only to learn she'd been locking lips with Richard Weston.

"You're welcome to him," he said, setting the mug down forcibly enough to send coffee sloshing over the sides. "As far as I'm concerned, you and Richard deserve each other."

"Oh, please, now you're acting like a jealous fool."

He was out the office door before he realized he'd had more than one reason for seeing Ellie. He walked back and leaned against the doorjamb, crossing his arms.

Ellie glanced up and waited.

"You going to the dance?" he asked finally, as if her answer didn't really matter.

"I...haven't decided yet. Are you going?"

"Yeah."

"Then I probably will, too."

"See you there?" he asked, his mood brightening.

She nodded. "Will you wait for me?"

He nodded, grinning.

She smiled back.

Five

As the evening wore on, Glen's feelings toward Richard Weston grew even less friendly. He resented the other man's putting Ellie at risk by escorting her to Bitter End. The more he thought about it, the more irritated he got. Richard's dating Ellie had never set right with him, either. Especially now, when she was at a low point in her life following her father's death and her mother's move to Chicago. Although Ellie generally had a level head, Glen didn't want Pretty Boy taking advantage of her.

And then there was his own unresolved—and unexpected—attraction to her…. But, no, the real concern was Ellie's vulnerability to a superficial charmer like Richard.

The only thing to do, Glen decided, was speak to Richard personally. Clear the air. Set him straight. He'd wait for the right opportunity. He was well aware that Ellie wouldn't appreciate his having a chat with Richard on her behalf, but she didn't need to know about it, either. Someone had to look after her interests. Glen liked to think of himself as her guardian.

Okay, *guardian* was probably the wrong word, seeing as they were close to the same age. What she could use was a sort of…advocate. A concerned friend. Yes, that was it. An advocate. Someone who had her best interests at heart. Stepping in where needed.

With his role clear in his mind, he held off until late Wednesday afternoon before driving out to the Yellow Rose Ranch and confronting the youngest Weston. This was between him and Richard. Man-to-man.

He turned into the drive and parked in the yard beside Grady's truck, then slowly climbed out of the cab. Savannah was in her rose garden wearing a wide-brimmed straw hat to shield her face from the sun. Richard sat on the front porch, strumming a guitar, apparently so involved in his music that he didn't see or hear Glen's approach. Rocket, Grady's old black Lab, slept on the porch, sprawled out on a small braided rug.

Carrying a wicker basket filled with fragrant pink roses, Savannah waved and walked toward Glen.

"Howdy, neighbor," she said, smiling her welcome.

"Savannah." He touched the tip of his Stetson. "Beautiful day, isn't it?"

"Lovely," she agreed.

"I'm here to see Richard," Glen announced, narrowing his gaze on the man who still lounged on the porch.

"He's practicing his guitar." She gestured unnecessarily toward Richard. He'd leaned the chair against the side of the house and propped one foot on the porch railing.

"Would you care for a glass of iced tea?" Savannah offered.

His throat was dry; something cold and wet would be appreciated. "That's mighty kind of you."

Richard's sister moved toward the house, then paused at the bottom step and turned. With a slight frown she said, "Is there trouble, Glen? Between you and Richard?"

"Not at all," he was quick to assure her. He was determined that this would look like nothing more than a friendly conversation between neighbors. And if he just happened to mention Ellie…

Obviously relieved, Savannah disappeared into the house, and Glen approached Richard. The younger man ignored him until Glen pulled at the chair beside his and plunked himself down.

Richard's fingers paused over the strings. "Howdy, Glen."

"Howdy." Although Glen had mulled over what he intended to say, he found that actually speaking his mind was surprisingly difficult. "Do you have a few minutes?"

"Sure." Richard set the guitar down on the porch, holding it by the neck. "I've always got time for a friend."

Friend. Glen hesitated since he didn't exactly view Richard that way.

"What can I do for you?" Richard asked companionably.

"Well…" Nope, he wasn't very good at expressing himself, Glen thought. "I've been concerned about Ellie."

"Really?" Richard asked. "Why?"

"Her father dying and then her mother leaving so soon afterward."

Richard nodded. "I see what you mean. She seems to be handling it pretty well, though, don't you think?" He picked up the guitar, laid it across his lap and played a couple of chords.

"That's the thing about Ellie," Glen explained, speaking with authority. After all, he knew Ellie far better than Richard did. "She can put on a good front, but there's a lot of emotion churning beneath the surface."

Richard chuckled. "You're right about that! She's a little fireball just waiting to explode. I've always been attracted to passionate women." His tone insinuated that he'd been close to getting scorched by Ellie a few times—as if he knew her in ways Glen never would.

Glen shifted uncomfortably, angered by the insinuation, but was saved from responding by Savannah, who carried out a tray with two tall glasses of iced tea and a plate of homemade oatmeal cookies.

"Thanks," Glen said, accepting a glass.

Richard had reached for his, plus a cookie, before Savannah could even put the plate down. "I can never resist my sister's cookies," he said and kissed her on the cheek. "No one bakes better cookies than Savannah."

His sister smiled at his praise, then quietly returned to the kitchen. Glen watched her go and realized that with very little effort, Richard had won over Savannah, too—despite all the grief he'd brought the family. No doubt about it, the guy was an expert when it came to manipulating women. Glen felt all the more uneasy, wondering how to handle the situation. He wanted Richard to keep his distance from Ellie, but he didn't want to be obvious about it. If he made a

point of warning Richard off, the bum would be sure
to tell her what he'd said. Probably snicker at him, too.

The best way, he decided, was to state his concerns
in a natural straightforward manner. "Ellie told me
you took her to Bitter End," he began, struggling to
disguise his anger.

Richard threw back his head and laughed boister-
ously. "I scared the living daylights out of her, too."

Glen hadn't heard about that and was forced to listen to Richard's story of how he'd blindfolded her, then
slipped out of the truck and hidden.

By the time he finished, Glen's jaw hurt from the
effort it took not to yell at the man. "I don't think it's a
good idea to be taking anyone up to that ghost town,"
he said as calmly as he could, realizing anew that he
actively disliked Richard Weston. He hadn't cared for
him as a teenager and liked him even less as an adult.

"I couldn't agree with you more," Richard said,
once his amusement had faded. "It was a mistake to
even mention Bitter End. Once I did, she was all over
me, wanting to see the place. When I finally said I'd
take her, she wasn't in the town five minutes before
she wanted to leave.

"Surprising how much of that town's still standing,"
Richard said next, helping himself to a second cookie.

Glen figured if he didn't take one soon, Richard
would devour the entire plateful before he'd even had
a taste. Deliberately he reached for a cookie, then another. He took a bite; they *were* as good as Richard
claimed.

"How'd you find the town?" Glen asked.

"Since you, Cal and Grady didn't see fit to include

me when we were kids, I didn't have any choice but to seek it out on my own."

"But why now?"

"Why not?" He shrugged as if it was of little consequence. "I've got plenty of time to kill while I wait to hear on my next job. I work for an investment company."

"I didn't realize that."

"I don't tell a lot of people," he said. "Most recently I was working with a smaller institution, specializing in loans and investments. Unfortunately, as you're probably aware, the larger institutions are swallowing up the smaller ones, and I was forced to take a short vacation while the company reorganizes. It seemed as good a time as any to visit my family."

"Investments? Really?" Richard certainly possessed the polished look of a professional. And he knew how to talk the talk. Glen was a bit confused, though; he'd been under the impression that Richard had a different sort of job—sales or something. Oh, well, he supposed it didn't matter.

"Yup." Richard ran the guitar pick over the strings and laughed easily. "I bet you didn't know I'd made quite a name for myself, did you?"

Glen sobered when he realized how smoothly Richard had diverted him from the subject of Bitter End, but he wasn't going to allow the other man to get away with it for long.

"You won't be taking Ellie back to the ghost town, will you?" Glen asked in a tone that told Richard he was in for a fight if he did.

"Not likely!"

"Good." Then, in case he might consider showing the town to others, Glen added, "Or anyone else?"

"Hardly." Richard's response was immediate; but Glen noted the way his hand stilled momentarily over the guitar. "I wouldn't have taken Ellie, but like I said, once I mentioned it she was all over me, wanting to see the place. It was either drive her there myself or let her go looking for it on her own."

That much was true, Glen conceded.

"Do you and Ellie have something going...romantically?" Richard surprised him with the directness of the question.

Glen hesitated, unsure how to respond. Before he allowed himself to confess what he'd denied to everyone, he shook his head. "We're just friends."

"That's what I thought." Richard sounded smug and satisfied.

"Any particular reason you're asking?"

"Yeah. I'm interested in her myself, and I don't want to step on your toes if I can help it."

Glen frowned. "Like I said earlier, this is a bad time for Ellie."

"She needs someone like me," Richard said, bending over the guitar and tightening a couple of strings. "What I'd like to see her do is sell that business and get on with her life. Her daddy stuck her with that feed store, but there's no need for her to hold on to it."

Glen shook his head. Ellie loved the store with the same intensity her father had. She recognized her contribution to the community and took pride in meeting the needs of the local ranchers. The feed store had become the unofficial gathering place in town, and that was because Ellie, like her father, made folks feel welcome.

Everyone dropped in at Frasier Feed, to visit, catch up on local news and gossip, swap stories. The large bulletin board out front offered free advertising space for anyone with something to trade or sell. The pop machine was there, too, with a couple of chairs for those who wanted to take a load off their feet.

Ellie sell out? Never. Apparently Richard didn't know her as well as he thought.

"She's interested in me, too, you know," Richard added.

This definitely came as a surprise to Glen. She'd admitted the two of them had kissed, but in the same breath had told him she preferred his kiss over Richard's. At least, that was what he *thought* she'd said. The last part of their conversation had been lost on him. They'd snapped at each other, gotten annoyed with each other and instantly regretted it. Glen had come to mend fences with her, not destroy them, and he'd turned back to ask her about the dance. He'd made it clear that he looked forward to spending the evening with her.

She'd told him basically the same thing. They'd meet there. He'd wait for her.

"She's attending the dance with me," Richard stated nonchalantly.

"With you?" Glen couldn't believe what he'd just heard. "The Cattlemen's Association Dance?"

"Yeah. She had some concern about the two of us being there together, though. Neither of us wants to start any talk."

"Talk?"

"About seeing one another exclusively."

"I see." Glen's hand tensed around the cold glass.

"You going?" Richard asked pointedly. "If I remember correctly, this dance is one of the biggest social events of the summer."

"I'll probably be there," Glen said. And he'd make damn sure Richard kept his paws where they belonged, because the first time he saw Mr. Investment Manager touching Ellie, Glen would be dragging him outside and rearranging his dental work. Even if Ellie *did* prefer Weston, as it now appeared.

"Who are you taking?" Richard probed.

"I...don't know yet," Glen confessed, and then because he didn't want it to look like he couldn't get a date, he added, "I was thinking of asking Nell Bishop."

"Sure," Richard said with an approving nod. "Ask Nell. I bet she'd be happy to go with you."

Glen gulped down the rest of his tea and stood. "Glad we had this conversation," he said, when in reality he was anything but. Only this time his anger was directed at Ellie. She'd played him for a fool. A fool! She'd led him to believe she didn't have a date. Moreover she'd indicated in no uncertain terms that she'd welcome his company there. *Wait for me,* she'd said.

What she intended, he now realized, was that he'd arrive and then stand there twiddling his thumbs while she danced her way across the room in Richard Weston's arms. Well, if that didn't beat all. The why of it wasn't too clear, but he figured Ellie was still mad at him and this was her revenge.

"Don't be a stranger," Richard said as Glen started toward his truck. "And don't worry about me taking Ellie up to Bitter End again, either."

"I won't." He wouldn't worry about a lot of things concerning Ellie, he mused, his anger festering. If it wasn't for Richard letting slip that she'd agreed to be his date, Glen would have arrived at the dance completely unawares.

Maybe Cal was right. Maybe women *couldn't* be trusted.

Frank Hennessey had been the duly elected sheriff of Promise for near twenty years. He knew everyone in town and they knew him. Because he'd been in office for so long, folks were comfortable coming to him with their problems. Minor ones and ones that weren't so minor. Sometimes he suggested they talk to Wade McMillen, the local preacher, and other times he just listened. Mostly folks felt better after they'd talked. More often than not a solution would present itself, although he'd barely say a word. Then folks would credit him when the answer had been there all along buried deep within themselves.

These days Frank had been hearing a lot about Richard Weston. Not that it surprised him. He knew Richard had absconded with the family inheritance the day Grady and Savannah had lowered their parents into the ground. Many a night he'd sat with Grady while the young man grappled with what to do— whether to press charges or not. In the end he'd decided not to pursue a case against Richard, but it had taken Grady damn near six years of constant struggle to work his way out of the red.

Now Richard was back, and Frank had heard from two or three of the local merchants that he was running up charges and not paying his bills. Frank didn't like the sound of this. What to do about it had weighed heavily on his mind for a couple of days.

He'd urged Max Jordan from Jordan's Town and Country outfitters to mention the bill to Grady, but Max didn't want to carry tales to Richard's big brother. Besides, he'd sold two vests like the one Richard had bought after he'd worn his about town. Frank would say one thing about the youngest Weston: he was a real clotheshorse. Max said he'd moved some other high-end clothing items because of Richard and was therefore willing to cut the young Weston a little slack.

For the moment, Millie Greenville was amenable about the money Richard owed her, as well. Grady had ended up paying for the flowers Richard had bought for his party; Frank knew that and had his doubts as to whether Grady would ever be repaid. Although Richard was already two months past due in paying her for the flowers he'd ordered since, she'd decided not to press the issue. He'd sent a huge arrangement for John Frasier's funeral and a number of other small bouquets to women around town. According to Millie, Richard had apologized and given her a plausible excuse; she'd chosen to believe him. But it was a little worrisome having four hundred dollars outstanding at the end of the month, all owed by the same customer.

Then there was the matter of the tab Richard was running at Billy D's. Apparently Richard had been more than generous about buying other people's drinks. It wasn't unusual for him to order a round for his friends and their friends, too, and then tell Billy just to add it to his tab. When Billy mentioned it to Frank, the money owed was close to five hundred dollars. Richard had fed the tavern owner some cockeyed story about being an investment broker, expecting a commission check that was due any day. Again Billy was willing to wait, seeing as Richard always drew a crowd. He was clever and amusing and people seemed to enjoy themselves when he was around.

Frank looked at his watch and eagerly shoved back his chair. "I'll be over at Dovie's," he said to his deputy on his way out the door. Ever since Dovie had opened her Victorian Tea Room, he stopped by each afternoon around four-thirty, after she'd finished serving tea and scones. The store was generally quiet then, and she'd usually offer him something to satisfy his sweet tooth.

Dovie was his friend. His *special* friend. If it was up to her they'd be married, but Frank wasn't the marrying kind. He had no interest in giving up his freedom, although if any woman could tempt him to relinquish his bachelor status, it'd be Dovie. They'd been dating more than ten years now, and about once a year she got uppity about the absence of an engagement ring. Frankly he liked their arrangement just the way it was, and if pressed, Dovie, he suspected, would admit she did, too. Twice a week he spent the night at her house—the two best nights of the week. No, he figured, this marriage business was a token protest on her part. The situation was ideal for both of them as it stood; Dovie liked her freedom as much as Frank liked his, and this way they enjoyed the benefits of a steady relationship. Best of both worlds.

Frank entered the antique shop and once again admired how Dovie had artfully arranged five tables in the corner of her compact store. To his relief, the tearoom was empty, and he hoped she'd take a few minutes to sit down and chat with him.

"Afternoon, Dovie," he said, pulling out a chair at his favorite table. She'd done the shop up all fancy. Real elegant. The tearoom, too. All the tablecloths and matching napkins were good linen, and tea was served on a china service with sterling silver.

Frank was impressed by Dovie's creative style. She'd taken several bulky pieces of heavy antique furniture—dressers and wardrobes and the like—and used them to display her goods. She positioned things attractively: fringed silk scarves dangled from open drawers, as did long jet necklaces of 1920s vintage. Linens and lace doilies, and large hats with feather plumes and nets sat on shelves. Mismatched antique china, porcelain oil lamps, silver candelabra—she had knickknacks everywhere. Pricey ones, too. Dovie didn't sell junk; she sold *treasures*. She made sure he understood that. Far be it from him to question such matters.

Frank had never seen a woman more in love with things. Every square inch of the shop was used for display. The ladies in town loved to browse there. Most men were afraid to move a foot inside for fear they'd knock something down and end up paying for it.

Dovie looked up from tallying her receipts to send Frank a welcoming smile. As always, it made his heart beat a little faster. He returned the smile and settled back to wait.

When she was finished, Dovie poured him a cup of coffee and brought it, with a slice of warm apple crisp, to the table. Actually he'd been looking forward to her bread pudding with brandy sauce, but since he never paid for these treats, he could hardly complain.

"You look like you've been busy," he said.

"I have." She took the chair across from him, removed her shoes and rubbed her tired feet. "Ellie Frasier was in and bought the Gibson-girl dress for the dance. My, she looked lovely. I know it was more than she wanted to spend, but once she tried it on, she was sold. I don't think I appreciated what a pretty young woman she is," Dovie said absently.

Frank sneaked a peek at Dovie's ankle. She had a fine pair of legs. He'd always been taken with her trim ankles, and never had understood why she insisted on wearing long dresses. It was criminal the way she hid those shapely legs of hers.

One bite of the apple crisp and Frank closed his eyes, savoring the combination of tart and sweet flavors.

"Good?" she asked even though Frank was sure she already knew it was.

"Excellent."

He ate the rest of it in record time.

"You've got something on your mind, Frank," Dovie said. "I can always tell. Are you going to say what it is?"

"Someone's going around charging a lot of money with local merchants," he told her reluctantly. "I'm not convinced he's planning to pay off his debts."

"Someone?" Dovie repeated. "You don't need to say who. I can guess."

He'd already said more than he should have, so he left it at that. He trusted Dovie. She wasn't like some women who just couldn't keep anything to themselves. He'd never known her to break confidences or spread rumors. It was one of the many things he valued about her.

"What are you going to do about it?"

"I don't know that I *can* do anything. He hasn't broken any laws."

"True," she said, looking thoughtful. "But you might have a chat with him. Man-to-man—or rather, sheriff to miscreant. I recall you had plenty to say to Laredo Smith not long ago."

Frank ignored the comment about his talk with Laredo, especially since he regretted having said a word. He'd made one mistake in judging character recently and didn't want to make another. He couldn't be one-hundred percent sure, after all, that Richard *didn't* have money coming in.

"I don't know what I could say to this guy." Frank didn't have any right to question Richard about his financial affairs.

"Frank, a lot of small businesses can't afford to take losses. Some months it's all we can do to pay the rent, let alone make a living wage. Let him know you're onto him."

"But he hasn't done anything that warrants my speaking to him."

"He doesn't know that. Let him think you have plenty of reasons. Put the fear of God into him before he robs the entire community blind," she urged. "Before he puts one of us out of business."

Frank knew how close to the edge some businesses operated. Dovie herself wasn't going to get rich with her antique shop, although it was one of the most popular stores in town.

"If nothing else," Dovie added, "it might make him think twice before charging something again."

"True." Frank rubbed his chin. It wasn't his place

to tell shop owners who they should extend credit to and who they should avoid, but he hated the thought of Richard's taking advantage of good honest folk.

Dovie drank a little more of her coffee, then carried the china cup to the small kitchen in the back room. Frank followed her with his empty cup and plate.

"You need someone to help you out here now you've got the tearoom," he said. It was clear to him she was working far too many hours, and while he'd encouraged her to add the Victorian Tea Room, he was concerned about the toll these extra hours took. The fatigue, the lack of private time.

"You're right, I could use another pair of hands," she said. "But I can't afford to put anyone on the payroll just yet."

Frank slipped his arms around her waist. "I guess you've picked out something special to wear to the dance," he said, nuzzling her neck. "I'm going to be the envy of every man there."

"You've been kissing the Blarney Stone again, haven't you?" Dovie teased.

"The only thing I'm interested in kissing is the widow Boyd." Not giving her time to object, he turned her in his arms and brought her mouth to his. She was soft and warm and her gentle kisses fired his blood to life.

"Frank," she whispered, breaking off the kiss. She looked flustered, her face red and her hands flying around her head checking that her hair was still tucked in place. "For the love of Ireland, it's the middle of the afternoon! Anyone could walk in."

"Let them."

"You're getting mighty bold, Mr. Sheriff." Her eyes

narrowed slightly. "Are you ready to take the leap yet?"

Marriage. She hadn't mentioned it in nearly a year. Her question had the effect of a bucket of cold water dumped on his head. His discomfiture must have shown in his face, because Dovie giggled and quickly kissed his jaw.

"You'd better go now," she said good-spiritedly.

"I've got to talk to a certain young man," he said. But he stole another kiss on his way out the door.

The antique white cotton-lawn dress, lavishly trimmed in lace, was quite possibly the most beautiful dress Ellie had ever owned. She hadn't intended to buy it. But every time she walked past the window of Dovie's store, she'd stopped and admired it. On impulse she'd decided to examine it up close. It was fate, she told herself. Fate. First of all the dress was her size, and when she tried it on, it fit like a dream. The moment she saw her reflection in Dovie's mirror, she knew she had to have it for the dance.

Perhaps she was putting too much stock in what Glen had said. He hadn't formally asked her to the dance, but he'd told her he'd be there. He'd also let her know he'd be waiting for her to arrive.

It was *almost* a date. She and Glen. Every time she thought about it, a warm feeling came over her. She and Glen together. Dancing. Kissing. A couple.

Her stomach fluttered and she pressed her hand over it, closing her eyes. So much had happened in the past few weeks. For a while, after her father's funeral and her mother's move to Chicago, Ellie had felt alone. Abandoned and unloved. She didn't feel that way now.

She realized that a lot of her new optimism was because of her changing relationship with Glen. If he'd stayed a little longer the last time he was in the store, they would've kissed again. All her instincts told her that. What surprised her was that she wouldn't have minded. In fact, just the opposite.

Maybe friends did make the best lovers, which she'd heard and read for years. She'd never thought of Glen in those terms before, but now she was ready to move on to a different kind of relationship with him—a romantic one. She thought he was, too. And if he had any doubts about his feelings, the moment he saw her in that dress his mind would be made up.

She grinned when she thought how smart a saleswoman Dovie was. If the woman had gushed all over her when she tried on the dress, she might not have purchased it. Instead, all Dovie had done was smile and escort Ellie to the full-length mirror.

Dovie didn't need to sell the dress; the dress had sold itself.

Ellie ran her hand down the sleeve one last time, then shut the office door. Tonight she'd take it home, hang it in her closet and look forward to Saturday the way a high-school junior anticipates her first prom. She could hardly wait to see Glen's reaction.

Near closing time Nell Bishop showed up with a list of needed supplies.

"I had a wonderful time at Ruth's party," Ellie told her as she looked over the list.

"Ruth's still talking about it," Nell said.

"And I think it's great you're going to start a dude ranch."

"Well, I don't have any takers yet."

"But you will." Ellie was sure of that.

"Are you going to the dance?" Nell asked suddenly.

Ellie smiled; the Cattlemen's Association summer dance appeared to be on everyone's mind. "I didn't think I would at first but... I had a change of heart. So I'll be there. What about you?"

Nell shook her head. "I don't know..."

Ellie understood Nell's indecision. While almost everyone came with a date, it wasn't necessary. Technically she herself was attending the function dateless.

"You don't need to worry if you don't have an escort," Ellie assured her and was about to explain her own situation when Nell continued.

"It's not that." She wore a puzzled frown. "I'm just wondering if there's something in the air, because I received two invitations in one hour."

It was time the men in this town woke up and realized what a wonderful woman Nell Bishop was. "That's great!"

"First Grady Weston phoned. Now, I like Grady, don't get me wrong, but I've always thought of him as..." Again she hesitated, as if unsure what to say next. "I just don't see Grady and me as a couple. If he's going to ask anyone, it should be Caroline Daniels. Those two are perfect for each other."

So Ellie wasn't the only one who'd noticed. "I've always wondered what's kept them apart."

Nell shook her head. "I can't figure it out."

"Do you think it's Maggie?" Ellie asked, referring to Caroline's five-year-old daughter.

"I can't imagine why."

"I don't think Grady's comfortable with kids," Ellie

said. She tried to remember seeing Grady with children and couldn't recall a time she had.

"Maybe, but I've got kids, too. In fact, he chatted with Jeremy for a couple of minutes first. Then when I got on the phone…he invited me."

"What did you tell him?"

Nell shrugged. "I didn't know what to say. No one's asked me out since Jake died, and I got so flustered I don't know if I made sense. I think I asked him to give me some time to think about it. He agreed."

"I like Grady," Ellie murmured. He wasn't an easy man to know, but he was fair and honest and hardworking.

"I'd no sooner recovered from that when I got another call," Nell said. "It was Glen Patterson."

Glen's name came out of the blue like a flash of lightning. "Glen?" Ellie repeated, the name buzzing in her ear. "Did you say Glen Patterson?"

"Yes. If Grady's invitation surprised me, Glen's knocked me for a loop." She laughed softly. "I think I must have done a fairly good imitation of a guppy. All I could do was open and close my mouth."

The fluttery sensation was back in the pit of Ellie's stomach, only this time it resembled nausea rather than happy anticipation. Ellie had assumed—*believed*—that Glen had wanted her to be his date.

"So you're going to the dance with Glen," Ellie said bluntly, struggling to hide her feelings.

"No. I told him the same thing I told Grady."

"Maybe you should go with both of them. Dangle one on each arm," Ellie suggested, trying for a lighthearted response.

Nell laughed. "Maybe I should. That'd really turn some heads, wouldn't it?"

Somehow Ellie managed a smile. The dress was going back to Dovie's that very afternoon. She'd been an idiot to spend that much money trying to impress a man who'd already approached another woman. Perhaps he thought he'd walk into the Grange Hall with a woman on each of *his* arms. Well, in that case, Glen Patterson had another think coming.

"There's a problem with Glen, though," Nell said, studying Ellie.

"What's that?" she asked, feigning interest.

"It's similar to the one I have with Grady. I always thought you and Glen would make a wonderful couple."

"Glen and me?" Ellie laughed as though it was the funniest thing she'd heard in weeks. "Nah, we're nothing more than friends. If you want to go to the dance with him, don't let me stand in your way. He asked *you,* didn't he?"

"Yes, but—"

"Don't worry about it," Ellie said, surprised how convincing she sounded. "It's no big deal."

"You're sure?"

"Absolutely."

On second thought, Ellie mused, as she rang up Nell's purchases, she was keeping the dress. Not only that, she'd be dancing every dance.

And she hoped Glen got a really good look at her, wearing her beautiful dress and dancing with every attractive single man who asked.

He could eat his heart out!

Six

This was bound to be an interesting evening, Cal Patterson thought. He climbed into his truck wearing fresh-washed Wrangler's, a string tie and polished boots. The big dance. Which meant there should be lots of entertaining activity as men and women of all ages flirted outrageously—making fools of themselves and each other. A few romances were always made at this kind of event, and a few broken. Yup, it was fascinating to watch, all right, especially if you were a disinterested observer. Like him.

But not like Glen.

Cal wasn't sure where Glen had gone Wednesday afternoon, but his brother had returned in one hell of a mood. While he might not know the particulars, Cal would wager a case of beer that his brother's rotten mood involved Ellie Frasier.

When Cal had made the mistake of mentioning Ellie in connection with the big dance, Glen had all but exploded. Even before Cal could ask any questions, Glen had slammed out the door, but not without dropping a couple of hints first. If Cal guessed right,

Ellie had decided to accept Richard Weston's invitation over Glen's.

While her choice surprised him, Cal was the first to admit that women were inconstant creatures who rarely knew their own minds. Best to keep your distance. Next thing Cal knew, his little brother had asked Nell Bishop; it hadn't done Glen's ego any good when she'd turned him down, too.

Cal himself had been fool enough to let one woman kick him in the gut and had found the experience as painful as anything he'd ever known. By God, he wasn't about to let it happen a second time. Glen, however, seemed destined to learn this particular lesson on his own.

Apparently his younger brother was a slow learner, because tonight he'd come downstairs in a new denim blazer and a pair of blue jeans so crisp they squeaked. His boots were polished to a gloss. One look dared Cal to comment.

He didn't, but he could tell it wasn't dancing that interested Glen. His brother intended to prove to Ellie, and quite possibly himself, that he didn't need her to have a good time. In other words, he was determined to act like a world-class idiot in front of the entire town.

Cal could almost guarantee that before the end of this night, Glen was going to do something really stupid. Now, that would have some entertainment value, but more important, Cal considered it his brotherly duty to be there to pick up the pieces afterward. He felt for Glen; he'd been through this, too. Heartbroken and humiliated.

Oh, yeah, *definitely* best to keep your distance from women.

Cal heard the band playing when he parked his truck in a long line of vehicles outside the Grange Hall. Cars and trucks were crammed bumper-to-bumper on both sides of the two-lane highway; obviously the parking lot had filled early in the evening. From the look of things everyone in town had shown up for the dance that traditionally kicked off summer.

The piercing strains of a fiddle cut into the night, followed by a banjo and Pete Hadley's melodic voice. Light spilled out of the open doorway and Cal could see a number of the married men clustered outside for a breath of fresh air. That, and a swallow or two of the hard stuff. Cal wasn't much of a drinking man himself. A cold beer now and again was more to his liking.

Someone shouted a greeting and Cal raised his arm in silent salute, but didn't stop to chat. He'd given his brother two hours—two hours during which he'd have his pride booted to hell and gone. If all went according to his calculations, Glen would be drunk soon or wish he was. Give him another hour. At that point Cal would step forward and haul him home.

The poor guy was in love, and while that alone guaranteed disaster, the worst of it was that Glen refused to admit it. Seeing his brother in such sad shape was akin to looking back two years and remembering the way he'd been with Jennifer. It amazed him now he hadn't seen her for what she was. He'd been so deeply infatuated with her he would have done anything to make her happy. Anything to prove how much he cared.

He'd asked her to be his wife, and six months later

she'd humiliated him by canceling their wedding at the last minute. All because he wouldn't give up ranching and move to San Antonio or Houston. Jennifer, who'd transferred from Phoenix, Arizona, to take a short-lived job as an assistant bank manager, had wanted out of small-town America. She'd wanted to move him to a city so crowded he'd never be able to breathe.

Cal had loved Jennifer, but he couldn't change who he was, not even for her. When he wouldn't dance to her tune, she pulled out of the wedding only two days before the event. Then she'd skipped town, leaving him to deal with the explanations and the embarrassment. Last he'd heard, Jennifer was living in Houston with some salesman.

He should have realized from the first she was a city girl at heart. But, like Glen, he'd been in love and hadn't recognized what was right there in front of him. Pushing thoughts of his ex-fiancée from his mind, he headed toward the hall.

The huge room was packed, forcing Cal to twist and turn as he made his way through the crowd. Men and women stretched across the hardwood floor in long rows, line dancing to the "Boot-scootin' Boogie." He remembered a few steps himself; Jennifer had insisted he learn the basics, despite the fact that he'd been born with two left feet.

When that song was over, the couples dancing started. Cal peered around, looking for Glen, and finally spotted him. His brother stood on the opposite side of the room, leaning against the bar, his narrowed gaze trained on the dancers. It didn't take a genius to figure out who held his attention.

Ellie.

Cal's eyebrows arched when he saw the object of his brother's affection. He'd never seen Ellie look prettier. The dress wasn't one with a Western flavor, which appeared to be the popular choice, but more old-fashioned. Elegant. She looked *damn* pretty, and Glen wasn't the only one who'd noticed, either.

Richard Weston had his arm tightly wrapped around Ellie's waist. From all appearances they were deeply involved with each other. This was worse than Cal had expected. He knew the type of man Richard Weston was, and he'd figured Ellie would've caught on fast enough herself. Apparently he'd overestimated her ability to judge character. It was a shame, too, because Richard was a user.

This protective feeling toward Ellie surprised Cal. He didn't want to have *any* feelings toward women. Whatever you did, you got your teeth kicked in. Wasn't worth it. No sirree, he'd learned his lesson the hard way.

As he looked back at his brother, his eyes strayed to the woman standing directly to Glen's left. It took him a moment to remember who she was. The new doc. The first time he'd noticed her she'd worn a power business suit to a barbecue; now she was dressed in jeans and a snap-button Western shirt. Not exactly appropriate attire for the year's most formal event. Cal couldn't help feeling sorry for her, even if she *was* a city girl, but suspected she found this hick-town dance highly amusing. He could picture her phoning her city friends and making fun of the way people dressed and talked in Texas.

The doc must have sensed his scrutiny because she glanced across the room and looked squarely back at

him. He glared in her direction, wanting her to know
that he didn't like her attitude—or what he assumed
her attitude to be.

The music ended just then, and before Cal could
stop him, Glen marched onto the dance floor and
headed straight for Ellie.

This was working out even better than Ellie had
hoped. Glen hadn't been able to take his eyes off her
all evening. Richard viewed Glen as competition. She
was well aware that his attentions had more to do with
one-upmanship than any real interest in her; nevertheless she found flattery a balm to her wounded pride.
She knew it was a superficial and childish reaction,
but she couldn't help it. Glen had really hurt her by
asking Nell to the dance. Temporarily, at least, being
with Richard was a way of assuaging that pain.

The one bad side effect was that Glen's presence
had brought out a possessiveness in Richard she wasn't
sure she liked.

The only man she wanted to dance with hadn't even
approached her. He'd followed her every move but
hadn't made one of his own. Glen must've been reading her thoughts, though, because as soon as the music
ended, he squeezed through the maze of people and
stopped directly in front of her.

"The next dance is mine," he announced, his grim
eyes challenging her to contradict him.

She stared at him, astonished. This was a side of her
friend she'd never seen. Demanding, intense. Generally he took everything in his stride, live and let live,
that sort of thing. But this... Ellie didn't know what
to think.

"You've danced with Richard three times now. It's my turn."

"You're counting?"

"Yes," he snapped. He grasped her about the waist, dragged her close and clenched her hands as if expecting Pete to break into the "Beer Barrel Polka."

"Isn't this dance mine?" Richard asked with a look of sardonic surprise.

"She's dancing with me," Glen responded before she had a chance to answer.

"Ellie?" Richard turned to her with lifted brows.

Glen's arms tightened around her defiantly.

"It's all right," she assured the other man. "I'll dance with Glen." She waited until Richard had left the dance floor, then burst out, "What's gotten into you?" She had to raise her chin to look him in the eye.

"Plenty," he responded gruffly.

The music started again and Glen whirled her to the opposite side of the room and as far away as possible from Richard. The dance number was a mournful ballad about love gone wrong. Ellie found it a fitting choice. Couples flocked onto the dance floor, their arms around each other like clinging blackberry vines.

Glen didn't say anything, but he held her close, arms tight, jaw tense. But gradually he relaxed and so did she. They'd just found their rhythm when Richard approached and tapped Glen on the shoulder.

"My turn," he said with the smug certainty of a man who knew he'd eventually get what he wanted.

Ellie saw Glen's eyes flare in annoyance before he slowly released her. With his high sense of drama Richard grabbed her about the waist and dipped her backward until Ellie gasped, thinking her feet were about to go out from under her. Then Richard pulled her upright and danced her to the other side of the room, away from Glen.

Just when she'd adjusted her steps comfortably to Richard's, Glen was back. Without a word he tapped Richard on the shoulder. Richard gave Glen a flinty-eyed glare, then unwillingly released her.

Glen gathered her back in his arms, but they hadn't taken more than a couple of steps before Richard interrupted a second time. The two men scowled at each other.

"This is ridiculous!" Ellie cried. "What's the matter with you, Glen?"

"Me?" he exploded.

"You heard the lady," Richard said with a mocking smile that suggested Glen was making a nuisance of himself.

"You're no better," she snapped, hands aggressively on her hips.

The music faded and the couples closest to them stopped dancing to stare at the unfolding scene. Ellie had never been so embarrassed in her life. Before another minute had passed, Frank Hennessey was standing between the two men. Although he wasn't at the dance in his capacity as sheriff, he was the law in town and no one questioned his right to intervene. Dovie Boyd, who was with him, cast Ellie a sympathetic look.

"Is there a problem here, boys?" Frank asked, placing emphasis on the last word. It was a not-so-subtle reminder that this sort of skirmish was generally reserved for adolescents.

"Nothing Richard and I can't settle *outside*," Glen said.

"Glen!" Ellie couldn't believe her ears.

"That's fine with me," Richard answered quickly, raising his fists.

"Just one minute." Frank put a hand on each man's shoulder. "No one's going outside. If there's anything to settle, we'll do it right here and now." He nodded at Glen. "What's the problem?"

"I'd like to finish the dance with Ellie without Richard cutting in."

"Hey, it's a free country," Richard said, his tone cocky.

"Richard and I can settle this between us, man-to-man." Glen flexed his hands a number of times, letting Richard know he welcomed the opportunity to shove a fist down his throat.

"Neither of you is leaving this hall," Frank stated in a friendly but unmistakably firm tone. "At least not in your present frame of mind."

"I asked Ellie to dance first," Richard insisted.

"The hell you did!" Glen shouted.

"Ellie?" Frank turned his attention to her. "Which one of them yahoos you want to dance with?"

She glanced from one man to the other. Richard wore a smug contemptuous look and Glen's dark brooding expression didn't make her feel much better. It was as if he thought he had squatter's rights or something.

"Neither one," she announced coolly.

Glen's mouth sagged open. "Fine," he muttered.

"But, sweetheart…" Richard objected.

Unwilling to listen to either one of them, Ellie

turned abruptly and muttered to Dovie and Frank, "I'm going to get a glass of punch." Glen and Richard were insufferable fools, she told herself, both of them plagued with oversize egos. She refused to allow them to make an idiot out of her, too.

Every eye in the room was focused on Ellie as she marched off the dance floor. She could feel the heat building in her face; she could hear the curious whispers all over the room.

Savannah and Caroline met her at the edge of the dance floor and gathered close around her. "Are you all right?" Savannah asked.

Ellie didn't know how to answer. Glen and Richard had made spectacles of themselves and a laughing-stock of her. "I'm so furious I could scream."

Savannah nodded. "I know exactly what you mean. Sit down and I'll get you a glass of punch. It'll calm your nerves."

In her present mood it would take a whole lot more than a cold drink to calm her. Thankfully the music had started again, and as people resumed dancing, they seemed to have forgotten the incident. To Ellie's annoyance, Savannah wasn't the one who returned with the punch; Glen brought it to her, instead. She glared up at him before accepting the glass.

He stood beside her for a couple of moments, then wordlessly claimed the empty chair next to hers.

Ellie crossed her legs and turned slightly, granting him a partial view of her back.

"You might have let me know," he said after several tense minutes.

"Know what?"

"That you'd accepted Richard's invitation to the dance."

"Oh, that's rich." She twisted around to face him, struggling to keep her voice under control. "You make a point of asking if I was going to be at the dance and I thought—I *assumed*... I spent a fortune on the dress, and the next thing I hear, you invited Nell."

"You bought that dress for me?" His face brightened and the beginnings of a smile edged up the corners of his mouth.

"You'd look pretty silly in a dress, Glen Patterson. No, I bought it for me."

He grinned roguishly at that, but his amusement faded when it became clear that Ellie was about to end the conversation.

"You'll note I'm not here with Nell," he said softly.

"Nell came with Grady, then."

"Grady asked her, too?" Glen's mouth snapped shut and he leaned hard against the back of the chair. He focused his attention on the dance floor. "I'd never have invited her if you hadn't agreed to go with Richard. I thought you and I were going to meet here."

"That's what I thought, too."

"But you said yes to Richard, anyway."

Ellie bristled. "I didn't until I heard you'd asked Nell."

Glen's face went blank, then his eyes narrowed suspiciously. "Why, that slimy..." he muttered. "Richard told me—" Glen stopped abruptly as if he'd already said more than he intended.

"Told you what?" Ellie pressed.

"Nothing. It doesn't matter," he muttered.

"There's no need to get short-tempered with me." Ellie crossed her arms and glared straight ahead.

Beside her, Glen crossed his arms, too, and scowled darkly at the other side of the room.

It was now or never, Caroline decided. Pete Hadley had just announced that the next dance was ladies' choice. Heart pounding, Caroline slowly approached Grady. He sat next to Cal Patterson, and they were deeply involved in conversation. Her guess was that it had something to do with Glen and Ellie, who were the subject of a great deal of comment tonight. Little wonder, considering the scene they'd created earlier. Both of them now sat at the end of a row of seats, arms crossed and looking about as miserable as any two people could get.

About as miserable as *she'd* been the past few days—since her most recent encounter with Grady.

Couples were already heading toward the dance floor, and if she waited any longer, she'd miss the opportunity entirely. Savannah, on Laredo's arm, cast her an encouraging smile and nodded in Grady's direction. Savannah had been the one to persuade her to clear the air with Grady.

Grady and Cal's conversation halted as she reached them. Grady looked up at her as if he couldn't imagine why she was standing in front of him, blocking his view.

"Would you care to dance?" she asked, gesturing weakly toward the couples already circling the polished floor. Her pulse increased by fifty beats a minute, and she was sure he was going to humiliate her by refusing.

Grady frowned.

"It's ladies' choice," she elaborated, her voice growing small.

Grady glanced to either side. "You're asking *me?*"

"No," she snapped, her anger saving her. "I thought I'd start at the front of the row and work my way down. If you refuse, I'll ask Cal next. Come on, Grady, it shouldn't be such a difficult decision."

It seemed for a moment as if he was about to decline, then, to her enormous relief, he got to his feet. "I'm not much good at this," he muttered.

He walked stiffly at her side to the dance floor. Then he put his arm around her waist, but maintained a space between them as if he feared she carried something contagious.

"I don't generally bite," she said, amused more than insulted.

"Really?" he asked and drew her somewhat closer.

The music was soft and mellow, and they shuffled their feet a bit, not really dancing, which was fine with Caroline. Her skill was limited, too. She looked out over the dance floor and recognized quite a few couples. Savannah and Laredo were lost in each other's arms. How she envied the happiness her friend had found. Caroline's heart ached with a sudden loneliness for that kind of love and contentment.

"Why'd you ask me to dance?" Grady asked gruffly.

"I figured I'd have to," she said. "The last time we spoke, you said *I'd* have to ask *you.*"

She felt some of the stiffness leave his body. "In other words the ball's in my court now."

Caroline grinned. "Something like that."

Grady's hold on her tightened and he gave a deep

sigh as he eased her closer. For several moments, neither one spoke.

Caroline knew she'd have to bring up the subject of
their last argument. This was her opportunity to mend
fences with Grady, and she didn't want to waste it. "I
felt bad after our conversation the other day."

"I did, too," he said. "I'm a bit of a hothead."

"And I'm too impatient."

They didn't seem to have much more to say after
that, and before long the dance was over.

"I didn't step on your toes, did I?" he said as they
walked off the floor.

"I seem to have survived."

He grinned, and she smiled back. Caroline held
her breath, hoping maybe now he'd ask her to dance.
He didn't.

"Thanks," he said when they returned to the sitting area.

"You're welcome." Caroline turned away, swallowing her disappointment.

Glen couldn't sit still. He'd been home from the
dance for an hour and hadn't stayed in any one position for longer than five minutes. He sat down in front
of the television, then bolted upright and stalked to the
kitchen, thinking feverishly.

He brewed himself a cup of instant coffee and carried it into the living room. Cal was watching the late-
night newscast and glanced curiously in his direction.

Glen sat back down, but was squirming a few minutes later.

"What in tarnation is the matter with you?" Cal

demanded when Glen bounded out of the recliner for the sixth time in as many minutes.

"Nothing's wrong," Glen lied.

"You're thinking about Ellie again, aren't you?"

He was, but Glen had no intention of admitting it. "What makes you say that?"

Cal gave a bark of laughter. "Because, little brother, you've got it written all over you."

"Got what?"

"You've fallen for Ellie."

Glen opened his mouth to deny it, but changed his mind. After the spectacle he'd made of himself in front of the entire community, he'd look like an even bigger fool claiming otherwise. He did have feelings for Ellie, but he hadn't decided what they were. He was protective of her, like a brother, but his reactions to Richard and his behavior that evening had proved it was more than that. He wasn't sure anymore what he felt.

"Richard drove her home," he muttered, stating for the first time what had been on his mind since leaving the dance.

"You don't trust him to be a gentleman?"

"Damn right, I don't." The more Glen thought about Richard alone with Ellie, the more agitated he got. It would be just like that scumbag to try something with her. Ellie knew how to handle herself, but she was vulnerable, and Richard was just the kind of man who'd try to take advantage of that.

"I'm driving into town," he announced. He wanted to reassure himself that Richard had gone—and he wanted to talk to Ellie.

"Now?" Cal glanced at his watch. "It's nearly midnight."

"I don't care what time it is." Decision made, Glen reached for his jacket and hurried to the door. He should have followed Ellie home, that was what he should've done, but they'd barely spoken after their big scene.

"You might phone her first," Cal suggested.

Glen paused and considered his brother's idea, then shook his head. "I have things to say, and that's best done face-to-face."

"What are you going to say to her this time of night?" Cal wanted to know.

"I'm not sure yet," Glen admitted, letting the screen door bang shut. He hadn't worked anything out; maybe the moment would bring some inspiration.

The drive into town was accomplished in record time. He parked on her street, drew a couple of shaky breaths and headed for her house. He rang the bell, and when she didn't immediately appear, he pounded on the door.

The porch light went on and then he heard Ellie moving about on the other side. "Who's there?"

"Glen!" he shouted loud enough to wake half the neighborhood. "Open up, Ellie. I need to talk to you."

"It's the middle of the night," she protested, but he heard the lock turn.

She was wearing a flannel robe cinched at the waist. Her hair was mussed and he could see he'd roused her from bed. She didn't invite him inside, which was just as well.

"I'm warning you," she muttered. "This had better be important."

"It is." Then to his acute embarrassment, his mind went blank. Not only that, he couldn't keep his eyes off her. Even without makeup, her hair flattened on one side, she was beautiful. It astonished him that he'd spent all that time with her week after week, year after year, and had never really seen her.

"Would you kindly stop staring at me!"

Glen hadn't realized he was. "Is Richard with you?" he asked and knew immediately that this was the worst possible thing he could have said.

In response Ellie slammed the door in his face.

Glen clutched the frame, knocked his forehead against the door and gritted his teeth. Hoping she'd give him the opportunity to redeem himself, he pressed the doorbell again.

"Ellie, I'm sorry, I didn't mean that," he shouted, praying she could hear him.

His apology was met with silence. Then finally, "Go away."

"I can't," he said, utterly miserable.

The porch light went out. Feeling completely dejected and the biggest fool who'd ever roamed the earth, he sat on the top step. He propped his elbows on his knees and dangled his hands between his legs, lacking even the energy to get up and walk to his truck.

He must have sat there a good ten minutes before he heard the door open softly behind him. If he hadn't been so thoroughly depressed, he would have leaped to his feet and begged Ellie to forgive him. But in his current frame of mind, he was convinced she'd phoned Sheriff Hennessey. He wouldn't have blamed her.

To his surprise she sat down next to him.

"I'm sorry, Ellie," he whispered, still not looking at her. "I can't believe I asked you something so stupid."

"I can't believe you did, either."

"I kept thinking about him driving you home, and I don't know, something crazy came over me." Even knowing he'd probably infuriate her further, Glen asked, "Did he kiss you?"

She groaned, and leaning forward, buried her face in her hands.

"Is that a yes or a no?"

"It means it's none of your business."

So Richard *had* kissed her. Glen would bet just about anything on that. It was obvious; otherwise she'd have been quick to deny it. His heart sank. At one time it wouldn't have bothered him, but now it did. A hell of a lot.

"What's happened to us?" she asked. "We used to be such good friends."

"We were," he agreed. "Good friends."

"And then you kissed me."

Talk about mistakes—but Glen really couldn't make himself regret that kiss. He'd relived it for days, remembering how it felt to hold Ellie in his arms, taste her lips, touch her hair. How it felt to be so *close*.

"Damn me if you want, but I'd give anything to kiss you right now," he whispered.

He was aware of her scrutiny and half turned to meet her gaze. "Because you think Richard kissed me earlier?" she asked.

"No," he said softly. "Because I need to." He reached for her, and his heart swelled with joy when she met his lips with an eagerness that matched his own. This was what he'd wanted, what he'd needed all along. Ellie in his arms. Ellie at his side.

"This is what I want, too," she whispered, her lips moving over his.

Glen kissed her again. For the first time that evening—that entire week—he was at peace.

Seven

Ellie slipped into the pew Sunday morning five minutes after the service had started. Organ music surged through the church as she took the last seat, reached for the hymnal and joined the congregation in song. At first she suspected the attention she'd generated was due to her tardiness. It wasn't that she'd overslept. Far from it. The night had been her most restless since before her father's death.

She'd tossed and turned and fretted, and when sleep finally claimed her, it was fitful. She blamed Glen for that—and for a whole lot more. It was because of him she was late, but at the moment she'd have been willing to blame him for global warming.

Even after the song had ended and Pastor Wade McMillen started his sermon, Ellie felt the scrutiny of friends and neighbors. That, too, could be directly attributed to Glen. The man had single-handedly made her the object of speculation and gossip. Wringing his neck would be too good for him. First he'd embarrassed her in front of the entire town by making a spectacle of himself fighting over her. If that wasn't enough, he'd woken her out of a dead sleep, insulted her—then kissed her senseless. Ellie couldn't recall a time anyone had confused her more.

Not that she was Richard's champion. No way! He'd intentionally provoked Glen, leading him to believe the two of them were involved when it simply wasn't true. Besides, Richard was selfish and untrustworthy, and Glen was... Glen. Her friend.

Naturally Glen had skipped church. Richard, too. No doubt the effort of carting around their massive egos had worn them out, she thought irritably. It might have helped had they shown up to divide the attention now directed solely at her.

By concentrating on Wade's sermon, she managed to pretend she didn't notice her newfound celebrity status. At the end of the service following the benediction, she hoped to slip away unnoticed; it soon became apparent that this wasn't going to happen. The organ music filled the church as the congregation started to flow outside and Ellie was surrounded.

"I saw everything," Louise Powell purred, sidling up to Ellie as though they were long-standing friends. "It isn't every woman who has two men virtually at each other's throats."

"I think you misunderstood what happened," Ellie said desperately.

"I've known Glen Patterson all my life," Ruth Bishop was saying behind Louise, "and when he wants something, he gets it."

"I wouldn't underestimate Richard Weston," Louise said. "He's a man of the world. Ellie could do worse."

Ellie hated it when people spoke as if they knew more about her life than she did.

"Stay close to me," Edwina Moorhouse whispered, suddenly slipping next to Ellie and taking her arm. "Lily," she instructed her younger sister, "go on the other side." Again for Ellie's ears only, she added, "Just keep walking. We'll have you out of here in no time."

Ellie found herself grateful for the Moorhouse sisters' protection. Especially from Louise Powell, the town gossip; a woman who enjoyed meddling in the affairs of others, often under the guise of concern.

"Ladies, ladies," Louise said in a sharp voice, tagging behind Ellie and the Moorhouse sisters. "*I* was chatting with Ellie."

"You aren't any longer," Edwina declared, stepping in front of Ellie.

If it hadn't been so ridiculous, and if she hadn't felt so tired and worn-out, Ellie would have laughed. Each sister positioned herself in a way that told Louise she'd have a fight on her hands before they'd willingly abandon Ellie. The two unlikely guardians were dressed in their Sunday best, with crisp white gloves and pillbox hats.

"All I wanted to do—"

"We know very well what you were doing, Louise," Edwina said in a voice that reminded Ellie of her school days.

"Louise," Lily said, not unkindly, "do you remember in sixth grade when Larry Marin…"

Louise's face turned beet red. "I remember," she whispered.

"It would be embarrassing if news of you and Larry somehow got around town, wouldn't it?"

"That was nearly forty years ago!" Louise protested.

"And just as scandalous today as it was back then," Lily said primly. "Now, as Edwina was saying, Ellie's with *us*."

"Oh, all right." The other woman flounced off with her rumpled dignity and returned to where her husband stood impatiently waiting.

"Lily!" Edwina gasped. "What happened between Louise and Larry in the sixth grade?"

Lily covered her mouth with her hand. "God's honest truth, sister, I don't know."

"Sister, you amaze me."

"You!" Ellie giggled. She could certainly have dealt with a busybody like Louise Powell on her own, but this was much more fun.

Edwina waited until Louise was out of earshot, then she turned around and regarded Ellie with deep affection. "Are you all right, Ellie?"

"Of course."

"I'd like to box a few ears," Lily said. "We didn't teach our students to stare, did we, sister?"

"Positively not."

"I hope you're willing to forgive everyone's curiosity?"

"It's only natural, I suppose," Ellie said agreeably. "Especially in light of what happened at the dance."

"Yes, we did hear about that." Lily patted Ellie's hand. "I realize you didn't ask Edwina's or my advice, but I feel compelled to offer you a few words of wisdom."

"Since your mother isn't here," Edwina inserted.

"Please do." Ellie had always loved the Moorhouse

sisters and wouldn't even consider turning down anything they offered.

"We may never have married, but Edwina and I do know a thing or two about love."

"I'm sure that's true."

Edwina caught Ellie's hand in her own. "Follow your heart, child."

"Yes, indeed, follow your heart," Lily echoed.

"I will," Ellie promised, and she would, just as soon as her heart had sorted everything out.

Still thinking about their advice, Ellie drove home, stopping first at the grocery store to pick up a few essentials. When she turned onto her street, she noticed the pickup outside her house. She groaned when she found Richard sitting on her porch, waiting for her return.

He was the last person she wanted to see. Not that she was ready to see Glen anytime soon, either. She refused to think about the kisses they'd shared or the reasons he'd come by her house after the disastrous dance. Her fear was that he saw Richard and himself as rivals for her. And that this had influenced his actions and his declarations.

What he didn't know was that Richard hadn't kissed her. Not for lack of trying, mind you, but because she was in no mood for him or his games.

Realizing she had no escape, Ellie pulled into her driveway and climbed out of the car. Richard glanced up, apparently surprised to see her loaded down with groceries.

"Ellie," he said, smiling brightly. He leaped to his feet and raced down the steps to take the bags out of her arms. "You should have said something," he chastised as if he'd waited all day for the honor of carrying her groceries.

Ellie tried to refuse his help, but he'd have none of it. "Hey, it's the least I can do." It also gave him the perfect excuse to follow her into the house, Ellie noted despondently.

He set the bags on the kitchen counter and immediately started unpacking them. "Look at this," he said as if finding a dozen eggs was akin to discovering gold. "I swear I was thinking just five minutes ago how much I'd enjoy a mushroom-and-Swiss-cheese omelet." Gesturing like a magician, he pulled a paper sack of mushrooms free of the bag, along with a slab of Swiss cheese. "It's fate," he said, his eyes twinkling.

"Richard, I don't think—"

"I'll cook," he said. He clasped her shoulders and backed her into a kitchen chair. "Sit down and make yourself at home."

"I am home," she interrupted, amused despite herself at his audacity.

He stopped a moment and smiled, then said, "So you are."

She started to stand, but he wouldn't allow it.

"I'm cooking," he said cheerfully, pushing her into the chair again.

"Richard—"

"I won't take no for an answer." He opened the cupboard door and took out a small bowl. Before Ellie could stop him, he was whirling about her kitchen as if he'd been cooking there his entire life.

To his credit he seemed to know what he was doing.

"You look especially lovely this morning," he said, pouring the eggs into the skillet.

"Yeah, yeah." Ellie was in no mood for empty flattery. "I've heard that before."

"Only because it's true." He whistled something jaunty as he edged a spatula under the omelet.

The doorbell rang and with a wave of his hand Richard motioned for her to answer it.

Ellie was too concerned with how to expel Richard from her home to be affronted by his peremptory manner—or to worry about who'd come calling unannounced. Hindsight being what it was, she wished later she'd given the matter some thought before she opened the door.

Glen Patterson stood on the other side.

Ellie's mouth fell open. She hadn't expected to see him.

"Glen!"

"Who is it, sweetheart?" Richard asked, stepping out of the kitchen, a dish towel tucked at his waist. He carried the frying pan and spatula in his hands and didn't miss a beat when he saw Glen.

"Howdy, neighbor," he called. "I'm stirring up a little brunch here. You're welcome to join us if you want."

Glen's eyes hardened as he looked at Ellie. She tried to tell him without words that it wasn't how it seemed; that she hadn't *asked* Richard to join her, he'd come uninvited. But Glen had already formed his own opinion, and nothing she did now was likely to change it.

"I'll be back another time," he muttered.

"Stay," Richard urged like a gracious host. "Cooking is one of my talents. Ask Ellie."

It was all she could manage not to wheel around and kick Richard in the shin.

* * *

Three days had passed since Glen had stumbled on Richard cooking Ellie's breakfast. Three miserable days. He still couldn't think about it and not get mad.

He hadn't seen Ellie, hadn't talked to her in those three days. Generally he dropped in the feed store for supplies on Tuesday afternoons. Almost always they'd spend a few minutes together, joking, teasing, laughing. There'd been damn little of that lately. He didn't drive into town on Tuesday, and he wasn't eager to make the trip on Wednesday, either. It would do Ellie good to miss his company, not that he'd received any indication that she had.

Ellie preyed on his mind, making him next to useless around the ranch. Disgusted, Cal sent him out to check fence lines. If that was meant to distract him, it hadn't worked. Grandpa Patterson used to say: Never approach a bull from the front, a horse from the rear or a fool from any direction. Well, Glen couldn't help feeling like a fool, and his mind seemed to be spinning in *every* direction.

His thinking was clouded with thoughts of Ellie as he trotted back toward the ranch. When he wasn't thinking about her, he was brooding about Richard Weston. Glen feared Richard was using the time he stayed away from Ellie to further his own cause.

If that was true, then so be it. If Ellie wanted Richard, fine, she was welcome to him but he'd figured she had more sense.

A man had his pride, too. Glen had kissed Ellie on two occasions now, and if he could recognize that they had something pretty special, why couldn't she? Okay, so they hadn't talked about their feelings, but Glen had been hoping to do that on Sunday. Only he couldn't because Richard was there, playing Julia Child.

The way he saw it, Ellie owed him an apology. She'd misled him, kissing him like she had, then cozying up to Richard. He'd never have taken Ellie for the type of woman who'd play one man against another, but he'd seen the evidence with his own eyes.

Cal was waiting for him when he led Moonshine into the barn.

"Are you picking up supplies this week or not?" Cal demanded.

"I'll get them," Glen replied without enthusiasm.

"If it's a problem, I'll drive into town myself."

"It's no problem," Glen said. Damn it, he couldn't stay away a minute longer, and he knew it.

By the time Glen cleaned up and drove into town, his throat was parched. More to fortify his courage than to cure his thirst, he decided to stop at Billy D's for a cold beer.

Billy D himself was behind the bar when Glen sauntered in. The ranchers tended to congregate here when they came to town, and there was usually someone he knew. Billy was the friendly sort and something of an institution in Promise. He baked a decent pizza, and his fried chicken was as good as any colonel's; but few people came to Billy D's for the food. It was the one place in town, other than the bowling alley and the feed store, where ranchers could shoot the breeze and unwind. And at Billy's they could do it over a beer.

"Well, if it ain't Glen Patterson himself," Billy called out when Glen walked in.

A couple of ranchers lounging against the bar raised their hands in greeting.

Glen tipped his Stetson a little farther back on his head.

"You want a cold one?" Billy asked.

"Sounds good." Glen stepped up to the bar and set some money down on the counter.

With practiced ease Billy slid the thick mug down the polished bar and Glen grabbed it before it flew past.

"Keep your money. It's on the house," Billy said, smiling broadly.

Glen arched his brows and lifted the mug to his lips. Nothing tasted better than a cold beer on a hot day, especially when it was free. It slid down the back of his throat, easing away the taste of several hours of eating dust.

"Any reason you're giving away beer this afternoon?" he asked when he'd downed half the mug.

"Only to you," Billy informed him.

"What's so special about me?"

Billy gave him a look that suggested he open his eyes. "I figure you're gonna set Richard Weston on his ear. In fact, I'm waitin' to see it."

Glen frowned. "I don't have any fight with Weston." Ellie would probably love it if he acted like an idiot— yet again—but he was finished with that game. Those two were welcome to each other. Glen had decided to wash his hands of the whole thing. If Ellie wanted to marry Richard, then he wasn't going to stand in her way.

"You don't care?" Billy looked as if he wanted his beer back. "Richard's been by, and to hear him talk, he's done everything but put an engagement ring on Ellie's finger. You aren't going to let that happen, are you?"

"What am I supposed to do about it?" Glen asked, hardening his heart in order to avoid showing his feelings.

Billy frowned. He braced both hands on the bar and leaned forward as though to get a better look at Glen. "You're serious about this?"

"Damn right, I'm serious."

"That's not the impression I got Saturday night. The three of you are the hot topic of conversation this week, dancing that Texas two-step of yours. Some folks've started placing bets on which of you is gonna marry Ellie."

"As far as I'm concerned Richard can have her." It was a bald-faced lie, but Glen considered it damage control. For his ego *and* his reputation.

"Personally I think you're the better man," Lyle Whitehouse said. His back was to the bar and he'd rested his elbows behind him. Lyle worked at a ranch closer to Brewster than to Promise, but he'd worn out his welcome at more than a few places. He had a reputation as a hothead, although he hadn't started any fights at Billy D's. Yet.

Jimmy Morris stood beside him, his stomach pressed to the bar and one boot on the brass foot rail. "When you're talkin' marriage, it isn't a matter of bein' better," he said ponderously. "Ladies choose who they choose."

"True enough," Lyle agreed. "But it doesn't hurt to try a bit of persuasion..." He winked. "You know what I mean."

"Richard seems to think he's got an edge on you," Billy informed Glen, "and no one likes a man who's too confident."

"Even if he does buy the drinks," Jimmy added.

"Richard's celebrating already?" Glen asked, wondering if Richard knew something no one else did. Maybe he'd already asked Ellie and maybe she'd given him an encouraging response. The thought twisted his gut. To this point he'd trusted Ellie's judgment. More or less. He was miserable and uncertain about her and Richard, but he'd always supposed that in the end Ellie would turn to him. Because of their friendship and everything they had in common...and their kisses.

Those kisses in the wee hours of Saturday night had been wonderful, the best of his life. He found it hard to believe they'd meant so little to her.

"Weston's so sure of himself he's taking odds."

"Making himself the favorite," Billy said, his mouth thinning with disapproval.

"Naturally," Jimmy muttered and took a swallow of beer.

"We were kinda hopin' you'd set him down a peg or two," Lyle said in a tone that suggested more than one rancher had pinned his hopes on Glen.

Glen didn't know what it was about Richard Weston. He'd never met anyone so likable, yet so universally disliked. He could be charming, witty and fun, and at the same time he was the biggest jackass in the state of Texas.

"What do you think?" Billy pressed.

"You're not gonna take this sittin' down, are you?" Lyle asked.

"You gotta do something," Jimmy added. "We got money on you!"

All three men looked to Glen. Unfortunately he didn't know *what* the hell to do.

One of the most difficult things Richard Weston had ever done was return to Promise—broke, his tail between his legs, seeking a handout from his family. Once he was home again, he figured he'd die of sheer boredom inside a month. Promise was about as Hicktown, U.S.A., as it could get. He stared at the walls of his old bedroom and sighed. Never in a million years did he guess he'd end up back here.

What intrigued him was how gullible folks in Promise were. Everyone—well, except for the sheriff and he couldn't *prove* anything—accepted his lies without pause or question. In fact, he'd gotten a little careless, but it didn't seem to matter. He'd certainly been right in assuming that he'd be safe here, at the ranch—safe from his troubles back east.

The boredom, though. He sighed. And the cows...

It'd taken him the better part of six years to get the stench of cattle from his skin. He'd never understood the attraction of following a bunch of pathetic-looking beasts from pasture to pasture. As far as he was concerned, cattle were headaches on the hoof. Yet his father and his brother had always acted as though there was nothing more wonderful in life than ranching. But it sure wasn't for him; never had been, never would be. The mere thought of sitting in a saddle all day made him want to puke, although God knew Grady had done his best to get him to do some work around the place. Thus far, he'd managed to avoid doing anything of consequence. He'd volunteered to run errands, which gave him free use of the pickup—something that had come in handy for other reasons. The tradespeople around Promise trusted him, assumed he was taking care of ranch business. And he was. But he was seeing to his own needs, as well.

To his surprise he'd discovered some pleasant distractions in Promise. Ellie Frasier, for one. She was a sweet thing, pretty, too, if a guy didn't mind small breasts and skinny legs. Personally he preferred a more voluptuous woman, but Ellie came with certain monetary compensations. A prosperous business, plus a healthy inheritance from her daddy, who'd doted on his only child.

It wouldn't hurt him any to get his hands on old-man Frasier's money. He could use it. He was in trouble, but all it took was money in the right places and his problem would vanish.

For now he was safe enough in Promise. No one knew about his family, and even if they managed to track him to Texas, they'd never find his hiding place.

He had Savannah to thank for that. He'd always been lucky—at least until his present difficulties. But then, everything had a way of working out. This latest episode was a good example.

No, he decided, lying on top of his quilt, hands folded behind his head, there could be worse things in this world than marrying Ellie Frasier. He'd ask her soon, and if she was opposed to selling the business, then he'd take it over. He could do well with it, too—aside from the fact that it would provide collateral for raising quick cash.

Actually Richard liked the idea of becoming a local

businessman. He could remember one of his teachers, Lily Moorhouse, telling him he should be a politician. The old biddy just could be right. In a year or two he might even consider running for mayor. Promise could use his kind of leadership. This hayseed town needed someone to bring it into the twenty-first century.

The town had real possibilities, if he could convince people to listen to his ideas. For starters they needed to close down the bowling alley; in his view it gave the place a white-trash image. He'd buy up land outside town and get some investors to build a shopping complex. If not that, he'd bet he could get one of the big discount stores interested in the area. It was time the local shop owners found out about competitive pricing.

Everything hinged on Ellie. They'd kissed a couple of times, and although she didn't exactly set him ablaze, she wasn't bad. He knew she was sweet on Glen Patterson. That might be cause for concern if Patterson wasn't so intent on putting his foot in his mouth, which he seemed to do with increasing regularity. Fortunately for Richard.

Poor guy was out of his league with women, unlike Richard who had the whole mating ritual down to an art. The way he figured it, Ellie would agree to marry him before the end of the month. Maybe sooner. When he turned on the charm, there wasn't a female within six states who could refuse him. Little Ellie Frasier didn't have a snowball's chance in hell.

And over at Billy D's Richard stood to pick up a few extra bucks betting on his own chances in the Texas two-step.

Altogether a sweet deal.

* * *

For most of his adult life Glen had been confident and self-assured. He'd taken over the family ranch with his brother, worked hard, kept his nose clean. Romantic involvements had been light and ultimately insignificant, causing no pain when they ended. Until now there'd been little to disrupt his calm existence.

Any problems he either solved himself or sought advice from Cal. This was the first time since he was thirteen years old that he felt the need to speak to his father about girls. Women. What his grandfather used to call "personal matters."

His parents had moved into town a few years ago. His father had suffered a heart attack, and although the doctors had said he was good as new following his bypass surgery, his mother wasn't taking any chances. For years they'd talked about moving into Promise one day. His father had insisted he wasn't ready to retire, so they'd bought the Howe Mansion, which wasn't really a mansion, just the largest house in town. Before another year was up it'd been renovated and turned into a bed-and-breakfast.

Glen had had his doubts about this venture. Cal, too. But their parents had proved them both wrong. The bed-and-breakfast was thriving, and so were Phil and Mary Patterson.

His mother complained that she didn't see near enough of her sons. That being the case, she certainly looked surprised to see Glen when he walked into her kitchen.

"Hi, Mom," he said, slipping up behind her and kissing her cheek.

Mary Patterson hugged him as though it'd been a

week of Sundays since his last visit. "Taste this," she said, sticking a spoon in his face.

"What is it?" Glen asked, jerking he head back. He preferred not to be part of a culinary experiment.

"Chili. I'm practicing for the cook-off."

"Mom, that's not for months yet."

"I know. This is a new recipe I've been playing around with. What do you think?"

Despite his better judgment, Glen tried the chili and tried to hide his response. It tasted…well, not like food. Not like something you'd seriously consider eating.

"It needs work, right?" she asked, studying him.

He nodded. For her guests his mother generally stayed with plain basic food. Good thing. "This recipe needs a rethink, Mom."

She sighed and tossed the spoon into the sink. "I was afraid of that."

"Where's Dad?" Glen asked, hoping to make the inquiry sound casual.

"Upstairs. The sink in the bathroom's plugged again." Her gaze didn't waver from his. "Something on your mind?"

He nodded. He could never hide anything from his mother.

"Does it involve Ellie Frasier?"

"Yeah."

She grinned and pointed toward the stairway off the kitchen. "Talk to your father, but if you want advice about how to romance her, talk to me. Your father doesn't know a damn thing about romance."

Hiding a smile, Glen headed for the stairs. Just as

his mother had said, he found his dad lying on the tile floor staring up at the sink, wrench in hand.

"Hi, Dad."

"I thought I heard you downstairs talking to your mother." Phil Patterson slid out from beneath the sink and reached for a rag to dry his hands. "And to think she was worried about me working too hard on the ranch. If anything's going to kill me, it'll be this sink."

Glen sat down on the edge of the tub.

"Did you have something you wanted to ask me, son?"

Leaning forward, Glen removed his Stetson, slowly turning it in his hand. "How many years have you and Mom been married?"

"Well, your brother's thirty-six, so this year we had our thirty-seventh anniversary. Thirty-seven years! Damn, it doesn't seem that long. Hell if I can figure out when I got old."

"You're not."

Phil smiled. "That's my boy. Buttering me up, are you? So what do you need?"

"Just some advice."

"Be glad to help if I can." With an exaggerated groan, he stood up, lowered the toilet seat and sat there.

Glen wasn't sure where to start. "When did you know you loved Mom?"

Phil considered the question for a moment. "When she told me I did." He chuckled and Glen joined in. "Don't laugh too hard, boy, it's the truth. We'd dated in high school some, but she was two years younger. After I graduated, I enlisted. Joined the navy. We wrote back and forth and I saw a little of the world.

Eventually your mother graduated and went away to college in Dallas. We didn't see each other for three years, but we kept in touch. I must say she wrote a lot more letters than me.

"Then one Christmas, we both happened to be home at the same time. It was a shock to see her again. We'd been friends, stayed in touch, but somehow I'd never noticed how pretty she was."

Glen nodded; his mother was still a pretty woman.

"I wasn't the only one who noticed, either," his father continued. "She got more attention than a prize heifer at the state fair. Until that Christmas I'd always thought of her as a friend. We'd dated from time to time, but it was nothing serious. That Christmas my eyes were opened."

"Did you ask her to marry you then?"

"Hell, no. I wasn't happy about other men paying attention to her, but I figured if she wanted to date someone else, I didn't have the right to stand in her way."

"You were sweet on her, though?"

"Yeah, but I didn't realize how much until we'd kissed a few times."

Now that was something Glen could understand. "Did you try to talk to her?"

Phil chuckled again. "I sure did, but all we seemed to do was argue. Nothing I said was right. I told her I thought she was pretty, and even that came out like an insult."

This story was sounding more familiar by the minute. "So what happened?"

His father grew thoughtful. "It was time to head back to the base, and I knew if I didn't try to explain myself one last time, I might not get another chance.

I called her all evening, but she was out—you can imagine how *that* made me feel, especially since I couldn't very well ring her doorbell in the middle of the night." He smiled at the memory. "So I stood outside her bedroom and threw stones at the window until she woke up.

"It's not a good idea to wake your mother out of a sound sleep, even now. It took me a while to convince her to hear me out. Luckily she agreed and sat with me on the porch. By that time I was so confused I didn't know what to say."

Glen edged closer to his father, keenly interested in the details of his parents' courtship.

"I stammered and stuttered and told her how much I valued her friendship and hated the idea of returning to Maine with this bad feeling between us. That was when she looked me full in the eye and asked if I loved her."

His mother had always been a gutsy woman and Glen admired her for it. "What did you tell her?"

"I didn't know what to say. It was the first time I'd ever thought about it. We were friends, hung around with the same crowd, exchanged letters, that sort of thing. She wanted to know if I loved her, and for the life of me I didn't have an answer."

It went without saying that wasn't what his mother had wanted to hear.

"When I hesitated, Mary leaped to her feet and announced I was the biggest fool who'd ever lived if I hadn't figured out how I felt about her after three years. My, was she mad." Shaking his head, he rubbed the side of his jaw. "Her eyes had fire in them. In all the years we've been married, I've only seen her get that riled a handful of times. She told me if I married some Yankee girl I'd regret it the rest of my life."

He paused a moment, lost in his memories. "Then before I could stop her, she raced into the house. By the time I'd gathered my wits and followed her, she was already running up the stairs. Her father and her mother both stood on the landing, looking down at me as though they wanted to string me up from the nearest tree."

"What'd you do?"

"What I should have done a hell of a lot sooner. I shouted up at her father for permission to marry his daughter."

That scene filled Glen's mind. His father a young sailor, standing at the bottom of the stairs, watching the love of his life racing away. "What'd Mom do?"

"She stopped, halfway between her parents and me. I'll never forget the look of shock on her face as she turned around and stared at me."

"She burst into tears, right?"

"No. She stood here, calm as could be and asked me when I wanted the wedding to take place. Hell if I knew, so I said that was up to her, and she suggested six months."

"I thought your anniversary was Valentine's Day."

"It is. Once we decided to get married, I wasn't willing to wait six months. By summer she was pregnant with your brother." He looked at Glen. "Why all these questions?"

"Just curious."

"You going to ask Ellie to marry you?"

"I've been thinking about it."

His father's grin widened. "Did she tell you you're in love with her yet?"

"Nope. I don't think she realizes it herself."

Phil stood and slapped him on the back. "Then start a new family tradition and tell her yourself, boy. It's about time the men in this family took the initiative."

Eight

Richard rolled out of bed and reached for his jeans. Savannah was making breakfast, and if his nose didn't deceive him, it smelled like one of his favorites. French toast.

Yawning, he grabbed a shirt on his way out the door and bounded down the stairs and into the kitchen.

"Mornin'," he said, yawning again. He glanced at the wall clock and was surprised to see it was after nine. A midmorning breakfast cooked specially for him meant his sister was planning on a little heart-to-heart. Damn.

"Morning," Savannah returned in that gentle way of hers. At times it was all he could do not to leap behind her, waving his arms and screaming at the top of his lungs. He wondered if he'd get a reaction from her even then. Somehow he doubted it.

"Grady needs you to drive into town this morning."

"No problem." Actually Richard liked running errands. They suited his purpose. Every time Grady sent him into town, he managed to pick up an item or two for himself and put it on his brother's tab without Grady's knowing a thing about it.

Savannah delivered a plate to the table where Richard sat waiting. He dug into the meal after slathering his hot toast with plenty of butter and syrup. Savannah didn't disappear, which meant the errand for Grady wasn't the only thing on her mind.

"There's been plenty of talk around town about you and Ellie," she said, clutching the back of the chair opposite his.

The tension in her fingers told him she felt awkward addressing the subject. Lord, his sister was easy to read!

"That so?" He stuffed another forkful of French toast in his mouth.

"Ellie's a real sweetheart."

He shrugged.

Savannah pulled out the chair and sat down.

Damn it, he'd asked for that. Knowing his sister was fond of the other woman, he should have talked her up, fabricated a few things, let his sister think he'd fallen in love with Ellie. He hadn't, but his interest in her was definitely high at the moment. A lot was riding on this, and if he managed to manipulate the situation to his liking, it meant staying in the community. After fixing his current problems of course. Yeah, he could see a future here. Become one of the leading lights in Promise. Turn this place around. And it all hinged on little Ellie Frasier.

"I don't want you to hurt her, Richard."

This was quite a statement from Savannah. "Hurt Ellie?" He tried to look shocked that she'd even suggest such a thing.

"Ellie's…fragile just now."

"I wouldn't dream of doing anything to hurt Ellie." He set his fork down as if to say the mere idea had robbed him of his appetite.

"Then your intentions are honorable?"

Leave it to Savannah to sound like she was living in the nineteenth century. She could've set up camp at Bitter End and fit right in.

"Of course my intentions are honorable. In fact, I intend to ask Ellie to be my wife." Richard assumed this was what Savannah wanted to hear, but she didn't react the way he'd expected. He'd hoped that when he mentioned words like *wife* and *marriage,* she'd go all feminine on him and start nattering about wedding plans.

"It's a big step for me," he added, thinking she'd be quick to praise his decision.

Savannah frowned. "I heard about this little lottery thing you've got going."

"Oh, that." He dismissed her concern with an airy gesture. Word traveled fast in small towns and he'd forgotten that.

"I don't think placing bets on…on love, on whether Ellie's going to marry you or Glen, is such a good idea."

"It was a joke," he said. What Savannah didn't understand and what he couldn't tell her was that the whole thing had gotten started when he'd had one too many beers. Naturally he'd taken a lot of ribbing about the fiasco at the dance.

The whole thing was Glen Patterson's fault. In Richard's opinion, the rancher owed him an apology.

Ellie had been *his* date and Glen had been way out of line butting in at the dance.

"Joking with another person's affections—"

"I'm not joking with Ellie," Richard interrupted. "I love her, Savannah," he said, doing his best to look and sound sincere. What he really loved about Ellie Frasier was the store and her inheritance. That Ellie wasn't hard on the eyes was a bonus. Marriage wasn't such a bad idea, either. He could grow accustomed to bedded bliss, not to mention regular meals. Savannah had spoiled him, preparing elaborate dinners and baking his favorite goodies, although she tended to do less of that these days.

"It isn't only Ellie I want to talk to you about."

"You mean there's more?" He tried not to sound perturbed, but really, this was getting ridiculous. He didn't need his big sister prying into his private life, nor did he appreciate this need she had to lecture him. He'd been out of the schoolroom too many years to sit still for much more of this.

His sister pursed her lips in exactly the way their mother used to. "I got a phone call from Millie about an unpaid flower bill."

"Millie?"

"You know Millie." Her tone left no room for argument.

"Oh, that Millie." He was walking a tightrope when it came to a number of charges he'd made in town during the past few months. He'd hoped to have moved on by now, but this romance with Ellie had fallen into his lap and he couldn't let the opportunity just slip through his fingers. He'd also made contingency plans—no fool he. He'd found the perfect hiding place when and if he needed it. But he couldn't leave Promise yet and perhaps not for some time. Keeping Grady and Savannah in the dark until he'd secured his future was proving to be something of a challenge.

"Millie said you owed her four hundred dollars. I realize your…check hasn't arrived yet—" she didn't meet his eyes "—but you *have* to make some kind of arrangement with Millie."

He toyed with the idea of being shocked to hear it was that much money, but thought better of it. "Well, I have just a little money left." He hoped that was vague enough so she wouldn't question it. "In fact, I was in just yesterday and made a payment," he said.

"I talked to Millie yesterday and she claimed she hadn't seen you in weeks." Savannah's eyes had never been that cool before.

"I didn't see Millie, just one of her employees."

"I didn't know Millie had anyone working for her." Savannah pinned him with her gaze.

"Summer help, I assume," he murmured. "I've got the receipt up in my room if you want to see it." He put the right amount of indignation into his voice to make sure she understood he found her lack of trust insulting.

"If you say you made a payment, then I don't have any choice but to believe you."

Richard shoved his chair away from the table. "I'm getting the distinct impression I'm no longer welcome around here." He stopped short of reminding her he'd been born and raised in this very house, fearing that might be overkill, even with a softhearted woman like his sister.

"It isn't that."

"I've come home," he said, tilting his chin at a proud angle. "It wasn't easy to arrive on your doorstep with nothing. Now that I'm here, I've realized that I made a mistake ever leaving. Promise is my home. I've fallen in love and I want to make a new life for myself with friends and neighbors I grew up with. People I've known all my life. If you want to kick me out, then all you or Grady need to do is say the word and I'll be gone." He drew the line and dared her to cross it. Basically it was a gamble, but one he was willing to take. He'd been a gambler most of his life, after all—one who usually had an ace up his sleeve.

"I won't ask you to move," she said after a moment. He hadn't really thought she would.

"But I'm giving you fair warning—tread lightly when it comes to Ellie."

He widened his eyes, disliking her brisk tone.

"And pay your bills. Once Grady gets wind of this, there'll be trouble. His nature isn't nearly as generous as mine."

"You haven't got a thing to worry about," Richard said, and as a conciliatory gesture, he carried his plate to the sink.

It had sounded so simple when Glen talked to his father nearly a week earlier. Asking Ellie to marry him had seemed the right thing to do. But Richard's interest in her had muddied an already complicated issue. From the gossip circulating around town, Weston had definitely taken advantage of the time Glen stayed away.

Fine. Great. Wonderful. If Ellie was so impressed with Richard, she could have him. At least that was what Glen told himself a dozen times a day, but no matter how often he said it, he couldn't quite make himself believe it.

"I don't know what the hell I'm going to do," he muttered. He sometimes did his thinking out loud, and talking to a horse was safer than talking to certain people. As he cleaned the gelding's hooves, Moonshine perked up his ears in apparent sympathy.

"You talking to me?" Cal shouted from the other side of the barn.

Glen didn't realize his brother was anywhere nearby. "No," he hollered, hoping to discourage further conversation.

It didn't work.

"Who you talking to, then?"

"No one!" he snapped. Glen was the first to admit he hadn't been great company lately. That was one reason he'd kept to himself as much as possible and avoided Cal.

"You still down in the mouth about Ellie?" Cal asked, sounding much closer this time.

It was on the tip of Glen's tongue to tell his brother to mind his own damn business. Lord, but he was tired of it all. Tired of being so confused by this woman he could no longer think. Tired of worrying she'd actually marry Richard. Tired of feeling miserable.

"How'd I get into this mess?" Glen asked hopelessly.

"Women specialize in wearing a man down," Cal said, peering into the stall.

"Ellie isn't Jennifer," Glen felt obliged to remind him. That was the problem with discussing things with Cal. His brother refused to look past the pain and embarrassment his ex-fiancée had caused him. Everything was tainted by their ruined relationship.

"I know."

Glen lowered Moonshine's foot to the ground and slowly straightened. The small of his back ached. He pressed his hand to the area and massaged the sore muscles before he opened the stall door.

Glen watched Cal carry a bucket of oats to his own gelding. Suddenly it was all too much. He couldn't stand it anymore. Damn it all, he *loved* Ellie and if she wasn't willing to come to him, then by God he'd go to her. The rush of relief he experienced was overwhelming.

"I'm asking Ellie to marry me," he said boldly, bracing himself for the backlash of Cal's reaction.

Cal went very still. Finally he asked, "Is that what you want?"

"Damn straight it is."

"Then…great."

Glen blinked, wondering if he was hearing things. The one person he'd expected to talk him out of proposing was Cal.

"You love her?"

"Of course I do," Glen said. "I wouldn't ask a woman to share my life if I didn't."

Cal laughed and slapped Glen on the shoulder. "So I guess congratulations are in order."

Glen rubbed his hand across the back of his neck. He didn't feel like throwing a party just yet.

"When are you going to ask her?"

"I… I don't know yet," Glen confessed. He'd only decided this five seconds ago.

He glanced at his watch. If he showered quickly he

could make the drive into town and talk to Ellie before she left the shop. It seemed fitting that he ask her
to marry him at the feed store, considering that most
of their courtship had taken place there. At the time,
however, he hadn't *realized* he'd been courting her.

"I think I'll do it tonight," he said. Feeling euphoric,
he'd dashed halfway out of the barn when Cal stopped
him.

"Have you got her an engagement ring?"

A ring? Damn, he hadn't thought of that. "Do I
need one?"

"It doesn't hurt."

Glen could feel the panic rising up inside him. Cal
must have seen it, too, because he offered Glen the
ring he had in his bottom drawer.

"I've still got the one I bought for Jennifer."

"But that belongs to you."

"Go ahead and take it. It's a beautiful diamond.
After Ellie agrees, then the two of you can go shopping and pick out a new one if she wants. Although
this one's perfectly good."

Things were beginning to fall nicely into place.
"Thanks." As Glen recalled, Cal had gone for broke
buying Jennifer's diamond. Damn shame to keep it
buried in a drawer. If Ellie liked that ring, he'd buy it
from his brother; she need never know the ring was
slightly used.

A quick shower revitalized him. He sang as he lath-
ered up, then raised his face to the spray, laughing as
the water rushed over him. When he'd finished, he
shook his head like a long-haired dog fresh from a
dip in the pond. Still smiling, he dressed in a clean
shirt and jeans.

He felt drunk with happiness.

Glen didn't sober up until he reached town. Then and only then did the seriousness of his mission strike him. Not once had he given any thought to how he would word his proposal.

This was quite possibly the most important conversation of his life and he hadn't even rehearsed it! His father had spoken to his potential father-in-law and not the bride. But even if Ellie's father were alive, that approach didn't really work anymore. Too old-fashioned.

He thought about getting down on one knee and spilling out his heart, but immediately dismissed the idea. No one did that sort of thing these days. Much too formal. By the same token, he didn't want to make an offer of marriage sound like an invitation to go bowling, either. All he could do was hope the right approach presented itself when the moment arrived.

It was nearly closing time when he got to the store. Ellie was on the loading dock at the far end of the building, giving instructions to a delivery-truck driver as Glen parked his own truck in front of the store and turned off the engine. She damn near fell off the dock in surprise when she saw him.

That was promising, Glen thought. She must've missed him. He'd missed *her* like hell, and telling her so was probably as good a place to start as any. Having decided that much, he climbed out of the cab and walked up the steps.

"Hello, Glen," Ellie's assistant greeted.

"Hi, George."

"Good to see you," George Tucker said, then added in a low voice, "Damn good."

"Glad to hear it." Glen sat down in one of the lawn

chairs by the front door near the soda machine, and waited until Ellie was free. It took almost ten minutes to supervise the unloading of a truckload of hay, but he was a patient man.

Ellie signed the necessary papers, then stood there for a moment, blinking into the sun. Her face was pink, and the hair at the back of her head was damp and clinging to her neck. It'd obviously been a long hot day.

"Do you have a few minutes?" he asked when she'd finished. "I'd like to talk to you—*privately*." He added this last bit in case Richard was anywhere around.

"Privately," Ellie repeated. Small vertical frown lines appeared between her brows.

"There's, uh, something I'd like to discuss with you. Privately," he said again.

"Do you want a cold drink?"

It was almost like old times, he told himself. Casual, relaxed, two friends talking.

"Something cold'd hit the spot," he said, answering Ellie's question.

She retrieved change from her pocket and slipped the coins into the pop machine. She handed him one of the cold damp cans and pressed the other to her forehead, then claimed the chair beside his.

Glen opened his drink, pulling back the tab with a small hissing sound, and took a long swallow.

George appeared. "Do you need me to do anything else?" he asked.

Ellie shook her head. "You're free to go, thanks, George."

"I'll see you in the morning, then," he said, turning the Open sign to Closed on his way past.

It might have been Glen's imagination, but Ellie's assistant seemed eager to be on his way.

Ellie answered his question before he could even ask it. "It's his bowling night," she explained.

His parents were like that, Glen mused. Often, his dad didn't need to voice his thoughts for his mother to know what he was thinking. Sometimes that was true of close friends, as well. With Ellie, he could have love *and* friendship, and surely that was the best way to enter a marriage.

The late-afternoon sun blazed, but the heat didn't seem nearly as bad, now that he was sitting in the shade with Ellie. A slight breeze stirred, cooling his skin, ruffling her hair.

"You wanted to talk to me," Ellie began.

"Yeah." Glen had hoped to make this as natural as possible.

"You haven't been in for a while," she said, staring straight ahead.

Ten days, not that Glen was keeping track or anything. Cal had taken care of the errands these past two weeks while Glen stayed close to the ranch.

"I've been busy," Glen said, deciding it probably wasn't a good idea to mention he'd been waiting to hear from her.

"So have I."

Glen could just imagine who she'd been busy with, but he didn't dare say that. Richard Weston wasn't a name he wanted to introduce into their conversation—although he did wonder how much she'd been seeing of the guy.

"I wanted to talk to you about the dance first," he said, and although he tried, he couldn't keep his voice

from sounding stiff. The events of that night still rankled him.

"I don't think it's necessary, seeing how—"

"I'd like to apologize," he interrupted. If she wasn't
willing to admit her part in the disaster, then he'd be
man enough to seek her forgiveness for his own role.

"Oh."

"I didn't mean to make us both fodder for gossip."

"I know you didn't," she said, her voice softening
perceptibly.

"You and I've been friends for quite a while now."

She nodded. "Very good friends."

Glen stuck his hand in his pocket and felt for the
diamond ring. Holding on to it lent him the courage to
continue. This was harder than he'd thought it would
be, but too important to ruin with nerves. All he had
to do was remind himself that this was Ellie, his longtime friend. In the years to come he wanted to be able
to tell his children and his grandchildren about this
day with the same sense of wonder and excitement
he'd heard in his father's voice when he'd relayed the
tale of proposing to their mother.

"Since your dad's gone, I feel a certain duty to
protect you."

"A duty?" A chill edged her voice.

"Well, not a duty exactly. More of…an obligation
to see that no harm befalls you." He knew he must
sound stilted, kind of old-fashioned, but he couldn't
seem to help it.

"What do you mean by harm?"

The hell if he knew. "Perhaps *harm* isn't the best
word, either. I want to look after you."

"I'm not a child, Glen."

"No, no, I don't mean to imply that you are." He could feel the sweat starting to break out across his forehead. Working his way up to this marriage proposal was harder than freeing a stuck calf from a mud hole. He swallowed painfully as he prepared to continue.

Ellie eyed him in consternation.

"What I'm trying to say," he started again, gulping down some air, "is— Oh, damn." He catapulted to his feet, finding it impossible to stay seated any longer. "Listen, Ellie, I'm not good at this. I'm the one responsible for embarrassing you and—"

"What the hell are you talking about?" she demanded.

Glen paced the porch, walking past the soda machine several times. "It hasn't been easy deciding what to do, I want you to know that."

"I'm not asking you to *do* anything."

"I know, but I feel responsible."

"Then I absolve you of all responsibility." She waved one arm as if holding a magic wand.

"It isn't that easy," he muttered.

"What's this all about?" she asked again.

Glen tilted his head back and expelled a long breath. This wasn't going well. He should have practiced on Cal first, at least gone over what he intended to say, sought his brother's advice.

Ellie had stood up, too.

It was now or never. Taking the plunge, he squared his shoulders and met her look head-on. "I think we should get married."

"Married!" The word exploded out of her mouth. Almost as if she'd been struck, Ellie sat back down,

gripping the sides of her chair with both hands. Then…
she began to laugh. A deep robust laugh.

Glen was deflated. This woman had a great deal to
learn about a man's pride, he reflected sadly.

"You're serious?" she asked when her laughter had
dwindled to a low chuckle.

"I have a ring," he said, pulling it out to prove his
point. He held it between index finger and thumb.

Ellie's eyes widened.

Dismissing his earlier plan, he decided she should
know the truth about this particular ring. "Actually I
borrowed it from Cal. This is the diamond Jennifer
returned when she broke the engagement."

She stared at him as if she hadn't heard a word he
said.

"I couldn't very well propose without a ring," he
explained. "If you don't like it, you can choose another one later, although I've got to tell you I think
Cal would give us a good deal on it. But I'll leave that
decision up to you."

Ellie blinked back tears and Glen relaxed. He knew
once he got the word out, everything would be better.

"Why now?" she asked, her voice cracking. "What
made you propose today?"

"We're friends," he said. "That's one reason. I enjoy
being with you more than any woman I've ever known.
You've got a lot of excellent qualities and…" He was
running out of things to say. "Basically it's time."

"Time?"

"To get married. I've been thinking along those
lines recently—"

"Because of Richard?"

Glen had hoped to get through this conversation

without any mention of the other man. He cleared his throat. "Not entirely."

Her responding smile was slight. "At least you're honest enough to admit he has something to do with this."

"Hey, it wasn't me who sat on a porch kissing one man and then having brunch with another the next morning." He wondered how *she'd* have felt if he'd shown up at her house with another woman on his arm. She wouldn't have liked it any better than he'd liked seeing her with Richard. He wanted to tell her that, but figured he'd come off sounding jealous. Hell, he *was* jealous.

"You didn't stick around long enough for me to explain."

"What was there to say?" It was obvious enough to Glen what had happened, and frankly he wasn't interested in hearing the details. Anyway, that was all in the past. What mattered now was the future.

"I'm flattered, Glen, that you'd ask me to marry you."

"What do you think about the ring?" He held it up so she could get a better view. Cal had spared no expense with this beauty, but Glen realized he'd prefer to have Ellie choose her own ring. Something unique to her. To them.

Ellie's hand closed over his. "Give the ring back to Cal."

"I'm glad because I'd rather the two of us shopped for one together."

She shook her head. "I'm sorry."

"I *said* I'd rather the two of us picked out a diamond together," he told her again, only louder.

"I heard you the first time," she said impatiently. "What I meant was that I'm sorry, but no. I can't marry you."

It took him a moment to realize what she was saying. "You're turning me down?" Each one of those words seared a hole through his heart. When he recovered from the shock, he asked, "Do you mind telling me why?" He had to know. Maybe he should have left things as they were, collected his shattered pride and gone home—but he couldn't. "I... I thought we had something special."

"We do. Friendship. You said it yourself, remember?"

He nodded.

"I don't want a husband who proposes marriage to me because it's an obligation."

"I didn't mean it like that." His voice sounded odd to his own ears. A little ragged and faraway.

"When and if I agree to marry anyone, I want it to be for specific reasons."

"Okay, that sounds fair." Weren't *his* reasons specific? Glen's ego came to the rescue, and the anger and pain in his voice were less evident now. More controlled.

"Reasons other than *it's time and you have excellent qualities.* Reasons other than *I should get married now and you'll do.*"

"I didn't say that!"

"No, but you might as well have. Oh, and I almost forgot, you said you *owed* me."

"Owed you what?"

"I might not get the words right so bear with me." He could tell she was being sarcastic but wasn't sure why. "Something about duty because you'd embarrassed me in front of the whole town."

"I... I didn't mean it to sound like that. Damn it, Ellie, you're putting words in my mouth."

"I don't need any favors, Glen."

He looked at her, afraid she was about to cry, but he was mistaken. Her face was strong and confident. She could give him all the excuses in the book, but he knew what was going on here and wasn't shy about saying it, either.

"It's Richard, isn't it? You're in love with him."

"That's it!" she cried.

"I thought as much." He shoved the ring back into his pocket. He'd tell his brother to bury it—the diamond must be hexed.

"The thing is, Glen, you're too late."

"Too late?" He didn't know what the hell she meant by that, but he wasn't sticking around to find out.

Ellie, however, insisted he hear her out. "Richard came by earlier and he proposed. Sorry, Glen, he beat you to the punch."

Nine

Not for a single moment would Cal describe himself as a romantic. Despite that, he felt good about encouraging his little brother to go and propose to Ellie Frasier. He'd even given him the ring!

Good enough to tell his neighbor. It wasn't often that Cal had reason to shoot the bull over a telephone; usually a beer at Billy D's served the same purpose, but even better. However, this news was too good to keep to himself.

Grady answered on the second ring.

"It's Cal," he announced.

"Something wrong?" Grady asked right off.

They'd been best friends since first grade, and Grady knew him about as well as anyone ever would. Over the years they'd been through a lot together. As kids, they'd explored Bitter End. Later Grady had talked to him about his parents' deaths, his problems with Richard, his concerns about Laredo. And it was Grady Cal had gone to when Jennifer canceled their wedding, Grady who'd gotten him home safely when he'd fallen down drunk. Grady who'd talked some sense into him when he badly needed to hear it.

"Glen's driving into town to ask Ellie to marry him," Cal said without preamble. He wasn't a man who wasted words.

"You're kidding!" Grady sounded shocked.

"No. He's been acting like a wounded bear for damn near two weeks and then I found him mumbling to himself in the barn, about as miserable as I've ever seen him. Tried to talk to him, but he damn near bit my head off. I'd had enough. I figured he should either fix what was wrong or forget Ellie."

"And Glen listened?"

"No, I didn't get the chance to give him my advice. He decided to marry her all on his own."

"That's great." Cal heard the relief in Grady's voice and knew his neighbor harbored his own set of fears when it came to Ellie Frasier. "At least she won't be marrying Richard, then."

"Not if Glen has anything to say about it." Cal knew Grady didn't trust his younger brother, and with damn good reason.

"I was thinking of celebrating," Cal continued. "You're welcome to join me if you want. There's cold beer in the fridge, plus a bottle of the hard stuff if you're interested." An invitation from Cal was about as rare as a phone call.

"I might just do that."

A couple of minutes later Cal hung up the receiver, feeling more like his old self than at any time since his broken engagement. Grinning from ear to ear, he reached for a beer and walked outside, where he leaned comfortably against the porch railing. In years past he'd spent many an evening in this very spot, looking out over the land, knowing that cattle grazed peacefully in the distance. In certain moods, wistful moods, he liked to imagine a wife standing at his side and the sound of their children's laughter echoing in the house.

Glen married.

Cal had known it would probably happen one day, and he'd always wondered how'd he react, seeing that, despite his imaginings, he'd likely remain a bachelor himself. In fact, he felt surprisingly good about having played a small role in his brother's romance. He'd known Glen was in love with Ellie months before it even occurred to Glen.

Glen's feelings for her had been apparent for a long time. He'd drive into town and return a couple of hours later and talk of little else. Ellie amused him, challenged him, comforted him. She fired his senses. And all that time Glen had insisted it was "just" friendship.

Right! Cal nearly laughed out loud. It was friendship and a whole lot more.

The sound of an engine broke into Cal's musings, and he looked toward the driveway as Grady's truck pulled into view. Good, his neighbor was going to take him up on his offer.

Grady leaped down from the pickup and raised a bottle of whiskey high above his head. "Glen getting married. Hot damn, this calls for a party," he shouted.

Cal lifted his beer in salute and let out a cheer.

"So Glen's really doing it," Grady said, taking the porch steps two at a time. "He's marrying Ellie."

"Unless the woman's a fool and turns him down."

"Ellie Frasier's no fool," Grady said with confidence.

"He took the diamond I bought Jennifer," Cal explained as he headed into the house for a couple of tumblers and some ice.

"Glen asked Ellie to marry him with Jennifer's ring?" Grady followed him, sounding worried.

"It's just a loan. I figure Ellie'll want to choose her own diamond later." He dumped the ice cubes into two mismatched glasses.

"You think that was wise?"

"Well, yeah. This way Glen wasn't proposing to her empty-handed."

The two men returned to the porch and Cal poured two generous measures of the honey-colored liquor over the ice, but he noted that his friend's worried frown didn't go away. "What harm could it do?" he asked.

"Probably none." Grady sat down with Cal in the white wicker chairs and relaxed. Leaning back, he stretched out his long legs and crossed his ankles, then with a deep contented sigh, raised the tumbler to his lips.

Cal tasted his own drink. His eyes watered as the whiskey burned its way down his throat.

"I have to tell you," Grady admitted, "it does my heart good to know Richard's out of the picture with Ellie."

"Mine, too." Cal wasn't fond of the youngest Weston. Richard was a difficult person to understand. Witty, amiable, a natural leader—and yet he'd squandered his talents, in Cal's opinion, anyway. Richard had taken a wrong turn and he'd never gotten steered back on course. It was unfortunate, too, because he could have been a success at just about anything he chose.

"I told Savannah," Grady mentioned casually, "and she's delighted for Glen." Then, looking as though he might have done something wrong, he glanced at Cal. "You don't mind, do you?"

"She won't tell anyone else, will she?" Not that it mattered; word would be out soon enough.

"I doubt it." Grady didn't seem to know for sure.

Cal wasn't really worried, though. Savannah—sensitive and kind, the complete opposite of Richard—would never say anything to ruin another person's happiness. She'd never cheat Ellie out of the pleasure of spreading the news herself.

"Which one of us is going to be next?" Cal asked, although he already had his suspicions. Grady. He'd seen the way his friend's eyes followed Caroline Daniels at the Cattlemen's Dance. Later, when she'd asked him to dance during the ladies' choice, Grady had been so thrilled he'd nearly stumbled all over himself. Not that he'd let on, but Cal knew. Yup, it'd be Grady for sure.

First Glen and then Grady. Soon all his friends would be married, and he'd be living on the ranch alone. The picture that formed in his mind was a desolate one but preferable to the thought of letting another Jennifer Healy into his life.

The sound of a vehicle barreling up the driveway caught Cal's attention.

"Glen?" Grady asked.

"I didn't expect him back so soon." Cal set his tumbler aside.

"You think everything went all right, don't you?"

"Don't know why it wouldn't." But Cal was beginning to feel some doubts, considering the speed at which Glen had been driving.

The slam of the truck door echoed through the quiet evening.

"I don't like the look of this," Grady said in a low voice.

Cal didn't, either. He dashed down the porch when he saw Glen moving toward the barn. "I wonder what happened," he said. "I'd better find out. Be back in a couple of minutes."

Cal didn't want to think about what might have gone wrong, but clearly something had. He opened the barn door and searched the dim interior. It took his eyes a moment to adjust, and when he did finally see Glen, his uneasiness intensified. His brother was pitching hay like a man possessed.

"I take it things didn't go so well between you and Ellie," Cal said, hoping he sounded casual.

"You could say that." Glen's shoulders heaved with exertion. "What's Grady doing here?"

"We're..." He almost slipped and said they were celebrating Glen's engagement. "We're just shootin' the breeze."

Silence.

"You *did* talk to Ellie?"

Glen stopped midmotion, the pitchfork full of hay. "We talked."

Cal wondered how to proceed. "Did she like the ring?" he asked and realized immediately it was probably a tactless question.

"She didn't say."

"I see."

"I doubt it." Glen stabbed the fork into the ground, breathing hard, his face red from exertion.

"Do you want to tell me about it or would you rather work this out on your own?"

Glen took a couple of moments to think it over. "I… I don't know," he mumbled.

Another silence. Cal knew it was up to Glen to talk or not.

"I owe you an apology," Glen surprised him by saying next.

"Me? What for?"

Glen looked him full in the eye. "When Jennifer walked out on you, I was secretly glad. As far as I was concerned, you got a lucky break. I thought she wasn't the right woman for you. I didn't stop to consider how you must have felt, how damn hard her leaving was on you."

Cal didn't quite understand how all this talk about Jennifer applied to the current situation, but he didn't want to interrupt Glen.

"Hurt like hell, didn't it?"

Cal wasn't going to deny it. "At the time it did. I don't think about it much anymore."

Glen reached into his pocket for the diamond that had once belonged to Cal's ex-fiancée. He stared at it for several seconds. "I wonder how long it'll take me to forget Ellie," he said, sounding as if he was speaking to himself. He raised his head as he handed Cal back the ring, and the look in his eyes spoke of blinding pain.

"Ellie's decided to marry Richard Weston."

* * *

Not once had Ellie said she'd *accepted* Richard Weston's proposal, but that was what Glen had immediately assumed. It hurt that he'd actually believe she would marry anyone else when it should be clear as creek water that she was in love with him!

She let herself into her house and slumped down on the sofa, discouraged and depressed. She'd always known that Glen wasn't much of a romantic, but she'd hoped he could at least propose marriage without making it sound like an insult. He'd said all the wrong things. He'd talked about an obligation to "take care" of her; well, no thanks, she could take care of herself. He'd said it was "time" he got married—so what did that have to do with her? He'd referred to her "excellent qualities" as though he was interviewing her for a job! Perhaps worst of all, he'd half admitted that his sudden desire to propose had been prompted by his effort to outdo Richard Weston.

The one thing he'd never said was that he loved her.

Crossing her arms, she leaned her head back and closed her eyes. It was at a time like this that she missed her father most. He always seemed to know what to do, and Ellie feared that in her anger she'd badly bungled her relationship with Glen. She feared that nothing would ever be the same again.

She knew about the lottery at Billy D's and all the Texas two-step jokes. She hated the idea of being in the middle of some stupid male rivalry, and everything Glen said only reinforced that. It bothered her, too, that he'd come to her with a used engagement ring, a leftover from his brother's failed romance. She'd drawn the only sensible conclusion, which was that he'd been in such a rush to get to her before Richard proposed, he hadn't taken the time to buy his own ring.

Now she didn't know what to do. She loved Glen and wanted more than anything to be his wife, but at the same time she needed to feel that she was more to him than a trophy, a way of triumphing over Richard. Deciding to marry someone wasn't like switching dance partners—even in the Texas two-step!

She needed Glen to acknowledge that he loved her, and she needed to understand that his feelings for her had nothing to do with Richard. She wanted Glen to look into his heart.

But she worried he wouldn't be able to see beyond his own disappointments.

Glen sat at the breakfast table and stared glumly at the kitchen wall, sipping his coffee. It was barely five and he was already on his third cup.

Cal ambled down the stairs, yawning loudly. "You're up early," he muttered as he headed for the coffeepot.

Glen didn't tell his brother that he hadn't been to sleep yet. He'd gone to bed and closed his eyes, but it'd done no good. He'd finally gotten up at three-thirty and sat waiting for the tightness in his chest to go away so he could breathe without this pain.

"You feeling all right?" Cal asked.

His brother was more awake than Glen had given him credit for. "I'm fine."

Cal leaned against the kitchen counter, holding his coffee mug with both hands, and studied Glen.

"I said I was fine," Glen said a bit more gruffly than he intended. He wasn't up to talking. In time the details would come out, the same way they had when Jennifer canceled the wedding. Cal had been tight-lipped for weeks, then gradually, bit by bit, Glen had pieced it all together until he had a fairly accurate picture of the events that led up to the final scene.

Cal's face seemed to darken. "It doesn't seem either one of us is the marrying kind," he said, then pushed away from the counter and left the house.

His eyes burning from lack of sleep, Glen toyed with the idea of taking the day off, but instinctively realized that would be his worst choice. He needed to stay busy. Otherwise thoughts of Ellie and Richard would drive him crazy.

Downing the last of his coffee, he followed Cal.

The day dragged. Glen had never felt wearier in body and spirit. By late afternoon he knew the only way to find peace was to seek out Richard Weston and congratulate him. Then he'd talk to Ellie and wish her and Richard every happiness. He was sincere about that; he loved her enough to want her to have a good life.

He didn't tell Cal where he was going when he was finished for the day. Nor did he bother to shower or shave.

Cal had just ridden in when Glen was ready to leave.

"Did Ellie mention anything about the wire cutters I ordered?" Cal asked, stopping him.

Glen froze at the mention of her name. He might as well get used to it. She was as much a part of his everyday life as this ranch.

"I'll ask her if you want," Glen said.

Cal looked as if he wanted to say something, but hesitated. Then, "I didn't mean… I forgot."

"Don't worry about it. Frasier's has been our supplier for a lot of years and I don't think we should change things now." He was man enough to accept being rejected, or he'd like to believe he was, anyway.

Ellie, ever sensitive and thoughtful, was probably worried about him. That would be just like her. Glen didn't want her to think her decision had ruined their relationship. They could still be friends. Sort of. Not the way they'd been in the past but…friendly.

Glen headed for the Weston place. He found Richard loading supplies into the back of Grady's pickup when he arrived. The other man looked mildly surprised when Glen sought him out. He stood there with a case of canned goods balanced on his shoulder, his stance defensive.

"You wanted to talk to me?" Richard asked.

"I came to congratulate you." No need to hedge. This wasn't a conversation he relished having, and the sooner he'd finished the better.

"Congratulate me?" Richard echoed. "Did I win the lottery and someone forgot to tell me?"

Glen didn't appreciate the joke. "In a manner of speaking."

Richard leaned forward and dumped the box onto the open tailgate. "What's up, Patterson?"

"It's about you and Ellie."

Richard scowled. "What about us?"

"I understand you asked her to marry you."

"What of it?"

"I also understand that she's accepted."

Richard had started to remove his gloves, one finger at a time. His head snapped up at Glen's statement. "Ellie's a hell of a woman, isn't she? I didn't realize she'd decided to let the word out." He nudged Glen with his elbow. "But then, that's just like my Ellie."

My Ellie. The words hurt like alcohol on a cut, and Glen flinched before he could hide his reaction. Recovering quickly, he forced a smile. "I couldn't agree with you more," he said. "Ellie's one of a kind."

Richard slapped him hard on the back. "I guess you could say the best man won."

"Yeah, I guess you could say that," Glen answered, clenching his teeth.

"I don't suppose she happened to mention a wedding date, did she?" He laughed. "Seems the groom's always the last to know."

"Can't say as she did."

"It'll be soon, if I have anything to say about it." Richard hopped onto the tailgate, his legs dangling. "The wedding will be a small intimate affair right here in Savannah's rose garden. Family and a few friends. You're invited of course."

"Thank you."

"Hey, no problem." Richard began whistling; Glen might not have much of an ear for music; but he recognized the "Wedding March."

He tried not to let it distract him. "I want to wish you both every happiness," he said formally.

"That's good of you, Glen, and I appreciate it. I'm sure Ellie will, too." Richard thrust out his hand. "I realize it was difficult for you to lose her, but I want you to know, I plan to make Ellie happy. The two of us would like to consider you a friend."

"I hope you will." This was what made Richard so

damn difficult to understand, Glen mused. One minute he was a jackass; the next, he was a regular joe. "If you need anything, give me a call," he offered.

"I will."

Glen climbed back into his pickup. Despite his dislike of Richard, he felt better for having cleared the air between them. Although he'd dreaded talking to the guy, he was glad now that he had.

He hoped everything would go as well with Ellie.

The ache in his gut intensified as he drove into town. When he entered the feed store, she was ringing up a sale for Lyle Whitehouse. She didn't notice Glen until she handed Lyle his package. Her hand froze in midair and she gaped at him as if she couldn't believe her eyes. Recovering quickly, she released the bag.

Lyle turned around, and when he saw Glen, he grinned broadly. Then he winked and gave him a thumbs-up as he walked out of the store.

"Hello, Glen," Ellie said tentatively.

"Ellie." He nodded once. "Cal wanted me to ask you about those wire cutters he ordered."

"They won't be in until Monday," she said, sounding oddly breathless.

"I'll tell him." He felt awkward and tongue-tied again, the way he had when he proposed. He waited a moment, just staring at her. "I have a few things to say. Is now a good time?"

"As good as any," she said stiffly. She remained on her side of the counter while he stayed on the other.

Damn she was beautiful. That wasn't the kind of thing he should be thinking, he told himself, and glanced away. "First, all I really want is for you to be happy."

"I am happy," she said a little too loudly.

"Good."

Ellie moved out from behind the cash register and started restacking blocks of salt.

"I was hoping we could remain friendly," he said, moving up behind her.

"I was hoping that, too."

Glen raised his hands to place them on her shoulders, the need to touch her almost impossible to resist. He paused, then with unprecedented determination dropped his arms to his sides. He had no right to touch Ellie anymore. She was engaged to another man.

"You've been my closest and dearest friend," she whispered and turned to face him. "I don't know what I would've done without you when Dad was so terribly ill...and since."

Glen wasn't sure if she'd come toward him or if he'd stepped toward her, but all at once they were standing mere inches apart. Their eyes avoided meeting, but their slow labored breathing seemed to keep pace.

"I needed you," she whispered, "and you were there for me."

Again he reminded himself that she was engaged to Richard, and yet all he could think about was kissing her one last time. Just one kiss, to tell her goodbye, to wish her well.

Everything within him yearned for her. It seemed natural to stand this close; it seemed even more natural to hold her, but he managed to resist. He mustn't feel these things any longer, mustn't allow himself to look at her this way. Mustn't kiss her again.

His heart went wild when Ellie stepped into his arms. When she raised her lips to his. Her kiss nearly buckled his knees. It began as a simple, almost chaste touch, her warm mouth on his. Unfortunately it didn't stay chaste long. Glen slipped his arm around her waist and against every dictate of common sense, urged her closer. If this was to be their last kiss, then he'd make sure it was one they'd both remember.

The kiss spoke far more eloquently of his need and love for her than any words he'd ever uttered. Ellie moaned and he cradled her face with both hands. The kiss grew molten-hot and would have grown hotter had they continued. Abruptly Glen released her, trembling with the restraint it demanded to pull away.

She stared at him, wide-eyed, then pressed the back of her hand against her mouth.

"I suppose you're waiting for an apology," he said, knowing that kiss should never have happened. "I'll give you one if you insist, but it'd be a lie. This is only the third time we've kissed, and it's the last. It has to be." He reached out to stroke her hair and whispered, "Be happy, Ellie. Be very happy."

Looking as if she'd been struck dumb, she continued to stand there, staring up at him.

"Richard doesn't deserve you," he said, his voice gruff with pain, "but I don't, either." He touched her cheek, loving the feel of her skin beneath his fingertips. Then he turned and walked out of the store.

Ellie didn't move for five solid minutes after he left. Her hand remained poised at her lips, the taste and feel of him still clinging to her mouth.

Little of what he'd said made any sense—but they hadn't been able to communicate effectively in weeks. Except when they kissed…. They'd been best friends for years, able to talk about anything, and then overnight it had all changed.

The big oaf. He'd screwed up his marriage proposal and now he was back, kissing her senseless and saying the most beautiful words she'd ever heard. He hadn't actually said he loved her, although his kiss was pretty persuasive. What he'd said was, "Be happy." And if he didn't love her, he wouldn't have told her that. Because Glen Patterson was an honest man.

Glen's kiss still lingered on her lips when Richard casually sauntered into the store.

"Darling," he said, flashing her an easy smile. He grabbed her in a bear hug and soundly kissed her cheek.

Furious, Ellie wiped away his kiss, not wanting his touch to taint what she'd shared with Glen. "Let go of me," she ordered. One thing she detested was being manhandled. When Richard didn't immediately comply, she elbowed him hard in the ribs.

"Ouch," he muttered, holding her at arm's length. "Why didn't you tell me yourself?"

"Tell you what?"

"That you'd decided to accept my proposal." He glared at her as if suddenly aware that something wasn't right.

"Who told you that?" Although she could almost predict his answer.

"Glen Patterson," he murmured. "It's all a joke, isn't it?" His lip curled into a snarl.

She *was* going to kill Glen, no doubt about it. "Not a joke," she said feeling genuinely sorry, "but a misunderstanding."

"Well, that's just fine," Richard spit. "I just went and bought myself a new suit for the wedding."

"Oh, Richard." She brought one hand to her mouth. "Glen didn't understand—"

"What the hell am I supposed to do about the suit?" He actually made it sound as though they should get married because of a new set of clothes.

"Can you return it?"

"I don't think so," he said, his voice tight with anger.

"I am sorry, Richard."

He looked as if he wanted to plow his fist through something. "It wouldn't have worked, anyway," he said. "You're too uptight. Making love to you would have been like warming up an ice cube."

Ellie had heard all she cared to. "I think you should go. And take your insults with you."

"Fine. Whatever. Patterson really had me fooled— he must've enjoyed playing me for an idiot. Tell him I'm not going to forget his sick joke." That said, he bolted out the door.

If Glen's actions earlier had confused her, Richard's outraged her. She hadn't missed the threat, but as far as she knew, Glen had nothing to fear from Richard Weston. He should worry about what *she* planned to do to him, instead.

George, who'd gone on an errand, was back fifteen minutes later. The minute he walked into the store, Ellie reached for her truck keys. "I have to go," she said. "Can you close up shop for me?"

"I… I guess."

It wasn't like her to walk out before five, but it couldn't be helped. She was in her truck and headed out of town in five minutes flat. She managed the forty-minute drive in thirty; half an hour was not long enough to cool her anger even slightly.

Glen and Cal must have heard her coming because both men stepped onto the porch when she arrived. She glared at Glen with undisguised fury.

"Ellie, is something wrong?" he asked, walking down the steps toward her.

With her hands planted on her hips, she yelled, "Did you actually believe for one minute I was going to marry Richard Weston?"

He hesitated, fifteen or so feet away. "That's what you said."

"I said," she returned from between clenched teeth, "that Richard had proposed. I did *not,* I repeat, *not* at any time state that I'd accepted his proposal of marriage."

Glen's face was stricken. "You didn't?"

"I most certainly did not. Furthermore, anyone with eyes in his head would know it's *you* I love."

"You love me?"

"Don't pretend you didn't know, Glen Patterson. I've loved you forever." But at the moment she wasn't particularly happy about it.

"Then you'll marry me, right?" Glen looked like he was about to fly across the yard and haul her into his arms.

Ellie stopped him cold in his tracks. "Give me one good reason why I'd want to marry a man who's got the brains of a tumbleweed."

"She loves you, all right," Cal shouted from the porch steps.

"You stay out of this," Ellie shouted back, pointing

an accusing finger at Glen's brother. "You encouraged him to do it, didn't you?"

"Yup." Cal seemed downright proud of himself.

"The next time Glen asks you for advice, ignore him." Then she threw open the truck door and climbed inside.

"Ellie!" Glen started toward her. But when she revved the engine, he apparently knew better than to press his luck. He stayed where he was. Good thing, because in her current frame of mind she was liable to run him over.

When the dust had died down, Ellie glanced in her rearview mirror and groaned. Cal and Glen Patterson were leaping about, hugging each other wildly.

Ten

Glen Patterson had never been happier. Ellie loved him. *Him.* Not Richard Weston. And by golly, she was going to marry him, too!

"I knew it," Cal announced cheerfully as though he was personally responsible for the unexpected turn of events.

"Did you ever see such a woman?" Glen asked, watching Ellie drive away. Damn, but she had spunk. It wasn't every woman who would've come out here to confront him the way she had.

Cal chuckled. "Don't think I've ever seen a female that mad." He glanced at his brother. "How're you going to get her to marry you?"

That was a question Glen hadn't considered. Of course Ellie would marry him. She loved him. He loved her. Marriage was the natural result of such feelings. Sure, she was mad at him right now, but she'd cool off and they'd sit down and talk this out and plan for their future together. "Any suggestions?"

"From me?" Cal adamantly shook his head. "Didn't you hear? Ellie wasn't too impressed with the advice

I gave you earlier, although I don't know what I said that was so wrong. Do you?"

"Nope." Women baffled him just as much as they did Cal. "So, who should I ask for advice?"

Cal thought it over a moment. "Mom?"

"Not Mom," Glen said. He loved his mother, but she was sure to meddle. All mothers did. Once she heard about this, she'd want to fix it; she'd want to talk to Ellie and act as a go-between and generally get involved. Glen shuddered. He preferred to handle the situation himself.

Cal shrugged. "Dovie, then. She's got a good head on her shoulders."

"Dovie," Glen repeated slowly. Yes. She was a good choice.

After a night without sleep, followed by one of the most emotionally draining days of his life, Glen nearly nodded off during dinner. As soon as the evening chores were done, he showered and went to bed. He'd figure out what he should say to Ellie. Tomorrow... He'd figure it out tomorrow. As he drifted into sleep, he actually felt happy for the first time in weeks.

The next afternoon Glen opened the door to Dovie's Antiques. Glancing around, he immediately removed his hat. Little wonder the women in town loved this place. It was full to the rafters with pretty things, and smelled a little like Savannah's garden. If his nose didn't mislead him, he caught the scent of some mighty fine brandy, too. Must be what she used to make that famous cordial of hers.

"Hello, Glen." Dovie was her usual lighthearted self. "What can I do for you this fine day?"

"Ah…" For the life of him, Glen couldn't think of a single way to start the conversation.

Dovie regarded him expectantly. "I'll have you know, young man, I have my money riding on you."

"I beg your pardon?"

"Do you think only the men are in on Billy D's lottery?"

"Oh, that." Glen had forgotten all about that silly lottery. He stood just inside the door, arms tight against his sides, for fear one wrong move would send hundreds of fragile little things tumbling to the floor.

"Come on inside, Glen," Dovie encouraged. "You aren't going to break anything."

He took a few cautious steps, then glanced anxiously around the store and back at Dovie.

"Is there a problem?" she asked with concern.

Glen had always liked his mother's friend. It was Dovie who'd suggested the bed-and-breakfast idea and who'd helped his mother decorate the old Howe Mansion.

"I need some advice," he finally said. The last time he'd been this unsure of himself—not counting the day he proposed to Ellie—was when he'd roped his first calf in the Brewster rodeo at the age of ten.

"The advice is free, but the tea will cost you a dollar."

"Tea?"

"I think best when I'm sitting down." Smiling, Dovie motioned toward the assembled tables and chairs in one corner of the shop.

"All right," he agreed.

"I take it this all has to do with Ellie?" Dovie asked,

leading him to a small table covered by a pretty floral cloth.

"You know, then."

"I know you and Richard made first-class fools of yourselves at the dance."

Glen wished folks would forget about that. "It's gotten worse since."

Dovie carried a blue-and-white china teapot and two cups to the table. "I was afraid of that."

"Cal suggested I talk to you about Ellie. You see, I want us to get married. I tried asking her and it didn't turn out the way I'd hoped. Can you help me?"

"I can try." Dovie poured him some tea, then served herself. "Milk? Sugar? Lemon?"

Glen shook his head mutely. He generally sweetened his tea, but he wasn't willing to do it with one of those miniature silver spoons. He already felt like an oversize buffoon in this dainty little shop.

"How would you like me to advise you?" Dovie asked.

"Can you tell me what I can say to convince Ellie to marry me?"

Dovie frowned slightly. "Perhaps you should tell me how you proposed the first time."

Glen recalled what he could of their conversation. "Best I can remember, she started getting hostile when I mentioned I felt responsible for embarrassing her at the dance."

Dovie nodded, and Glen continued, "I told her I admired her and I wanted to marry her. That was when I brought out the diamond ring I borrowed from Cal."

"You *borrowed* an engagement ring?"

"Just so I'd have something to offer. I wanted Ellie

to know I was serious, and a man doesn't get more serious than diamonds."

Dovie was frowning again.

"Was that so terrible?" Glen demanded. "All I want is for Ellie to know how much I love her."

"Why don't we start with telling her that this time?" Dovie suggested.

"Ellie already knows how I feel about her." It was incomprehensible to him that she wouldn't. He'd made himself the laughingstock of the entire town over her. When she'd rejected his marriage proposal, he'd swallowed his pride and wished her happiness, even at the cost of his own. A man didn't say those kinds of things to a woman he didn't love. "She's *got* to know," he added.

"A woman likes to hear the words, Glen."

It was that simple? Of course he loved Ellie, and if all he had to do was tell her how much... He reached for his hat and got eagerly to his feet. "Great. I'll let her know right now."

Dovie grabbed his shirtsleeve. "I'm not finished yet."

"Oh." He sat back down.

"Is there anything else you plan to tell Ellie?"

Glen wasn't sure he understood the question. Perplexed, he gave it a moment's thought. "Just that I can't get married next Tuesday because the farrier's coming."

"Oh, dear." Dovie briefly closed her eyes.

"That's the wrong thing to say?"

"Well...yes."

"Thursday's not good, either. I play poker at Billy

D's on Thursdays, but I'd be willing to give that up if Ellie decided she wanted to get married then."

"Have you considered that Ellie might want a church wedding?"

He hadn't, and the mere suggestion made his blood run cold. All this time he'd been thinking they'd fly off to Vegas and get married the same night. A quickie wedding, because now that the decision had been made, he was ready. Strike while the iron's hot, as the farrier might say.

"Besides, I think you might be getting ahead of yourself," Dovie murmured. "First you've got to convince Ellie to be your bride."

"Right." If the truth be known, he'd given more thought to the honeymoon than the wedding. He was in love, and damn it all, he wanted to make love to Ellie. "Why does this have to be so complicated?" He wanted to know. "I love her, and she's already confessed she loves me."

Sighing, he took a careful sip of his cooling tea. "When she was going through her father's things, she found this old Bible passed down from his family," Glen said, thinking out loud. "She showed it to me and turned to the page where her family's names and dates are listed. Weddings, deaths, births—you know. All day, I've been thinking about Ellie and me entering our names in that Bible, and someday, God willing, writing down the names of our children. I love Ellie, and it's a love that'll last all our lives. Maybe a hundred years from now one of our great-great-grandchildren will come upon that Bible and wonder about us. I'd want them to know—just from the way we lived—that despite everything life threw at us, our love survived."

"Oh, Glen, that's beautiful," Dovie said softly and squeezed his hand.

"It was?"

"Tell Ellie that."

"About putting our names in her family Bible?"

"Yes. Speak from your heart and don't mention the farrier, all right?"

"I'll do it." Glen felt immediately better.

Grady relaxed against the back of a molded plastic bench in the bowling alley. Lloyd Bonney had asked if he'd substitute for him the next two weeks while he was on vacation. It'd been ages since Grady had last bowled, but Lloyd was a likable guy and he hated to turn him down. That wasn't the only reason, either; for the first time in six years, he was able to indulge himself with a few leisure activities. He used to enjoy bowling and had been fairly good at it.

He was a bit rusty, but he'd bowled a decent series tonight. It felt good to be with friends, to laugh again. Finally he had the financial security and the extra time to make it possible. This evening had whetted his appetite for more.

He was on his way to Billy D's afterward when Max Jordan followed him outside.

"Grady, you got a moment?"

"Sure."

Max shifted his gaze away from Grady. "Listen, I realize this is a bad time and all, but I need to talk to you about Richard."

"Yeah?" Grady didn't like the sound of this.

"He charged a few things at my store—clothes and boots—when he first came back to town and he hasn't paid me and…well, it's been almost three months now."

Grady's grip tightened on his bowling bag. "How much does he owe you?"

Max stated an amount that made Grady's stomach clench. His brother must have picked out the most expensive clothes in the store.

"Earlier this week he charged a new suit," Max continued. "It's a pricey one, and—"

"You let him do that even when he hadn't paid you for the other things?" Grady was furious with his brother and with Max, too.

Max lowered his eyes to the pavement. "I feel like an old fool now. Richard stopped in the store and told me he was getting married. I was pleased for him and Ellie. It wasn't until later that I learned they weren't engaged, at all."

"It isn't your fault." Grady blamed himself as much as anyone. It'd been a mistake to let Richard stay at the ranch for even one night. He knew the kind of man his brother was, and still he'd allowed Richard to take advantage of him. Well, no more. He was sending that bastard packing.

"I'll take the suit back," Max said.

"I'll personally see that he returns it," Grady told him. "I can't tell you how bad I feel about all this."

"And the other money he owes? Richard had me put it on the family account, but so far I've mailed all the bills to him."

"I'll make sure he takes care of it right away," Grady pledged. Richard would pay one way or another, he decided. He should have realized sooner what was happening. His no-good brother arrives in town, throws himself a party and buys some fancy duds to go along with everything else.

Max Jordan wasn't the old fool; Grady was. Why hadn't he guessed where Richard's clothes had come from? Why hadn't he known Richard would pull something like this?

The evening that had started out with such promise was ruined. Grady changed his mind about meeting his friends for a beer and headed directly back to the ranch, instead. He was having this out with Richard once and for all.

The lights in the house were off when Grady got home. He attacked the stairs with a vengeance and didn't bother to knock on his brother's door. It shouldn't have surprised him to find the bed empty, but for some reason it did. Although it was about midnight, Richard wasn't anywhere to be found. Why the hell shouldn't he party half the night, seeing as he hadn't done a lick of work all day, or any day since he arrived? Grady resisted the temptation to slam the door shut.

He lay awake half the night, listening for his brother's return. Eventually he'd fallen asleep and never did hear him come home. But then, Richard seemed to have a sixth sense about such things; even as a child, he'd been able to smell trouble and avoid it.

In the morning another check of his brother's room showed that Richard hadn't been home that night.

"Have you seen Richard lately?" he asked his sister when he went downstairs for breakfast.

Savannah shook her head. "He's probably still sleeping."

"His bed is empty." Grady used his fork to grab

a pancake from the stack in the middle of the table. "When you see him, tell him I need to talk to him, all right?"

"Problems?"

Grady didn't want to involve Savannah in this, but she knew him too well not to realize something was wrong. He tried distancing her with another question. "Did Laredo leave the house already?"

"What's Richard done?" Savannah asked, ignoring the question.

Grady sighed and set down the jar of maple syrup. "Max Jordan talked to me last night about some money Richard owes him. Apparently our dear little brother has charged a few things at Max's he hasn't bothered to pay for."

Savannah didn't comment, but he saw sadness on her face.

"It makes me wonder if he's been doing the same thing with anyone else in town." Grady grabbed another pancake and picked up the syrup again.

"He has," Savannah confessed in a small voice.

"And you knew about it?"

"I…" She bit her lip. "I just found out about it myself. Millie Greenville talked to me last week. She suggested that perhaps we could trade something for the money Richard owes her. My roses, for example."

Grady slammed the syrup jar down. "You didn't agree to this, did you?"

"No."

"Good."

"But—"

"I won't hear of it, Savannah, and neither will Laredo. Richard's the one who owes that money, not you and not me. He's going to repay it, too, if it's the last thing he ever does. Every penny."

"I know," she said. "Laredo and I've already discussed what to do, and he's as adamant as you are."

Grady's fork sliced viciously across the pancake. He forced himself to relax, knowing his anger would ultimately hurt him far more than it would Richard.

Laredo had saddled the horses and was waiting for him outside when he finished his meal. Savannah walked out, too, and with an agility Grady envied, her husband leaned over his horse's neck and kissed her.

"If Richard shows up, tell him…" Grady paused, then shook his head. "Don't tell him anything. Let me do the talking this time."

Savannah nodded. "He's been making himself scarce lately."

"Now we know why, don't we?"

The sadness was back in his sister's eyes before she turned away and hurried into the house.

Richard dominated Grady's thoughts for the rest of the day. By the time he got home, he was ready to read his brother the riot act. To his surprise Richard was there waiting for him.

"I understand you want to talk to me," his brother said.

Grady was so angry he needed every bit of self-control not to explode with it. "Damn right I want to talk to you."

"It's about the stuff I charged in town, isn't it?"

"Yes. I can't believe you'd take advantage of our good name to—"

"Listen, Grady, you've got every right to be mad, but I don't need a lecture."

"That's too bad because—"

"Before you get all bent out of shape, let me say something. I've been sick with worry about those charges. Ask Savannah if you don't believe me. I have some money owed to me, quite a bit as it happens—you know that. It was supposed to have been mailed to me long before this." He frowned thoughtfully. "It must have been misdirected. I've spent weeks trying to track it down."

If anyone knew what it was like to be low on cash, it was Grady, but he wasn't falling for his brother's lies again. He opened his mouth to tell him so when Richard continued.

"I figured I'd have those bills paid off before now. I haven't charged anything in weeks."

"What about the suit?" Grady flared.

His brother's expression became pained. "That was a...mistake. I was tricked into thinking Ellie had agreed to marry me and didn't learn until later it wasn't true." He inhaled sharply. "In my excitement I went down and bought myself a decent suit for the wedding."

"Max said he'd let you return it."

Richard smiled slightly. "As it happens the money was at the post office when I picked up the mail this afternoon. The first thing I did was pay off all the bills." He slid his hands into his jeans pockets. "I realize it was a mistake not to discuss this with you earlier."

"Yes, it was." Grady's relief was tremendous. The problem was solved and the family's good name redeemed. And none of the business owners was losing any money.

"I'm sorry you had to find out about it the way you did."

While reassured that the money matters had been properly dealt with, Grady wasn't willing to make any further allowances for his brother. Richard had worn out his welcome. "Now that your money's here, you'll be reimbursing me—and then moving on, right?"

"Yes. I appreciate you letting me stay this long. I know it's been an inconvenience, but I didn't have anywhere else to go. We've had our problems over the years, and I'm hoping we can put those behind us now." He held out his hand for Grady to shake.

Grady accepted it, glad to see that his brother had revealed the maturity to confront him man-to-man.

Perhaps there was hope for Richard, after all.

Ellie had been restless all day. With the big Fourth of July weekend coming up, business was slower than it had been in weeks. She found herself waiting, watching, hoping to see Glen—and was furious with herself for caring.

She was finished with men, Ellie told herself. She'd rather herd goats than be married, but even as she entertained the thought, she realized it was a lie. Although she was fond of Savannah's goats, she was more than fond of Glen Patterson. Not that he deserved her affections!

Once the store had closed for the day, she returned home. The afternoon heat was intense, so she made herself some iced tea. She tugged her shirt free of her waistband, propped her bare feet on the coffee table and let the fan cool her. But it was going to take more than a fan and a glass of iced tea to revive her sagging spirits.

Because of the fan's drone she didn't hear her doorbell. When she finally realized someone was at her door, she got to her feet and hurried across the room. She threw open the door and on the other side of the screen was the largest bouquet of flowers she'd laid eyes on. While she couldn't see the man behind it, she could easily identify him by his boots.

Glen.

He waited a moment, then peeked behind the flowers and beamed her a smile. That slow sexy smile of his, capable of melting the hardest hearts, the strongest wills.

"Hello, sweetheart," he said, his smile growing wider. "Aren't you going to let me in?"

Wordlessly she unlatched the screen door and opened it for him.

He carried in the flowers and set them in the middle of her coffee table. They towered over it, filling the room with a profusion of glorious scents. Then he kissed her cheek and said, "I'll be right back."

When he returned, his arms were laden with gifts. She noted the chocolates, the basket of exotic fruit, the bottle of champagne. He set everything down next to the flowers and added three wrapped gifts.

"What's all this?" she asked, glancing at the table and then at him.

"Bribes," he said, looking very pleased with himself.

"For what?"

"I'll get to that in a moment." Taking her by the

shoulders, he guided her back to the sofa. "Sit," he instructed.

She complied before she realized she should have made at least a token protest about being ordered around, but curiosity won her over.

"Here," he said, handing her the smallest of the wrapped gifts. "Open this one first."

Christmas didn't yield this many presents. "Don't think you can buy my love, Mr. Patterson."

"I don't need to, Ms. Frasier," he said confidently. "You already admitted you love me."

For the fleetest of seconds Ellie wanted to argue, tell him she'd been emotionally distraught at the time, but it was the truth—she did love him.

Inside the package she found a pen. An attractive-looking ballpoint pen. Puzzled, she raised questioning eyes to him.

"Do you like it?" he asked.

"It's very nice," she said, puzzled but nevertheless excited. Before she had time to say anything more, he thrust another package at her. "This one is next." He knelt on the floor beside the sofa while she unwrapped a shoe-size box.

"Are you going to tell me what this is all about?" she asked. She tore away the paper and stared in utter amazement at the mismatched items inside.

The first thing she pulled out was a Cal Ripken baseball card. Next she removed a shoelace, followed by rose-scented bath salts from Dovie's store, and last, an ordinary key. Ellie examined each thing again, wondering what she was missing. As far as she could tell, the items weren't linked in any way.

"Is there a reason you're giving me one shoelace?"

He grinned. "It's blue."

She would have described it as a dark navy, closer to black—but that was beside the point. "The key?" she asked, holding that up next.

"That's to Bob Little's vacation home on the Gulf."

"Why do you have it?"

"I borrowed it," he replied as though that answered the question.

"I see." But she didn't. Changing tactics, she reached for the pen. "What about this?"

He gazed into her eyes. "The pen is for something special. I was hoping we'd use it to write our names in that old family Bible of yours. Maybe Wade should do it for us after the wedding ceremony, but then—" He stopped abruptly and leaned back on his heels. "I'm doing this all wrong again, aren't I?" Not giving her time to answer, he continued, "I spoke with Dovie earlier and she advised me how to go about this, but now I've forgotten almost everything."

"You spoke to Dovie?"

He ignored her question. "Honest to goodness, Ellie, I don't know what I said that was so terrible when I asked you to marry me before, but whatever it was I couldn't be sorrier. I love you. I mean that."

"I know." She felt tears brimming in her eyes. She'd waited a long time for Glen to tell her how he felt.

"You do?" His relief was evident. "Dovie said I needed to tell you that, but I was sure you already knew. And I want it understood that my proposal doesn't have anything to do with the bets Billy D's taking over who you're going to marry."

"I'd forgotten about that."

"I had, too, until Dovie reminded me. I love you, Ellie," he said again.

"I know, but it doesn't hurt to say the words every now and then. Or to hear them."

"Dovie said the same thing." He brightened at that, then clasped both her hands in his and got back on his knees. "Will you marry me, Ellie?" he asked solemnly.

When she didn't immediately respond, he reached for the box she'd just opened. "I wanted to be kind of traditional about this," he said. "The baseball card is something old. I've had it since I was in junior high. The scented bath salts is something new. The key's something borrowed, since Bob said we could use his house on the Gulf for our honeymoon. And the shoelace is something blue."

"Oh, Glen."

"I'm miserable without you. Nothing seems right."

It hadn't been right for her, either.

"I know Dovie said I shouldn't mention this, but I want you to know that even though we've waited two months for the farrier's appointment, I'd cancel it if you decided Tuesday was the day you wanted to get married. I'm that crazy about you."

"You're sure this isn't because of Richard."

"Yes," he said firmly. "Very sure. Although I'm grateful to him, otherwise I don't know how long it would've taken me to realize I love you."

"Then I'm grateful to Richard, too."

"We'll buy an engagement ring together, anything you want. Only please don't make me wait much longer." His eyes filled with such hopeful expectation she couldn't have denied him anything. "Ellie, you're my friend, the best friend I've ever had. I want you to be my lover, too. My wife. The mother of my kids. I want us to grow old together."

Rather than respond with words, Ellie wrapped her arms about his neck and lowered her mouth to his. She'd yearned for this from the moment he first kissed her. She understood now, with all her heart, what poets meant when they wrote about being completed by a lover, a spouse. She felt that. He completed her life.

Glen placed his arms around her waist and pulled her from the sofa so that she was kneeling on the floor with him. They kissed again and again, each kiss more fervent than the last.

"I hope," he said, drawing back from her a fraction, "that this means yes."

"Mmm. Kiss me."

"I have every intention of kissing you for the rest of our lives."

"That sounds nice." And it did. She tightened her arms around his neck. "What's in the other box?"

"It's for the honeymoon," he mumbled.

"You were sure of yourself, weren't you?"

"No," he countered, nibbling her neck. "I was a nervous wreck. We *are* getting married, aren't we?"

"Oh, yes." She sighed as his hands closed over her breasts. "Married," she repeated, liking the sound of it.

"We're going to have a good life together," Glen whispered. He kissed her. "I promise." Another small kiss. "I'm crazy about you, Ellie."

Ellie grinned. "You already said that. But for the record, I'm crazy about you, too."

She pressed her lips to his.

Eleven

Time was running out and Richard knew it. He had to leave Promise and soon. It wouldn't take Grady more than a few days to discover there *was* no money. The check Richard had given him was written on a closed account; it was going to bounce like a rubber ball, and when Grady found out... Nor would he be able to hold off paying his creditors much longer. All he needed was a week or so to get everything ready. No one would think to look for him in that old ghost town. He'd just quietly disappear.

Until then, he had to keep the wool pulled over his brother's eyes. Even if it meant doing work he'd sworn he'd never do again. That morning Grady had insisted Richard fill in for one of his summer hands who'd suddenly taken ill. This time Grady wouldn't listen to any excuses, and Richard was forced into what he considered slave labor.

"I don't know how much good I'm going to be," he told Laredo as he saddled Roanie.

"A little extra help is all Grady is looking for," Laredo said.

Savannah's husband hadn't made any effort to disguise his dislike of him. It hadn't bothered Richard to this point. He wasn't a big fan of Laredo's, either, although he had to admire the way the wrangler had finessed himself a partnership with Grady. Smith had apparently sold some land in Oklahoma and was investing it in stock for their quarter-horse operation. There'd been a celebration the day Laredo discovered his newly purchased mare was pregnant with Renegade's foal. From all the fuss, anyone might assume it was Savannah who was pregnant, not some horse.

"Grady wants us to weigh calves and get them into the holding pens," Laredo said as they rode toward the pasture.

"What for?" Richard demanded, bouncing in the saddle. He'd never been able to get comfortable on a horse. If he was going to be working his butt off, quite literally, then he wanted an explanation of his duties.

"They need to be weighed."

"Is he selling them?"

"Eventually. He wants to be sure they're healthy and gaining weight the way they should before we send them to market."

Richard stifled a groan. Anyone looking at those smelly animals could see they were doing fine. Better than he was, Richard thought bitterly. Already his backside hurt. By the end of the day he was bound to have blisters in places people didn't normally talk about—but then that was exactly what Grady had planned.

His brother was punishing him, Richard knew, for Grady was vindictive and a sore loser. He'd been jealous of Richard's skills and talents for years. The only reason he'd insisted Richard mount up this morning was to get back at him for the embarrassment of being confronted by Max Jordan a few nights earlier.

It would do no good to complain about it now. He didn't want to give Grady the satisfaction of knowing he'd succeeded in making him miserable.

After they'd ridden for several minutes, they came to the holding-pen area. Laredo told him to dismount, then had him sort through the calves. It was his duty to separate the steers from the heifers. No easy task, and it irked Richard that his son-of-a-bitch brother-in-law took such delight in the trouble he had. Even the dog seemed to be working against him, instead of with him. Laredo was at the gate while Richard herded the cattle one way or the other. All too frequently, Laredo had to correct him, but then, Richard had never been any good with animals. He hated ranch life, and Grady knew it. His brother was unfairly trying to make him pay for circumstances beyond his control.

When they'd finished sorting the calves, they broke the steers into twenty-head lots and weighed them. Nothing hurt Richard's ears more than the sound of ill-tempered cattle thundering onto the scale. They weren't any more interested in being weighed than Richard was in finishing the task.

"Are they loaded?" Laredo shouted.

"Isn't it lunchtime yet?"

"No. Answer the question."

"They're on the scale," he shouted back, waving his hand in front of his face. Not only were cattle stupid and nasty, their stench gave him a headache.

Laredo did whatever he did with the controls of

the scale and checked the balance. Richard watched it bob back and forth until the correct weight was found. Then the steers were moved into the holding pen.

Laredo seemed pleased with the results. "They've gained an average of fifty pounds in the past twenty days," he said.

"Whoopee."

Laredo ignored him. "At this rate they'll weigh around six hundred pounds by the sale date."

"Great," Richard muttered, seeing that his sarcasm was lost on the wrangler. He stared at his watch. "Isn't it lunchtime yet?"

"Soon." Laredo shoved back his hat with the heel of one hand. "When we're finished here, Grady wants us to vaccinate the steers."

"*What?* You mean my brother actually expects me to give them shots? With a needle?"

"So it seems."

"I hate needles." Damn it, Laredo hadn't mentioned this earlier, and Richard just knew the omission had been on purpose. Probably figured he was saving the best for last, the bastard.

"I don't suppose the calves are fond of being vaccinated, either," Laredo said calmly.

"Fine, then let's skip the entire procedure."

Laredo didn't bother to respond, and Richard accepted that there was no help for it. But down the line, his big brother was going to pay for the trouble and humiliation he'd caused. Oh, yes. Grady had learned about the bill with Max, but he didn't know about the others. Not yet. And by the time he *did* discover the amount of money Richard had charged...well, Richard would be long gone. Bye-bye Yellow Rose.

Who'd be smiling then? Who'd be feeling smug and superior? It was enough to carry Richard through the rest of the day.

Ellie spent as much time as she could with Glen, but not nearly enough to satisfy either one of them. A September wedding date had been set, and she was busy making plans. At the moment Glen and his brother needed to get the herd to market; that was their immediate priority and not something Ellie could help with.

"I thought I'd find you in here," Glen said.

Ellie, who was in the sick pen with a couple of calves, smiled up at her fiancé. He wore his Stetson and cowhide chaps. His approach warmed her heart.

"Are these two going to make it?" she asked. Most calves had slick hair, bright eyes and big bellies, but the calves in the pen looked dull-eyed and thin.

"They don't have anything a little bit of medicine and some tender loving care won't cure."

"Good."

Glen joined her in the pen. "When did you get here?"

"Fifteen minutes ago. George is closing up this afternoon."

He kissed her briefly. "Thank him for me."

"He's going to have to get used to it. When we're married, I'll be leaving early sometimes."

Glen wrapped his arm around her waist. "I like the sound of that word."

"Married?"

He nodded and, opening the gate, ushered her out of the barn and toward the house. "I like the sound of it more and more every day."

"So do I," she admitted softly. And she thought to herself that her father would have liked the idea of his Ellie married. To her friend, who was his friend, too. She imagined him smiling, telling her she'd chosen well. John Frasier had liked Glen and respected him. Her only regret was that her father wouldn't be there to walk her down the aisle or dance at his daughter's wedding.

"Give me time to shower," Glen said as they entered the house. "I'll be back before you know it." He smiled down at her and then, as if he couldn't restrain himself, kissed her once again.

While Glen cleaned up, Ellie went into the kitchen to start dinner. Since they'd made their engagement official, she'd stopped by the ranch two or three nights a week. It only made sense for them to eat together. She'd taken a few cooking lessons from Dovie on preparing basic meals. Meat and potatoes, mostly. Next thing, she'd tackle pies. She enjoyed practicing in the big ranch-house kitchen, especially with Glen there to cheer her on. Ellie found she begrudged every minute she couldn't spend with him, and she knew he felt the same way.

She had a roast in the oven and was peeling potatoes when Cal walked into the kitchen. "Hey, Ellie, how's it going?" he asked.

"Great," she said, dropping a freshly peeled potato into a kettle of water.

"You don't have to do this, you know. But let me tell you I appreciate every morsel."

Ellie grinned up at him. She was discovering that she liked Cal. Actually she always had, but he could be a difficult man to understand because he often seemed so remote, and sometimes even gruff. She'd been spending more time with him lately, and they'd developed a comfortable rapport. Ellie had even talked him into attending the Fourth of July celebration with her and Glen. To all appearances, he'd enjoyed himself, although he hadn't asked anyone to dance at the evening festivities. It was a well-known fact that he didn't trust women, although he was obviously pleased for her and Glen.

"You're welcome to join Glen and me for dinner anytime after we're married," she told him. They'd already decided it would be most beneficial, considering her business, for Glen to move into town after the wedding and commute to the ranch every day. Soon they'd be setting up an appointment with a Realtor and looking at houses. Glen hoped to have the deal closed by August so that once they were married, they could move right in. Ellie hoped that was possible, too.

As soon as Glen reappeared, his hair wet and glistening from the shower, Cal quickly left the room. Glen's arms circled her from behind and he kissed her neck. "Damn, but I love you."

Now that he was comfortable with the words, he said them often; he seemed to delight in sharing his feelings.

"I love you, too." The words had no sooner left her lips when she turned in his arms to face him. "I'm worried about Cal."

"Cal? What's wrong with my brother?"

"Nothing love wouldn't cure."

Glen frowned and took Ellie by the shoulders. "You've got that look in your eyes. I've seen it in my mother's and Dovie Boyd's."

"What look?"

Glen kissed the tip of her nose. "I don't know what it's called, but it's what comes over a woman when she thinks she knows what's best for a man."

"I'm not trying to be a...a matchmaker, Glen!"

"But you think Cal needs a woman."

"He needs to fall in love."

"He did once," Glen reminded her.

"Next time it needs to be with a woman who'll love him just as much in return. Who'll appreciate him for who he is without trying to change him."

"And where do you intend to find such a woman?" Glen asked, his gaze holding hers.

"I don't know, but she's out there and just waiting for someone like Cal."

Glen eased Ellie back into his embrace and kissed her with a thoroughness that left no question about his own love for her. "You're a terrible romantic, Ellie Frasier-soon-to-be-Patterson."

"I'm a woman in love and I want my almost-brother-in-law to find happiness, too."

"He'll have to look for his own partner if he wants to do a Texas two-step."

Glen drew her closer still.

She smiled up at him. "Well," she said, "that's the thing about the two-step. There's no changing partners if you do it right." She raised her mouth to his in a teasing kiss.

"You can bet on that." And he kissed her back.

* * * * *

#1 *New York Times* bestselling author

DEBBIE MACOMBER

**returns with the eleventh novel
in the beloved Cedar Cove series**

Dear Reader,

You've probably heard that my wife has left me. Rachel is pregnant, and she says she can't handle the stress in our household anymore. My thirteen-year-old daughter, Jolene, is jealous of her. Maybe it's my fault. As a widower I spoiled her—

Jolene was reading over my shoulder just now and says that's not true. She claims Rachel ruined everything. But *that's* not true. The real question is: How can I get my wife back? I don't even know where she is. She's not with Teri Polgar or any of her other friends from the salon. The other question is...when will Jolene grow up and stop acting like such a brat?

Available now, wherever books are sold!

#1 *New York Times* Bestselling Author

DEBBIE MACOMBER

Planning the wedding will be the easy part!

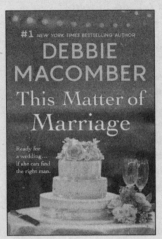

If Hallie McCarthy is going to get married and start a family the way she wants to, she's going to need a plan. And a man. Since Hallie is an organized, goal-setting kind of person, she gives herself a year to meet Mr. Knight-in-Shining-Armor. But all her dates are absolute disasters. Aren't there any nice, normal guys out there?

Too bad she can't just fall for her good-looking neighbor Steve Marris. He's definitely not her type. Anyway, Steve's busy trying to win back his ex-wife, who's busy getting married—just not to Steve. Life would be so much simpler if he could fall for someone else. Like...Hallie.

They are friends, though—and sometimes friends become more...

Available now, wherever books are sold!

Turn your love of reading into rewards you'll love with
Harlequin My Rewards

**Join for FREE today at
www.HarlequinMyRewards.com**

Earn **FREE BOOKS** of your choice.

Experience **EXCLUSIVE OFFERS** and contests.

Enjoy **BOOK RECOMMENDATIONS**
selected just for you.

PLUS! Sign up now
and get **500** points
right away!

Earn
FREE
REWARDS
Join
Today!
HarlequinMyRewards.com

MYR16R

DEBBIE MACOMBER

36869	CHOIR OF ANGELS	___	$7.99 U.S.	___	$9.99	CAN.
33125	NAVY FAMILIES	___	$7.99 U.S.	___	$9.99	CAN.
33121	NAVY BRIDES	___	$7.99 U.S.	___	$9.99	CAN.
33032	HANNAH'S LIST	___	$7.99 U.S.	___	$9.99	CAN.
33019	ALASKA HOME	___	$7.99 U.S.	___	$9.99	CAN.
33018	ALASKA NIGHTS	___	$7.99 U.S.	___	$9.99	CAN.
33017	ALASKA SKIES	___	$7.99 U.S.	___	$9.99	CAN.
32918	AN ENGAGEMENT IN SEATTLE	___	$7.99 U.S.	___	$9.99	CAN.
31926	THE SOONER THE BETTER	___	$7.99 U.S.	___	$9.99	CAN
31917	BECAUSE IT'S CHRISTMAS	___	$7.99 U.S.	___	$9.99	CAN.
31913	CHRISTMAS IN ALASKA	___	$7.99 U.S.	___	$9.99	CAN.
31903	WEDDING DREAMS	___	$7.99 U.S.	___	$9.99	CAN.
31894	ALWAYS DAKOTA	___	$7.99 U.S.	___	$9.99	CAN.
31888	DAKOTA HOME	___	$7.99 U.S.	___	$9.99	CAN.
31883	DAKOTA BORN	___	$7.99 U.S.	___	$9.99	CAN.
31860	THE MANNING BRIDES	___	$7.99 U.S.	___	$9.99	CAN.
31624	ON A CLEAR DAY	___	$7.99 U.S.	___	$8.99	CAN.
31580	MARRIAGE BETWEEN FRIENDS	___	$7.99 U.S.	___	$8.99	CAN.
31551	A REAL PRINCE	___	$7.99 U.S.	___	$8.99	CAN.
31535	PROMISE TEXAS	___	$7.99 U.S.	___	$8.99	CAN.
31441	HEART OF TEXAS VOLUME 2	___	$7.99 U.S.	___	$8.99	CAN.
31413	LOVE IN PLAIN SIGHT	___	$7.99 U.S.	___	$9.99	CAN.

(limited quantities available)

TOTAL AMOUNT	$ _____
POSTAGE & HANDLING	$ _____
($1.00 for 1 book, 50¢ for each additional)	
APPLICABLE TAXES*	$ _____
TOTAL PAYABLE	$ _____

(check or money order—please do not send cash)

To order, complete this form and send it, along with a check or money order for the total above, payable to MIRA Books, to: **In the U.S.:** 3010 Walden Avenue, P.O. Box 9077, Buffalo, NY 14269-9077; **In Canada:** P.O. Box 636, Fort Erie, Ontario, L2A 5X3.

Name: _____

Address: _____ City: _____

State/Prov.: _____ Zip/Postal Code: _____

Account Number (if applicable): _____
075 CSAS

★
▶ mira
Harlequin.com

MDM0519BL

*New York residents remit applicable sales taxes.
*Canadian residents remit applicable GST and provincial taxes.